THE BODY IN THE HOLE

by

JONATHAN B ZEITLIN

JONATHAN B. ZEITLIN

OVERKILL PRESS
WASHINGTON, DC

ISBN: 978-0-9834672-7-4

ACKNOWLEDGMENTS

I want to give a special thank you to Edward and Barbara Bierhanzl, Mark and Tracey Tremblay, Deirdre Fike, John Novak, Steve and Necois Penn, and to all those who pre-ordered my book. Thank you for the faith you had in this project, and for waiting patiently while this interminable process ground its way to the finish line.

I also want to thank a few people whose technical support and assistance were priceless: Forensic Pathologist M. Scott McCormick, M.D., for his obvious contributions, Author Jim Ball and Genevieve Kazdin for reading and offering suggestions for my manuscript, Robert Blake Whitehill, Author/Screenwriter, The Ben Blackshaw Series, www.RobertBlakeWhitehill.com, for his technical and editorial guidance, and of course my wife Stephanie, who read every version of my manuscript, tolerated my late night tapping on this keyboard, and convinced me people might actually buy it.

THE BODY IN THE HOLE

╬

CHAPTER ONE

"Ah, Randall. Randy, Randy, Randy, what a day!"

Yvgeny glanced at the words chiseled into the grave marker's face, then turned and leaned against it, legs straight out, ankles crossed.

"Still feels like summer up here. They say it's a heat wave. I say it's global warming."

Yvgeny shimmied across the mossy, pock-marked headstone to take advantage of the shade cast by a nearby weeping willow. Then he crossed his arms, shook his head, and after a polite pause, made a clucking sound with his tongue.

"That grand-daughter of yours, she's late again."

He received no response, and spent a minute listening to the rise and fall of the crickets rubbing their wings together. He re-crossed his ankles, one foot kicking over the desiccated remains of a bouquet of flowers.

"You hear that chirping, Randy? They're trying to attract mates. Those are the boy crickets. It's their way of making music. You and me, all we see is a cemetery, but to them, it's one big insect disco."

Again, Yvgeny's ramblings were met with silence,

and he squirmed against the headstone. The shade kept the sun at bay but not the humidity, and the sweat began to pool in the small of his back.

Yvgeny, or Geny to his few friends, looked across the cemetery, glanced toward the street, then took out his iPhone and checked his hair using the camera's *selfie* feature. Then he patted the top of the headstone and re-crossed his ankles a third time.

"You know, Randy, she's a real looker. I was thinking, well, I've been meaning to ask you - you know what? Never mind."

He yawned, scratched his cheek, then sniffed loudly, his nose starting to run from all the smells of autumn.

"What's that? Ah, Randy, maybe she overslept. Or got stuck in traffic. I wouldn't worry."

Yvgeny chuckled and again changed position on Randall's headstone, rolled his neck in one direction, then the other. He cocked his head.

"I gotta tell you, I think she'd be perfect for me, too. And you'd make a great grandfather-in-law."

Yvgeny pushed off the headstone and stood, then stretched. He felt the need to urinate, twisted away from Randall's marker to handle his business, then turned back to look over his shoulder while relieving himself.

"We could have it right here, surrounded by all our friends. And hell, pretty soon, maybe you and Mama will finally be able to meet." Yvgeny paused, and then muttered, "sooner, with luck."

Yvgeny reflexively glanced back toward the mortuary, shook, then buttoned up his Livingston trousers.

"Well, Randy old pal, gotta go grab a cold one- get it?"

Yvgeny laughed, then slapped the headstone with

the palm of his hand as he left, adding, "I put the fun in funeral!" He took a few steps, then called out behind him, "Toodles!"

Yvgeny returned to the mortuary just in time to see Alfred, the gravedigger, pacing on the stoop, holding a shovel caked with red clay. The moment he saw Yvgeny approach, Alfred stopped pacing and called out, "Nnng! Ungh ungh nnng!"

Alfred was a deaf mute who spoke mostly by gesticulation and facial expressions. Yvgeny tried to interpret Alfred's rudimentary language; sometimes successfully, sometimes less so. He watched as Alfred poked a long, brown finger toward the cemetery grounds and stamped his feet. His pale blue and rheumy eyes pinned like a nervous robin's. The grunts and clicking in his throat emphasized his level of distress.

Yvgeny followed the direction of Alfred's finger, then shrugged.

"Dunlap? My dear Alfred, the funeral isn't until 2 pm. That's hours away!"

Alfred's nostrils flared and the clicking in his throat grew louder. His expression reminded Yvgeny of an agitated bull seeing the matador. He resumed his pacing, rhythmically smacking his shovel against the wood with each step, leaving a sprinkle of moist clay in his wake.

Yvgeny glanced over Alfred's shoulder toward the Dunlap plot again. He took measure of the faded green canvas canopy, and beside it, the discolored tarp covering a mound of dirt. Beside the mound, poles and velvet ropes marked the hole that would soon receive Mr. Dunlap, followed by the mound of dirt. The canopy swayed gently against the deep blue Middle Georgia sky.

THE BODY IN THE HOLE

Alfred examined Yvgeny, growing more impatient, now pounding the shovel against the stoop, wet earth falling from the shovel in clumps upon the warped wooden boards. He thrust his gnarled index finger over and over toward the Dunlap family plot. His clicking and wordless mumbling grew louder.

Yvgeny cast a furtive glance toward the upstairs windows of the mortuary. Then he held out his hand, motioned with his palm down, and whispered, "OK, OK, Jesus Alfred, come off the stoop, you could wake the dead with that racket!"

Alfred clopped down the two steps onto the ground, smacking the shovel with each step, and when Yvgeny outstretched his hand toward the Dunlap plot as if to say 'be my guest,' Alfred loped ahead like a dog that had successfully lured his master out for a romp in the grass. One of his legs was almost an inch shorter, exacerbating his odd gait. His head was on a swivel as he repeatedly turned back to Yvgeny, motioning for him to follow, dragging the shovel beside him. The sticky humidity glued Yvgeny's Edwardian collared shirt to his back.

Watching Alfred's hunched and withered frame, Yvgeny wondered how old he was. He had memories of Alfred as a younger man, when he still had his hair in a tight afro, when he had all his teeth. He was the only black man he had ever seen with blue eyes.

Alfred had aged to a point where his race and age were no longer apparent. His afro had all but disappeared, and his skin had the cracked, brownish appearance of a dried out Medjool date. The whites of his eyes had yellowed like old parchment, and were set deep within his face. The irises had faded over time to a milky, grayish blue. It seemed life in the cemetery was gradually digesting his humanity, consuming more of him each year, and Yvgeny believed one day he would come outside to find Alfred frozen between two headstones, carved from granite, immovable, with chalky dried excrement from countless pigeons decorating his shoulders.

It had rained all night, and the clay was too dense to absorb the water, leaving it standing on the grass for him to slosh through in his shoes and gray felt spats. Luckily, he didn't have too far to walk. The Dunlap family plot was close to the mortuary. The first dead Dunlap was buried there generations earlier, in 1912. By Yvgeny's count, he and his father buried around a dozen Dunlaps, give or take. Alfred probably dug over half those holes.

He followed Alfred to the grave site, shaking his head. The old man had always been strange, but this was unusual even for him. Yvgeny peeled his shirt away from his damp and overheated skin; in Middle Georgia, autumn was a long way from winter, and the humidity ruined an otherwise beautiful morning.

As they stood still, tiny gnats hovered in large clusters right at face level in another impressive display of reproductive competition. Waving at them with his hand, his thoughts again turned to Brianna Schtumpf.

Yvgeny imagined Brianna in one of his top of the line coffins, the Goliath 20 gauge thirty-six inch Galaxy model, champagne velvet and satin interior, continuously welded bottom, brushed aluminum hardware. He had a beautiful dove gray floor model upstairs that could easily accommodate both of them. His mind began to wander.

Unfortunately, his fantasy was interrupted when he noticed his gray spats rimmed red from the wet Georgia clay.

That will never come out!

Alfred stood before the hole, his arms stretched out, shovel in one hand, as if presenting royalty to a swooning crowd. Yvgeny looked around, a bemused expression on his face. Alfred's triumphant smile faltered.

"So what's so important, Alfred?"

Alfred's shoulders slumped. He pointed into the hole, then pantomimed digging while nodding hopefully at Yvgeny. Yvgeny crept closer and looked down into the hole. He could smell Alfred, who seldom bathed, and briefly evaluated whether he smelled worse than the corpses he serviced each day.

The grave was empty, as it should have been, but it was at least a foot too shallow. He glanced over at Alfred, shaking his head. Beyond him, Yvgeny saw movement behind a headstone; another stray cat. At least a dozen lived around the property, and they usually followed Alfred around as if he was the Pied Piper. This one watched them intently.

"You brought me all the way out here to show me an empty hole? Come on, Alfred, you know it's a foot too shallow. Just finish it, there's still plenty of time. And perhaps a bath would be in order before the guests arrive?"

Alfred stared intently at Yvgeny's mouth, reading and translating. There was always a slight delay between spoken word and comprehension, and a moment after Yvgeny finished talking, Alfred's mouth opened and the sounds came again. His gesticulations grew even more agitated and he began stomping his feet and pointing at the earth. The clicking in his throat was insistent, angry. Yvgeny watched him carefully, trying to divine the meaning behind his movements.

"Did the rain fill it in? That's OK, Alfred, just dig it back out. There's nothing to worry about. Seriously. You have hours."

When Alfred grew frustrated enough, he sometimes raised his head and made a blood curdling howl, like a wolf. He made one then, fists clenched, eyes squeezed shut, rousting dozens of birds from the nearby trees. The nosy cat froze, stunned by the sound, then scurried behind a headstone.

Alfred deflated, then took his shovel in two hands and hopped into the hole. Yvgeny winced at the sound of Alfred's body creaking and cracking from the impact. Yvgeny sighed and took a step closer to the hole. He could just see the top of Alfred's head as he dug.

After a short time, just seconds, Alfred stopped, and stood straight, staring down, his mouth open, breathing heavily, and then he did something Yvgeny had never before seen, not in all the years he had known Alfred; he made the sign of a cross over his chest. Yvgeny took another step forward, to the lip of the grave, and looked down. There was a depression where Alfred had started digging, and in the hole he saw pale white flesh.

⚼

CHAPTER TWO

Yvgeny turned back to the mortuary, scanned the windows and, seeing no movement, sighed in relief.

"Alfred, quickly, load it up and bring it inside."

He then leaned closer and in a hushed tone added, "and do it quietly!"

Yvgeny ran ahead to change and prepare the embalming room. Alfred climbed out of the hole and trudged past his shed into a small barn like structure. He placed his shovel against the wall, then approached a large object covered by a tarp, which he lifted to reveal a golf cart, modified to carry coffins. Instead of a passenger seat, it bore a platform that rested long ways across the cart and had straps permanently attached for securing a coffin. Until that morning, the cart had never been used to bring a body *away* from the cemetery, and certainly had never been used to transport a body without a coffin.

Alfred drove the cart to the grave site, then stared into the grave, contemplating his options. Again, lifting bodies out of holes was an unfamiliar task.

Meanwhile, Yvgeny rushed back to the mortuary, giddy over the find.

Buried treasure!

He shut the door slowly, carefully, tiptoed into the kitchen, then stood, motionless, listening for movement. After a short pause, he sighed with contentment; the house was still silent.

With a little luck, he thought, *she will sleep until noon, as usual.*

He plucked his rubber apron from its hook and placed it over his head, then went to the window to watch from afar as Alfred pulled up to the gravesite with the golf cart. *The slab cab,* as Yvgeny liked to call it. Yvgeny rubbed his hands together in expectation as Alfred stood over the hole contemplating his options.

Yvgeny was practically buzzing with anticipation. *Who could it be? How was he killed? Who did it?* He channeled his inner Holmes as Alfred continued to process his options. *My Watson!*

After some internal deliberation, Alfred decided on a mixture of brute force and stubborn determination to lug it out of the hole. He first walked to the edge of the property to check the street, then again jumped into the grave. He cleared away most of the soil, stared at the body, then lugged it up over one shoulder, hoisted it over the lip of the grave, then climbed out. Squatting low, he grabbed the arms and tried to drag it all the way out. Unfortunately, his hands slipped on the body and it went tumbling back into the hole.

Yvgeny's anticipatory grin faded as he watched Alfred lose the body. Yvgeny sighed, and started tying the waist laces of his apron as he jogged down the hall and out the back door to help him.

He arrived just as Alfred draped the body over the lip of the grave again. Without speaking, Yvgeny and

Alfred each grabbed an arm and together, they lifted the body all the way out and onto the ground. They each took a breath, then dragged the body beside the cart, propped it up, and heaved it onto the platform.

Yvgeny returned inside while Alfred finished securing the body and driving the slab cab toward the rear double doors of the mortuary. Yvgeny paced until he heard the squeak of the doors, followed by Alfred's shuffling footsteps. Yvgeny had stepped up to his mirror to check his hair as Alfred entered to retrieve the cart, and by the time Yvgeny turned away, Alfred was gone, his retreating footsteps now accompanied by the sound of rolling casters against the tiled floor. Yvgeny returned to the window, smiling, then his smile melted.

Alfred had left the slab cab parked outside in clear view from the street, the body draped across it, uncovered. Yvgeny stomped toward the front of the mortuary and into the main receiving room and looked out the large windows overlooking the street. Checking in each direction, he sighed in relief; the streets were empty.

Yvgeny jogged back down the hall and out the back doors. Alfred had positioned the gurney beside the slab cab, and had steadied the gurney with a foot on the lower crossbars. He had just begun to drag the body off the slab cab and onto the gurney when Yvgeny emerged, and Alfred froze when he saw him, his ancient joints struggling under the weight of the dead body and the awkward position.

"Alfred!" Yvgeny exclaimed, then, while glancing left, then right, then left again, whispered, "I said hurry, but don't be stupid! At least put a sheet over it!"

Alfred blinked several times but otherwise remained still. Yvgeny let his air out with a whoosh and shook his head, then muttered something about plucking an oyster from its shell as he turned and passed through the doors.

As his father had taught him, and his mother incessantly drilled into his head with every breath, reputation was everything in the mortuary business. One little old lady out for a stroll seeing a body draped across a golf cart would be all it would take.

Dead bodies were as ubiquitous to Yvgeny as shoes to a cobbler, although his insouciance toward them took years of exposure to acquire. As a queasy child stumbling into the embalming room and seeing his father working on a body, he could barely stifle his urge to retch. At the sound, his father would turn his head toward him in slow motion, blink a few times, then pull the trocar out of the body and say, *Yvgeny, these bodies are just broken machines. Broken, unplugged machines.*

Now, given the population of Comstock and his study of actuarial tables, he could accurately estimate he would be sharing his home with three to five of those broken, unplugged machines at any given time. They laid in chilled lockers while Yvgeny slept in his back office on a second-hand cot purchased from the army surplus store in town. He had slept upstairs until his father died, after which Mama gradually acquired living space like a real estate developer in a buyer's market.

Relegated to the main floor, Yvgeny had nowhere to put a bed. For a time, Yvgeny equivocated about sliding one of the display coffins into his room; the better ones would have been more comfortable than his Army surplus cot, but the floor models were simply too expensive and besides, Mama would not have approved.

Yvgeny's cot was good enough, however. He got it for a song from Rocko, who ran the Army surplus store. Yvgeny liked him. Rocko lost an eye during his service in Vietnam. A broken machine.

Rocko saw the world through a stark lens of black and white, one to which Yvgeny could relate. Mama called him retarded, but Rocko once told Yvgeny his story about how he lost his eye, and Yvgeny could only assume the injury took more than an eye.

Rocko usually referred to himself in the third person, which, when combined with the man's size and somewhat grumbly voice, made Yvgeny think of him as a white and less fuzzy Cookie Monster. Yvgeny recalled Rocko's sales pitch when he purchased the cot.

"Rocko say cot is good. Beat sleeping on floor. Dogs sleep on floor. You are not dog."

"Yes, Rocko, I am not a dog. How much do you want for the cot?"

"Ten dollars for cot. Rocko give you good deal. Not like crooks at Walmart. Crooks charge you fifty."

"Yes, Rocko, they are crooks. Can you help me get it into the car?"

Rocko nodded and on his way out, stopped by a display of dull machetes. Rocko abruptly grabbed and hefted one and turned back to Yvgeny, giving him a start, and asked, "Undertaker man need machete? Good for cutting. You can chop up dead guys, fit them in smaller boxes. Save money. Buy better cot."

"No, thank you, Rocko, I don't need to chop up any bodies at the moment."

"Chop, chop! Good machete."

By the door was a large wooden Indian statue. As Rocko passed by to follow Yvgeny outside, he smacked the machete into the side of the Indian and left it, blade wobbling in the wood.

Yvgeny's daydream crashed to a halt when Alfred pushed the shiny steel gurney into the embalming room and parked it beside the supply cabinet. Alfred glared at him a moment, then turned to study the contents of the cabinet, sweating and dirty. Behind him, on the gurney,

₃ody lay under a sheet. Yvgeny shook his head as he ₃ticed several orange and red smudges on the sheet from Alfred's clay caked hands. One whitish blue foot peeked out from beneath the shroud. *At least he remembered the sheet.*

While looking in the mirror to check his hair again, Yvgeny said, "Thank you, my dear Alfred. That will be all for now. Is the Dunlap site ready?"

Satisfied, Yvgeny turned to Alfred, who had been staring at the body. Yvgeny extended his arm out toward the body and waved a hand to get his attention, waited for Alfred to look in his direction.

"Are the chairs all set up?"

Alfred shook, then lowered, his head, and with a deep breath, turned and shuffled away, taking one more look at the body before leaving. Yvgeny approached the body and lifted the shroud. His eyebrows raised in surprise. There was no head.

He pulled back the sheet completely, discovering there were no hands, either. He tossed the sheet into the corner and inspected the body. It was dressed in old slacks and a knit crew sweater, threadbare but serviceable. Streaks of clay ran along the pants and sweater, either from Alfred or the killer, or perhaps both. The pants were torn at the knees. The body looked to be male, but he couldn't be certain about gender until he looked beneath the clothing.

Yvgeny stood, hands on hips, trying to envision what his beloved Holmes would do next. *Perhaps light a cigarette, then stroll around the body, his hands clasped behind him? Produce a large magnifying glass and inspect the wounds? Yes, yes!*

THE BODY IN THE HOLE

Yvgeny opened one of the drawers of his Snap On tool chest and withdrew a large magnifying glass, dropped it into his apron pocket, then returned to the body. With his hands clasped behind him, he walked around the body, inspecting the wound sites, the feet, the clothing, occasionally nodding his head sagely, as he imagined Holmes would do. As he passed by his mirror he turned to admire himself in his role. Once he had made a complete pass around the body, he stood a moment, smiling and tapping his foot.

A vague thought bubbled up to him, that his grave was now a crime scene, and that he should notify the police, but after he glanced at the clock, he shrugged off the thought. Dunlap was at 2 pm. He couldn't risk having the cops crawling all over the cemetery, especially considering the Dunlaps had not yet paid in full. *I will call them after the ceremony*, he thought, then donned a pair of rubber gloves.

He ran his hands down the body, over the pockets. All empty. He reached for his glass, then crouched and took a closer look at the extremities. The head and hands were removed by something fairly sharp, the bones cut cleanly. *Like a machete*, he thought.

The neck was messier and must have taken a few chops, as the blade grazed the left shoulder a couple of times. The chops were *post mortem*, in his estimate. No real struggle, not too bloody. He ran a finger along the wound, the skin already beginning to recede from the body. *Yes*, he thought to himself, *sharp, but not too sharp*. And a strong hand.

As he removed the pants he could hear creaking from the second floor. He cringed and froze, waiting for footsteps on the stairs. Fortunately, none came and he relaxed a bit. But one thing was certain: *she was awake*.

Yvgeny inspected further and confirmed it was a male, probably early eighties, in fair enough shape for his age, not overweight, but not emaciated, either. Other than the missing parts, there were no other apparent injuries. He glanced back at the pants and sweater; neither could be repurposed. And no hands meant no rings. He clucked with his tongue and shook his head. Nothing of value.

Yvgeny learned all the tricks of the trade from his father, who had never been squeamish around bodies, having acquired the gift of detachment by necessity as a young man in Poland. It took Yvgeny longer to fully embrace his father's dispassionate perspective, but by grade school, Yvgeny was fascinated by the bodies of the dead.

While other children played stick ball and ogled girls, Yvgeny made alterations to clothing so they would fit properly for loved ones' funerals. When he was a little older and his hopeful peers asked girls to the junior prom, Yvgeny pedaled around Comstock looking for road kill upon which to practice his embalming skills. Unfortunately, his work with the dead did not prepare him for the revulsion expressed by the living, especially those of the opposite sex.

Yvgeny, a virtual outcast by high school, spent his formative years watching funerals from behind thick red velvet curtains; his friends and only company were the stiffs he or Alfred rolled into the mortuary, relationships that generally expired after a few days, epitomizing the old adage comparing house guests to fish.

The more alienated he became from the living, the more Yvgeny focused on the dead. He poured himself into his work, taking advantage of any opportunity that presented itself. A closed casket funeral became free embalming practice. Cremations were even better, allowing him to take bigger risks and to learn from his mistakes.

An artist that spent all his time on still life paintings would quickly grow bored. Such was the case for morticians. Working on the elderly eventually loses its charm. Luckily for Yvgeny, some people die terrible, gruesome deaths, whether by accident, homicide, even suicide. Yvgeny liked the variety. And on that rare occasion when the decedent's family insisted on an open casket funeral, Yvgeny accepted the challenge with gusto.

He credited his father for helping him hone his talent. His father had been a master. An artist. A virtuoso. He could piece together bodies, faces, limbs, with the ease of a child working on a jigsaw puzzle. But it required practice, and it was a perishable skill.

When Yvgeny was a teenager, his father somehow got on the list of approved morticians maintained by the Georgia State Department of Corrections. To those lucky few came the bodies of expired inmates that had no family to claim them.

Like an artist provided with free canvasses, Yvgeny sharpened his skills on these murderers and rapists, and he always made sure not to waste one inch of flesh. Of course, Georgia required an affidavit certifying the body had been treated with dignity and was disposed of properly, but that was but a formality, and one that did not deter Yvgeny's father; he had always put his son's training and experience first.

Yvgeny removed the corpse's sweater. First one sleeve, then up and over the space where the head should have been, then he peeled the whole thing off over the remaining arm. The sweater got hung up around the forearm, and when Yvgeny grasped the sleeve to give it a tug he felt something hard, metallic. He tugged harder and the sleeve gave way, revealing the glint of metal. Gold. A watch had snagged on the rough seam of the sweater.

The watch looked old. He held it up to his ear and

heard the rhythmic tick of a proper timepiece. He turned it over, saw an inscription, but it was too small to read. He turned it around in his hands several more times, and was about to slide it over his hand to test its fit when he heard shuffling footsteps behind him. He twisted around quickly, hiding his hands behind his back, and came face to face with his mother. *How did I not hear her on the stairs,* he thought, then cursed at himself for not tossing a sheet over the body.

"Mama, what are you doing down here?"

His mother stopped a foot away and spied him with a raised eyebrow. In a heavily accented voice she said, "What, I need permission to come downstairs in my own house?" Then she looked over Yvgeny's shoulder toward the body.

"*Gówno,* where's Dunlap's head?"

"It's not Dunlap, Mama."

Mama shook her head.

"*Oi,* my *tygrysek,* this is no time for playing around. Guests will be here soon. Put away your toys and get back to work! And what did you do with his head?"

When Yvgeny didn't respond, his mother smiled and shook her head.

"Always the comedian, *tygrysek.* Just make sure you put it somewhere the guests won't find it."

Mama glanced at the body one more time, smiled, tousled Yvgeny's hair, then turned and shuffled away. Yvgeny waited for her to leave, then slid the watch over his hand and onto his wrist. He would bring it to Reuben.

In the kitchen he heard his mother start slamming cabinet doors, and he returned to his task, relieved. He tossed the sweater onto a pile with the remainder of the victim's clothes on the lower shelf of the rolling gurney, then stood back and inspected the body from neck to foot. Some of his colleagues preferred "modesty towels" to cover a corpse's genitals, but Yvgeny scoffed at the practice. Dead men had no modesty. They didn't care.

Alfred shuffled back into the room, his muddy shoes squeaking on the white tile. He had a camera in his hand. He looked down at the body again, then looked up to Yvgeny, said, "nng, nng," his Adam's apple bouncing with the effort. Yvgeny knew what he meant this time and smiled, nodded his head, and walked toward the phone on the wall.

"Yes, of course, Alfred, I was about to call them. I do hope you've finished preparing the site for the Dunlaps."

Alfred glanced out the window, in the direction of his shed, then began absently picking his ear. When Yvgeny picked up the handset from the cradle, Alfred dropped the camera on the body and shuffled quickly out the door.

He watched Alfred leave, then replaced the handset and turned back to the body. But then he stopped, equivocating. He didn't like cops. Never had. *Irreconcilable differences,* Yvgeny thought to himself, a fitting euphemism, the same one used by angry divorcees tired of their slovenly husbands.

Plus, cops were bad for business. But. . . .

He began tapping his foot, glancing between his watch and the body, then finally cursed and lifted the phone again. *Alfred was right,* he thought to himself with a groan, *if I wait they will only ask more questions, cause more problems.* He made the call, then quickly photographed the body.

╬

Yvgeny replaced his rubber apron on its hook, hid his camera, then changed into a proper outfit: black suit, black shirt, black tie, somber and professional. He had barely cinched the tie into place when he heard sirens. Cursing to himself, he fumbled with his polished black wingtips.

Why must they rush to a dead body? He thought, then added, out loud, "He's not getting any deader!"

He stood, straightened his coat, then headed toward the door, still grumbling softly.

"Speeding through Comstock will only lead to the corpse having fresh company!"

Yvgeny placed his stovepipe hat in place on his way to the door, and fixed a neutral expression on his face, which took a fair amount of effort.

"Then again, that would be good for business."

He opened the door and stepped outside.

He heard the acceleration of the Ford Crown Victoria before he saw it, and managed to hold his tongue when the officer slammed on his brakes. Then he heard another, and barely stifled a reprimand when that officer screeched to a halt in the street. He swallowed the invective boiling inside him; it would only create a bigger spectacle, and the last thing a proper mortuary needed was a spectacle!

He cleared his throat and waited for them to emerge from their patrol cars, his hands clasped behind him, still the outward epitome of patience and repose.

One officer spoke into his radio, then they both collected their clipboards and began to fiddle with their uniforms. *Provincial hayseeds,* he muttered to himself.

And two! Why two? He's already dead! Two officers meant they dispatched the entire day shift. To someone as frugal as Yvgeny, it was a terrible waste of resources. But still Yvgeny stood, impassive, resolute, the outward embodiment of serenity.

But when the unmarked Gilbert County cruiser pulled into the driveway, Yvgeny lost his composure. Three was too many. His shoes squeaked on the asphalt as he approached them from the carport.

"Only three of you? You sure that's enough? Where's the fire department? No ladder truck? What, no ambulance? Hurry, hurry, he might not be dead! Which one of you is a doctor? Come, quickly!"

He took a breath, but was far from finished.

"Wait, no doctors?" Yvgeny asked as he turned to each officer, feigned shock on his face, "that's OK, let's get Madame Jezelda, the palm reader off Main Street, maybe she can bring over a witch doctor, spit some rum on the body, shake a chicken leg at him and bring him back to life!"

The two startled officers stared at him, open mouthed. Their eyes wandered up to his stove pipe hat, then back down again. He was used to it. *Star power,* some called it. The stove pipe hat hadn't been in vogue for over a hundred years, but Yvgeny recognized true fashion, and so would everyone else.

Yvgeny regretted his outburst once he calmed down, but was relieved the deputy had still been in his unmarked cruiser and missed out on most of Yvgeny's diatribe. The Gilbert County sheriff also served as coroner, which meant relatively frequent contact with his office, and Yvgeny didn't want to lose any of the coroner's business to some mortuary in Macon or Warner Robins. He already lost the Department of Corrections contract after a petty disagreement with a nosy warden. He couldn't afford to lose any more clients. Times were lean.

But he couldn't mask his sneer as the three lawmen walked up his driveway. The source of his dislike for the police was a combination plate of Eastern European DNA tossed with a healthy dose of parental influence. His parents grew up in a land where the police were not to be trusted, not to be relied upon, and he was counseled from an early age to avoid them.

The only other contributions his parents provided were his name and his accent. He hated both. As a child growing up near Atlanta, nobody could pronounce his name; teachers and friends instead called him Geny, pronounced with a hard G.

Everyone else called him Jenny, usually with a snicker. His parents told him he should embrace his name, that it was part of his family heritage, like his accent. But like any child, he hated anything that made him different. Sitting in classrooms full of country folk and blacks, he was always the one that was different.

As he grew older, more mature, he realized it wasn't merely the differences themselves that irked him; it was the fact that those differences were only skin deep. His parents buried the horrors of communist Poland deep inside, long lines in foul weather for moldy turnips and onions, riots between the people and the police, loudspeakers blaring communist slogans, and everywhere, barbed wire.

His parents traveled to America with nothing, fought for everything, learning a strange, new language in the process, only speaking their mother tongue in soft whispers before going to sleep each night. They adapted and assimilated, eliciting respect by suffering and surviving.

But Yvgeny was born in Georgia, and they never

taught him their mother tongue. They never shared with him their experiences and their suffering. They wanted him to be fully, completely, American, yet they named him Yvgeny, and he had their accent and their Slavic features. They branded him Polish, but gave him nothing that made him a Pole. In this, they were hypocrites. He balanced on a wall between America and Eastern Europe, a product of both, fully accepted by neither. He felt like an impostor. An actor.

The two police officers stopped just outside of social distance from Yvgeny, hands in their pockets, clipboards under an arm, kicking at the dirt and looking around uneasily. Finally, the man in the unmarked cruiser stepped out. He walked past the two officers without a glance and approached Yvgeny.

He was tall and did not wear a uniform. He wore his gun and badge exposed on his belt, the six pointed star worn by deputies of the county sheriff, setting him apart from the two city officers. Yvgeny did not extend his hand, instead keeping them clasped together behind his back. The watch felt heavy on his wrist.

"Inspector, good of you to come so quickly."

Yvgeny preferred *inspector* to detective, *constable* to officer, just as he preferred *undertaker* to *mortician*; Yvgeny fully embraced his Victorian image, from vocabulary to apparel, having read his treasured copy of *Sherlock Holmes* so many times he had even adopted a grandiloquent spoken version of Sir Doyle's punctilious writing style.

The time for physical introductions having passed, he slowly reached into his pants pocket to find his good luck charm, turned it around a few times in his pocket. With his free hand he motioned for the three lawmen to come inside, then led the way, his back straight, again clasping his hands behind his back.

The deputy stifled a grimace and stepped inside,

followed by the two policemen, shuffling and keeping their eyes averted as if expecting to find a body in every corner. Yvgeny stepped forward in between two of his display coffins and drew their attention by clearing his throat. The younger officer's complexion paled when he looked up and saw Yvgeny standing surrounded by coffins. Yvgeny smiled.

"Right this way, constables."

They followed him toward the back and through a set of double doors set in mahogany. The other side of the doors were sterile stainless steel. Yvgeny walked slowly, purposefully, almost able to feel the officers exchanging uneasy glances as they followed him into the embalming room, each clutching their clipboards more and more tightly. Yvgeny's smile broadened and he stifled the urge to turn abruptly and yell *boo!*

The embalming room had been fashioned from a large butler's pantry combined with what once was called a sleeping porch. Eldred Junior contracted for the remodel long before Yvgeny arrived with his parents, and Yvgeny's father later retrofitted it with stainless steel surfaces and more modern equipment.

"What's that?" asked one of the city cops, pointing at a machine in the corner beside a low sink no higher than knee level. Yvgeny could see the regret on the officer's face almost instantly as Yvgeny cleared his throat to answer him.

"Excellent question," Yvgeny began, rubbing his knuckles.

"You see, back when this house was built, the embalming process was a messy, smelly affair that required a high degree of physical exertion and even higher degree of, well, detachment. Gravity was one's only assistant in the draining of the body's fluids. Lucky for me, times have changed!"

Yvgeny took a step closer to the officers, sucking them in like the hawker in an infomercial.

"Today, the gravity method has been replaced by that machine you pointed to. Here's how it works. It's kind of like an artificial heart machine."

Yvgeny walked over to the machine and lifted two tubes attached to its side.

"So, when it's time to embalm a corpse, I shove this end here into the jugular."

He made a stabbing motion with his hand.

"Then this one here, I stab into one of the major veins. Doesn't matter which one. Then I just push this button here. This hose sucks out all the blood, and this one here, well, it pumps the body full of embalming fluid. Pure genius, really. It does all the work for me! Suck and spit, suck and spit, kind of like, well . . . ."

Yvgeny made a sucking sound followed by a whoosh, repeating the sounds several times in rhythm. Then he reached over and grabbed a bag of Doritos from a small table and started munching while he talked.

"When you get a really old person, you know, emaciated, it's like hooking up an air compressor to a deflated kiddy pool. Magical, don't you think?"

Still holding his bag of Doritos, he walked toward a small table and again faced the officers.

"Of course, it's not quite that easy. You still have to deal with the organs."

He waved his hand over a small handheld tool on the table.

"Now, this tool right here is called a trocar. It works kind of like a shop vacuum. Now, what you do is take the trocar-"

The deputy cleared his throat and interrupted Yvgeny.

"So this is the body?"

Yvgeny deflated and turned to find the deputy standing before the table bearing the nude, headless corpse.

"Clearly."

The deputy stood with his hands on his hips staring at the body. The two city cops avoided looking directly at the body, suddenly fascinated by the walls, floor, and each other. One tried to breathe into his clipboard, and the other held his breath, both clearly more accustomed to the mild odors of spilled antifreeze and burned tire treads on pavement.

The deputy walked up to the table, still staring. Yvgeny remembered him from another incident, when a body was found on a street just outside the Comstock city limits. He had been shot in the chest, and given Comstock's proximity to Interstate 75, the mayor announced it was clearly another killing out of Macon, *what else*? It was an election year, and the impact Macon's crime had on poor Comstock became the incumbent's rallying cry.

Yvgeny suffered no righteous anger about the crime rate, only disappointment that Lenny Updike's shop in Warner Robins got the ticket for stuffing that stiff. Lenny poured a lot of cash into the mayor's campaign so what would one expect?

The deputy reached into a pocket and smeared a dab of Vicks Vapor Rub into his mustache, then tossed the jar to one of the city cops. He moved in closer to inspect the wounds on the body, then turned his attention back to Yvgeny. If he remembered him from that murder, he didn't show it.

The city cop fumbled as he opened the jar, and the lid scuttled across the floor and came to rest under one of Yvgeny's tables. As the cop scrambled to retrieve it, Yvgeny snorted, muttered, "amateurs," and walked over to the officer.

"Oldest trick in the book. Go ahead, smear it all over your uniform. It might mask the smell all right, but nothing can mask the taste."

Yvgeny smacked his lips and smiled.

"See what I mean? You can actually taste the death. It's in the air!"

Yvgeny delighted in the officers' baleful expressions of horror, but it was short lived, for the detective interrupted his reverie.

"So if you found the body out there," he asked, "how the hell did it get in here?"

"Well, I had to recover it because-"

"Because why? Why did you have to recover a murder victim and remove him from the crime scene?"

Yvgeny crossed his arms.

"Because I have a funeral scheduled for 2 pm today and I need that hole!"

"That hole is a crime scene!"

"Oh Yvgeny, you brought friends!"

Everyone turned as Yvgeny's mother walked into the room.

╫

CHAPTER THREE

One of the city officers straightened up his posture and cleared his throat. The deputy gave one more hard look at Yvgeny before turning and acknowledging the woman with a nod and a "Ma'm."

The old woman had adopted a vacant and somewhat bemused smile as she stood in the doorway, then, having been acknowledged, she took mincing steps toward the deputy, thumping her cane on the floor with each step. She was barely five feet tall, and her long brown hair was meticulously braided and pinned. She stopped in front of the deputy, then smoothed out her formal blue dress, straightened her flowered apron.

"And what is your name, young man?" she asked the deputy.

"Harold Newsome. I'm a detective with the sheriff's office."

"Oh, a detective, how lovely! Did you hear that Yvgeny? A detective! And he brought police men!" She glanced at her son, then turned to the detective with a conspiratorial wink, motioned for him to come closer, and said in a low voice, "I've always told my little *tygrysek* one is judged by the company he keeps! And if he has friends like you three, then I will sleep very well tonight indeed!"

"Tee-gree-sek?" asked the detective.

The old woman turned to her son and pinched his cheek lightly, then patted it, chanting, "yes, yes, yes, he's always been my little *tygrysek*, my little tiger!"

Yvgeny's face flushed in anger and embarrassment at her display. Before he could respond, his mother pinched his ear and drew him closer to her face where she planted a wet kiss on his cheek and hissed, "Cool off, *idiota*, I'm saving your ass!"

She turned to face the detective again, wearing her simpleton's smile.

"Detective, let me get you each a nice cup of tea! I was just baking a few sweets for the function this afternoon. Surely you will all stay for it! It will be very nice. Tasteful, of course, my Yvgeny always throws such a lovely party!"

The two city officers stared at the detective in alarm.

"No ma'am, we can't really stay. We just came to take a look at this body here. Don't worry, we won't be long."

"Very well, detective. Yvgeny, didn't I tell you to put away your toys? Now come wash up, guests will be arriving soon!"

"Of course, Mama."

As Mama shuffled off, the deputy returned his attention to the body, crouched slightly, and took a closer look at the spot where the head should have been, then down at the arms, where the hands should have been. He nodded slightly, then produced a notepad and started writing. He had a choppy, messy scrawl; Yvgeny leaned in to snoop but could not read one word of it. *Holmes never wrote anything down,* he scoffed to himself.

After a few minutes, the detective straightened and again turned to Yvgeny. He reached up and twirled the tip of his bushy mustache.

"You got all his clothes?"

Yvgeny pointed down below the table.

"Right there."

The detective nodded and reached into his back pocket, removed a pair of blue nitrile gloves. He was taller than Yvgeny, with short brown hair and a strong brow, casting his eyes perpetually in shadow. Combined with his thick mustache, he looked more like an old cowboy than a detective. Yvgeny glanced down at his gun.

Newsome pulled on the fingers of the gloves while looking around the room.

"How long you been running this place? Twenty years?"

Yvgeny shrugged.

"Something like that."

To be exact, it was twenty two years, but by nature, Yvgeny was circumspect when speaking with law enforcement. Schmidt and Sons became Yvgeny's upon his father's death in 1994. Many years earlier, when Yvgeny was a child, his father bought the place out of probate. His father kept the name out of respect for the family that ran the business for a hundred years and for the man who took him in and taught him everything about it.

When the place became Yvgeny's, he continued to

honor the family name as a sign of respect. However, he did file papers to change the name from Schmidt and Sons Funeral Home to Schmidt and Sons Mortuary. He did not believe in false advertising. Homes were for the living, not the dead, and he had no interest in the sappy whitewashing the moniker, *funeral home*, implied.

Newsome's eyes settled on the alcove with the drain, saw shampoo and soap. His gaze lingered there a moment, but he said nothing. Newsome turned back toward the body. The two officers had shrank into a corner, their backs to the others.

Newsome crouched underneath the body and examined the clothing Yvgeny had piled on the tray.

"Was he dressed when you found him?"

Yvgeny nodded. The deputy stared silently at him, then he stood, lifted one of the corpse's arms, and began inspecting the body, inch by inch. No injuries were apparent, other than the obvious. He muttered to himself as he did so.

"Maybe shot in the head? Strangled?"

He continued to work, then glanced over Yvgeny's head and took a hard look at the blue uniformed officers in the corner. He made as if to yell something at them, then shook his head and turned to Yvgeny with a smirk.

"Hey tiger, would you mind helping me turn this guy over?"

Yvgeny ignored the detective's bait and jeer, and helped him without speaking. Newsome paused when he noticed Yvgeny was not wearing gloves. *I suppose that will go into his report,* Yvgeny thought to himself.

Newsome continued examining the body while Yvgeny watched. After a while, he turned to the officers and called out, "One of you boys want to make yourself useful and call Flowers out here to get the body?"

Dr. Flowers was the local physician. He had his own general practice in town and achieved the unfortunate status of being the only doctor in Comstock after old man Smithers died. On the bright side, after Smithers's death, Flowers acquired his old contract with the sheriff to perform coroner's duties and, on rare occasions, autopsies. The sheriff quickly regretted awarding the contract to Flowers on account of his tendency to complain, self-aggrandize, and generally annoy.

Flowers's most recent request was for the sheriff to provide him an ambulance, which the sheriff flatly refused for months until Flowers convinced him his wife would leave him if he didn't stop loading dead people into the back of the family Ford Bronco. The sheriff finally caved and used drug forfeiture money to buy Flowers a used van from the county auction.

The old van had been part of the county school system's fleet and was beat up from years of hard use, but Flowers didn't care. The sheriff paid to make it roadworthy again, but Flowers bartered with a local mechanic to make some additional improvements in exchange for the doctor's services (which consisted mainly of a frequently renewed prescription for a healthy dose of pain killers), then took the van to Earl Scheib in Warner Robins for their $199 paint special. Fire engine red. Flowers asked them to get as close as they could to the color of Tom Selleck's Ferrari in Magnum PI, his favorite television show.

Soon after picking up his new van (which he referred to as his ambulance), he developed a penchant for Hawaiian shirts and grew a bushy gray mustache. The sheriff grumbled with disgust, but remained silent on the subject.

Flowers then ordered a magnetic door sticker from a sign company in Macon that said "COUNTY MEDICAL EXAMINER" in big and bold capitals, Arial font.

The sheriff blew a gasket when he saw the finished product driving through town. He despised showboating; he was a fourth generation Gilbert County man, conservative, fond of bow ties and oblivious to the fact it visually enhanced the size of his large gut. To make things worse, he tended to pull his pants up high and cinch down his belt, making him look like a balloon sheriff created by some talented clown at a child's birthday party.

Throughout town, people followed Flowers's arrival in that red van from behind drawn blinds, holding their breath as the harbinger of death passed by, a Chevrolet-powered ATM card about to be swiped for the ultimate withdrawal. But no-one cared when it pulled into Yvgeny's drive to make a deposit. At that point it was no more interesting than the pizza guy ringing a neighbor's doorbell.

The first time the sheriff saw what had become of Flowers's van, he stopped in the street, his thumbs in his pockets, and stared. His first inclination was to have one of his deputies hook a wrecker to it and take it away. Flowers saw him staring, parked, and came ambling over, all smiles, to greet him and ask for reimbursement for the cost of the paint job. The sheriff stared at Flowers, mouth agape, then turned without a word and walked away.

But the last straw for the sheriff came when Flowers submitted paperwork requesting a county permit to operate red lights and a siren on his "emergency response vehicle." In a one sentence denial, the sheriff personally wrote *your patients are all dead already. No need to rush.* He also crossed out "emergency response vehicle" and scribbled in "van." Flowers decided not to appeal the decision after consulting one of the three civil lawyers in town.

Newsome stood straight again and walked toward the waste can, removing the gloves.

"Geny, you see anything else on this guy or around the body?"

Yvgeny stood quietly a moment. He shook his wrist, un-snagging the watch from his cuff button, the movement causing Newsome's eyes to briefly flick down to Yvgeny's arm, then back up.

"Nope. Alfred pulled the corpse out of the earth himself."

Newsome nodded slowly. Took a breath.

"Alfred. That old black guy that works here?"

Just as he asked the question, there was a metallic scrape, followed by the sound of wheels rolling against a hard surface. The sounds grew louder, then the door opened and a very filthy, very smelly Alfred lumbered into the room pushing a cart. The timing of his entrance was so perfect, Yvgeny thought, it was almost theatrical, as if choreographed, straight from a modern adaptation of a Shakespearean tragedy.

This cart was different from the one upon which the headless body had been resting, made with thicker gauge piping and bigger, sturdier wheels. A casket rested on top. He pushed the cart past the officers, one of the wheels turning in circles and squeaking as it rolled.

Yvgeny pursed his lips when he noticed Alfred's muddy footprints on the tile floor and caught his odious scent as it wafted by. A reprimand was on his tongue for Alfred's slovenly appearance and foul smell, but when he saw the officers' reaction to Alfred, he had to make a conscious effort not to shudder with anticipation.

THE BODY IN THE HOLE

Alfred arranged the cart against the far wall and walked toward the refrigerated drawers, oblivious to the officers' worried stares. Yvgeny watched them watching Alfred, amusement on his face. He knew what was about to happen.

Alfred reached up and opened one of the doors, then wheeled out the pallet containing the remains of Mr. Dunlap. One of the city officers inhaled sharply as he saw the big lump covered with a white sheet. Alfred was about to execute a maneuver Yvgeny had seen many times, and Yvgeny watched gleefully as the play unfolded.

Alfred slowly rolled the body out about half way, then back in about a foot to gather momentum, then pulled hard on the pallet, sort of like starting a lawn mower. The pallet shot forward, then slammed into the rubber stops. Like a driver in a crash without a seatbelt, the body continued to slide forward from the impact and came to a stop about a third of the way off the pallet and remained there, the head and shoulders dangling free from the sheet and pallet, just inches above the coffin.

Hanging upside down, mouth wide open, old man Dunlap's lifeless eyes seemed to stare straight at the two officers while Alfred finished the job. He had mastered the move, like a short order cook cracking eggs, with just the right amount of force. Alfred steadied the cart, locked the wheels, lifted the lid of the coffin, angled it just right, then grabbed Dunlap's fleshy arms and hauled him the rest of the way out and guided his fall into the open casket. The body landed with a wet thud.

As Alfred slammed the pallet back into the bin and shut the door, the younger officer pressed his hand to his mouth and made retching noises. The second officer turned a shade somewhere between green and yellow.

Yvgeny stepped in front of the officers, assumed a professorial expression, and began to narrate like PT Barnum standing on a crate before a crowd.

"Ah, closed casket. It's best for us all with that one," began Yvgeny, pointing his thumb back toward the coffin where Alfred still hovered.

"He was a real stinker. You know, poor habits during life lead to poor results after death. You rot more quickly, and with the rot comes the smell. That fat bastard cost me a small fortune in embalming fluid and deodorizer. And as if that wasn't bad enough, he kept clogging my machine."

Yvgeny crept toward the officers, slowly, drawing their attention to him like rubberneckers passing a crash on the highway.

"Imagine, if you will, trying to suck up a gallon of oatmeal through a straw."

Yvgeny emphasized his point by making sucking and slurping sounds, in and out, just a foot away from the two pale, trembling officers.

"Only it wasn't oatmeal, if you follow me. Clogged up my machine real good."

Then he stood up straight and clapped his hands together, causing them to jump.

"So, constables, if we are through here, I'd like to get in there and scoop out the rest. Funeral's in a couple hours, gotta finish him quick."

Then he leaned in even closer, almost close enough for them to feel his breath, and whispered, "probably just use my hands. Scoop it out the old fashioned way."

Yvgeny chuckled as the first officer finally turned and ran out of the room. Newsome watched him leave, pursing his lips together in disgust. Then he turned back to Yvgeny.

"You already embalmed him."

Yvgeny, still smiling, glanced over at the deputy.

"Of course. But the look on their faces was priceless."

The deputy rubbed his hand across his chin, then pulled on the corner of his mustache again. Then he shook his head.

"You mind if I take a look at my crime scene before you toss another body in it?"

"Not at all. Like I said, the funeral isn't scheduled to begin for a couple hours."

Alfred began to push Dunlap toward the double doors, but Yvgeny called out to him, then turned to Newsome to say, "Just one moment, inspector," then lifted the lid of Dunlap's coffin. He reached inside, bent his head to inspect something beyond Newsome's view, then stood up straight, leaving the lid open. He noticed Newsome's stare and explained, "You saw Alfred's methods. Just had to make sure Dunlap wasn't leaking. Happens sometimes."

"Ain't you going to dress the guy?"

"Why? Like I said, it's a closed casket."

In fact, Yvgeny thought to himself, the family brought over Dunlap's Armani tuxedo, which Yvgeny estimated would fetch $500 on eBay with little effort.

Newsome did not respond, and Yvgeny walked halfway toward the door, then turned and with a flourish extended an arm out as if to say, 'Be my guest.' Newsome took a few steps, then stopped and turned toward the remaining officer.

"Come on, Princess."

The officer shuffled across the room, past Yvgeny, and out the door. His partner was waiting in the hall fiddling with his smartphone, and glumly fell in behind them as they walked outside to see the crime scene. Both officers jumped as they heard Alfred slam the lid back down on the coffin. When they heard the squeaking of the wheels growing closer, they started to walk faster.

They stepped outside into a warm soup of a day, the air moist and heavy. It settled down over them, their shirts clinging to their skin as they waved away clouds of gnats. The blue sky had clouded over and resembled one of Alfred's milky blue corneas; unstable weather fronts in Middle Georgia were not unusual in the fall months and Newsome glanced heavenwards to gauge the likelihood of a deluge.

They trudged through the grass toward the Dunlap plot and gathered around the canopy to stare into the hole. Alfred appeared in the distance, making his way slowly toward the gravesite in the slab cab, Dunlap's coffin strapped in beside him. Next to the grave, Alfred had set up a contraption with four sturdy belts that would help him unload the coffin, then eventually lower it into the earth. Newsome put his thumbs behind his belt buckle, then turned to the younger officer.

"Let's get on with it, Frankie."

Frankie looked up as if he had been struck.

"Me?" he asked, while looking around for a sympathetic face, and after finding none, added, "I ain't got no shovel."

Yvgeny smirked and looked past them toward Alfred, then began wind-milling his arms over his head to get Alfred's attention, and when the modified golf cart rolled to a stop, Yvgeny made digging motions with his arms, and put his hands on his hips. His smile broadened.

"Not to worry, Alfred is on his way."

Alfred detoured toward his shed, parked, and retrieved a shovel. He headed over on foot, trudging through the grass, weaving around headstones, crosses, and statuary, surprisingly nimble despite a withered leg and ambling gait. The thought occurred to Newsome that watching Alfred in action was like watching an ungainly penguin struggling on the shore, then becoming an acrobat in the sea.

Yvgeny took the shovel from Alfred's dirt caked fingers, then held it out to Frankie. Alfred appeared confused, then looked expectantly toward the hole.

"Ask and ye shall receive!"

Frankie's expression looked more like that of a kid in trouble with his mother than a police officer. He sought support from his partner, then Newsome, turning to them like a convicted man silently pleading with his jury, and finding no sympathy, hung his head and with a groan, took the shovel and stumbled into the hole. Newsome turned to Yvgeny and asked him, "How much earth you think was dropped in over the body?"

Yvgeny considered, looking down at the hole. Frankie stood inside the hole frowning at the earth all around him. His lower lip began to quiver.

Yvgeny wanted to say two feet, but decided not to lie, if only to get rid of the cops sooner than later.

"No more than a foot, maybe thirteen inches."

Newsome looked down at Frankie and said, "You heard the man, thirteen inches."

Frankie sighed, then slammed the shovel into the earth, lifted a scoop, then looked around as if unsure where to place it. He eventually tossed the earth behind him and, having heard no objection from above, continued in that manner.

Frankie spent the next half hour looking up, shovel in hand, while his overseers stood around the hole above him pointing toward anything that caught their eye. He would sift through one area, then another, burying himself past his shins. The Georgia red clay clung to his navy pants. Alfred hovered at the edge, continually turning his attention from Frankie up to the heavens, as if he was communing with some gravedigger's deity. Or perhaps he was divining the time before the clouds spewed forth to soak them all.

Yvgeny glanced down at his watch and realized Alfred, whose studious expression had gradually changed to impatient, anxious, may actually have been studying the sky not to prognosticate the weather but to determine the time in his own rudimentary way.

Once Alfred began repeatedly turning from Frankie in the hole to old Dunlap on the golf cart, Yvgeny looked across the hole at Newsome and called out, "Are we about finished here?"

Frankie had trouble climbing out of the hole, mainly due to the wet earth, but his rotund belly and heavily laden gear belt didn't help. He clawed handfuls of moist earth from the sides in his struggle to escape, which greatly irritated Alfred, who shook an accusatory and mud-caked finger at the officer while shouting, "nnnng! Ngh!"

Newsome walked around the hole toward Yvgeny, and they both looked down into the hole together.

"You gonna tell them there was another body in that hole?"

Yvgeny did not look up from the hole when he spoke.

"Dunlap was a fat slob and his wife is a whore. I'm not telling them anything."

Newsome nodded. He had heard the rumors about her.

"I don't know how you do this for a living, Geny."

Yvgeny looked out across the headstones.

"It's a living, inspector. I don't know how *you* do *your* job. With all of *them*."

Yvgeny cocked his head toward the officers. As they watched, the older one crouched and extended an arm to Frankie as he fought to get out of the hole. As they struggled, Alfred bounced from one foot to the other, grunting and pointing at the two officers, and occasionally looking up at the sky.

"Well, I usually don't have to work with *them*."

Eventually Frankie made it out of the hole and began brushing himself off like a terrified girl who had walked into a spider web, then they both shuffled sullenly to their patrol cars. Newsome watched them, a smirk on his face, then put his hands on his hips and hollered, "Hey, cowboys, one of you needs to wait for Flowers! Chain of custody and all. You know the rules."

The two officers looked at each other again, horrified, and Frankie slowly lowered his head, his shoulders slumped. Seniority had its benefits, and the older officer almost ran toward his car and sped away.

"How inspiring," Yvgeny muttered.

Newsome watched the car speed away, then held out his hand again to Yvgeny. When Yvgeny offered his limp hand, Newsome squeezed hard, causing Yvgeny to squirm, then leaned in and whispered, "You ever pollute another crime scene of mine, I'll put you in a cell the size of that there hole, ya' hear?"

Newsome squeezed harder for a moment, then

released Yvgeny, stared at him silently, then turned and left. As Newsome walked by Frankie he muttered, "Don't let Flowers carve this guy up. Tell him the body goes straight to the GBI. Kincaid needs to handle this one."

Flowers arrived thirty minutes later. The magnetic signs were gone, having been replaced with his name in all caps and the words *Medical Examiner* stenciled in a garish yellow cursive font. He had tinted the windows limousine black. Flowers stopped in the street, then backed into Yvgeny's drive. Plumes of black smoke rose from dual chrome-tipped exhaust pipes.

Frankie, who had been leaning against the wall of the funeral home, pushed off and stood, one hand resting on the butt of his gun. The mortuary door swung open and smacked against Frankie's boot, knocking him off balance and into the bushes as Yvgeny emerged.

Frankie recovered and brushed himself off. As the van backed up the drive toward him, he stared at the stenciled words on the van and said, "looks like a bowling shirt on wheels!"

Yvgeny continued staring at the van and muttered, "Henry Ford was right."

"Huh?"

"All cars should be black."

"Yvgeny, why is a plumber here? What's wrong? Is there a leak? I told you this place was falling apart!"

Yvgeny closed his eyes and took a deep breath as his mother continued to yell from the second story window. Flowers shoved the van into park and began revving the engine, glass packs rumbling like a busy wood chipper. Flowers had his arm out of his open window, jeering at Yvgeny through the side mirror.

Frankie, finally identifying a situation with which he had some experience, jumped into action and came after Flowers bellowing Georgia traffic code citations with a wagging finger.

Flowers dutifully shut off the engine and hopped out, then walked back to the rear double doors. He had the cocksure foot-bouncing strut reminiscent of the jocks Yvgeny remembered from high school, but the similarities ended there. Flowers was a rail of a man in his sixties who wore his gray hair bushy with a matching mustache. He wore jeans and a Hawaiian shirt, un-tucked, channeling his inner Magnum PI.

Like the sheriff, Yvgeny didn't approve of his flashy van or his radical appearance, but tolerated Flowers to preserve their relationship, one he maintained out of business necessity.

Yvgeny met Flowers at the back of his van. He could feel his mother's eyes watching every move from her window. Frankie stood to one side, eyes alert like a humorless school teacher monitoring a high school dance.

"Mr. Undertaker," Flowers said with a smirk, "I understand you have a package for me."

Yvgeny shook his head and rolled his eyes, then checked his watch.

"Come on, we are on a tight schedule this morning."

Flowers retrieved a collapsible gurney, the legs of the contraption dropping into place as he pulled it out, then he rolled it toward the mortuary behind Yvgeny.

"Yvgeny, what would your father say about bartering? And what kind of plumber dresses like that?"

Both Flowers and Frankie looked at Yvgeny, who squinched his eyes shut and tried to ignore his mother's questions. Frankie placed a Skoal Bandit behind his lip, turned to spit into the bushes, then fell in behind Flowers. The three of them plodded along through the doors and down the hall toward Yvgeny's work room.

Frankie equivocated outside the room's entrance, looking in, then back out, his face pale. Finally, he stood sideways at the entrance, leaning against the threshold, too uncomfortable to come in, but too nervous to remain outside by himself.

Yvgeny brought Flowers into the work space, then directed him to the body. Flowers walked around it silently, then stopped, cocked his head to one side, and said, "He's missing his head."

Yvgeny looked at Flowers a moment, stony-eyed, before crying out, "That's strange, it was there a minute ago. Frankie, what did you do with his head?"

Flowers pursed his lips, muttered, "Just help me move him over."

He pushed his gurney toward the body, and just as they turned to move it, a rattling sound came from outside the room. Frankie, still posted at the threshold, straightened up and whispered, "What was that?"

Yvgeny, still irritated by his mother, by Newsome, and everything else, said, "Oh, that's nothing, just one of the corpses stacked down the hall. Sometimes, after *rigor mortis* diminishes, they shake and jerk around like they're having a seizure. They knock stuff over, make burbling noises, why, sometimes they even sit up! Why don't you go check it out? Might be fun!"

Frankie's face turned green and his mouth moved like a caught fish on the bottom of a boat, and he ran. The door remained propped open. Yvgeny and Flowers looked out the open door as Frankie's footsteps grew softer, then they heard a door slam shut. Flowers muttered something under his breath and turned back to the body.

The rattling grew louder, then Alfred came into view, his arms laden with stacked chairs. Seeing activity inside, Alfred lowered the chairs to the floor and came in to watch, curious.

Flowers produced and unzipped a body bag and arranged it on the gurney, then tried to slide the body across Yvgeny's table and into the bag, but the table slid away each time. Flowers fiddled with the wheel locks, then resumed his struggle with the body. Yvgeny and Alfred both watched, and more than once Flowers glared at them as they stood motionless. Finally, Flowers stopped and cried out, "You gonna help me or not?"

Yvgeny approached and held the gurney steady so Flowers could pull the body into the bag and zip it closed. He rolled it toward the door, then stopped and turned back to Yvgeny.

"Where's the head?"

"How the hell would I know? Probably with the hands."

Alfred took a couple steps back and stared intently at the chairs.

Flowers hissed through clenched teeth and smacked the gurney against the external doors hard enough for them to swing wide open, then started to push it through. Alfred looked up and, breathing out of his mouth, stared at the body bag.

Yvgeny took several strides toward the doctor, one arm raised, a finger pointed in the air, and called out, "Oh, Flowers, Flowers! Newsome told me to tell you to take the carcass to Macon. He wants Kincaid to chop it up."

Flowers punched the side of the body, causing the gurney to slide to one side, the body within rustling as it settled.

"Dammit! So now I'm just the taxi service? What's he giving it to Kincaid for?"

Flowers scratched his head with both hands, something Yvgeny had seen him do when irritated, then turned back to Yvgeny, an insalubrious smile on his face, and growled in a low voice, "It's the sheriff, isn't it? I bet he's still pissed about the van. You know, he didn't complain when the fire chief painted all *his* trucks from yellow to red."

Yvgeny shrugged his shoulders.

"He's the fire chief. You're not. You're not the coroner either. Or the ME. Or the sheriff. Come to think of it, you're not anything, really."

"You're a real buzz kill, Geny."

Flowers deflated, then steadied the body. He heaved the gurney against the doors again, then stopped and looked back toward Yvgeny.

"Wait a minute, where's all his crap?"

Yvgeny pointed back toward the table. Flowers saw the bag beneath it, cursed softly, and on his way back to retrieve the bag his eyes darted toward Yvgeny as he said, "You were gonna just let me walk out the door without it?"

Yvgeny smiled and shrugged his shoulders.

"Well, silly me, I figured someone with your education and experience would eventually figure it out."

Flowers stared at Yvgeny a moment, then turned and grabbed the bag, muttering as he left, "A pleasure, as usual. You seem more like one of these corpses every day."

He dropped the bag on top of the body, knocked the door open for the third time, then chocked it with his foot. He paused, then turned back one last time, a strange smile on his face.

"What time are they coming back?"

"Who?"

"The police! They always get a search warrant for crime scenes like this. Probably tear the whole place apart. Might even dig up a few bodies, just for sport. Make a real mess, just in time for Dunlap's funeral."

Yvgeny sputtered but remained silent.

Satisfied, Flowers pushed the gurney through the doors and shuffled off, whistling softly. Frankie dolefully watched Flowers from his defensive position behind the door of his patrol car.

Yvgeny's mind began to race at the possibility of the police returning with a search warrant. He thought of his goody can in the kitchen cupboard, and the plush cushions in the living room.

He turned to find Alfred watching Flowers's progress with an odd expression on his face. Yvgeny inspected the man's unkempt appearance, and was not pleased.

"Damn Alfred, you look worse than Dunlap. Go set up those chairs, then get cleaned up. If anyone sees you like that, they will think you've risen from the dead. Come on, those idiots will be here any minute."

Alfred glared at him, his Adam's apple bouncing, then he grabbed the chairs and shuffled away in silence. Still irritated by Flowers's parting words, Yvgeny approached the doorway to watch him struggle to load the body into his van.

Yvgeny's eyes strayed over to Frankie, who was still hunkered down behind the door of his patrol car. Yvgeny snorted, poked his head out, and yelled, "Inspiring, constable. Truly."

Mama was waiting for him when he returned, tottering with one hand on her hip, the other on her cane. He sighed, then adjusted his rubber apron. He knew what was coming. She checked her watch.

"The Dunlap clan will start arriving soon, you still have a lot to do."

"I know."

"And where is Maude?"

"Airing out in cold storage."

"And Dunlap? You even package him yet?"

"Already at the gravesite."

His mother gave him her best "Humph!" but didn't further comment.

Maude Oliver made it to ninety, a ripe old age, far older than old man Dunlap, a testament to proper living and diet. Maude could have lived inside Dunlap like Jonah in the whale. With her size, she only needed to chill half a day before her "coming out" party, as he liked to call it.

Yvgeny worked the math in his head while approaching his cabinet, trying to ignore his mother's withering stare. At her age, her emotions wavered unreliably like a rusty canoe in choppy water.

His first shelf contained his main arterial chemicals: preservatives. His preference was formaldehyde, but he kept a supply of glutaraldehyde and a few bottles of phenol; whatever was on sale. He counted the bottles, glanced at the clipboard hung from the top shelf, then re-counted the bottles. Then he counted them again. One was missing.

He immediately thought of those bungling city cops, but then discounted them; they wouldn't have the guts to filch a bottle of embalming fluid. He looked toward the door, in the direction of Alfred's shed, then shook his head and clucked his tongue. *Poor Alfred,* he thought, *I'll have to have a talk with him.*

He checked his stash of methanol, which would keep his formaldehyde from evaporating. There was more than enough for his solution, which, for Maude, he would hand mix like an accomplished chef. *No recipe necessary.*

His mother shuffled closer, shaking her head.

"Your father always knew just what to mix. Such a professional. Zip, zip, zip!" she said, pretending to grab bottles and toss them over her head like a mime. His mother was a consummate professional at disguising insults that targeted him within compliments toward third parties.

"He would handle his business and be at the table before I could serve breakfast."

"It's not like making soup, Mama. Each job is different and requires careful –"

His Mother rolled her eyes and mimicked the tossing again, "Zip, zip, zip!"

Ignoring her, Yvgeny continued, "careful calculations depending on the body and the circumstances."

Yvgeny's mother had always been more interested in the cash flow than the business itself. She had never appreciated the details; even seemingly minor factors, such as the length of time a body must remain above ground, were crucial: the longer the time before burial, the higher the index of the solution.

His mother waved her hand dismissively.

"The whole town loves Maude. She taught half of them! Your father, God rest his soul . . . ."

Yvgeny tuned her out, thinking back upon a passage from one of the moldering books on old man Eldred's shelf, words that stuck with him over the years:

Embalming is only a temporary reprieve from the inevitable decomposition that will eventually return us all to those basic building blocks that keep the world full of life. Your preservatives will keep colonizing bacteria at bay for a week or two, but not much longer.

Yvgeny repeatedly tried to defend himself from her attacks by trying to convince her of the mathematical precision required to properly embalm a body, but in fact, Yvgeny didn't have a great mind for numbers. It therefore came as a relief to him that the calculation of dilution levels was as much art as it was science. A little fudging on the numbers rarely mattered. It was more about appearances and the bottom line, similar to used car salesmen clutching their big button calculators. *All part of the dance.*

Ignoring her critical eye, Yvgeny adopted an expression of deep concentration, muttering about Maude's size, weight, condition, time of death, then pretended to calculate the required concentration level of his solution, counting off with his fingers to maximize Mama's frustration with him.

"Yes, around 20% should maximize preservation," he declared, and ignored his mother's tongue clucking and impassioned descriptions of his father's work acumen.

"This one needs to be special!" His mother called out abruptly.

Oh, this will be special, Yvgeny thought. In fact, he had something very special planned for Maude, something Lenny Updike couldn't have envisioned in his wildest dreams. He spent hours of research, development, and planning with the guys at *Jumpie's, Inc.* in Macon.

The *Jumpie's, Inc.* fabricators were virtual

magicians, experts in their field of expertise. Yvgeny had seen what they could do to a 1978 Monte Carlo; once they applied their engineering skills to Yvgeny's project, it would truly put Schmidt and Sons on the map. *Ah, but it was time to get back to business.*

"Don't worry, Mama, it will be special."

One could fudge the dilution numbers quite a bit, but some things needed serious consideration. Maude had been in her home a while before anyone noticed, and she was polluted with months of chemotherapy, which left her body very acidic. Acidity caused the formaldehyde to have to work twice as hard, so he set aside a bottle of special water conditioner which would balance her out. He also added a bottle of dye to give her a little more color.

He stopped to reflect on a time, years before, when he had found an electric blue colored dye and, in a fit of artistic flair, had tried it on a burn job (what he affectionately called those due for cremation) just to see what would happen. He was hoping for a giant Smurf, something to add some levity to his photo album, but instead he only achieved the look of an asphyxiation victim.

Glancing back at his disapproving mother, he snapped up two bottles of humectant as a final touch. It would fill out Maude's thin, crepe-like skin; otherwise she would give her grandkids nightmares for months.

"Two bottles? A little overkill, if you ask me."

Yvgeny cringed, then snatched a third bottle out of spite, smiling at the reaction it aroused in her, then his smile increased as he heard the tapping of her cane as she finally left.

"Now then, where was I . . . Ah, yes," he said, then grabbed a bottle of SaniSol 5 just in case. An excellent product, like Lysol for bodies. He loaded his things on a small wheeled cart he kept just for this purpose, then wheeled it over to his Snap On tool chest and opened the big middle drawer. He sorted through his collection of trocars and chose a couple he thought would be best for Maude.

Next, he set everything up in the corner next to his embalming machine, rehearsed the steps in his mind to make sure he hadn't forgotten anything, then nodded to himself with approval. By the time he was done with her, she would look better than she did alive. He returned his rubber apron to its hook and retired to his parlor. He needed to straighten up before Dunlap's party.

╬

CHAPTER FOUR

The Dunlap affair went without a hitch. Alfred waited for the family to toss their flowers and leave, then he lumbered over to finish him. Yvgeny remained in the parlor to observe the visitors, wearing one of old man Eldred's better black suits and a new cravat he recently had purchased. Eldred must have put on a great deal of weight toward the end, as, unlike the others, this suit required significant alterations. Yvgeny of course handled the adjustments himself, another talent passed down from father to son.

Throughout the event, his mother lurked in the shadows, casting disapproving glares at him whenever he glanced in her direction.

Yvgeny believed an undertaker to be part artist, part scientist. He also believed his only client was the corpse on the table. Once the client was in the ground, the rest was formality and appeasement.

The fat, obnoxious Dunlaps consumed a truckload of meat and hors d'ouvres and, of course, copious amounts of booze, walking cadavers looking for coffins. His whore of a wife was stuffed into a black dress and when no one was looking, she guzzled her wine, then checked her lipstick using her reflection in one of the silver platters. Yvgeny watched her ogle one of the young male caterers.

He suffered through the ritual, silently counting the minutes, then stood in the carport seeing them off with a waving, limp hand, all the while keeping an eye on Alfred to make sure he was focused on the caterers. Caterers were an untrustworthy lot, notorious for leaving kitchen surfaces dirty and drawers empty. His mother hated the affairs and used to remain upstairs, much to Yvgeny's satisfaction, but that all changed after the Wakefield funeral.

The Wakefields were a suspicious lot. Old man Wakefield had walked with the assistance of a cane, so when the attendees heard his mother shuffling about on the second floor, and heard the rhythmic pounding of her cane, one of them screamed, and that scream whipped the others into a frenzy, and they fled the building thinking his ghost was preparing to make a grand entrance. The caterers took the opportunity to reward themselves with some of the family silver. Naturally, the police did nothing.

As Yvgeny stood watching the cars drive off, one by one, he saw a vehicle approach from the street, its blinker on as it waited for an opening in the traffic. It was a tiny red Smart car, and his heart jumped in his chest at the sight of it. The car was about the size of the Goliath Galaxy, a high end coffin for the most discriminating of cadavers. Yvgeny fantasized about sharing a Galaxy with the Smart car's driver, Brianna Schtumpf, his friend Randall's forty five year old granddaughter. He all but ignored the remaining Dunlap posse as they filed out.

Brianna parked her car and the door opened. She flicked a cigarette butt out, and he watched it arc across the lawn, reminding him of a little lightning bug in its quest for a mate. The whole car then rocked back and forth as she slowly emerged, huffing and squeezing, the suspension of the tiny car squawking in protest, then settling with a squeak of relief.

And there she stood, holding a bouquet of flowers for her grandfather. She mopped the sweat from her brow that had collected from her effort, then started her hike toward her grandfather's final resting place.

See Randy, I told you she'd be here.

Yvgeny anxiously waited for the last few stragglers to leave, then checked his watch; 4:30. *Perfect!* It was nap time for his mother, and, as if on cue, he heard her cane thumping away toward the parlor where she took her rest. Yvgeny wasted no time and headed out into the cemetery.

In early October, the four o'clock hour was the hottest of the day, and by the time Yvgeny caught up with Brianna, she looked like a monstrous candle melting beneath an invisible wick. She held her cigarette between her lips as she furiously texted a message into her phone. She leaned against Randy's headstone, the afternoon sunshine transforming her curly blonde hair into flaxen, spun gold in a feat worthy of Rumpelstiltskin himself.

Yvgeny stood, transfixed, watching her as she texted, then waited, then flushed with the response.

"That no good son of a-"

Her thumbs attacked the phone with a vengeance, her eyebrows knitted, her mouth twisted into a beautiful mask of rage, her cheeks colored with righteous indignation, *like some Teutonic warrior princess in battle,* he mused, *or perhaps a sumo wrestler trying his hand in a* Noh *drama.* Or, Yvgeny imagined with a flash of color rushing to his own cheeks, *like a cigarette smoking plus-sized geisha.* Yvgeny felt his palms growing moist.

She suddenly felt his presence and jumped, almost knocking her head into Randall's stone. Her cigarette fell from her mouth and bounced off her bosom before hitting the ground. She eyed him suspiciously, clutching her phone to her body with both hands in a defensive posture.

"What are you doing?"

"These are my grounds."

"What the hell does that mean?"

"I am the undertaker, and this is my cemetery."

Brianna stared at him like a deer crossing paths with a child, frozen into submission, curious, but coiled like a spring.

"And I am a friend of your grandfather's."

Brianna made a prune face and spit out, "Are you kidding me? He died over seventy years ago. What are you, some kind of nut job?"

"My name is Yvgeny, and no, what I meant to say is, I come out here and talk to him sometimes. He's a good listener."

Brianna stared at him a moment, then pulled a pack of Marlboros from a pocket and fiddled with the packaging. Tossing the cellophane into the breeze, followed by the inner freshness foil, she pulled a cigarette from the package, tapped it against the box, then fixed it to the corner of her mouth.

Brianna spoke slowly, still guarded.

"I know. That's why I come here. It's, well, peaceful."

Yvgeny nodded, like that same child coming upon that skittish deer, recognizing the magic of the moment. He took one small, ever so small, step forward.

"Yes, yes it is."

She produced a package of matches and as she lifted the flap, Yvgeny rushed in.

"No, please, allow me."

He closed the gap and took the matches from her, produced a flame, and held it out as she lit her cigarette. He sniffed but was unable to catch her scent. She took a deep drag, exhaled over his head, then gave him a somewhat confused expression, and said, "Thanks." Then she glanced down at his outfit.

"Is that your uniform?"

"In a manner of speaking. I believe appearances are important. I am guessing that you agree," he added, looking down at her outfit. She wore an ankle length black cotton dress with black Reebok sneakers, no doubt chosen for her trek to Randall's spot. *Sensible.* Brianna started to relax, but kept her eyes on Yvgeny.

"I'm Brianna."

"Yes, I know."

"I never even met him, you know. Hell, my Dad didn't really know him, either. He died when Dad was like a year old."

Smoke curled up from her nostrils as she glanced away for a moment and muttered, "I know, it's stupid."

"Not at all. It is a tribute to your sense of family obligation and values."

"Is that a shot?"

"Of course not!" Yvgeny said, aghast.

She smoked quietly, occasionally glancing at him, and then turning away.

Her phone began to vibrate and she checked the screen. A flash of anger spread across her face, but quickly dispersed. She muttered something guttural and unintelligible. She noticed him watching her, and explained, "ex-husband. He's a real A-hole."

Yvgeny nodded, trying to remain stoic.

Brianna sucked once more from her cigarette,

smashed it against her grandfather's tombstone, then flicked it away into the grass. She looked around, shrugged her shoulders, and turned to leave. Yvgeny rushed forward to escort her, turning to wink at Randall's tombstone. He couldn't help but lag behind a few times just to watch her walking with her flat footed clopping stride, like a beast of burden under the yoke; so different from his diminutive mother.

Arriving at the driveway, Yvgeny avoided Mama's baleful expression as she surveilled them from her parlor window. He instead focused on his prey, watching as she squished herself into the tiny opening of her car, her ample belly pressing against the steering wheel. The process reminded Yvgeny of a snake consuming a large mouse. The car gave another loud creak of protest but accepted the load. He shut her door as she fumbled with her keys.

"Perhaps I will see you again next week?"

Brianna stopped fumbling with her keys and looked hard at Yvgeny, as if seeing him for the first time. Her expression was sharp, appraising. *Calculating.* It gave him a shiver.

"Are you hitting on me?"

In all things but love, Yvgeny was a direct man. But standing there, with his conquest within his grasp, his lack of experience showed and he went mute. After a moment, she nodded, as if his silence was answer enough. She leaned forward and looked through her windshield at his mortuary, then asked, "Do you make a lot of money here?"

"I want for nothing I cannot obtain."

"Huh?"

"Yes, I earn a proper income."

She fumbled with her cigarettes again, waving off his attempt to assist her, punched the lighter button in her car, then turned back to him.

"All these dead people. You're not some kind of freak, are you?"

Yvgeny remained silent until he realized she was asking a real question.

"What? Of course not."

She eyed him suspiciously one more time, then nodded. The car lighter popped out, and she brought the red hot eye to her cigarette and dragged until it lit, then blew the smoke out the window, where it wafted up toward Yvgeny's face.

"OK, fine. I have to work tomorrow until 10 pm. You can meet me there."

"Where is there?"

"The Golden Pantry on SR96 in Bonaire. You know where it is?"

"Of course."

She fumbled a moment with her seatbelt and started her car. She gave him one more up/down appraising look, then added, "If you come right before Ricky gets there, I can sell you gas at 10% off. One of the fringe benefits of the job."

When Yvgeny didn't immediately respond, she put her cigarette between her front teeth, crunched her car into gear and lurched off down the driveway. Yvgeny watched her leave, speechless.

He wandered back inside, a self-satisfied grin slowly appearing on his face. He replayed the exchange in his head, looking down as he recalled her reference to his *uniform*. He led her to believe he was well off, which was true depending on one's perspective.

His life would have been well beyond his means if he had had to pay for it all. He inherited Schmidt and Sons from his father, acquired his extravagant wardrobe of formal wear from a combination of former clients and his original benefactor's ancient collection. *Ah yes, living the golden life on a pig iron budget!*

Back in his kitchen, he set the tea kettle to boil, then stood by the window imagining Brianna in the green smock all the cashiers at the Golden Pantry wore, her yellow plastic nametag pushed to one side by the swell of her enormous bosom.

This image led to others, and then his imagination took over, and her green smock melted into chain mail, her head bearing a horned Viking helmet, her arm brandishing a battle axe, the star of a dark Wagner opera, one foot resting on her slain enemy.

He was ripped from his fantasies by the sound of his mother behind him.

"Ugh, my son with a *spaślak*," his mother called out from the entrance to the kitchen. He turned to find her leaning against the wall, also dressed in black. Her accent was even thicker than normal, which generally meant she had just woken up or had taken too many of her pills again.

"Not now, Mama. I'm having tea."

"Your father wouldn't approve of her."

"Of course, Mama, invoke father's name. Because naturally you have no opinion."

His mother checked her watch and began counting under her breath. Yvgeny knew what was coming. He had heard it a million times.

"Thirteen, fourteen. There goes another one. That could have been me."

"I know, Mama, every fourteen seconds someone dies."

"The Census Bureau knows, Yvgeny."

"Yet here you are. Must not have been your last fourteen seconds after all."

"Keep it up, Yvgeny, I will end up in one of those caskets."

"You're not going to rain on my parade."

Yvgeny prepared his tea, then passed his mother, holding the mug in both hands as he walked into the parlor and eased himself into a large chair. His mother hobbled behind him, unwilling to drop the issue. She settled herself into the chair opposite his, then bounced on it several times.

"Something is different. Yvgeny, did you redo these chairs? Is that how you spend your father's hard earned money?"

"Didn't cost a dime. Pure ingenuity and frugality, Mama."

"If you only had your father's business acumen. He could make a silk pig out of a sow's ear."

"You mean a silk purse."

"Correcting your mother, Yvgeny? I grew you in my *matka* for nine months so you could correct me?"

Yvgeny looked away, sighed, then took a sip from his hot teacup. He smacked his lips in satisfaction, trying to pretend she wasn't there. He kicked his feet up on the polished mahogany coffin that functioned as his coffee table, although not an effective one, as anything placed on the convex lid slid immediately off. He leaned back and shut his eyes.

The cushions were stuffed tight, as his Mother noticed. The mortuary had offered cremations ever since old man Eldred had the cremator installed, and Yvgeny used his ingenuity to make it into an entirely new income stream.

On those lucky afternoons when Yvgeny had a burn job, he always started with a simple visual inspection to identify any jewelry; some families forgot to remove it all, while others actually insisted on cremating their loved ones with their valuables. Yvgeny never asked, but figured they were like the ancient Egyptians, thinking somehow their dearly departed would be able to take these trinkets to the Afterlife.

After his visual inspection, Yvgeny was supposed to review the Georgia state cremation form completed by the family that listed anything metal inside the body. The only thing he really cared about were pacemakers, as they tended to explode when exposed to the 1,400 degrees generated inside a cremator. State law required proper disposal of such items, and on occasion he honored the requirements, just enough to avoid the notice of the authorities. Or an explosion.

Artificial joints, fillings, skeletal pins, steel plates, he left them all in; he cremated the body, and trashed whatever survived the heat. On the increasingly rare occasion he found gold or silver fillings, he would be sure to remove them, along with the teeth. He stored them in an old can of green beans.

The process always brought back a childhood memory of a vacation to Atlantic City, where a young Yvgeny would wake up each day and look out the hotel room window to see the old men in their plaid Bermudas and tall black socks combing the beaches with their metal detectors.

Once everything worth keeping was removed, Alfred hauled the bodies down to the cremator, where Yvgeny would initiate stage two of his recycling mission. Yvgeny carefully shaved their heads and collected the results in a bag, storing them for later use. It was an ideal method for buttressing the sagging padding of the furniture that had come with his father's purchase of the mortuary.

It came to Yvgeny as an epiphany a long time ago, while sitting in his barber's chair watching a young man sweeping mounds of hair across the floor. After twenty years of cremations, the furniture was better than new. It was his own little secret; not even Alfred or Mama were aware of how everything got so comfy! A penny saved was a penny earned.

Yvgeny's penchant for recycling didn't end there. Once the body was his, clothing could be taken and later sold on consignment, or even stocked for sale to other families so their loved ones could rot in style (for an additional fee, of course).

Every few months, he would take down the green bean can and shake out the contents, count the number of silver, of gold, then send them off to a few of his more favored recyclers, never too much to any one place. Leaning back in his chair, he silently applauded himself for his adherence to the Go Green movement.

Yvgeny sipped his tea and took stock of his surroundings. *Ah, yes,* he reflected, *this place was built back when construction meant something, the work of true artisans, journeymen who paid just as much attention to aesthetics as efficiency.*

After growing up in dilapidated and sterile apartments, Yvgeny appreciated his surroundings like a hungry man appreciated a sumptuous meal. He glanced up to admire the finish carpentry, nodding his head in appreciation.

Just look at that crown, it's the product of an era when carpentry was the work of hand saws and planes, not chop saws and bulk purchases from some big box store. And it was all real wood, not MDF, that modern abomination of sawdust and glue that you couldn't even hammer a nail into.

"You're doing it again."

"And what's that, Mama?"

"Calculating. Gloating."

"So you can read minds too? You should consider a second career in show business."

"Read *my* mind," she said in response, then offered him her best expression of disgust.

Having had enough, Yvgeny stood up and returned to the kitchen. He stood over the sink finishing his tea and looking out the window. He glanced over his shoulder, then opened the cupboard and removed his other can, the one containing the jewelry. Mostly women's, but occasionally he snared a pinky ring or a decent wedding ring. His teeth guys were strictly into dental metal; he had another guy for the decorative stuff.

Reuben's pawn shop was all the way up in Macon, but he was worth the drive, and now, thanks to Maude, he had a full can, justifying another trip. *Quite a haul,* he thought to himself, depending on how much he got for the watch.

Yvgeny knew nothing about watches, and was a terrible judge of value. He had presented Rolexes to Reuben only to discover they were worthless fakes, but on other occasions he emerged from the pawn shop with hundreds paid for a watch whose name he couldn't even pronounce. *Either way,* thought Yvgeny, *the stuff was worthless to the client. They're all just irreparable, unplugged machines; computers with smashed hard drives.*

His mother believed in the Afterlife, in Heaven and Hell. *But even if she's right,* he thought, *nobody's taking their broken, rotting carcass with them, nor anything else, for that matter.*

Maude had been practically oozing with gold when he got her; perhaps she was expecting Clark Gable or Fred Astaire to be waiting for her on the other side of the pearly gates.

To Yvgeny, the jewelry was nothing more than his tip for a job well done. *And Maude had been particularly generous,* Yvgeny thought as he shook the green bean can. *I will take special care of her,* he decided, and made a mental note to place another bottle of deodorizer on his work tray.

He never specifically told Reuben where he got his trinkets, but he was no fool. He walked Yvgeny out of the store once, all the way to Cerberus, as he affectionately called his Cadillac, a late model hearse edition, and Yvgeny saw the recognition in the man's rheumy, old eyes. Sometimes Reuben shook his head, but he was a business man, and business was business.

After getting paid, Yvgeny often stopped at Rocko's to do some shopping. Rocko's good eye was sharp enough, but his head was soft and he didn't care where Yvgeny got his money. Rocko, like Reuben, was a practical man, a quality Yvgeny appreciated.

After cashing in on Maude, and maybe that watch, I'll treat myself to something nice. Maybe a bigger cot, one big enough for two!

Yvgeny fixed himself a meager dinner of Ramen noodles cooked on his ancient gas range, then mixed in a can of tuna. He shunned the Old World concoctions his mother made, and found her company incompatible with proper digestion.

Afterwards, all alone in his study, his mother thankfully asleep upstairs, the lights dimmed, the blinds drawn, under a framed photograph depicting the propped-up corpse of John O'Connor preserved by one of Yvgeny's idols, the great Ed Livingston, he leaned forward and reached down between his legs and under his chair. He withdrew a dusty leather bound album, and looked behind him to confirm the drapes were drawn before opening it.

The book was redolent from decades spent in a steamer trunk in the attic of Schmidt's, and represented what Yvgeny personally believed contained some of the greatest forms of art, albeit one with few admirers. He flipped through the aged and brittle black paper pages, glancing at the daguerreotypes set upon them, followed by several dozen early examples of black and white photography. What thrilled him the most were the before and after shots, which no doubt old man Eldred's father never showed anyone.

Such artistic perfection! Such natural talent, expressed without any of the modern conveniences we now enjoy!

Yvgeny found the album many years earlier, soon after his father buried old man Eldred. Eldred was a practical man; at his request, there would be no funeral, no embalming. Alfred dug the hole, and he was unceremoniously dropped in, then covered with a sheet, the dirt shoveled back in over the top.

Yvgeny was still a boy, then, and on one of his romps through the old Victorian, he came upon a weathered steamer trunk. Two, actually, side by side, leather and wood with steel frames. The first contained the album, a pocket watch on a chain, and two stovepipe hats that were all the rage a hundred years earlier. Beneath one of the hats was a pristine early copy of Doyle's *The Adventures of Sherlock Holmes.*

The next chest was a jackpot of a different variety. For young Yvgeny, it was love at first sight. Neatly folded among scores of mothballs, impeccably maintained, having survived the ages, were at least a dozen perfectly preserved examples of Victorian formal wear, presumably once worn by the original Schmidt.

Yvgeny remembered a much younger version of himself sitting on the trunk that day, a morning coat draped across his child's frame, thumbing through Doyle's masterpiece. It was the first day of a lifetime of infatuation with the Victorian age and Sherlock Holmes. As the years passed, he grew into his wardrobe, and finally became the man he fantasized about becoming.

He remembered the first time he officiated as undertaker. In fact, it was several Dunlaps ago; the brother of the soon to be interred had died prematurely of natural causes. *Ah, the splendor,* Yvgeny reflected, emerging from his work room in his black Edwardian club collar shirt, black notch collared vest, black cravat, and, to top it off, a black velvet trimmed and silver buttoned Edwardian morning coat that hung at mid-thigh and angled open at the bottom to expose the black pinstripe pants beneath.

The drawing in of breath from the crowd, the shocked expressions and immediate hushed silence, spoke volumes to him. Had he remembered his tall stovepipe hat, it simply would have been too much for his adoring fans.

In full Victorian regalia, he blended into his mortuary like an inmate in orange overalls standing in his cell. When he presided over an internment, he was like a doctor in green scrubs in the OR, or a conductor standing before his orchestra, baton in hand. The comparisons were endless. He was the very Platonic form of

Undertaker.

Shaking away the memories and fantasies, Yvgeny replaced the ancient album and felt around beneath the chair again until he found the other one. *His* album. Some of his best work, captured for all eternity.

For example, there was Becky, a gorgeous specimen from 1999. Breathtaking. *Yes,* he thought to himself, *Father would have been proud.* Blond hair, curled perfectly across her shoulders and, ever so carefully, askew across her temple just enough to hide the blunt force trauma that killed her. No makeup or subcutaneous ministrations would have fooled her loving family. He added the slightest touch of rouge on her cheeks, as if he had just whispered a slightly off-color joke in her ear.

Ah, the magic! The perfection! Such a shame his priceless works of art must each be hidden beneath a mound of earth to rot in a box.

In every coffin, a Monet, in every urn, the ashes of a Picasso.

He listened carefully for movement, prayed he would hear none.

He imagined Becky seated at the very chair upon which he was sitting, legs crossed demurely, one hand gently stabilizing a cup and saucer balanced on the top knee, glass eyes open, mouth relaxed into the hint of a smile.

Ah yes, now that would be a viewing, one that would truly showcase my unique gift.

Art should be displayed for all to see, not wrapped in a present never to be opened. Perhaps he could convince his mother to indulge him when that day came. He turned the page.

But don't forget Adam, from 2003, Yvgeny thought to himself. *Another work of art.*

He sifted through his muses, one after another, finally closing the album with the reverence of a preacher completing his sermon, palms resting on the cover, then he replaced it carefully beneath his chair. With a self-satisfied smile, Yvgeny retired to the study, where he lay in his cot with his cherished Holmes, reading until sleep arrived. Unfortunately, it didn't stay long.

╬

Laying on his surplus cot that night, even after all the years, Yvgeny was seven again. Seven, and not like the other children in his neighborhood. In his school. His accent was strong even though he was born in the United States. He sounded like his parents. The other children made fun of him. They pushed him around because he was smaller than them. They taunted him. They called him Jenny. And then there were the dreams. Always, the dreams.

His subconscious superimposed the nightmares of his ancestors upon his own experience; mental snapshots taken from his parents' hushed conversations, eavesdropping from the hallway while they spoke.

He wandered among the ruins of their world, seeing it through a lens filtered through a seven year old's imagination. He ran down dark Polish streets suffering the ravages of Nazi occupation, a Poland now dead. He cringed behind burned out buildings as unshaven police men passed by with slivered clubs and shiny buttons.

Then there was Uncle Albert's excitement after getting hired to work at the great marvel of Chernobyl, and his slow, painful death two years later. Yvgeny's subconscious used these stolen vignettes as the backdrop for his dreams.

Between his generally unhappy childhood and the haunting stories passed down from lost generations, each night became a crucible of horrors both experienced and acquired; on that night, it was set in a twisted Polish Atlanta, a misty world filled with Russian speaking and grotesquely disfigured soldiers wearing APD uniforms, angry pus filled faces melting as they chased him and his parents through a dying, radiation poisoned world.

In the small hours, in between nightmares, he lay awake in his cot imagining Newsome and his blue shirted sidekicks were his pursuers.

⊥⊦

CHAPTER FIVE

When Yvgeny opened the door to Reuben's shop, a large bell hanging from the inside door handle jangled as if attached to an anxious cow. Reuben looked up, then raised his hands into the air exclaiming, "Ach! Yvgeny, you look like a *Hasid*! Grow your beard a little longer, and I'd be back in Crown Heights!"

Reuben was a short old man with a New York accent and numbers on his arm. He owned a small pawn shop on Riverside Avenue just north of Macon. He and Yvgeny's mother were the only people left on earth who called Yvgeny by his true name and pronounced it right. Yvgeny enjoyed the Yiddish Reuben always sprinkled into his conversations because it reminded him of his father's voice.

Yvgeny removed his stovepipe hat, turned it upside down and, like a magician, waved his hand around it, then reached in and produced a small felt bag. Reuben nodded his head.

"Ach, more *chazerai*!"

Yvgeny placed the bag in Reuben's waiting hand, and the old man shook it slightly, a broken smile creeping across his face. A stroke had caused the left side of his face to sag.

"Ah, Yvgeny, *zaftig!*"

Yvgeny just shrugged. Reuben's eyes drifted down to Yvgeny's black suit, shirt and tie, then away. His half smile faded.

"Well, let's see what we have."

The old man reached into the bag and started removing the items one at a time, glancing at each piece before placing it on a worn felt-covered tray. Reuben fished in his pocket for his jeweler's glass and inspected each item, turning them slowly in his fingers while softly grunting, then placed them on the tray, forming two distinct piles.

Reuben stopped, put down his glass and stared at all the items, then knife edged his hand and slid over the items on his left and waved at them.

"Rubbish."

Then he placed the other items on a table scale, squinted at the digital readout, and started to count to himself, his lips moving silently, eyes unfocused. Finally, he nodded.

"Three hundred for all of it."

Yvgeny looked at the items, trying to figure out if it was a fair sale. He had little patience for negotiating, and experience taught him rising Reuben's numbers just wasn't worth the aggravation and haggling. Then he remembered his watch.

"Ah, Reuben, I almost forgot."

Reuben watched Yvgeny fiddle with the catch on the band, then finally remove it and place it on the felt. Reuben took the watch and inspected it.

"Nice watch, Yvgeny, nice watch. Laco. One of their first models. I haven't seen a Laco in a very long time."

The old man looked more closely, inspected the jewel face, the band, then held it up to his ear. Smiling, he turned the watch around. He brought the watch closer to his face, squinted.

"Ah, it's engraved, let me see, very small letters, so small."

Yvgeny tried to decipher the old man's expression, and guessed it was disappointment. Unless it was someone famous, personal engraved messages reduced the value of jewelry, and removing them damaged the material.

Reuben set his jeweler's glass and scrutinized the message.

"Hmm.... 1936. Yes, a true Laco, Yvgeny. I can feel it. *Oy gevalt*, the message is in Hebrew."

He looked away, rubbed his eyes, then looked back through his glass.

He squinted at the message, and Yvgeny watched as Reuben's mouth set in a strange expression. His olive skin grew pale. He slowly moved the watch away from his face, and let the jeweler's glass pop out of his eye socket and hit the counter. He placed the watch on the felt, squared it in the center, and stepped away, staring at it as if he expected it to grow feet and hop off the counter.

"What's wrong, Reuben, is it rare? Wait, is it a one of a kind? What does it say? Was it someone famous?"

The old man did not seem to hear him. Yvgeny began tapping on the glass counter until Reuben blinked heavily and looked up.

"I cannot help you, Yvgeny. Did these other items come from the same, uh, the same place?"

"No, just the watch. That's it."

"Are you certain?"

Yvgeny cocked his head and shrugged again.

"Reuben, the rest of it was all ladies' jewelry."

Reuben glanced at the other items on the felt tray as if seeing them for the first time.

"Of course. Three hundred for the rest of it, but please get this watch out of my sight. Now. Please. God help me."

"Reuben, I . . . ."

"Now!"

Yvgeny snapped his head back as if he had been struck, then grabbed the watch and started fumbling with the band. Reuben watched him with his mouth agape.

"Yvgeny, you can't wear it. Take it back to wherever you got it. Please, for the love of God Yvgeny, promise me."

Yvgeny stopped, holding the watch over his wrist, and exclaimed, "Jesus Christ, Reuben, what's got into you? It's a damn watch."

"Yes, Yvgeny, yes, a damned watch. Yes indeed. Take it off, and take it back to wherever you found it."

"What does it say? What is so terrible about this watch?"

The old man took a deep breath, then stared down at his hands.

"Ani l'dodi, v'dodi li."

"What does that mean?"

Reuben looked away, but not before Yvgeny saw the sadness in his watery, red rimmed eyes.

"I am my beloved's and my beloved is mine. Song of Solomon. Old Testament."

Yvgeny waited for the rest of the explanation, but none came. He fidgeted, then put his hands on the counter. He was still holding the watch and it made a metallic smack on the glass, causing Reuben to blink, then resume staring down at the tray. Yvgeny waved a hand before the old man's face to get his attention.

"Great quote, Reuben, really, but what's it worth?"

"Don't you see?" Reuben pleaded. "1936? Song of Solomon? This was a gift from a wife to a husband. A Jewish wife to a Jewish husband. In 1936."

Reuben's eyes were pleading, but still Yvgeny squinted at the old man, not understanding.

"Tell me something, Yvgeny, did you see any numbers on his arm? A tattoo?"

"What? No, he didn't have any tattoos. What difference does it make?"

"The Nazis marked Jews for a time with numbers. Not all of them, and not for a long time, but it would have made it more likely this man was a Jew."

"Well, he was clean. So that's all you know about the watch?"

"It's German, Yvgeny, so whoever wore it was probably German. Very few German Jews who remained in Germany survived the War, and even less would have survived with a Laco like this."

"So maybe he was a Jew, maybe not?"

"Maybe he was one of the lucky ones, Yvgeny, maybe he escaped before it all went to hell, moved to the States. Or maybe, maybe he was not so lucky."

Reuben blinked slowly, eyes cast down. For a moment, the store was silent, then Yvgeny clapped once and started rubbing his hands together.

"Wow! This is so exciting! If I could find the right buyer, tell the right story," Yvgeny mused, then walked along the counter, arms outstretched theatrically, "imagine, a watch owned by a real victim of the Nazis! Some collector out there would probably pay, what, Reuben, a thousand bucks? Two?"

Yvgeny clapped his hands together again and bounced on his toes several times and crooned, "Oh, this is too good to be true!"

"Don't be such a schmuck, Yvgeny! I know where your trinkets come from. I'm not going to help you steal from a Jew, and certainly not a survivor of the *Shoah*! If that man made it through that living hell with this watch, then dammit, it belongs in the ground with him!"

"I didn't know you were so sentimental, Reuben."

Yvgeny collected himself and tried to form a serious expression; he needed Reuben, so he would have to endure his maudlin beliefs and pretend he cared; *but dead men don't need watches, because time means nothing to them.*

"Reuben, does it say who owned it?"

Reuben shook his head, and said softly, "No. Just initials, from whoever gave it to him. BK. 1936."

The old man punched a button on an old cash register and riffled through the contents. He took out a stack of $20 bills, counted out $300, slid it across the counter.

"Please take that watch and go. I don't ever want to see it again, you hear me? Yvgeny, do you hear me?"

⊥⊤

As Yvgeny meandered back toward the highway, he was so lost in his own thoughts he didn't notice the smell of Macon's largest paper plant, which belched out its noxious mixture of wet newspaper and astringent from its base right off Interstate 75.

Yvgeny was also oblivious to the stares of passersby as he drove Cerberus; they stared as if he was the Grim Reaper himself, scythe in hand, visiting a neighbor whose time had come. When people heard the sirens of an ambulance, it brought hope, but Yvgeny was always last to the party. Hoping to add some levity to his arrival, he had affixed a bumper sticker to Cerberus, *LAST RESPONDER.*

Reuben was the only Jew Yvgeny had ever met. Yvgeny had never seen a synagogue, and assumed there were none in Comstock. He doubted the town had any Jews at all.

The Jew they tossed into Dunlap's grave came from somewhere else, Yvgeny mused to himself as he headed south on the highway. *Imported.*

The two constables that showed up were worthless, but at least the inspector, Newsome, had a whit of sense. He wasted too much time criticizing my handling of the crime scene, but it was possible, a long shot, but possible, the inspector was sharp enough to stumble into the killer and maybe even manage to arrest him before getting plugged himself.

Yvgeny estimated that in all of Gilbert County, there couldn't have been more than a couple of Jewish families. If one was missing, surely they would have made a huge stink about it, and Newsome would have known. *Yes,* Yvgeny thought, *it must've been a dump job from somewhere else.*

But then again, Comstock sprouted up from the Georgia pine forests a hundred years earlier, built along the path of old State Route 41. Schmidt and Sons set up shop at the mortuary soon after the road was paved, and plunked down a huge sign for everyone passing through to see.

It was prime real estate until Eisenhower came along and ruined it. The interstate system chose a different path, and the old state route became Main Street in what would soon become a dead end town. Comstock was, overnight, marginalized from pit stop on the great King's Highway to a customer-starved backwater.

What that meant, in Yvgeny's opinion, was that Comstock was too inconvenient a place to dump a body unless you lived there. When the Mayor told everyone the drug deal dump job was an example of Macon exporting its problems, it made sense: the body was found well outside the city limits along the edge of Gilbert County near the highway. But in this case, why would anyone risk driving a body all the way to the center of Comstock?

Sounds like a job for the great Sherlock Holmes!

Yvgeny returned home in a funk, and decided to take a walk to clear his head. He stepped out into the cemetery, wandering between the headstones, lost in his thoughts. Living people just weren't his forte. Or his preference.

To Yvgeny, most people were at their best after their expiration. Exsanguinated, embalmed, then decorated, even the most insufferable boor could be quite tolerable. Even Dunlap himself was pleasant enough on Yvgeny's stainless steel table.

Yvgeny stopped before Randall's hole and leaned against his headstone. Randall was born in 1924 and died in 1944 in Normandy, before even making it onto the beach. Beside him was a headstone with the chiseled name of his wife, Beatrice Schtumpf, now almost ninety years old. Her birth year of 1927 was chiseled, but not the ending year.

Beatrice had visited every week until a year or two before, when she had to move into a nursing home. *And the lovely Brianna Schtumpf took up the slack, making her grandmother proud.* And making Yvgeny's heart race.

"Whatcha think, Randy? Think the good inspector can solve it?"

He strummed his fingers on top of the headstone.

"Maybe they'll find a missing person report, maybe he will connect the dots and figure it out."

He looked around, then straightened up, excited.

"Hell, Randy, maybe the dead guy is a Dunlap! That'd give him squatter's rights!"

Yvgeny chuckled softly and changed position on Randall's headstone, then rolled his neck in one direction, then the other. Then he cocked his head.

"What's that? Ah, Randy, the Gilbert Globe . . . well, nobody's talking, so nobody's writing about it."

Yvgeny shook his head.

"You know reporters, they don't care when Flowers pays me a visit. Just ain't news."

Nodding, Yvgeny added, "No doubt, sooner than later someone will spill their guts after a few rounds at the VFW. But I'll tell you something, Randy, you'd think if some old coot was missing, somebody would've called it in, and somebody would be asking more questions."

As he pushed off from the headstone, he sniffed loudly and cracked his knuckles.

"If Holmes was here, they'd already have caught the killer!"

Yvgeny rounded the corner of the mortuary and glanced out toward the street. Eisenhower killed Comstock, but it was bouncing back. In fact, there was a continual stream of strangers going to and from town, and the nosy bastards always looked to see who had died.

The rubberneckers were irritating, but Yvgeny grudgingly acknowledged the mortuary's location and status as a local landmark and source of gossip was good for business.

On the bright side, the cemetery abutted acres of undeveloped land no-one wanted to buy, and beyond lay the virgin forests of western Gilbert County, which would never be for sale. The forest was mostly oak and pine, and even in the winter, there were enough evergreens to ensure privacy.

Yvgeny had respect for Eldred as an undertaker, even as a surrogate uncle, perhaps, but the two had little else in common.

Eldred cultivated a holistic approach to his work; losing a loved one was an occasion to be marked by pomp and circumstance, a celebration of remembrance.

He was also a dedicated member of the local small business association, the Lions Club, and the Loyal Order of Moose. He was, in short, fully engaged in his life and in his town.

In contrast, Yvgeny believed business was business. A mortuary was a place to embalm and dispose of bodies. Nothing more. Whereas Eldred was a steward of the dearly departed and a combination grief counselor, financial adviser, and overall master of ceremonies, Yvgeny was merely a purveyor of holes in the ground and headstones.

Where Eldred volunteered his time and efforts to

those less fortunate, Yvgeny contributed no more than what the state and federal governments required on April 15.

Eldred's prices covered all necessaries and required little negotiation. The basic fee Yvgeny charged included only the use of his leather furniture and walnut lined walls of the mortuary, and of course the hole of their choice. Everything else was extra.

Families were welcome to have whatever type of service or wake they desired. But his mortuary was not a Chuck E. Cheese, and he wasn't hosting birthday parties. He didn't inflate balloons and didn't serve tea. If you want a party, hire caterers. And he did not accept credit cards. Cash or check, usually paid in advance.

If you wanted prayers, sermons, positive messages, hire a priest or a pastor. It wasn't his department.

Yvgeny returned to the embalming room and changed into more comfortable clothes. He removed the watch, turned it around and looked at the inscription. He could barely see the tiny and unfamiliar letters engraved on the back. He thought about the old man that had been wearing it, in his sodden pants and shirt. A survivor. But his luck ran out. It always did. Yvgeny held the watch up to his ear again, heard the ticking, then placed it on the counter beside his jacket.

Yvgeny saw the emotions flashing across Reuben's face like distant lightning. But despite his sympathy for the old man, he had no intention of burying a perfectly good watch, and he certainly would not hand it over to the police just to get arrested for some trumped up charge of evidence tampering.

Yvgeny flashed back to Flowers's words. Could the detectives return with a search warrant? Would they dig up Dunlap just to spite him? Yvgeny chewed on the possibilities. *Until they found the killer*, Yvgeny mused, *me and my cemetery would be fair game.*

Yvgeny started to pace. *The quicker they find the killer, the quicker I can be rid of them.* Back and forth, deep in thought, he worried on his situation, picking at it from all sides like a knotted shoelace.

Where's Holmes when you need him? They just don't make men like that, not anymore.

As he paced, an idea began to form, quickly taking root and springing forth from his mind, complete, like Athena emerging from Zeus's head.

What if I helped them solve it? Pushed them in the right direction? I could be Holmes!

Yvgeny evaluated his situation and determined he had several distinct advantages over Newsome. *I have the watch, and of course there's my superior intelligence.* He stopped pacing and puffed himself up in front of his mirror. *And surely, none of them had ever even read Holmes.*

As he was admiring his reflection, Yvgeny was distracted by the sound of flipping paper, and sighed. His mother was awake. She saved her copy of the Globe for after her nap each day, turning to each page, then whipping the paper back and forth to straighten it. It was a habit that grated on his nerves like fingernails on a chalkboard.

Flip, shake!

Flip, shake!

He peeked around the corner to find her looking up over the top of the newspaper, glaring at him.

"So much pacing, *tygrysek*, you are going to wear a hole in the floor."

He walked into the room, but did not respond.

Talking would only make it worse.

"Are you still upset over that detective?"

He resumed his pacing under his mother's narrowed eyes.

"No. Yes."

He shrugged.

"Some detective. He was more interested in criticizing my work than solving the case. But I have a plan."

"*No co ty!*"

"No, Mama, I know exactly what I'm doing. You'll see."

In a low voice he continued, grumbling, "I don't need a fancy badge and gun to solve a simple murder."

She shook her head and turned back to her newspaper and snorted, muttered, "my son, the detective."

Flip, shake!

But Yvgeny wasn't paying any attention to her. He was thinking about search warrants. *If they screw up Dunlap, that will cost a fortune. And Maude, Maude's big day is right around the corner.* Yvgeny wasn't about to push any business toward Lenny Updike. He wouldn't give him the satisfaction.

Yes, I'll give them a little hint, tell them the victim was a Jew. Just a push in the right direction!

Yvgeny nodded, but continued pacing.

But how?

He thought briefly about using his watch, but quickly dispelled the idea.

No way I'm giving it up. The watch is mine!

Flip, shake!

Yvgeny reviewed his conversation with Reuben, about tattoos, about the War. He needed a basis to justify to Newsome his belief the victim was a Jew. And he needed to do it quickly to keep them away from Schmidt and Sons, and out of his life!

There was probably scant evidence for them to go on at this point: Flowers had no doubt already carved the poor guy up, tossed the parts on the scale one at a time, then stuffed them all back inside all jumbled up, like Humpty Dumpty.

Yes, it was all up to me now.

Yvgeny stopped pacing as a foreign sentiment crept into his mind, something he couldn't identify, not at first. Then he realized what it was. *Sympathy!*

Yvgeny didn't generally care about the living, but he knew about the Holocaust. Hitler did the same thing to the Slavs that he did to the Jews.

How many millions of his own people were murdered by the Nazis? *Yes,* Yvgeny thought to himself, *I will throw the inspector a bone. It's the right thing to do. And I will be a hero.*

Yvgeny wondered to himself whether Reuben was part of a synagogue.

"*Ojej!*"

"What is it now, Mama?"

"Did you see this? Frank Dowling died."

"Who cares?"

She looked up at him with her mouth open.

"Who cares? He owned sixteen Burger Kings!"

"OK. Like I said, who cares?"

"He died right here at Comstock Memorial, but Updike's is burying him. Lenny Updike? All the way out in Warner Robins? Are you kidding me?"

His mother paused for effect, then snorted, adding, "Might as well hire a taxidermist!"

His mother tossed her paper onto the table and leaned back, staring at her son.

"You need a sale. Get on Craigslist. And buy some space in the Globe, offer a special. Maybe a coupon, ten percent discount."

"That's distasteful, Mama. You don't run a mortuary that way."

"Your father would have done it. Your father, may he rest in peace, he advertised."

"Yes, Mama, he advertised. But he didn't offer a sale. And he certainly didn't do coupons."

"Well, he never would have lost business to Lenny Updike."

She pushed Yvgeny's buttons, but he just smiled.

Ah, wait until you see what I have in store for Maude. People won't even call Lenny for taxidermy jobs!

⚏

Yvgeny disengaged himself from his mother and shut the door, then leaned back in his chair with the Greater Macon area phone book. There were sections for Gilbert and Houston Counties, and he thumbed between them looking under headings for religion, churches, temples, even Jewish, but found nothing anywhere in Gilbert County. Houston County also had nothing.

He expanded his search to Macon, the Bibb County seat, and finally found a few listings. There were three in north Macon, and one was large enough to have separate phone numbers for their childcare office and another for their day school.

Then he found what he was looking for. There was one temple in Byron, a small town on the border of Bibb and Houston Counties. Byron was the closest you could get to Comstock while in Bibb County, around twenty miles drive. *A good place to start.*

Yvgeny moved to his computer, an older model Apple with a plastic coffin-shaped mouse. He typed in the address, then furrowed his brow. The address associated with Temple B'Nai Israel also linked to a UPS Store, a CVS drugstore, and a Winn Dixie supermarket. Google Maps confirmed his suspicion; it was in the middle of a strip mall a couple miles off the highway.

The temple did not have a website but it did have an informative Facebook page. Temple B'Nai Israel was a reform temple which, according to Google, meant it followed a more liberal variety of Judaism.

Google also taught Yvgeny that orthodox Jews did not work on the Sabbath. They also did not drive cars, flip light switches; they didn't even use their stoves on Saturdays.

In contrast, reform Jews spent their Saturdays like any other day of the week. They wore jeans to Saturday morning services, not coats and ties. Less Hebrew was spoken during services, the preference being for English, so those repeating the words would also understand them.

Temple B'Nai Israel's Facebook page included a few photographs, and they revealed a handful of families in attendance. Yvgeny scrutinized the photographs looking for any familiar looking old men. At front and center was the rabbi, Shalom Shachter. According to his bio, he was a retired orthodontist from Atlanta who had resettled in Crawford County over twenty years earlier. He bought an old house that sat on a few hundred forested acres.

Yvgeny stared at the photograph a while before concluding the rabbi was not his headless victim. He was too chubby.

Why should anything be easy!

The other synagogues in the area had no web presence, so Yvgeny switched gears. He researched for something he could use to convince the inspector his victim was Jewish. He had to wade through a fair volume of white supremacist garbage, but eventually he found exactly what he was looking for.

Success! Let the games begin!

⸸

"Not one word?" the rabbi asked, while looking out his window toward the trees beyond.

"Nope."

The old man shook his head and turned to face the others. His grandson Jacob was at the head of his kitchen table. Seated at either side were the Cohen brothers, Isaac and Albert. Each was a year apart, friends since they were small children. Albert was oldest and was a senior at Byron High School. His brother Isaac was a sophomore, and the rabbi's grandson Jacob was a junior.

Rabbi Shachter was a reform rabbi, but he was raised by conservative parents, and his furnishings were Spartan and functional; his living room contained a religious painting, a large tapestry, a sofa, chair, and table, nothing more. He had no television.

"So it's as if it never happened?"

Albert shrugged, said, "Well, *we* know it happened!"

"Of course *you* know. It's *them* I worry about."

Isaac shrugged and said, "Maybe it's better just to forget about it."

All eyes turned to the old rabbi, expecting a retort. Instead, he shuffled over to the table, creaking as he lowered himself into a chair.

"Well, young Isaac, a wise man once said, 'Those who cannot remember the past are condemned to repeat it.' So tell me, do you think your generation doesn't need to know about the *Shoah*?"

"Of course they need to know!" Jacob said. "One kid in my class told me it never even happened. Said it was fake, that the Jews made it up. That it's a big conspiracy!"

The rabbi nodded. "Ah, yes, I have heard that before. Some cannot accept that something so terrible could actually happen. 'He fills them with lies, that his idea is the best, and everyone hears what they want to hear, and disregard the rest.'"

Albert looked up.

"Talmud?"

The old man chuckled.

"Papa Turner and the Crazy Eights. Best blues band there ever was."

The older boys then laughed with him while Isaac, the youngest, looked at them all with a vacant look on his face. After a moment, the old man clapped his hands on his knees and said, "so nothing about the *Shoah*."

It was not a question, and the children remained silent.

"Grandpa, you tried."

Albert nodded his head and added, "Yeah, the principal talked about your letters for days!"

When the rabbi learned his grandson's public school education would not include any mention of the Holocaust, he was livid. He and his congregation engaged in a letter writing campaign decrying this profound gap in their learning. Dozens of letters were written and mailed to the Governor, county officials, the state superintendent of schools, congressional representatives, asking them to commit to educating Georgia's children about the Nazis.

The responses they received were lukewarm and, in some cases, patronizing. There were simply too many other, more important topics, like the idea that Christopher Columbus found the New World, and how important Harvey Milk was to gay rights.

"Well, talk is talk. Either way, it is done. And we have other things to discuss. Come, let's sit in the living room."

At least a few times each month, Jake and his parents came to visit and made a big family dinner for everyone. While Jake's parents unloaded bags of groceries, the rabbi and his young entourage settled in the living room.

Just as they sat, Jake's mother dropped a can of green beans, which hit the counter with a loud crack. The noise startled Jake, who shot back up and turned to glance uneasily in her direction.

The rabbi locked eyes with each teen in turn, drawing them in.

"You three need to stick together, now more than

ever. Like a cluster of lilies in a field of wheat, you flourish together, but apart you will starve."

Albert nodded, confident.

"Now *that* was the Talmud!"

With a smile, the rabbi said, "Nope. That was Jake's Grandpa!"

There was some muted laughter, but they quickly settled into a nervous silence, until Jake broke it by asking his grandfather, "Grandpa, tell me a story about the war."

His grandfather chuckled.

"Bah! Again with the war. I barely even saw it. By the time they called my draft number, it was almost over. VE Day came before I made it across the Atlantic."

"Come on, Grandpa, you had to see *some* action."

"Sure did. In the kitchen! I guarded a mess hall in Germany for a few months, then they shipped me across another ocean so I could guard a mess hall there."

The rabbi got nothing but wan expressions from the teenagers seated around him.

"Look, it is done. *C'est la vie.*"

Albert crossed, then uncrossed his legs, unable to get comfortable.

"But what do we do now?"

"Do? About what? There's nothing to do. We tried to resolve a problem to the best of our abilities. Sometimes the best thing; the only thing to do, is move on and put it behind you."

"It's that easy?" asked Isaac.

"I didn't say it would be easy. Sometimes the past is a great weight upon your shoulders that doesn't lighten until you're six feet under."

Jacob began picking at imaginary things on his pants.

"Grandpa, what if God is angry with us?"

Jake's mother poked her head into the living room.

"Who's hungry?"

The old man sighed and sat silently a moment, gathering his thoughts. Jake's mother walked in and tousled her son's hair, smiling at her father the rabbi, who smiled back, then turned back to the boys.

"Listen to me carefully, children. It isn't always what you do, but how you do it, and why. Our teachings are very clear on this subject. Consider the Ninth Commandment. Thou shalt not murder. If I kill an animal so I may eat, it does not violate God's laws. If I kill an animal for sport, it is murder. If I kill in self-defense, it is not murder. If I kill out of anger, it is murder. Do you see the distinction? In most cases, God cares only for *why* you act, not the act itself."

The Cohen boys nodded their heads slowly.

"Dad, what in the world are you talking about?"

Jacob cringed, but the rabbi spoke up before his mother noticed.

"Your son is worried that we didn't do enough to try to convince their school to add the Holocaust to the curriculum."

Jake's mother shook her head.

"That again? Come on, Jake, what else could you have done? Why don't you write a paper about it or something. Educate them in your own way. But for now, no more talking, dinner's getting cold!"

╬

CHAPTER SIX

Yvgeny chose his attire carefully for his evening with Brianna: muted gray pants with a casual Victorian cutaway coat and gray Fleetwood shirt, perfect for a night out on the town. After much thought and consideration, he decided to leave the hat at home; it would not have been tolerated in the Victorian era, but for 2016 in Georgia, it would be acceptable.

He had scrubbed Cerberus until it was a shining stallion, and ignored his mother's withering stare as he passed by on his way out. Minutes later, he was galloping up Interstate 75 toward his date with destiny.

He approached the on-ramp from State Route 96 onto the interstate. To his left was a dilapidated motel, and across the parking lot, an adult entertainment business. They shared a partially paved parking lot. Both were owned by an Indian man who invested a small fortune in billboards for a hundred miles up and down the highway.

The signs had been there for decades, directing discerning travelers to Chateau Lolita (called Chateau Ho by local cops), where, according to the billboards, the women were always beautiful and friendly. Once you crossed the state line, the billboards added, *We Dance Without Pants.*

Although not advertised on his billboards, his hotel offered reasonable nightly *and hourly* rates. This poorly advertised but well known trait, combined with its proximity to Chateau Lolita, led local law enforcement to bestow upon it some uncharitable, but not inaccurate monikers, including the Hush and Tush, the Spilt-more, the Tits Carlton, and the Humpin' Hilton.

As Cerberus rolled to a stop at the intersection, Yvgeny heard the muted thump of country music straying from the windows and doors of the Chateau. A few token street lights in the parking lot of the hotel cast everything in a dim orange glow, including the handful of trucks and rusty cars patronizing one business or the other. Or both.

The orange glow did nothing to illuminate the rest of the intersection, being surrounded in all directions by sod farms. It was so dark, Yvgeny felt like he was underwater. He flipped on Cerberus's brights and punched the accelerator.

By 9:50 he was pulling into Bonaire's Golden Pantry. There were several cars at the pumps, and in the corner he saw Brianna's Smart Car. The windows of the station were too obstructed with advertisements for him to see her inside. He passed through the parking lot slowly, turning heads as he parked.

Should I wait in Cerberus? Should I go inside?

For a moment he was wracked by indecision. Then he saw her face in the window, scanning the parking lot, finding him. She gave him a raised single index finger, the universal sign for *wait there*! Problem solved.

Yvgeny waited outside Cerberus, trying not to fidget. Customers pulled in, pumped their gas, walked inside to make their purchases, then returned to their car, each casting uneasy glances in his direction. Some kept their head down to avoid making eye contact. One held his breath as he walked by. Yvgeny chuckled.

A few minutes later, Brianna shuffled out the door without looking back. She fumbled with a cigarette as she walked, the jeans covering her thighs rasping together with each step. Yvgeny presented his lighter for her as she arrived.

"Punctual, aren't you?"

"Ten o'clock means ten o'clock."

She responded by looking him up and down.

"You always dress like that?"

When he didn't answer, she sighed and said, "Well, whatever floats your boat."

She took a deep drag, exhaled, and asked, "Well, what do you wanna do?"

He smiled.

"I have an idea. Shall we?" Yvgeny motioned with his hand toward his hearse.

She turned to Cerberus and balked.

"In that?"

"Of course."

She winced, then her eyes traveled down to the corner of the rear window glass, where Yvgeny had affixed a diamond shaped sign.

"Body on board?" she asked.

"A little levity never hurt anyone, right?"

Yvgeny tried a disarming smile but it did not have the desired effect on Brianna, who looked behind her one last time, glumly scanned the parking lot, then hung her head, defeated. She flicked her cigarette across the pavement, then followed him toward the passenger seat. He opened her door.

She removed another cigarette, then asked, "You

mind?"

He paused, then muttered, "if you must."

She pursed her lips, then replaced the cigarette in the pack and squeezed inside.

As Yvgeny hurtled back down SR96 toward the highway, Brianna turned to him and asked, "So where are we going?"

"Macon."

"Why?"

"It's a surprise."

"I don't like surprises."

"You will like this one."

Several more minutes passed, and soon enough Cerberus was racing north on the interstate. Brianna occasionally glanced at Yvgeny, who tried to focus on the road, but her presence made him like he was sitting beneath high voltage power lines.

"So, all that death, do you ever wonder when you're going to die? What will happen? How?"

Yvgeny considered her question.

"Not really. Nobody lives forever and there's nothing you can do about it anyway. When it's your time, that's it."

"Pretty bleak view."

Yvgeny shrugged, said, "It's realistic. Face it. This could be your last drive on the highway."

He pointed out his window and added, "See the moon? This could be the last time you ever see it."

"You're starting to get creepy."

"Seriously. Think of all the repetitive things we do. We do them every day, over and over, without thinking about it. But have you ever stopped and thought to yourself, *what if this is the last time I do it?* Every time you smoke, each cigarette might be your last one.

They drove in silence a moment, then Yvgeny stole a quick glance at her, then said, "I see it like this. Imagine a chart, a huge finite chart, and every cigarette you will ever smoke is on the chart, and some supreme being ticks off each one as you smoke it. Eventually you will smoke your last one."

"And why in the hell would anyone want to think like that? That's about the most depressing thing I've ever heard."

"On the contrary! It makes me appreciate every little thing just a little more. Every moon. Every sunrise. Every cremation."

Brianna picked at her ear and stared at Yvgeny while he drove, then said quietly, "You are one odd duck."

When Yvgeny glanced over at her, she was smiling.

Around thirty minutes later, Yvgeny merged off the highway at the Riverside Drive exit. Toward the end of the trip she tentatively removed a cigarette and held it out to Yvgeny, who grimaced but waved his hands in a defeated gesture. Brianna consumed it quickly, careful to blow all the smoke out the window, then tossed it.

As he navigated toward their destination, Brianna grew more and more uncomfortable. After several side-long glances, she turned toward him and growled, "I really don't like surprises. Where are we going?"

Yvgeny pointed straight ahead through the windshield and said, "right there."

Brianna squinted at an empty parking lot, one street light intermittently flashing on and off. Then she saw the sign.

"Humperdink's Waxen Personalities?"

Yvgeny could no longer hide his glee and began to squirm in his seat.

"This is going to be fantastic!"

"Geny, it's almost 11 pm. The place ain't open, look at it!"

"Ah, but that's part of the surprise! Come, come!"

"I ain't getting out of this damn car until you tell me what's going on."

Yvgeny sighed and said, "Fine. I want you to meet Louise, and, hopefully, my father."

Brianna's eyes grew wide. "He's here?"

"Essentially."

Brianna equivocated, then slumped in her seat. Yvgeny took her posture as acquiescence and double parked Cerberus right in front of the doors and practically launched himself out of the hearse before she could change her mind. He raced around the hood and opened the door for Brianna, who squeezed herself out and checked her hair in the side view mirror. As he chirped the hearse's alarm, the door to Humperdink's opened with a creak and a withered old woman peered around it.

"Geny!"

"Louise!"

They embraced briefly, then Yvgeny turned to Brianna with a flourish and said, "This is my companion, Brianna Schtumpf."

The old woman shuffled all the way out and fiddled with a pair of thick glasses hanging from a beaded chain. She squinted at Brianna, up and down, inspecting her like a side of beef hanging from a butcher's ceiling.

"Mmm hmmm. Yes, yes, mmm hmmm," she said to herself, then reached out and grabbed a wrist, lifted Brianna's arm, then inspected her large bicep.

"She'd be a good one."

"Good one for what?" Brianna asked, yanking her arm away and retreating from the old woman.

"Model, of course! Haven't never done a big boned German girl."

Brianna stared at her a moment, then launched at Yvgeny.

"I knew you were a freak! I knew it! I'm calling the cops."

Brianna started rooting through her purse looking for her cell phone as Yvgeny held up his hands.

"Wait, wait, you don't understand. Louise is a sculptor. She makes wax models of people. Haven't you ever heard of a wax museum?"

Brianna, who had found her phone and had already dialed 911, stopped, her thumb on the send button. She looked from Yvgeny to Louise and back again, then hesitated.

"Wax museum?"

"Yes, she's a sculptor. She and her late husband opened the museum years ago. My father used to bring me here."

"Oh, that rapscallion!" Louise gushed, brushing a stray gray hair back behind her ear.

Yvgeny's cheeks colored, but his smile remained.

"Well, come on in!" the old lady said, then tottered

back inside. Yvgeny held the door open for a hesitating Brianna, then locked the door behind them. As they caught up with Louise, Yvgeny began to explain.

"My father taught me how to make molds of faces. He was a master. He learned from Louise. And she, in turn, learned from Eldred Junior himself."

"Eldred?" Brianna asked, confusion clouding her eyes.

"The son of the original owner of the mortuary. He used to make molds from faces, then create a wax bust to present to the family during the funeral service. They could take it home, like a party favor!"

Brianna continued staring at him, mouth open. He smiled at her, but when she frowned in response, he dropped his smile and he quickly continued.

"Anyway, my father kept up the practice after taking over the shop, but people slowly lost interest in the art. Frankly, they took forever to make, and they weren't cheap."

Then, with a quick conspiratorial glance toward Louise, he added, "You know, once I had this great idea to turn them into candles, but Louise talked me out of it, she said it would trivialize the art."

Brianna made a horrified face and said, "A candle? Someone dies and you turn their head into a candle? So you can watch their head melting?"

"A wax mold of their head."

Brianna's expression did not change. Yvgeny tapped his foot a minute, then looked away, adding, softly, "Artists are seldom appreciated by their own generation."

Brianna reached for her cigarettes, but Yvgeny grabbed her hand, trying to push the package back out of view. He looked over at Louise to see if she noticed, then shook his head quickly at Brianna, who reluctantly dropped the cigarettes back into her purse, whispering, "Freak!"

They followed Louise toward a black velvet set of curtains. Louise turned to wait for them, leaning against the wall, a proud expression on her face, chin up, chest out.

With a flourish that made Yvgeny smile, she tossed back the curtains and beckoned them to follow her.

"Remember when these were all the rage, Yvgeny?"

Yvgeny nodded sagely. Brianna looked around at the collection of funerary busts, all flesh colored and realistic. She walked up to one, crouched, and inspected the face.

"So real," she whispered.

Her irritation with Yvgeny vanished as she inspected the bust. She remained crouched before it for a solid minute before straightening and approaching the next one. She studied each one, then finally stood and faced Yvgeny.

"Amazing," Brianna said, then after a brief pause, added, "so when do I get to meet your father?"

Louise clapped her hands together and made a strange sound in the back of her throat.

"Wheee! You want to meet him? Come on!"

Louise turned and stepped through another doorway into a smallish room with a few figures standing within the shadows. Louise flipped on the lights and walked right up to one of the figures.

"Here he is! Say hi to your father, Yvgeny!"

Brianna slowly approached the wax figure, holding her breath. She stared at the face, then walked around it, inspecting the creation carefully. She glanced at Louise and Yvgeny several times with an odd expression.

"This is what you meant? A *wax figure* of your father?"

"I wanted you to meet Louise. And I wanted you to see something you've probably never seen before."

Brianna stared at him for so long she began to remind Yvgeny of one of Louise's waxen personalities. Then she cocked her head, first one way, then the other, and finally said, "I can't tell if you're completely insane, or just weird."

Louise then cackled and grabbed Brianna's shoulder, whispering "He's just weird, sweetheart. Just like his father." Then, she cried out, "Come on! I want to show you my landscapers."

The next room contained exactly that: three Hispanic men wearing overalls. One pushed a lawn mower across a strip of fake grass; another raked a collection of real leaves, and the third leaned against a lone fence post. Brianna muttered, "You gotta be kidding me."

"Splendid, just splendid!" Yvgeny exclaimed to a beaming Louise. He leaned in close to one of the figures, then walked around it slowly before asking, "Raw umber?" Louise clapped her hands together and gleefully cried out, "Yes! Yes! Winsor and Newton, of course."

Yvgeny returned to Brianna's side and leaned in to mutter, in a conspiratorial tone, "A wax figure takes months to complete. She likes to reuse, refresh, recycle. Last time I was here, these four were a white barbershop quartet."

Then he frowned.

"Louise, where's the fourth guy?"

Louise's smile faltered and she growled, "Teenagers," then shook her head. Yvgeny nodded sagely.

As they left the building, Louise grabbed Yvgeny around the shoulders and asked him, "So, did you tell her?"

Brianna stopped and turned to Yvgeny with dread on her face and asked, "Tell me what?"

Yvgeny glanced toward Louise in confusion, then asked, "you mean, you mean our plan?"

Brianna took a step backward, rummaging nervously in her purse for her cigarettes. Again she popped one in her mouth, then dug around for her matches.

"Of course! It's brilliant, really. Only a genius like Geny here can come up with such a plan."

Louise cooed and murmured, "if your father could only see you now!"

Her eyes alive with excitement, the old lady stepped over and took Brianna by the arm before she could light her cigarette.

"Theme funerals!"

Brianna's mouth opened in shock, the cigarette falling to the pavement. Louise had her arm in a strangle hold, and all Brianna could do was look down at her hands, longing for a drag.

"Funerals have become boring, even passé! But Geny, he's going to make them exciting again! Imagine if dear old Pe Paw finally kicks the bucket. Say he was a big John Wayne fan. What do you do?"

Before Brianna could respond, Louise barked, "a wild west funeral! Dress Pe Paw up like a cowboy, stick him in a pine box, prop it up against the wall, silver dollars over his eyes, a rifle balanced beside him. It's just perfect!"

Louise let go of Brianna to clap her hands together in delight. Brianna immediately retrieved and lit her cigarette and sucked like a drowning man finally reaching the surface. But Louise wasn't finished.

"The possibilities are endless! Instead of cremation, what about the Salem witch trials? Imagine your old Wiccan grandma being burned at the stake!"

Louise turned to Brianna, pensive, and added, slowly, "Wait, Geny, I have an idea."

Studying Brianna, she said, "What about a real Viking funeral? We could do it at Lake Sinclair! Gunther could make us a shield, a Viking axe, even a boat, we can send them off to Valhalla in style!"

Yvgeny's face was beaming with excitement as Louise prattled on about her ideas. Louise began pacing around Brianna as she spoke.

"Imagine your lovely lady friend here dressed as Bruennhilde, a shield in one hand, a sword in the other. She would be the very epitome of Wagner's great Valkyrie!"

Brianna escaped Louise's whirlpool of words and stood beside Yvgeny, then leaned in and muttered, too softly for her to hear, "Jesus, she's as twisted as you are. Maybe even worse."

Yvgeny gave her a vague nod, too engrossed in Louise to pay attention.

Louise continued for several minutes longer, energized by Yvgeny's goading and encouragement.

Finally, she took a deep breath and after some small talk she hugged Yvgeny goodnight with a fierce embrace, patted Brianna on her arm, and went back inside.

Yvgeny waited patiently as Brianna finished her cigarette, sucking, then spewing the smoke out of her open mouth. She occasionally glanced in his direction, then finally flicked the butt across the parking lot. It came to rest next to the curb, pushing a lazy trail of smoke up into the sky.

"You are one weird dude."

She paused, then added, "but not bad for a first date."

"Ah, so perhaps there will be a second?"

"Don't push your luck."

⚞⚟

As usual, the weather reports were wrong, and the following morning brought sunshine and warm weather instead of the rain they predicted. Autumn was nowhere to be found. Yvgeny drove the six miles out to the sheriff's department, figuring a personal visit would be more effective than a phone call.

Following him into the lot was an ancient school bus repainted white, with bars over the windows. The bus hit a pot hole and creaked like an ancient tree in a stiff breeze. The windows were tinted too dark to see inside, but Yvgeny imagined the prisoners within; *future clients*.

He wondered whether they sat on the same bus on their way to elementary school. Eventually, some of them would land on one of Yvgeny's tables.

Circle of life. Ashes to ashes, dust to dust, and all that crap.

Yvgeny walked into the lobby and approached the counter. Behind it was an overweight, middle-aged woman

108

with her hair in a bun. There was no ballistic glass, just a wooden desk. She glanced up at the sound of the door, but was too absorbed in her cell phone to actually focus on him. After waiting a while, he leaned in and announced, "I would like to speak with Deputy Newsome."

She looked up, surprised, then let her eyes slide down across his black tie, black shirt, black morning coat, and matching trousers. He had left his derby in the hearse.

He waited patiently while she soaked him in; Yvgeny knew it took time for some people to process the vision presented to them. Many, if not most, were unaccustomed to seeing a properly attired undertaker.

Image was important in the service industries; a proper image led to a proper reputation, and reputation was everything for a successful business. His father used to tell him, 'A slovenly dresser lives a slovenly life.'

As far as Yvgeny could remember, the only living people in the county that had seen him wearing anything informal was Alfred or Mama, and only after the mortuary emptied out for the day and all the holes were filled.

For Yvgeny, however, it was about more than appearances; it was a way of life, requiring complete immersion. An undertaker should always look the part, just as a country priest should always be in his Roman collared shirt and a surgeon should be in green scrubs.

The receptionist slowly inched her chair away from the counter and reached for the telephone. No-one answered, so she hung up and reached for another machine, pushed some buttons, and leaned toward a microphone on a stalk.

In a shaky voice, she called out, "Deputy Newsome, signal 35. Newsome, 35."

Her cheeks flushed as she swiveled in her chair and preoccupied herself with her phone. She avoided looking up at Yvgeny, who stared at her a moment, glanced down at her bloated form stuffed into her polyester uniform, then back at her face. He thought of Brianna in all her glory, and shook his head. *No comparison.*

Apparently feeling his eyes on her, she looked up with raised eyebrows that were drawn on in a permanent expression of surprise. *Amateur,* he thought.

From his vantage point he noticed her gold and white box of Marlboro 100s on her desk by her phone. *The hard stuff. Cowboy killers.* He leaned in close and in a conspiratorial tone said, "be seeing you sooner than later," then turned and sat, back straight, in one of the thinly upholstered wooden chairs in the lobby. He ignored the stack of magazines on the table and the stunned expression on the receptionist's face.

Some minutes later, Newsome poked his head into the lobby beside the woman. They exchanged a few words, then he disappeared, emerging from another door in the lobby ten seconds later.

"Geny? What brings you here?"

Newsome did not extend his hand.

"I was wondering whether you've caught the killer yet."

Newsome's half smile faded.

"Still waiting on autopsy results. Why?"

Ignoring the question, Yvgeny asked, "Well, do you have any clues? Any witnesses come forward?"

Newsome canted his head to the side.

"What do you care?" he asked, then he paused. "Wait a minute, you been holding out on me? You find something else when you buried the other guy? Am I gonna need that search warrant?"

"No, I was just thinking about the body. I think he was Jewish."

Newsome squinted and said, "Jewish? There ain't no Jews in Comstock. Hell, probably ain't no Jews in all of Gilbert County. How'd you come up with that idea?"

Yvgeny had been practicing how he would respond to that question. He took a deep breath and tried to adopt a concerned expression.

"Well, the way he was dressed, something about him, and of course, well, you know, his particulars."

Newsome's face clouded for a moment before it registered.

"Geny, a lot of people get circumcised. Don't make 'em all Jews."

"Maybe not. But I did a little dabbling on the Internet. Back when this guy was a baby, the circumcision rate was less than 50%. But all Jews get it done, right? So that raises the odds."

Yvgeny leaned forward and added, "The other thing is, Jews like to bury their dead as soon as possible. So I'm thinking, maybe it was a Jew on Jew thing. One of them kills another, then he rushes to bury the body real quick."

Yvgeny waited for a response, but the detective just stared at him. Finally, Yvgeny waived a hand dismissively toward him and said, "Look, call it a hunch if you want. But trust me, I've seen a lot of dead people."

"Yeah Geny, but how many dead Jews?"

Yvgeny shrugged.

"Not many. Like I said, they like to bury them fast. They rarely require my services."

Newsome nodded, set his hands on his hips.

"Anything else you got for me?"

Yvgeny remained quiet a moment, then squinched his mouth together.

"No, I just wanted you to know I think he was a Jew. Maybe you should ask around and see if one's missing."

Newsome's eyes narrowed.

"I'll do that, Geny. You have a good day, ya' hear?"

Yvgeny nodded, and as Newsome turned away, he called out again.

"Inspector. What did that lady behind the counter tell you?"

The deputy stopped and turned back to Yvgeny with a smirk he couldn't conceal.

"She said you made a pass at her."

Yvgeny smiled then, chuckled softly, more of a rasp than a laugh.

Right before Newsome stepped through the door, he turned to take one more look at Yvgeny, who was still standing in the lobby watching the deputy go.

⊥⊦
⊤⊦

CHAPTER SEVEN

Newsome returned to his desk and sat down. He steepled his fingers together and watched as Yvgeny passed by the window on his way back to his black Cadillac.

"That dude gives me the creeps," his partner, Bubba, called out from behind him. "Looks like he's dressed up for Halloween."

"Bubba, he dresses like that every day."

Bubba just whistled.

"There's something else I don't like about him."

"What, the fact he mucked up your crime scene?" Bubba asked.

"Well, that too. But you should see how he looks at me. And the city cops, too. He thinks he's smarter than all of us."

"Well, you was over there with Frankie and that other clown, what's his name? I don't like *them* neither."

The Cadillac's reverse lights came on, and they watched as it backed up slowly, then disappeared down the street. The windows were blacked out. It was technically against the law for them to be so dark.

"So why'd he come out here?"

Newsome put his feet on his desk and pushed back in his chair, turned toward Bubba.

"Well, our newest detective believes the victim was a Jew."

"Seriously?"

"Yup. He ain't never buried no Jew, ain't probably ever even met one."

"Well, maybe he's just nuts. I mean, just look at him!"

Newsome shook his head.

"No, he's an ass, but he's no idiot. Gave me a history lesson about circumcision. At least we know he can read."

"Circumcision? You kidding me?"

Newsome just rolled his eyes.

"I think he's running some kind of angle on us. And I'd like to know what it is."

"Maybe he's trying to help," Bubba offered.

"Nope."

Newsome rocked in his chair, tapping his fingertips together.

"That crazy Russian knows something. Why drive all the way out here with that crap when he could have called me on the phone?"

Bubba listened to the squeaking of Newsome's chair for a while, then cleared his throat and asked, "'bout time to call Flowers, ain't it?"

Newsome checked his watch and let his chair drop

back down onto all four legs.

"Yeah. Thanks, Bubba."

Newsome called the Georgia Bureau of Investigation's regional office in Macon, which handled most of Gilbert County's autopsies. Many of Georgia's 159 counties simply did not have the resources (or need) to have their own in-house pathologists.

Gilbert County, however, was part of a recent trend toward minimizing reliance on the GBI. As such, they recently started doing some of the work themselves.

For example, the sheriff and coroner for Gilbert County (the same person, as in most of the smaller counties) signed an on-call agreement with an old local physician, who would handle autopsies when no foul play was expected.

All the old doctor wanted was to be given the title of deputy coroner, and a shiny badge to put in his wallet. When that doctor died, the sheriff had to choose between the two remaining physicians in town. The first was Indian; the sheriff didn't like Indians and could barely understand the man, so making his choice was easy.

Only later did he regret his decision.

If the victim was eighty and died in a nursing home, Deputy Coroner Jimmy Flowers (he also insisted on the title and badge) would get the ticket. If the victim was twenty and killed in a car crash, for Flowers it was money in the bank. But for a murder, the body had to go to Macon.

"GBI. How can I help you?"

Newsome asked for Dr. Rufus Kincaid, one of the senior pathologists. The operator transferred him, and the line rang three times before being answered by Rosy, the doctor's assistant.

"Dr. Kincaid's office."

"Is the doctor available?"

"He's with a patient. Can I take a message?"

Newsome chuckled.

"Maybe you can help me, Rosy. Might be a strange question, though."

"Whatcha got, Harry?"

"My John Doe ... any chance he's more of a John Goldberg, or John Goldstein?"

"What do you mean, was he Jewish?"

"Yeah. Was he?"

"How the hell would we know that?"

Newsome cleared his throat, and waited. After about ten seconds it hit her.

"Oh. Oh! Um, I don't know, he's on ice, I could go check, but, well, Rufus might have already started his survey. Let me go ask him."

"You sure his patient won't mind?"

This time Rosy chuckled, then put the phone down on a counter. Newsome heard her footsteps as she walked away from the phone.

Rufus was at least 70 years old, thin as a rail, and over six feet tall. He was black, but with his beard and his frame, he resembled Abraham Lincoln. Raised on a farm south of Valdosta to a sharecropper and his wife, Rufus couldn't even read until he was fifteen, and barely passed medical school. He felt more comfortable around crops than people: his bedside manner destined him for a career in pathology.

"This Newsome? Harry? You there?"

Kincaid was terrible with modern technology. The GBI had equipped his examining room with a speaker phone that Rosy would set up for him when he was in an autopsy. He never quite understood the way it worked, so the first minute was always the same.

"Yes, Rufus, it's me, Harry. How are you?"

"Harry, I can hear you, but can you hear me? Harry, are you there?"

"Yes, Rufus, I'm still here, I can hear you five by five."

"Five by five? What the hell does that mean? Don't give me no cop talk, you know I don't understand none of that. Can you hear me OK?"

"Rufus, I hear you just fine. Do you remember that body we sent up to you a couple days ago? You get a chance to take a look yet?"

"Him? Nope, just a survey. White guy. Older than me." He paused, then added, "no head."

Newsome had to take the handset away from his ear. As usual, the old doctor sounded like he was pressing his mouth against the phone.

"I noticed that. Listen, was he circumcised?"

"Was he what?"

"Circumcised?"

"Dammit, Rosy, come get this liver, I just got bile on my tie!"

Newsome heard some loud crinkling sounds, then Rosy let out a grunt, after which the doctor yelled, "What in the hell difference does *that* make?"

"You talking to me?"

"Who else?"

"I'm just asking. I've got a hunch."

"A hunch about what? Death by circumcision?"

"He might be Jewish."

"Jewish? Jesus Christ. Can you hold on a minute? Rosy, how the hell do you put this thing on hold?"

Newsome turned to Bubba as he waited, a sour look on his face.

"I spent ten minutes with that body, why can't I remember if he was cut?"

Newsome heard muttering, then a click, followed by thready music, like a radio between two stations. He waited for a couple of minutes, then there was another click.

"Harry, you there? Is this thing still on?"

"Yes, Rufus, I'm still here. Whatcha got?"

"Well, good hunch, young man. Or maybe you took a quick peek. I don't know. He's cut. Terrible job, too, from what I could see. Rabbi must have been in a hurry. Poor bastard."

"So when do you think you'll be able to take a closer look at this guy?"

"Look here, Harry, they kill 'em in Macon quicker than I can study 'em. Probably a week, unless they get rowdy again this weekend. Yours is the only white guy in the whole damn morgue, me included. Oh, and he's the only one without a head. Thanks for the variety. You know he ain't got no hands either?"

"Yes, I noticed that."

"Just checking, seeing as you weren't sure the guy was cut."

"Very funny. So he's a Jew?"

"Like I said, how the hell am I supposed to know that? He's cut. So what? Lots of people get cut. Course, whoever whacked his johnson gave him a high and tight instead of a trim."

When Kincaid laughed it sounded more like a wheezy snort, and Newsome pursed his lips and waited for him to finish. Finally, the old pathologist calmed down and said, "Look, give me a few hours, maybe I'll find something."

Newsome sighed and looked out his window. As he watched, he saw a Ford F-150 King Ranch pass by and leave the parking lot. The truck had a set of blue and red lights over the cab.

"Must be time to check his nuts again."

The Gilbert County Sheriff's Department had nineteen deputies plus the sheriff, an elected official who spent most of his time working on his next election and checking on his pecan trees, the latter being almost a daily affair.

He was preoccupied with his trees suffering from disease and inspected them like a doctor scrutinized his patients. He was an avid surveyor of the skies and an accomplished predictor of the weather. He was a good farmer, a decent manager, but a lousy investigator.

That's where Newsome and Bubba Johnson came in. They generally divided the county in half, Newsome taking the eastern side, and Bubba, the west.

They covered everything, from burglaries to truancies, domestics to murders. The majority of their cases were more the truancy and burglary variety. They worked one or two deaths each year, but they were usually farming or traffic accidents and the occasional suicide. The last bona fide murder they worked was the body they found a few years earlier toward the interstate the mayor claimed was a drug deal gone bad. They never found the killer.

After Newsome hung up the phone, Bubba piped up, "Damn, Newsome, gotcha another dead guy. Maybe we can solve this one."

His battered desk was pushed right up against Newsome's and when they both were seated, they faced each other. Newsome nodded his head, looked over Bubba's shoulder and out the window. Bubba was younger than Newsome, pure country, but he had a good head on his shoulders and his hillbilly diction and vocabulary belied a keen intelligence.

"Maybe, but the last guy had a head *and* fingerprints and we *still* never identified him."

Bubba leaned back and kicked his feet up on his desk, laced his fingers together behind his head.

"Yessir, but this is gonna be different, I can feel it. Jewish, you think? Ain't never met me one. We don't got no Jewish churches around here, do we?"

"No Bubba, no we don't. They call them synagogues. Looked it up this morning. Closest one I can find is up in Byron."

"Byron? They got Jews in Byron?"

Bubba pushed back onto the two rear legs of his wooden chair, then rocked as if he was on his front porch.

"I reckon. They wouldn't have a synagogue there if they didn't."

They just stared at each other for a moment, then Newsome shuffled some papers on his desk.

"I printed out the address, figured it can't hurt to

120

ask around, maybe some old man is missing, maybe we get lucky."

Newsome paused a minute, then added, "but I ain't doing it because that freak undertaker said it!"

"I hear ya', Hoss," Bubba responded, still rocking in his chair, then added, "I'm telling you, Harry, we gonna have this in the bag by Friday. Easy case."

"Ain't no such thing as an easy case. Not when you find a body with no head. And some wing nut messing with your crime scene. I'm telling you, Atlanta's getting closer to us every day."

╬

As Yvgeny turned into his driveway, he saw Alfred round the corner from the back of the mortuary. Alfred wiped his hands on his dingy shirt while shifting his weight from one leg to the other. Yvgeny approached him, his face a study in chagrin.

"Well, my dear Alfred, it appears our good inspector was disinclined to accept my offer of information. That means I will likely have to solve this terrible crime myself and save the day."

Alfred clicked and grunted his sympathy, then turned to the sky. Yvgeny followed his gaze, then turned back to Alfred.

"What do you see when you look up there?"

Alfred glanced down at Yvgeny briefly, then refocused his attention on the heavens.

Yvgeny left Alfred frozen outside the mortuary and went into his kitchen to make some coffee. On the counter, where he left it, was a scrap of paper upon which he had jotted down the address of the synagogue closest to Comstock. With a sigh, he stuffed it into his pocket, then headed toward his easy chair to sip his coffee.

Such a burden, having to do everything myself.

He passed a small mirror and glanced at his reflection. As he admired himself, he was reminded of a funeral a few years earlier when an old man with dementia had waddled up to him, smacking his cane against Yvgeny's heart of pine floors. The man squinted up at him, then turned to yell, "Marge, it's Johnny Cash!"

Yvgeny sat for a while, clutching his warm mug and sipping his coffee, thinking about the body he found. Yvgeny knew corpses like a mechanic knew Chevys.

They're all pretty much the same under the hood, and after you've been up to your elbows inside them for a while, you come to realize they each might look a little different, might age at various speeds, but really, they're all alike.

A car is a car is a car. *Yes*, thought Yvgeny, *no maudlin sentimentality for me. Corpses and cars, at least a car comes with a warranty.*

His thoughts brought to the surface a disappointing experience he had at the national mortician's conference some years earlier. Several hundred practitioners at a hotel in Atlanta, each in their crisp blue suit, starched white shirt, and news anchor hair styles. Limp noodles. Salesmen.

He remembered following the signs down the escalator, around the corner, then down a hallway into what felt like the bowels of the hotel, far away from the other guests.

Once inside, he roamed, uninspired, past coffin displays and booths staffed by insurance companies and the top names in morticians' tools and supplies. When it was time for lunch, he wandered around the plastic tables until he found his folded cardboard name plate.

As his table mates pontificated about business, their cheap wine fueling ever more solemn and profound commentary on their chosen profession, Yvgeny kept his silence.

Finally, an older mortician sitting beside him tried to elicit from him a similar testament, poking and prodding until finally, having lost patience, Yvgeny sighed and said, "Look, we're all just a bunch of Chevrolets, Fords, Hondas, chugging along the great highway. We break, we get fixed, then one day we can't be fixed. Then we go to the junk yard. That's where we come in."

The entire table stared at Yvgeny, open mouthed, forks and spoons hovering above plates in surprise. Then one of the suits put down his utensil and cleared his throat, furrowed his brow, then asked, in a tremulous voice, "Aren't you trivializing your life's work? *Our* lives' work?"

Yvgeny shrugged, and said, "It's an ambiguity I can tolerate."

His esteemed colleagues then launched a withering assault, regaling Yvgeny with arguments and defenses, soliloquies and pontifications. Servers placed the main dish before them but the plates remained untouched, ignored, as they attempted to sway the jury of one.

Yvgeny finished his soup, picked at his salad, then finally, when their artful protests had petered out, he raised his fork and said, "When I go, just dig a hole and throw me in. Save your embalming fluid. And don't waste my suit, take it off and use it on someone else. Only worm food should go in that hole!"

Yvgeny countered their stares with a toothy grin, then attacked his Chicken Kiev.

"Then why keep at it? Why not find a different

career?" the old man had said, crossing his arms. "If it's such a big waste of time, then why bother?"

Yvgeny adopted a thoughtful expression and said, "Why does anyone do anything? For the money. Because I'm good at it. Come on, it's a job!"

Yvgeny sighed when he realized his table mates were staring at him in shock.

"OK, it's like this. You get some dead guy, make him look and smell like he's still alive. The rest of it's kind of like a birthday party. You stuff the guy in a box, wrap him up real nice, then take him to the party. The guests all look inside, ooh and ahh, and you're done. You put the lid back on and drop him in a hole. The guests go eat some snacks, drink a little wine, then you bury him and move on to the next one."

It was the last conference he attended.

Yvgeny took another swig of his coffee, and his mind wandered away from the convention and back to Reuben. Thinking of Reuben made him think of their last conversation, which made him think of the Nazis.

The Nazis had no respect for life, or anything else. Yvgeny made a career out of putting dead people in holes, but he didn't believe in killing. To him, life was too valuable precisely because there was no Afterlife.

It bothered Yvgeny that someone could survive the Holocaust only to be murdered in the middle of Georgia seventy years later. It also bothered him someone had the gall to dump the body into one of his holes. It bothered him that Reuben would not tell him what the watch was worth. It even bothered him the inspector shined him on when he visited him at the precinct.

Yvgeny sighed, sipped the last dregs of his coffee,

and felt in his pocket for his scrap with the address to the synagogue. It had wrapped around his charm, which he turned around in his fingers, then dropped it back into his pocket.

Holmes's assistance wasn't always gladly accepted by Scotland Yard, either, he thought glumly.

He stopped in his work room to check on Maude, who was chilling in cold storage. He pulled out the tray with his free hand, then placed his coffee mug beside Maude's head to take in a deep whiff.

"Ah, Maude, much better. Tomorrow we will get started. I have everything right here," he said with a flourish of his left hand toward his work tray.

"I just have a few errands to run. It appears that I am expected not only to do my job here, but to do the work of an unqualified public official who was too proud to accept my generous offer of assistance. You would think he'd be thankful."

Yvgeny leaned in close to Maude's face and whispered, "And he threatened to come back with a search warrant. Can you imagine what that would do for business?"

Yvgeny leaned in even closer, right up to her ear, and said, "Not to mention, we all have skeletons in our closets, now don't we?"

Yvgeny was so engrossed in his one sided conversation with Maude that he did not hear Alfred shuffling down the corridor in his muddy boots. Alfred turned to enter, then froze when he saw Yvgeny hunched over one of the cold storage drawers. He could not hear what Yvgeny was saying, but watched him sweep the air with his left hand to emphasize some point he was making, then return to his one-sided conversation.

Alfred glanced over at the cabinet to his right that contained all Yvgeny's embalming chemicals, then back to

Yvgeny. He made several clicks in the back of his throat as he stepped backwards out of the entranceway, then turned and squeaked down the hall toward the cemetery, leaving muddy prints on the marble tile.

⚔

As Yvgeny stepped outside, keys in hand, he saw Brianna in her Smart Car pulling up in the street. He smiled and approached while she began the laborious process of squeezing out of her car. By the time she emerged, her face was glistening from the effort. She put her cigarette to her lips and smoothed out her polyester smock with her palms. There was no bouquet this time; she came to see *him*.

"I had an hour to kill before work, figured I would stop by."

"That's lovely. Would you like to come in?"

She glanced toward the mortuary with an uneasy expression on her face.

"You *live* in there?"

She followed him inside, flicking her cigarette into the flowers before entering. She looked around, sniffed and scoffed, "It smells old."

"This mortuary was originally built to be the estate of Julius Weaver."

"Some rich guy?"

"A wealthy farming magnate. He died right after the turn of the century. He had no heirs, no will, so Georgia got everything. By the time they got it to auction, Franz

Ferdinand was shot and we got sucked into the First World War. Suddenly a mansion in the middle of nowhere wasn't worth a whole lot."

Brianna stood in the entry hall scratching her arms and trying to maintain eye contact with him.

"So it escheated to the state?"

"Well, yes. You know about such things?"

"Intestacy? A little. Enough to know it's important to have a will."

Yvgeny nodded, pausing long enough to smile, then cleared his throat.

"Anyway, the house changed hands several times and eventually landed in the lap of Eldred Schmidt, and it's all history from there. So I give you," he turned and raised his arm toward the hall, "Schmidt and Sons Mortuary!"

Brianna adjusted the hem of her shirt and leaned against the wall, crossing her arms.

"How do you know so much about this place? Did you actually meet this guy?"

"The original owner? No, no, if he were alive today he'd be about," Yvgeny paused trying to do the math, "160 years old. I never met Eldred either, but a long time ago I met one of his sons. I was just a kid."

Yvgeny heard footsteps upstairs and winced, then cleared his throat again and continued speaking to distract her from the squeaks and groans of the floor joists.

"I still remember that first day. We had packed everything we owned into our old dumpy station wagon and left Atlanta."

Yvgeny walked over to the banister that circled around and up the stairs.

"Eldred Junior was ancient, older than any of the stiffs my father rolled into the parlor."

As Brianna grimaced and looked away, Yvgeny seized the moment and let his eyes wander down to her ample bosom.

"Poor sap. It's a sad story. When Eldred Senior retired in 1936, his other sons refused to take over the family business. All but Eldred Junior, that is. The others were all drafted into the Second World War, and never came home. Eldred Junior framed the letters from the War Department and placed two headstones just down the way from your grandfather's to mark their empty graves."

Brianna snapped her fingers and started walking toward the door.

"That reminds me, I should go down there."

"Where?"

"His grave."

Yvgeny watched her walk outside with a mixture of curiosity and relief. He knew his mother could come lurching down the stairs at any moment, so to avoid a confrontation, he jogged up to Brianna as she followed the sidewalk toward the cemetery.

"Such dedication to your grandfather. I am very impressed."

Brianna continued walking, silent.

As they passed Alfred's shed, Yvgeny prayed he would be out of sight. Brianna trudged down the path toward her grandfather's headstone. When she arrived, she lit a cigarette, then balanced it on the top of his headstone. She rummaged through her purse and produced her cell phone, and as Yvgeny watched, she crouched beside the headstone and took a selfie. She noticed Yvgeny staring as she stood to retrieve her smoke.

"It's part of the will."

"What?"

"I have to visit him at least once a week to collect."

"Collect what?"

"His estate, what else?"

Yvgeny continued watching her, uncomprehending. Brianna sighed, mashed her cigarette butt against her grandfather's headstone, then flicked it toward Eldred Junior's brothers' graves. She glared at him and spit out, "What?"

"Your grandfather died seventy years ago."

"I didn't say it was *his* will!"

"I don't understand."

"My father died last year."

"I'm sorry."

"He was serving a life sentence in Jackson, so I never really knew him. But he wanted to make sure I'd come visit his Dad every week since he was never able to."

"So he makes you visit every week?"

"Yup. Pain in the ass, but I figure it's the easiest money I ever made."

"How much?"

She shrugged.

"Dunno, but the lawyer told me it would be worthwhile for me to do it."

"What kind of work did your father do?"

"He never really had a job. But I know he always had a nice car."

"So what do you do with your selfies?"

"I text them to the lawyer every week."

On the walk back to her car, she asked, "So what happened with that old guy? You bought this place from him?"

"Well, it's complicated."

Brianna flicked her cigarette butt into the dead leaves and dug through her purse for another.

"Eldred Junior, he ran the place for around thirty years, but never married, never had any kids. My Dad was like a son to him, but when he died in '74, he didn't have a will, so the state got the place again. My father told me the city was going to restore it and make it a historic landmark, but, well, back then, the embalming business was a pretty messy process. I'm guessing the state figured out how much it would cost to clean the place up and balked. They sold it as is, and my father was the only interested buyer."

"So your father bought it?"

"Yes, he was working for Eldred Junior."

Brianna glanced around the grounds, exhaling smoke from her nostrils, then asked, "So you actually live in there?" Her jaw remained partially open in a sneer. "With all those dead bodies?"

"Well, compared to where we lived in Atlanta, it's a palace."

Brianna turned and flicked ashes into the grass, then checked her watch.

"I have to get to work."

"Perhaps one day I could give you a tour of the

place?"

"Perhaps."

She briefly stood staring at him, then after an awkward silence, Brianna muttered, "I have to go."

As the Smart Car sped away, he heard one of the windows opening from above him.

"Ach. My son with a *wieloryb*! Just bury me next to your father now and save me the heartbreak!"

╫

CHAPTER EIGHT

Bubba opened Newsome's passenger door, then snorted hard and spit something over the car and into the grass. He sat down and ratcheted the seat all the way back, and while struggling with his seat belt asked Newsome, "You ever wash this thing?"

Newsome pretended not to hear him, and as he started the car, Bubba asked, "Where to first?"

"Macon," Newsome answered. "I want to see if Kincaid has anything yet. Maybe after, we can stop in Byron."

Bubba glanced over at Newsome.

"What's in Byron?"

Newsome took a breath, closed his eyes for a moment before responding.

"Remember? The synagogue?"

Newsome felt Bubba's blank stare, and without taking his eyes from the road, explained, "It's like a church for Jews."

"Oh yeah."

Newsome made his way toward Interstate 75 and headed north. Yvgeny was already on the highway a few miles behind them, and as the deputies continued toward Macon, Yvgeny pulled off, on his way to Byron. Clutching his handwritten directions against the steering wheel as he drove, Yvgeny navigated through town and beyond it, out into the country, past several miles of rolling pastures and sod farms, until he reached the strip mall.

He rolled through the parking lot, bouncing over one cracked, yellow speed bump after another. A Winn Dixie supermarket anchored the shopping center; he slowed to a crawl and found what he was looking for sandwiched between a UPS Store and a CVS Pharmacy, just like he saw on Google.

Thick blue drapes hung behind windows that bore Hebrew lettering in gold paint. Most of the shops in the strip mall were just opening for the day, so there was plenty of parking. An upbeat elderly woman left the drugstore with two bags and, upon seeing Yvgeny's hearse between her and her car, altered course to maximize the distance between herself and him.

Yvgeny figured there was no need to check the time, as he had no idea when synagogues opened for business. Plus, Yvgeny didn't like repetitive gestures like checking the time, because, as he described to Brianna, he believed each person had a finite number of movements in their life. He liked to use them sparingly.

He approached the entrance to the synagogue and tried the handle, expecting it to be locked. To his surprise, it was not only unlocked, it was standing ajar. As he pushed it open and looked inside, two people passing him on the sidewalk slowed, took in his outfit, then hurried past.

It was fairly dim inside and Yvgeny had to take a moment for his eyes to adjust. The interior slowly came into view; it reminded him of a church, with rows of pews, prayer books on the backs of each bench, and a dais up front. Yvgeny estimated the place could comfortably hold perhaps twenty congregants, give or take. He stood still for a moment, listening for movement.

Across the room, an interior door opened, and a younger man emerged wearing denim overalls and a suede work belt laden with tools. He held a length of PVC pipe in one hand and a bucket in the other. He took a few steps into the room before noticing Yvgeny.

At first, the man froze, then his jaw opened, shut, opened again, then finally the man asked in a shaky and small voice, "Um, can I help you?"

"I am looking for the rabbi."

Yvgeny took a few steps forward, and the man reflexively took a step back, smacking his heels against the door.

"He's not here."

"Well, does he have an assistant?"

The other man looked around, then shrugged.

"I, I don't know. I'm just here to fix the plumbing. What, what do you need?"

The man shifted his weight from one leg to the other, holding his pipe and his bucket. He could not keep his eyes from wandering down to Yvgeny's vintage outfit, which triggered an old childhood fear of Dracula. Yvgeny glanced around, oblivious to the man's fear, then his eyes fell back on him.

"I am wondering whether your synagogue is missing anyone. Anyone old."

The young man's jaw opened again, and he pressed himself against the door as if he could melt into it and escape. Without taking his eyes off Yvgeny, he slowly put down the bucket, but kept his grip on the pipe.

"What d-do you m-m-mean, missing?"

"I found a body down in Comstock. Had no head. No hands, either. But he was old. And we think he was a Jew."

Yvgeny looked around, as if looking for someone, and asked, "Anyone missing here?"

The man's eyes widened and his free hand reached behind him, fumbling for the door knob.

"Who- Who are you?"

"I'm Yvgeny Jedynak, I am the undertaker of Schmidt and Sons Mortuary. I found the body in one of my open graves."

The man muttered something unintelligible to Yvgeny while his fingers continued scrabbling against the door, searching desperately for the knob.

His mouth moved, but no sound emerged. Then, finally, he squeaked out, "undertaker?"

"Yes," said Yvgeny, growing impatient. "So is anyone missing? Unaccounted for?"

"No. Well, I don't think so, not that I know of. You should ask the rabbi."

"Where is he?"

"He's not here."

"Where can I find him?"

The man struggled a moment longer, then finally began to overcome his terror. He dropped his pipe and began rooting through his work belt, his nerves fueling a stream of consciousness babble as he fished through his pockets, finally coming out with a construction pencil, the kind that was more flat than round so it could be sharpened with a knife, and a scrap of paper.

"Why don't you give me your name again, and a number, I will have him call you when I see him. He's not here, ain't going to be here today at all, nope, no sir, I'm just here making some repairs, yup, broken pipe, water everywhere, the plastic done cracked, this place was built back in the early eighties, must've had a bad batch of plastic, half the pipes done been replaced over the last few years. Yessir, I will make sure he gets the message, what's your name again?"

Yvgeny watched the man fiddle with his pencil, repeated his name and number, then left without another word. The plumber watched him leave, shivered, then walked briskly to the door and locked it.

Just as Yvgeny left the synagogue, Newsome and Bubba pulled into the GBI office in Macon.

╬

Bubba and Newsome passed through the dingy lobby and split up, Newsome heading toward the stairwell, and Bubba getting into a tired elevator that squeaked rhythmically as it lurched into the bowels of the building.

Kincaid's lair was at the end of a windowless hallway in the basement of the GBI building; a setting equally suited for a horror movie.

There was a battered metal desk in a small vestibule at the end of the hallway that reminded Newsome of his own desk at the office. Rosy usually posted there as gatekeeper, but she was nowhere to be found, so they passed through the swinging double doors behind the desk.

The hallway continued another twenty feet and ended at another set of swinging doors; each with a square viewing window. Halfway down that corridor was Kincaid's office and the deputies' destination.

Kincaid was so tall his wooden desk looked like it was designed for a child. His afro was gray and over two inches high and unkempt, and he was rubbing his eyes when Newsome walked into his office.

"You look like hell, Doc."

The man continued rubbing his eyes, then coughed before looking up at Newsome.

"You ain't exactly the picture of health yourself, Harry."

Newsome smiled, then rolled over an old office chair missing one arm and took a seat across from Kincaid. Bubba glanced around the room looking for another place to sit, but the only remaining chair was stacked with books and papers. He leaned against the wall.

Kincaid's desk was a morass of paper, folders, photographs. Kincaid rooted around in the mess, pushing the paper around like a mystic pushing a planchette across a Ouija board. He finally pulled one brown folder away from the others, looked at the name on the outside, then slid it toward Newsome. As Newsome opened the folder, the doctor began reciting as if he had memorized its contents.

"Doe, John. White, probably in his eighties.

"That the closest you can get on his age?"

"He ain't a tree, Newsome, I can't cut off his arm and count the rings."

The doctor glared at Newsome a moment, then his eyes unfocused and he continued reciting from memory.

"Bad teeth, bad health, and seeing as you already reminded me of it, he kind of reminds me of myself."

He paused, then added, "if I was a cracker like you."

Bubba snorted.

"And also, seeing as you already pointed it out, he's got a hell of a circumcision."

He paused, then declared, "cause of death due to not having a head."

The doctor paused, and Newsome looked up from the file, one eyebrow raised.

"Are you serious?"

The doctor smirked and shrugged his shoulders.

"Well, you can't live without one. Ain't no trauma other than the missing parts. He could've been choked out, punched out, had his head smashed in, shot, clubbed. . . let's see here."

Newsome tossed the file back on the desk and asked, "Are you finished?"

The old doctor cleared his throat, then started picking at something on his cheek, muttering to himself as if he hadn't heard Newsome's question. After a moment, the doctor looked up.

"Oh yeah, they could've hung him. Or maybe he died of natural causes, then someone found him and took a few souvenirs. I could keep going."

"No, I think we get the picture. A guy who might be in his eighties might have been killed. You've been a huge help, Doc, you pretty much solved the case."

"Cool your jets, Newsome, I'm not finished. Now, try

to keep up. Maybe your friend there can translate for you."

Bubba smiled as the old man leaned back and clasped his fingers behind his head, his chair squeaking from the movement.

"I drained a little over a gallon of blood out of that body. That's quite a bit. Most of it, I'd say. Didn't see much clotting. And plenty of lividity. Either of you brain surgeons want to take a stab at what that means?"

Bubba responded immediately.

"They cut him up after they killed him."

"You win the prize, lawman. Probably an hour or two later. Now try this one on for size- I think he was seated when he was killed, and he was moved a few times."

"Lividity?"

"Yup, that's part of it. Plus, like I said, he still had most of his blood. Seems to me, if they cut his head off while he was alive, he'd been missing a lot more. Heart would've still been pumping, at least until they cut through his spine. Aorta would've sprayed everywhere. This guy's clothes were pretty clean."

"Assuming he was wearing them when he was killed."

The doctor nodded, and mumbled, "Well, you're the detective, not me."

Newsome asked, "So, any idea what they used to chop him up?"

"Something sharp. But not surgical. Big blade. Machete, axe. Maybe even a sword."

"Jesus," Bubba muttered.

"I took some pictures, in case you want to send them to the FBI."

Newsome nodded, then asked, "You didn't get

anything from his clothes?"

The old doctor shrugged and leaned back in his chair.

"Well, traces of lead, nitrocellulose."

"I thought you said you couldn't tell how it happened. Sounds to me like he was shot."

"I didn't say that. I said there were traces of those elements. On his shirt. Maybe someone shot him. Maybe one of you two transferred that residue when you touched him. Maybe he liked going to the gun range. Maybe it was his friend's shirt. How long you been at this job, sport?"

Newsome sighed.

"Great. Sounds like he will be John Doe forever."

The doctor absently picked at his ear, then suddenly stopped.

"Oh yeah, one more thing. His last meal was sausage, cabbage. Coffee. Probably had it a couple hours before he was killed, I'd guess."

Kincaid's chair was on little rollers, and he pushed himself away from the desk and went through the slow process of getting onto his wobbly legs. He walked over to a cart and picked up a large brown paper bag, brought it back over and placed it on the desk. The red evidence tape had been cut cleanly with something sharp, slicing Newsome's signature across the tape and bag in half. Newsome stood and opened the bag, peered inside at the threadbare clothing that the victim had worn.

"Who the hell was this guy?" Newsome wondered.

Kincaid had remained standing and reached up to pull on his patchy beard.

"I'd say a pensioner, myself. And an outdoors-man. I bet his hands are all calloused from manual work. He ain't fat, and at his age, that's saying something. Just look at me. He had him a good amount of muscle for his age, too. Bet he didn't go down easy."

Newsome nodded, and Kincaid approached him and pointed into the bag.

"He wasn't rich, assuming those are his clothes. Probably was sitting around at home, maybe watching some TV. Quincy, ME, if he had some taste."

Newsome glanced up at the old doctor and rolled his eyes but remained silent, then put a hand into the bag, working his fingers through the clothing. Then he sat back down and re-opened the file Kincaid had slid across his desk. As he read, Kincaid re-sealed the bag, signed his name across the top of it, and replaced it on the cart.

Kincaid walked over to a corner of his office to take a drink from the water fountain. It took him a while to get into the crouch necessary for his mouth to reach the water. Newsome thumbed through the pages, and his eyes stopped on one sentence.

"Hey Kincaid, what's this about a watch?"

The old man finished his drink and stood up slowly, smacking his lips, then ambled back toward his desk.

"Oh yeah. He was probably wearing a watch before he was killed. Now it's gone. Lividity. Clear outline of a round object on his wrist."

"So someone killed him, chopped off his head and his hands, then stole his watch?"

The old man sat in his chair, squinching his face at Newsome. He launched into a sing-song "Well..."

"Well what?"

"The lividity was pretty clear. I'd say he was dead for a while before they took the watch. Few hours, maybe."

"Same time they took the guy's head and his hands?"

"Hard to say. Could've been later."

"Don't suppose he had a pacemaker, maybe a fake hip, something with an ID number?"

The old doctor chuckled and said, "You wish. You ain't getting off this one so fast."

He watched Newsome nod his head, and as he turned to leave, Kincaid called out, "I'll send the stomach contents to the lab. Maybe you'll get lucky."

⚜

Newsome had grown up in Houston County, Georgia, the home of Robins Air Force Base. He remembered his father in his Air Force uniform leaving for work each day in his old Chevy 3100 pick-up. Blue and white, with a rusty muffler that made it rattle as it pulled into traffic. It was his father's last assignment; he was due to retire in 1970, when Harry was only four years old. Instead, he was retired by a would-be car thief at a red light on Moody Parkway.

Harry's only memory of his father was of him leaving for work in that truck, in his uniform, a red plaid thermos in one hand, his keys in the other. He had convinced himself his memory was of his father that last day he saw him alive, but with all the years that separated him from that memory, he could not be sure.

Harry wanted to become a police officer to find the man responsible for killing him. As it turned out, the Houston County Sheriff's Department found the man long before he was old enough to carry a badge and gun. They would not let him testify at the man's sentencing hearing, but he was in the courtroom.

Harry had been too young to understand the difference between a deputy and a police officer, other than the color of their uniforms. But that experience was enough for him to change his mind. He wanted to wear the brown uniform.

When he was still in high school, Harry remembered watching them bulldoze an old farm and start building the strip mall that would later house the county's first synagogue.

The first business to open was the anchor, Winn Dixie. It was also the only surviving original tenant. The other businesses came and went. A Revco drug store, a dollar store, a Mexican restaurant, they all moved in, moved out.

Then the Radio Shack closed its doors. A year later, he saw a few old men in black suits and strange hats poking around. It wasn't long after that Newsome saw the strange lettering on the window and beneath it, in English, *Temple B'Nai Israel*. It was the first and only synagogue Newsome had ever seen.

He read in the newspaper that a synagogue was where Jews gathered to pray. It was the talk of the town for a few days, then people got used to it. That was five years ago. He had almost forgotten it was there.

He parked in the fire lane in front of the synagogue, tossed his placard on the dash, and he and Bubba made their way to the door. It was locked, but they could hear banging coming from inside.

Newsome knocked, waited, then knocked again, louder. Bubba reached for his asp baton to rap it against the doorjamb, but Harry held up his hand to stop him. *God's house, regardless of the flavor.*

Newsome knocked a third time and finally the banging stopped. The door was made of glass with a pleated curtain, and after a moment someone pushed a corner of the curtain aside and looked out at him. Bubba stood off to one side, bladed to keep his gun away from the door. The man studied the deputies carefully, then unlocked the door.

"Help you?"

"Hi. We're with the Gilbert County Sheriff's Department. Is the, um, rabbi around?"

Newsome displayed his credentials for the man, who glanced briefly at them without reading or looking closely at the photograph. He wore overalls and a work belt with tools. Newsome estimated the man to be no older than twenty-five.

The young man shook his head, his eyes darting about into the parking lot behind Newsome.

"Rabbi? Nope, he ain't here. Be back tomorrow."

The man tried to close the door but Bubba put his foot against the jamb to stop him, then leaned against the door frame.

Harry asked, "You mind if we come in? Only be a minute."

The man paused, shrugged, then stepped back to let him in.

After they entered, the man poked his head out and surveyed the parking lot, then studied the sidewalk in either direction. Satisfied, he shut and locked the door, and as Bubba and Harry exchanged glances, the man tugged on the door to confirm it was locked.

Newsome took a few steps into the place and looked

around at the walls. No art, and given its position in the middle of the strip mall, there were no windows. Nothing but chairs, and a dais up front with a big armoire.

Newsome turned to the man, who then sneezed, and while wiping his nose against the sleeve of his flannel shirt, muttered, "So I guess you're here about the body, eh?"

Newsome furrowed his brow.

"What body?"

The man cocked his head.

"Well, the one in the hole. The other guy told me, he was here a couple hours ago, asking for the rabbi. Wanted to know if we was missing any Jews."

The man shut his eyes for a moment and shuddered as he relived the encounter.

"What did this guy look like?"

The man shuddered again and put his hands in his pockets.

"One of those cemetery guys. Creepy, too. Wearing all black. Long coat. Even a black tie. Reminded me of Dracula. Ain't Halloween for another couple weeks."

Newsome sighed, asked, "Was his name Yvgeny, by chance?"

"Something like that. You two working together?"

"You kidding me?"

Newsome gave the man his business card.

"Have the rabbi call me when he gets in, OK?"

They left the temple, and the plumber quickly bolted the door behind them.

Bubba stepped over to a large concrete urn on the sidewalk and spit tobacco juice into the bushes growing inside. An old woman walking by pursed her lips and shook her head, then sped up her pace when Bubba glared at her.

"What the hell is Geny thinking?"

"Beats me. Maybe he thinks it's a race."

"He's supposed to bury 'em. That's it. What's his angle, you reckon?"

Bubba sniffed, looked at his shoes.

"Maybe he figures we ain't getting anywhere."

"So now he thinks he's a detective? I'm starting to wonder about this guy. I'll tell you this much, he ain't doing himself any favors."

"Whatcha mean? You think he did it?"

They walked toward the car, but halfway through the parking lot Newsome stopped, stared off into the distance. Bubba watched him a moment, then said, "What?"

"We're gonna go pay the undertaker a visit."

"When?"

"Right now!"

Newsome resumed walking, and Bubba shrugged his shoulders and followed.

⚓

Yvgeny heard a car and looked outside, seeing Newsome pulling in behind the wheel of the same brown Ford Taurus.

Perfect timing, Yvgeny thought to himself. Then he

saw someone in the passenger seat.

Oh goody, he brought a friend!

The driver's and passenger's doors opened in unison and Yvgeny focused on the passenger side. The man was at least a head taller than Newsome, with a buzzed haircut and a flannel shirt. Around his neck was the sheriff's star on a chain.

As Yvgeny watched, this new cop pulled a tin of Copenhagen from his back pocket, then slid a pinch behind his bottom lip. He stood a moment, his tongue exploring the dip, then he spit onto the pavement. Yvgeny's pavement. He opened the door and stood waiting for them with his hands on his hips.

"Afternoon, Geny," said Newsome as he approached.

"Good afternoon, inspector."

Bubba raised one eyebrow when Yvgeny returned the greeting, but said nothing.

"This here's my partner, Bubba Johnson."

Yvgeny looked the man up and down, hands still on his hips, and muttered, "Tobacco juice stains concrete."

Bubba glanced over at Newsome but remained silent.

"I hear you were poking around that Jewish temple today, looking for the rabbi."

"Yes, I was. Is that a crime, inspector?"

"No, ain't no crime that I know of. But why are you visiting rabbis? You trying to do my job for me?"

Yvgeny smiled.

"No, just curious about the body. I've never buried a Jew. I wanted to know their customs."

Newsome stared at Yvgeny, and when Yvgeny didn't flinch or fidget, Newsome relaxed somewhat.

"Professional curiosity, huh?"

"Something like that, yes."

"Did you satisfy that curiosity?"

"Yes, I did."

"You plan on visiting any more rabbis?"

"No."

"You find anything else, Geny? Or hear anything more about that body?"

Yvgeny paused.

"Should I go get me that search warrant?"

Yvgeny shook his head and said, "No, inspector, I have told you everything I know."

Yvgeny and Newsome stared at each other while Bubba turned from one to the other as if it was a tennis match.

"Guess I'll be seeing you, Geny."

"Goodbye, inspector."

Newsome took a few steps, then stopped and turned.

"Oh, almost forgot. Don't suppose you found a watch out there, maybe near that body?"

Yvgeny felt his face flush, and hoped the inspector was too far away to notice. He feigned surprise.

"A watch? Did you lose yours? I can have Alfred poke around if you like."

Newsome cocked his head, then nodded and said, "sure, couldn't hurt. See you later."

Before turning away, Bubba spit one more time onto the pavement, aiming for dead center. When he got back to the car and stood waiting for Newsome to unlock the doors, Bubba muttered, "inspector?"

╬

CHAPTER NINE

Isaac and Albert Cohen met Jake at his grandfather's house. The three acknowledged each other quietly, then took off for the tree line. Rabbi Shachter watched them leave through the slider and go toward the woods.

The rabbi's house sat on two acres of scrub that bled into almost one hundred acres of forest, all his. Beyond that, more forest. It was the *de facto* playground for the teenagers, who mostly trudged back to find rabbit tobacco to smoke or chew depending on the season, and to drink when they were lucky enough to score some alcohol.

A few months earlier, when the area was thick with summer greenery, the three had walked until the trees began to thin. Soon after, they came upon a clearing, and about fifty yards past the tree line, a house.

Dilapidated, forlorn, the house stood at the end of a long gravel drive that connected to State Route 81. It couldn't be seen from Route 81 or any other street, or any other neighbor, for that matter. Unless you were given specific directions, you'd never know it was there.

It wasn't a stick built house, either, but a single wide, its wheels camouflaged behind corrugated aluminum trim pieces to give the illusion of a proper foundation.

That first time, the boys were surprised when they found it. The second time they walked that far, they heard the sound of someone chopping wood, and approached until they could see a man holding an axe in one hand, settling a piece of wood on a tree stump, then watched as he lifted, then slammed the axe down, splitting the wood in two, then repeating the move, over and over. They remained for a while, transfixed, then moved on. The man was facing away and never noticed them.

The third time they wandered as far back as the trailer, the man was nowhere to be found. They slowly crept out into the curtilage, toward the tree stump where they had seen the man chopping wood. The axe was sticking up on the stump, having apparently been swung hard into the wood, the handle sticking out like a lever.

They almost made it to the stump when they heard the sound of an engine approaching. They back pedaled, hitting the trees just as a rusty yellow Ford Bronco came around the side of the trailer and slid to a halt in the dirt and gravel. The driver's door creaked open and the man they had seen before emerged.

This time they could see his face, but like most teenagers, they saw the man as one of indeterminate age, anywhere from forty to eighty. He was holding a grocery bag, and walked inside the trailer, leaving the driver's door open. He shuffled back and forth, bringing bags inside, and on the last trip he slammed the door shut.

They turned back and began to head in the direction of Rabbi Shachter's house, but diverted to follow a narrow path that curled around and followed the street a ways.

Less than a quarter mile from the rabbi's house was a small body of water, too big to call a pond, too small to call a lake.

During the summer, the teens swam in it and couldn't find the bottom. They approached the water's edge and Isaac found a stone and tossed it in. The three stared into the water for a while, silent. Each started tossing stones into the water, the ripples subsiding almost immediately. Finally the eldest called out to the others, "Let's go."

⸸

BK. 1936. Germany. They were clues, Yvgeny supposed, but most likely dead ends. Newsome had the body, but there wasn't a lot he could do without the hands or the head.

Yvgeny estimated they were about equal in the evidence, neither having enough to solve the case. Yvgeny thumbed through the phone book looking for people with the initials BK and quickly realized it was pointless. Yvgeny tossed the phone book down on the desk, sighed.

Yvgeny's phone rang, loud and startling in the silence. Yvgeny answered, and heard a man clear his throat before speaking.

"Is this Yvgeny Jedynak?"

The accent was familiar to Yvgeny's ears, filled with the old world, like the Polish his parents spoke when he was a child.

"Yes. Who is this?"

"This is Rabbi Shalom Shachter. You left your business card at my *shul*."

"*Shul?*"

"Yes. My temple. My synagogue."

"Ah, yes."

There was a moment of silence, then the rabbi cleared his throat again. Yvgeny had to pay close attention because of the man's accent.

"You almost gave my plumber a heart attack."

Without a pause, Yvgeny responded, "If it happens again, I can take care of him for a discount."

The rabbi, unsure whether it was a joke, asked, "So what can I do for you? What does an undertaker need from an old rabbi?"

"A man was murdered, then dumped in an open grave at my mortuary. I believe he's Jewish. Well, was. The police are trying to identify him."

"Ah yes, that. And there is no name?"

"No name."

"Why do you believe he was Jewish?"

Yvgeny paused. He glanced down at the Laco on his wrist.

"Well, he was circumcised."

"I see. How old was this man?"

"He was old. Probably in his eighties."

"Yes, yes. You know, at his age, he probably had a 50/50 chance of being circumcised. At least in the United States. Any other reason why you think he was a Jew?"

Yvgeny considered the question. Took a breath to answer, then stopped. He chose his words carefully.

"Rabbi, I think we should meet in person."

"What is there to meet about? The police have already been here asking the same questions. There are no old men missing from my congregation. In fact, I am the oldest of them all. I do not know of any missing Jews here. Have you discussed your concerns with the police?"

"I am the one who called them. I have additional information I would like to share with you, but only in person. Not on the telephone."

This time the pause was on the other end of the conversation.

"I am not sure what you could share with me but not the police. Jews don't have confessionals, if that is what you are seeking."

"Hardly. I am no Christian."

"Well, if it's curiosity, I can tell you we have our own burial customs, very different from yours- I mean Christians, but as I said, I have no idea whether the man was a Jew. I-"

Yvgeny cleared his throat and interrupted the rabbi.

"Listen, rabbi. The thing is, I don't trust the police and would prefer to share information with you, not them. I don't think they believed me when I told them he was a Jew."

"Well, Mr. Jedynak, I don't see how I can help by meeting with you. The police-"

"Will never solve this case on their own," Yvgeny finished for him. "That is why I'm calling. I need your help."

"Mr. Jedynak, I am not convinced this man was a Jew. Please, let the police do their job. Good day."

The rabbi replaced the handset on the cradle and stood a moment, still clenching it, knuckles white. Finally, he released his grip and walked back to his office.

He wiped the sweat off his brow, then rooted around his desk until he found Newsome's business card. He dropped heavily into his chair and stared at the card. Then, with a sigh, he turned to gaze out the window, looking at the trees; unlike his childhood home of New England, these were pine forests, and the woods remained green year round.

The rabbi wanted nothing to do with that *meshuggeneh* undertaker, or the detective, for that matter, but he knew how persistent investigators could be, and putting him off would only increase their suspicion. The sooner he made the call, the sooner they could put it all behind them.

The telephone rang several times, then there was a click as the call was routed to the dispatch center.

"Gilbert County 911, what is your emergency?"

"Um, well, there's no emergency, I was calling for Detective Newsome."

"Who's calling?"

"Shalom Shachter. Rabbi Shalom Shachter."

"Stand by."

The dispatcher keyed up her microphone and radioed Newsome in his car.

"Some guy is calling for you, he has a thick accent, says he's a rabbi."

Newsome smacked his steering wheel and turned to Bubba, who was spitting into an old Gatorade bottle, said "hold on," then spun the steering wheel and slid the car 180 degrees and headed toward the highway. He asked the dispatcher to patch the rabbi through.

"Rabbi, this is Detective Newsome. Harry Newsome.

How are you?"

"I am doing as well as an old man can do, given the circumstances. What can I do for you, detective?"

Newsome got straight to the point.

"Rabbi, I was wondering if you would mind coming out to the GBI's morgue up in Macon. I'd like you to take a look at this body, maybe tell us, well, tell us what you think."

There was silence, then a crackle, and the rabbi's voice returned.

"Detective, I'm not sure I will be of any help to you. There is no-one missing from my congregation."

"I understand, rabbi, but maybe you will see something else relevant to our investigation, maybe something we wouldn't have noticed."

There was another pause.

"Detective, I am no longer a young man. I want to do my part, but driving is a great burden for me. Surely there are other Jews to whom you can direct your questions?"

Bubba rolled his eyes.

"Rabbi, as I'm sure you already know, there aren't a whole lot of Jews in these parts."

The old man sighed and in a defeated voice, asked for the address.

╬

The old rabbi drove slowly. As he headed north on Interstate 75 in his twenty-year old burgundy Toyota, he craned his head toward the windshield to get a better view of the road. He was oblivious to the brown Taurus that passed by him at a much higher rate of speed.

It took the rabbi a while to find the dilapidated government building. Newsome and Bubba posted outside the glass main doors, and took turns looking at their watches and watching the cars pass by until finally, an old Corolla puttered up the street, other drivers jamming on their horns and passing around him. As the rabbi turned into the lot, the anxious Macon driver behind him rolled down his window and launched a barrage of curses at him.

The rabbi had a brief exchange with the guard, who checked a clipboard, then raised the barrier so he could pass.

As Harry and Bubba started walking toward the car, a small, elderly man emerged wearing a black suit and sporting a close cut gray beard. He had a black hat in one hand that he placed on his head as they approached.

"Rabbi Shachter, I presume?"

The old man squinted up at Newsome through a pair of round glasses with numerous smudges across the lenses. Newsome reached into his pocket and displayed his identification. The rabbi inspected the badge and the identification card, glanced at Bubba, offered a pained smile.

"Detective Newsome, good to see you."

The rabbi had a thick northern accent mixed with something else; to Newsome it was similar to Yvgeny's inflection.

Newsome smiled and nodded.

"Thanks for meeting us up here. And I'm sorry for all the trouble."

The rabbi waved his hand as if smacking a pesky insect, and said, "Bah! It is nothing."

"Well, we really appreciate it."

There was a slightly awkward pause, then they walked together toward the entrance. The rabbi removed his hat and held it in both hands as Newsome opened the double doors leading into the building. He stopped, then turned to the rabbi and said, "Before we go any further, I just want to make sure you're prepared. You may find it, well-"

"I am aware the man is dead."

Newsome turned to Bubba, who nodded, then turned and spit more tobacco juice into his Gatorade bottle.

"Well, I guess follow me."

And for the second time that day, Newsome walked through the building and toward the morgue. There was an elevator in the lobby, along with two flights of stairs leading down into the basement. Newsome paused, then turned to the rabbi.

"Rabbi, you are welcome to use the elevator, but I had a bad experience with it and would prefer to take the stairs."

The rabbi narrowed his eyes and asked, "What kind of bad experience?"

The rabbi didn't notice Bubba's smirk, which Newsome erased with a withering glance.

"A few months ago the elevator got stuck. Took someone two hours to get me out."

The rabbi nodded slowly, studied the elevator one

last time, then shrugged.

"Guess I could use the exercise anyway."

The stairwell was built from cinder block bearing layers of industrial paint somewhere between white and tan, resulting in a uniformly dingy appearance. Newsome led the way, worried the old man might lose his balance.

Several of the rusty bolts securing the banister to the cinder block wall had come loose, and when the rabbi first grabbed it, the metal clanked and rattled freely. The rabbi froze, then tugged on the banister one more time, inspected the hanging bolts, then shrugged and began gingerly taking the stairs.

They reached the bottom and walked past a small windowless break room where they found Kincaid slumped in a chair, his chin against his chest, arms dangling at his sides. On the table was an empty coffee cup beside a wrapper from a vending machine honey bun with a fifty year shelf life.

Bubba said, "Is he still alive?" and approached Kincaid, then crouched down to make sure he was still breathing. As if in response, the doctor snorted in his sleep, smacked his lips, and was quiet again. Bubba stood and shook his head, then walked behind the sleeping doctor to spit tobacco juice into the sink, then nonchalantly picked up one of the plastic chairs and smacked it against the linoleum.

The loud bang woke the old doctor with a snort, his head snapping back. He fixed his eyes on Newsome, not yet realizing anyone else was in the room.

"Jesus Christ, Newsome, what the hell's the matter with you?"

It took Kincaid a few moments to collect himself, and finally he stood up, his knees cracking loudly from the effort. The chore of moving to a standing position was at least a thirty second ordeal, requiring him to lean against the table, slowly lift off the chair, then push backwards with his rear end to slide it across the floor, the plastic legs chattering on the linoleum. His efforts and his tall, gangly frame made him look like a huge, ancient praying mantis rearing up to catch a meal.

"Twice in one day. Lucky me."

As Bubba came around the table, Kincaid glanced at him, then noticed the old rabbi, and groaned.

"Lucky me. You've brought friends."

Newsome just smiled, causing the old doctor to groan again. Kincaid looked at Bubba but continued talking to Newsome.

"Well this one looks like another one of Gilbert County's finest, but your other friend there looks like he belongs in one of my chillers. What is it, bring your pe-paw to work day?"

Kincaid glared at the old man, then after a moment recognition set in.

"No offense, father."

The old rabbi grimaced but did not speak.

"He's a rabbi, Kincaid. And this is business. We want to see if Rabbi Shachter can tell us if our John Doe was a Jew."

Kincaid's eyes flashed over to the rabbi, then back to Newsome.

"Christ, Newsome, rabbis don't autograph their work, how the hell is he going to tell you that?"

Newsome shrugged his shoulders. The rabbi remained quiet but stiffened at Kincaid's tirade. Kincaid pursed his lips.

The doctor sighed, then started picking at an ear, and said, "Well, father, I guess you came this far, might as well take a look."

Kincaid shuffled out of the break room, followed by the deputies and the rabbi. They walked down the hall, turned a corner, and passed through the double doors leading into the lab. Kincaid stood before a wall of cold storage units, looking up at the yellowed ceiling tiles, muttering to himself and seemingly counting with his fingers. After a moment or two, he nodded and shuffled over to one of the drawers and tugged it open. The body of a black man laid upon it. He shook his head and tried another drawer, found the same thing.

"Dammit. Rosy!"

There was a bustle from down the hall, then Rosy arrived. Rosy was a big woman with curly red hair and a long face that always had the hint of a smile, like a modern red haired Mona Lisa.

"Whatcha need, Rufus?"

"The John Doe. White guy. No head. Where is he?"

"Locker number 4, where you left him."

Kincaid shook his head, grumbled a thank you, and reached for locker number 4.

"Only white guy in the morgue, you'd think I'd remember where I put him."

Kincaid pulled out the tray, and they all looked down at the lump beneath the sheet. The doctor pulled the sheet back quickly with a theatrical snap, revealing the body of a headless old man, and announced, "Voila! Behold the headless dead guy."

The rabbi took a step backward and almost lost his balance until Bubba reached out to brace him.

"Where's his head?"

"Ain't got one, father," said Kincaid. "At least not

anymore."

"What was he wearing?"

Newsome said, "a gray sweater, pants."

The rabbi muttered something in a foreign tongue under his breath.

"Are you OK, rabbi?" Newsome asked.

The rabbi leaned in closer. He crouched over the body, inspected it for a moment, then stood straight again, a grave expression on his face.

"I'm sorry, detective, I wish I could be of help."

Newsome deflated, and the rabbi began plodding toward the door.

"Rabbi, wait, is there anything you can tell us?"

The rabbi took a deep breath, and tried to smile.

"He's dead, detective. That much is certain. And he was circumcised. And it was a terrible job. But whether he was a Jew, only God knows for sure."

Bubba spit into his Gatorade bottle, sniffed loudly, then turned toward Kincaid and said, "Hey, doc, is Gino's still around?"

"The one on Orange? Of course, been there since '75."

"Hey Harry, might as well hit it on the way back, get the rabbi a slice for his troubles."

Bubba turned to the rabbi and added, "Best pepperoni pizza in town!"

"Sorry, detective, pepperoni is not kosher."

Bubba's face clouded, then he smiled.

"They make a mean sausage calzone, too."

"Most likely not kosher."

Bubba's smile faded, and Newsome narrowed his eyes.

"What do you mean?"

"Most sausage is made from pork. Jews don't eat pork, or the meat of any other cloven hoofed animal. It violates the laws of *kashrut*."

Newsome ignored Bubba and turned toward Kincaid and asked, "Didn't you say my vic had sausage?"

"Yeah, but I just sent it off for testing."

"Will they be able to tell us what kind of meat?"

"Don't see why not. But I will call up to Atlanta and make sure."

"See rabbi, I knew you would be a big help!"

⚏

Rabbi Shachter returned to his home, sweat beaded on his brow. His grandson was playing a video game with his two friends, Isaac and Albert. None looked up at him, for which the old rabbi was thankful. He passed them en route to his bedroom, shut the door quietly, then stood before his dresser, staring at himself in the mirror. What would his dear wife have said, God rest her soul? What words of comfort would she have for him, in such dark times?

Thought fragments danced through his aged and addled mind.

If I said he was a Jew, I would have to sit Shiva. That would be sacrilege. But I could not say he wasn't a Jew, either. What a dreadful situation.

He plodded toward his bed, fell heavily upon it, looking down at the carpet.

And who cut off the man's head?

Outside his bedroom, Isaac and Albert looked at Jake. On the screen their video game characters stood still, weapons in hand.

╬

CHAPTER TEN

"Come on, Harry, what do we have to go back there for?"

Bubba chewed his nails as he focused on the wavy fog line on the pavement outside.

"Gimme a break, Bubba. Just wait in the car if it's such a big deal."

"It's not a big deal. I just don't see the point in going back there."

"You heard the rabbi. Jews don't eat sausage. This guy ate sausage before he was killed. So the guy ain't a Jew. Right?"

"Maybe it was chicken sausage."

Newsome grunted, and said, "You're missing the point."

"What do you mean?"

"Think, Bubba! Geny thinks the guy was a Jew. If we convince him it's impossible, he will drop it and go back to doing whatever he does when he's not pissing me off."

Bubba responded with an unintelligible grumble.

"Look, I want this guy a million miles away from this case, and so do you. You want to keep running into him every step of the way or do you want to nip this in the bud now?"

When they arrived, the black Cadillac was gone.

Newsome parked in the street to wait, and Bubba's fidgeting increased in intensity as the minutes ticked away.

They only waited around ten minutes before the Cadillac arrived. It overshot the driveway, then began backing in. Yvgeny slammed the hearse into park and hopped out, glanced at Newsome and Bubba, then opened the rear door and bent into it. He briefly remained out of view to the two deputies, then came up holding something wrapped in a rough blanket. He shut the door with an elbow and carried his package to the stoop.

"What the hell?" intoned Bubba.

They both rushed out of the car and jogged across the street, catching Yvgeny just outside the entrance to the mortuary. Bubba approached the package cautiously and asked, "Whatcha got there, Geny?"

Yvgeny fixed him with a strange look, almost a smile, but not quite, and he turned and crouched, slowly peeling back the folds of the blanket, revealing a freshly killed opossum, its teeth and jaw crushed, a mess of flesh, gore, and insects. Bubba turned green and took a step backwards. Newsome just shook his head.

"Poor creature was run over and left on Highway 74 to rot. That's no way to treat the dead. I'm going to clean him up and give him a proper burial. An innocent soul."

He stood, leaving the blanket open, gleefully watching Bubba try to control his urge to retch.

Newsome had his hands on his hips, still shaking his head disapprovingly at both Bubba and the undertaker.

"Are you kidding me? It's road kill."

Yvgeny continued smiling at Bubba, but it became more of a display of bared teeth as he said, "Semantics, inspector, we're all just corpses looking for coffins, aren't we?"

Yvgeny tore his gaze away from Bubba, and he and Newsome stared at each other a moment before Newsome finally broke the silence.

"Look, Geny, you can call off your amateur detective show, the guy ain't no Jew."

What was left of Yvgeny's smile faded from his face.

"And what led you to this conclusion?"

"Trust me. He ain't no Jew. We just left the GBI."

Newsome had intended to tell Yvgeny about the man's stomach contents, but at the last moment had a change of heart.

"So you came all the way over here just to give me this update? I'm flattered."

When Newsome didn't respond, Yvgeny clapped his hands together and said, "Very interesting. Thank you for sharing. And good luck with your investigation."

Newsome glanced over at Bubba, who shrugged.

"Didn't do it for my health, Geny, I'm trying to tell you politely you can back off and let us handle this. We can take it from here."

"Of course, inspector, I have every confidence in you and your colleagues, I'm sure you are on the verge of breaking it wide open. Good day."

He turned his back on the detectives, knelt, waved away the flies, then began collecting his road kill.

╬

Yvgeny carried his package inside and placed it on the gurney that previously carried the headless body. He took a step back and rubbed his hands together. Then he rolled the gurney toward Maude, who was still on her own table.

Of course, he lied to the detectives. They wouldn't have understood; besides, his love life was none of their business.

As he started arranging his tools, he heard someone coming down the hall toward him. It was a limping, shuffling gait that stopped just inside of his work area. He did not hear the tapping of a cane.

"Not now, Alfred, I have work to do. A labor of love, my dear Alfred, a labor of-"

"Alfred? You call the woman that gave birth to you a gravedigger? You should have him start digging my hole now, Yvgeny, nice an deep, and make you sure he drops me in face down."

Yvgeny rolled his eyes and turned around, trying to block her view of his prize.

"Ah, Mama, you sounded like Alfred."

He looked down at his mother's foot and furrowed his brow. "What happened?"

She looked down at the white immobilization boot on her foot and shook her head.

"Well Captain Ahab," she spat, "while you were out swimming with your whale, I almost fell to my death down those stairs." She poked her finger behind her toward the staircase. "I was barely able to drive myself to that idiot Jimmy Flowers's office."

She craned her neck to one side to look at what was

on the table, but Yvgeny shifted his weight to block her view. She returned her attention to him and crinkled her nose.

"Ugh, what is that smell? Is that Maude? I thought you said you took care of her!"

When he didn't respond, she leaned a hand against the wall to stabilize herself.

"Your father would have been there for me, would have carried me to the car in his arms and taken me to Macon to a real doctor instead of that clown."

She shuffled away, muttering to herself.

Yvgeny watched her leave, then turned back to his prize, smiling. He slid his rolling tool tray closer and was about to pick up his scalpel when he got the urge to check his reflection in the mirror.

He ran his fingers through his hair, then frowned. He checked his watch, then glanced back down at his little furry friend. He equivocated a moment, then made his decision.

First me, then my new friend.

With a quick pat on the opossum's head, he grabbed his keys and walked out. If he timed it just right, it would be almost sweeping time at the barber shop.

╬

Yvgeny's favorite barber had a two chair shop in a small converted house. He rented his second chair to another barber, an overweight, middle aged woman that had quit smoking twenty years ago, but held an unlit Marlboro 100 in her mouth when she cut hair. The two barbers argued and bickered constantly; one of their regular topics was whose turn it was to sweep up all the hair. The practical result of this feud was that neither swept until the end of the day, when the debate over whose turn it was would finally end with one barber gloating and the other sweeping.

Yvgeny enjoyed listening to their banter, but, mainly, he went because they were such slobs. He timed his arrival for roughly 4:00, toward the end of the day but before the broom came out. He would step gingerly across the sea of trimmings that built up, curly and straight, brown and blonde, gray and artificially colored. It didn't matter to Yvgeny.

Yvgeny was mesmerized by the floor like a leprechaun standing before the open doors of Fort Knox. After climbing into the barber's chair, he fantasized about stuffing all that cushiony keratin into huge bags and bringing it home to satisfy his dream of having a bed stuffed completely with human hair.

Ah, the delight! The comfort!

Unfortunately, he could not concoct a story convincing enough for his barber to believe, so he remained silent: he glumly admired the field of hair lining the shop floor, like a resigned sharecropper harvesting the landowner's crop.

Usually, it was a quasi-religious experience for him, but this time, he found himself staring ahead, oblivious to the carpet of human hair. Ever since the inspectors left, his subconscious had been processing their visit, and he had eventually concluded something stank.

At first, Yvgeny just accepted their message as fact: the GBI conclusively determined the man was not a Jew. Perhaps the GBI actually employed men with some competence. When science spoke, Yvgeny usually listened.

But the more the exchange percolated, the less

convinced Yvgeny became. In fact, Yvgeny began to wonder whether Newsome was just trying to throw him off the scent with a convenient reference to a scientific explanation. *Yes*, Yvgeny thought to himself, *the man had to be a Jew*. He was wearing the watch, and he was cut. *What else could he be?*

The lady trimmed his bangs while he chewed on his ideas. She yammered away, the cigarette bouncing in her mouth, but Yvgeny didn't hear a word.

Those deputies are trying to get rid of me, they must think I'm a fool.

He started fuming quietly as his situation began to solidify.

Or maybe they are afraid I will solve it before they can figure it out themselves.

He chuckled then, which the barber thought was in response to her story, because she took the cigarette out of her mouth and held it as if it was lit, and said loudly, "I know, right?" then launched into the next chapter of her story, goaded on by his chuckle. But Yvgeny heard none of it.

I bet they will pretend the man was a Nazi. Then they can claim whoever killed him did it in self defense. And then they can sit around the precinct eating donuts instead of trying to solve a real crime. How lazy!

Yvgeny seethed.

Could they devise such a plan? Such a bold plan? Ingenious, even! Perhaps I have underestimated them.

Yvgeny went straight home after his trim, and began working on the opossum. Embalming a wild animal was no different from a human, but it was much easier because he did not have to worry about making the creature look exactly as it did in life.

The recipient of this gift would not compare it to

dear old dad, or granny, or whoever, then cover her mouth in abject horror because what was in the coffin was some twisted caricature of the dearly departed.

In this case, it would even be easier, because the animal would become a vessel, a repurposing of one of nature's creatures. In a sense, Yvgeny was giving him a second life.

Yes, my little furry friend, you will become my little messenger, my furry, embalmed Cupid!

After the dirty work, Yvgeny fashioned a skeleton from a collection of wire coat hangers, then began the painstaking task of mounting the opossum into a standing position, his arms out before him in a tight circle, as if hugging something.

Using a special epoxy, he replaced the animal's teeth, favoring aesthetic appeal over accuracy. Tiny, straight, perfect, white teeth, as if the opossum had worn braces.

He finished with several healthy handfuls of polyester fiber stuffing, then took a step back to admire his work.

"Magnificent. And now for the *pièce de résistance!*"

Yvgeny picked up the two marbles he had purchased for the occasion, and plugged them into the sockets. They fit perfectly.

Yvgeny jumped in the air and clicked his heels together, then snatched the animal by the wooden base and headed toward the cemetery to grab some flowers. Before he opened the door, he noticed Alfred wandering among the headstones, head down, as if looking for something. Yvgeny let go of the doorknob and watched.

He frequently found Alfred pacing outside, and depending on Yvgeny's mood, Alfred reminded him alternately of an eccentric professor deep in thought, or a stray dog sniffing for the right spot to do his business.

Alfred could not read or write, and only spoke in grunts and clicks, but on occasion Yvgeny wondered to himself whether it was all an elaborate charade. Some hid from the world by sequestering themselves in a monastery and taking a vow of silence. Perhaps the mortuary was Alfred's version of escape. From what, Yvgeny couldn't imagine.

Yvgeny didn't want Alfred to see him snatching flowers from one of the gravesites, so he killed some time wandering around the display coffins. Each paced, Yvgeny among the coffins, Alfred among the headstones, buried in their own minds.

Yvgeny was still stewing about Newsome and his friend. In order to keep them off his back, the killer would have to be found, and the only way *that* would happen, Yvgeny had convinced himself, would be to find the killer himself.

Newsome wasn't a complete idiot, but if Yvgeny was to wait for the man to hit a stroke of luck and solve the case, he would be waiting a long time. It was unfortunate Newsome had ordered him to leave it alone. He would have to be more careful, more circumspect, moving forward.

He glanced out the window again, seeing Alfred stopped between two headstones, looking up into the sky, turning his head this way and that, as if reading some celestial writing only he could see. His mouth was moving, like he was sounding out a foreign word, and his hands were balled into fists.

He's sharing his secrets with the dead.

Yvgeny's hand reached involuntarily into his pocket and he twisted his little good luck charm, feeling comforted just knowing it was there. It always made him think of his father, made him feel closer.

I miss you, Dad!

He continued watching Alfred, wishing he was more communicative, more *useful*. He would have been a great ally in his search for the cadaver's identity. There was simply no-one else he could trust, or even ask.

Just as he framed that thought, however, the moment the resignation set in, he had an epiphany.

Perhaps I'm not all alone!

He grabbed his opossum and stovepipe hat, then headed toward the main hall to grab his car keys. He walked past stacks of arrangements left by florists in advance of Maude's party. He reached the door, then froze.

He slowly walked backwards, then turned to the arrangements, a smile on his face.

No need to have to deal with Alfred!

He carefully inspected each of the arrangements, and once he made his selection, he donned his hat, gingerly placed his opossum on the floor, and with his free hands grabbed his chosen display. Among the blossoms was a small, sealed envelope addressed to Maude. He snatched it and ripped it open, pulling out a card bearing a message: *We love you Grandma!*

"So precious!" Yvgeny said, then chucked it down the hall. He retrieved his opossum, shoved his floral arrangement under an arm, then headed out the door.

Once he climbed into Cerberus, he laid the bouquet in the passenger side floorboard, then balanced the opossum standing up in the passenger seat, carefully securing it in the seatbelt, whispering, "Sorry, my little furry friend, rules are rules!"

It was not a long drive to Rocko's store, but Yvgeny drove slower than normal, careful to avoid any unnecessary jolts and bumps. At a red light, a woman pushing a stroller began to cross the street. She slowed when she saw the hearse, but once she realized what was sitting in the passenger seat, she burst into motion, shoving the stroller through the crosswalk at a brisk jog.

When Yvgeny walked into Rocko's shop, he found him in exactly the same place as last time, standing behind the counter like an automaton that only activated when the door was opened. When the cow bell attached to the door jangled, he came alive.

"Mr. Geny undertaker man, how's cot?"

"The cot is quite comfortable, thank you. Listen, I have something to tell you."

Yvgeny rested his arms against the top of the glass counter, looked around with a conspiratorial air, then leaned in and whispered, "something important."

Rocko's face remained impassive, waiting.

"Rocko, someone was killed a couple days ago. Well, I don't know when he was killed, but we found him two days ago. An old man."

Yvgeny smacked his lips, then added, deadpan, "possibly a veteran."

Yvgeny stood quietly, and smiled when Rocko leaned in toward him, narrowing his eye.

"War veteran? Killed? Who did it? Who was he?"

Yvgeny shrugged and tried to smother his smile.

"The police don't know. They're trying to investigate, but they're not very good at such things."

Yvgeny dug in his ear, trying to appear nonchalant, and added, "Sometimes a man has to deal with such things himself."

Rocko straightened up again behind the counter and placed his hands on top.

"Rocko knows how to deal with murderers, killers, thieves. Rocko has skills."

I bet you do, thought Yvgeny. He smiled, a sad smile intended to arouse sympathy, and added, with as much theatrics as he could muster, "Oh Rocko, that poor man. He was very old. Possibly a World War Two veteran, maybe Korea. That poor man, murdered after serving his country."

Rocko's hands clenched into fists. He stood even taller, straighter, filled with righteous indignation, and briefly glanced toward the American flag perched in the corner of his store. A vein pulsated over his good eye.

"Rocko mad!"

Rocko lumbered out from behind the counter and approached the wooden Indian by the front door. He reached into a nearby wicker basket and grabbed a machete. He hefted it, then brandished it in the air, causing Yvgeny to take a step back.

Then, in a dizzying display of speed, Rocko swung the machete at the Indian's head, so hard that the head splintered and fell off, fell to the Indian's wooden feet with a loud "klunk!" then rolled across the floor. It smacked into the front door, hard enough to ring the bell that hung from the handle.

Rocko winced at the sound, then dropped his machete wielding arm and in a low voice mumbled, "uh oh."

Rocko glumly dropped the machete into the basket, unaware of the smile on Yvgeny's face. He had his Golem.

"OK Rocko, here's what we need to do."

╬

Next stop, the Golden Pantry!

It was only a fifteen minute drive from Rocko's store. He edged Cerberus around the gas islands first, straining to see past the cigarette advertisements and venetian blinds blocking his view to the register. Her car was not on the premises and he considered returning later, but decided against it; he did not want to make multiple trips and arouse suspicion.

He parked in front of one of the pumps, then emerged and jogged around to the passenger side. It was a busy afternoon, and drivers seeking gas stared as they passed.

Cerberus was always an attention getter, Yvgeny thought with pride.

He hefted the opossum, cradling it in one arm, then reached in for the flowers. He tried arranging them while still holding the opossum, but it was impossible. He placed the animal on the hood of Cerberus, then opened up the animal's four legs, thankful he chose the thicker gauge wire for its limbs.

He placed the bouquet between the animal's legs, then wrapped the legs around the flowers tightly to secure them. Just as he finished adjusting them, he noticed movement from behind him.

Yvgeny turned to see a young, bearded attendant holding a cigarette and staring at him, his mouth wide open, completely frozen, a classic look of horror on his face.

Yvgeny turned back to his opossum and made one more minor adjustment to the arms so the bouquet was canted to one side. That way, Brianna would see the animal's face, which he had fixed in a big grin, its eyes crinkled at the corners with mirth. He took a step back, admired his handiwork, then scooped the package up in his arms and started to head inside. The attendant met him at the door, incredulous.

"You can't bring that in here!"

"It's a gift for Brianna."

Yvgeny looked past the man's shoulder toward the counter behind the register, then added, "You have plenty of room."

"Yeah, well, not for that!"

Yvgeny sized the man up, sneered, then gestured toward the door, where a line of impatient customers was beginning to form.

"The natives are getting restless."

The attendant glanced behind him, indecisive.

"Come on, this guy's heavy. Hold that door open."

The attendant crossed his arms.

"I'll call the cops."

Yvgeny adjusted his grip on his present.

"Ah, of course you will."

Yvgeny looked down at the nametag on the attendant's smock, then smiled.

"Ricky, is it? Ah, Ricky, I've heard all about you. Go ahead and call them. I look forward to it. I'm sure we will have a nice chat. We can talk about the science of embalming, the art of taxidermy."

Yvgeny took a step closer.

"Oh, and we can also chat about that pound of weed you have hidden in the cooler, behind the beer. Conveniently packaged in quarter bags, I might add. How enterprising."

The attendant turned an amusing shade of red, sputtered a moment, then stamped his feet and cursed.

"I'm gonna kill Brianna and her big mouth!"

He turned and yanked the door open and held it there for Yvgeny, adding, "But I ain't touching that thing!"

Yvgeny walked inside, then followed Ricky to the cashier's station and placed the opossum beside the large safe. He smoothed out his fur, arranged the flowers one more time, then nodded his head.

"You know what, Ricky? You've inspired me. I think I will name my little friend Ricky Junior.

"Very funny."

"I'm serious! Now make sure Ricky Junior is not disturbed until Brianna arrives."

"Don't worry, ain't nobody gonna touch that thing."

Yvgeny nodded again, satisfied. On his way out the door he stopped, door half open, and turned to Ricky and added, "I was just thinking, perhaps I will take a bag of that weed for my trouble."

He waited for Ricky to slump forward, defeated, then left the station with a cackle.

⌗

It was close to 4 pm when Newsome's desk line rang. Newsome was away, so Bubba stared at the phone, then snatched it off the cradle and answered, "Sheriff's Department."

"Newsome? That you? Don't sound like you."

"Depends who's asking."

"Ah, you must be the other lunk-head. Listen, the lab called. Got good news and bad news."

"I'm listening."

"Bad news, you got crap on the body."

"Crap? Wasn't any crap on it when we saw it!?"

"Dammit, cowboy, I mean I ain't got crap. Your victim was clean. No matchable DNA, no usable fibers, nothing at all. Got crap."

Bubba cursed under his breath. Newsome walked in and Bubba motioned for him to take the phone. Bubba covered the mouthpiece with his hand and whispered, "Kincaid."

"Thanks, Bubba. Hey Doc, it's Newsome. Got something already?"

"Bubba? Is that his real name? You kidding me?"

"Doc, focus."

"Right," Kincaid said and after a pause, said, "Anyway, I just told your friend there, ain't nothing from the lab on your body, no good DNA."

"Well, that's great Doc. Got any good news?"

"Matter of fact, I do. The lab analyzed the stomach contents. They like to call it leftovers. They've been saying that for twenty years and they still think it's funny. Anyway, they ran that sausage. They still have to type up the report, but it looks like it was pork."

"Pork?"

"Yeah. But not just any kind of pork. It was uncured

pork, packed in natural casings. You ain't getting that stuff at Kroger. That's some real high end butcher type shit. Maybe imported. Whoever your guy was, he sure had fancy taste in meat."

"Thanks Doc, that actually does help."

"I ain't done!" said Kincaid, in that special indignant tone reserved for (and generally only accepted from) the elderly.

Newsome waited.

"I sure enough grew up on a farm but I ain't one of them hayseed Negroes. Matter fact, 'twas my farming days made me think damn, they run DNA on everything else, why not run it on them leftovers!"

"You gotta be kidding me."

"Nope. Ordered it myself. Had 'em conduct a microscopic, morphologic examination on them there contents. Then they ran them some brand new tests, amplified fragment length polymorphism."

The old doctor wheezed into the phone a moment, then in a haughty tone muttered, "Wouldn't 'spect you to have any idea what that means."

When Newsome didn't respond, Kincaid continued.

"Unfortunately, it didn't tell us anything. Just said he ate some heirloom tomatoes. And some damn sausage."

"Well, again, Doc, that's great, thanks a lot for sharing, Wonder how much those fancy tests are going to cost the county."

"Boy, you gotta editorialize everything I say, don't you? Now shut up and listen, you might learn something. That DNA test didn't tell us shit, but remember I said they conducted a microscopic examination? Well, turns out whoever made those fancy sausages autographed them."

"You're kidding me."

"Do I sound like I'm kidding? MJ."

"What?"

"MJ. That's what the casing had marked on it. Written in ink, but somehow they figured it out. How 'bout *them* apples, son?"

Kincaid let out a self-satisfied snort, then hung up while grumbling something unintelligible.

While Newsome spoke with Kincaid on the phone, he had been staring out the window watching an old Ford Bronco back into a spot in the dusty strip mall across the street from the precinct. Plumes of bluish smoke belched out from the rear of the truck as it idled. The truck was battered from years of abuse and its once white paint job was reduced to a vague, flat swirl of grays and off-whites speckled with Georgia clay. It blended perfectly with the vehicles parked nearby, and Newsome eventually turned away, barely noticing it.

Behind the wheel, a large man studied the station with his one good eye. He wore a long, blonde wig and dark sunglasses, per Yvgeny's explicit instructions. Rocko shut off his engine, then texted Yvgeny. Strangely, Rocko texted in first person.

I'm here.

Yvgeny had just returned home from the Golden Pantry, and received the text as he emerged from Cerberus. He looked up from his phone, smiling, and watched Alfred, still engaged in his commune with the heavens, wandering among the aisles of the dead like some morbid usher in a macabre theater. Occasionally he stopped and looked down around him, as if looking for something.

⨼⊤

CHAPTER ELEVEN

"MJ? Guess we start with the phone book?"

Bubba spit into his Gatorade bottle, then leaned back in his chair. Newsome stood, leaned against Bubba's desk.

"Come on, we got bigger fish to fry. Let's get Maggie on it. She needs something to do besides screw with her iPhone and play tiddlywinks with the undertaker."

"Undertaker?"

"Never mind," said Newsome, and picked up the phone.

"Hey Maggie, listen, can you get on the net, see if you can find a butcher, or deli, or someplace called MJ, or with the initials M and J? I'd start around here, then maybe work your way up toward Atlanta. Can you see what you can find?"

"Why? You starting a catering business? I ain't handling your personal-"

"Maggie, it's work. It's for that murder caper. Now can you just handle it?"

Maggie hung up with a scoff. Newsome turned to find Bubba grinning at him wide enough to show the top of the dip beneath his lower lip.

"I don't want to hear it, Bubba."

"She's still sweet on you, hoss. Can't you just give her a little bit of that Harry Newsome charm?"

Newsome gave him the most baleful glare he was capable of, but it didn't diminish Bubba's smile at all. Bubba finally smacked the desk and screwed the cap back on his Gatorade bottle with a chuckle. They stared at each other a moment longer, then Bubba said, "So...."

"So what?"

"So, what are we going to do if we find this MJ? What exactly are we asking? Can't really show him a picture of the guy, being that he ain't got no head and all."

"Yup, you got a point."

"So we just tell 'em we're looking for some old guy in his eighties that might be missing. And might not be a Jew."

"Right."

Bubba reached for his Gatorade bottle again, then pushed off his desk with his feet, leaning back in his chair. He unscrewed the cap and spat into the bottle, then said, "a non-Jew in his eighties, with no hands or head, who liked sausage."

"You got it."

They stared at each other, Bubba rocking back and forth holding his Gatorade bottle, Newsome leaning against the desk.

"Maybe it's someone local."

"Maybe," Bubba said, then let his chair down with a

clunk. He began to get up, muttering, "Let me get the phone book. Maggie might take a while."

"Maybe the killer, I mean."

Bubba stopped and turned back around, said, "How you figure?"

Newsome returned to his seat and leaned back, scratched his cheek, said, "Well, that cemetery is about five miles, maybe six from the highway. Ain't even a gas station off the exit. Just a sleazy hotel and a strip club."

"Yeah," Bubba agreed.

"And Dunlap had money, but ain't nobody heard of him outside Gilbert County."

"OK."

"So, ain't no way some mope from Atlanta kills a guy, drives him all the way down here, then happens to find the cemetery, then happens to find Dunlap's open grave, and dumps him."

"Mm hmm."

"In the middle of the night, too! I'm tellin' you, too unlikely by my reckoning."

Bubba nodded slowly, pursing his lips, then said, "Well, anybody reading the paper'd know Dunlap was going in the ground."

"What paper, the Globe? That circulation ain't further than Macon. And who reads the obits? Nobody but old people and-"

Newsome stared at Bubba, tapping his fingers against the desk. The more he stared, the more uncomfortable Bubba got, until finally he asked, "What?"

Newsome continued tapping a moment longer, then stopped and let out his breath in a whoosh.

"Nah. Doubt it."

"Whatcha talking about?" Bubba asked.

"Well, I was thinking about that damn undertaker. I bet he reads the paper to see who kicked the bucket."

"Yeah, but they're his holes," Bubba retorted, "so he already knows who he's putting in each one. And when."

Newsome paused a moment.

"I know, and he's the one that called it in. So it wouldn't make any sense."

"Nope," Bubba agreed.

"Would've been perfect, Bubba, dump the body beneath a coffin. You'd never find him."

"Yup. Imagine sending a cadaver dog into a cemetery."

They sat in silence a moment before Newsome said, "He's so cocky, you know, what if he called it in just to try to test us?"

They looked at each other a moment, appraising the idea.

"Nah. He ain't that devious."

"And he ain't that smart."

Bubba nodded slowly, and added, "So it ain't some out-of-towner. It's a local. But it ain't the undertaker."

Newsome nodded.

"Well, Harry, that narrows it down to what, 'bout 5,000 give or take, if you include babies and old folks. Guess it's a good start."

Newsome smirked.

Bubba sat forward in his chair.

186

"I been doing some thinking, too. A guy that old, if he had grandkids, maybe a wife, even a drinking buddy somewhere, they'd have called it in by now. Maybe he ain't got no wife, maybe he lives alone. For all we know, he lives over yonder and nobody knows he's missing. Maybe we just gotta wait until some cops like us run out of ideas and put a BOLO out on NCIC. Or the old coot stops paying the water bill, or the rent, or whatever."

Bubba had turned away while he was talking, digging in his cuticles, then glanced back at Newsome to catch him staring at him.

"What?"

"Bubba, you're a damn genius," said Newsome, as he walked out the door.

⚏

"What are they doing now?"

"Can't tell. Police are still in police store."

"Precinct."

"That's what I said. Police store."

Yvgeny sighed.

"Well, stay on them, Rocko. Don't lose them."

"Rocko hungry, but Rocko brought food."

"Good to know, Rocko. Goodbye."

Yvgeny stood and checked his watch. He had a date with Maude Oliver. No sooner did he reach for his rubber apron when his phone rang. It was Rocko's number. Yvgeny had saved Rocko's number in his contacts as *Lurch*.

"Hello Rocko."

"Coppers left police store."

"Where are they going?"

"Tell you when they get there."

Rocko ended the call. Yvgeny put down his phone and started to rub his knuckles.

Rocko followed the unmarked Taurus to the highway, then up Interstate 75 until they entered Crawford County. Rocko tried to stay back a ways, but didn't want to lose them, either.

⚜

"Why are we going to Peach County?"

"You know the list of BOLOs that comes over NCIC each day?"

"Yeah, of course."

"They take them off the teletype and stick 'em in a folder. You ever actually look in it?"

Bubba remained silent a while, then shrugged and said, "sometimes."

Newsome pursed his lips.

"Well, I look in it, and I just checked it again. Peach County just reported a couple old dudes, missing persons."

Bubba considered for a moment, mouth open, then made the connection. He rolled his eyes and said, "Aw, hell, don't tell me we gotta go talk to B-B-B-Barry."

Newsome chuckled but didn't respond.

"Harry, can't they just email us the photos?"

"It's Peach County."

Bubba shook his head, and was about to respond when he noticed Newsome glancing in his rear view mirror once, then again, then a third time.

"We got trouble?"

Newsome glanced again and said, "White Bronco, been on us since we left the office. I think it's that idiot from the army navy surplus store."

Bubba raised his eyebrows.

"The guy that always talks about himself? 'Rocko hungry!' 'Rocko want five dollars for axe.' That guy?"

Newsome nodded.

"What the hell is he following us around for?"

"Guess we will find out soon enough. And he's wearing a wig."

Bubba turned to look at Newsome, speechless.

As they drove, Bubba started to fidget with increasing intensity, and finally Newsome glanced over at him and said, "Something on your mind, chief?"

"You know, it might be the guy was injured in some battle, maybe he's some kind of war hero."

Newsome snorted.

"Rocko was lucky the Army even took him, Bubba. He was an E2 cook's assistant. Wasn't even the damn cook."

"How do you know all that?"

"He's got his DD214 framed on the wall."

As they arrived at the Peach County Sheriff's Department, Rocko pulled across the street into the county yard, backing in between two bucket trucks. Rocko waited for them to enter the building, then picked up his phone. The detectives pretended not to notice him.

Lieutenant Barry Jameson was waiting for them. Barry and Harry Newsome were academy mates many years before, and they remained friends. Barry was an excellent investigator with an excellent reputation until 1997, when his career came crashing to a halt.

Barry was hit by a drunk driver while he was on a traffic stop. The first responders did not expect him to survive the trip to the hospital.

Not only did Barry survive, he returned to work just a few months later, with only one catch: he acquired a terrible stutter, making it difficult for him to interrogate subjects, and impossible to get promoted.

Despite his limitation, his solve rate was higher than any of the other detectives in Peach County; in addition to having a keen intellect and dogged determination, most suspects underestimated him because of his stutter.

Finally, after several failed promotional cycles, Jameson visited a local attorney, who fired off a well worded letter that indirectly threatened hell fire and damnation in a way only a skilled lawyer can pull off. Two weeks later, he made sergeant. From there it was easy.

"Well, Ha- Ha- Ha- Ha- Harry, been a whi- whi- whi- while."

Newsome shook his hand and patted him on the back.

"Yes it has, Barry, too long. How ya' been?"

"Well, I'm working on my stutter, and if I foc- foc- focus on it, I can ju- ju- ju- just about control it."

"That's great Barry, mind over matter right?"

The small talk continued for a few minutes, then Bubba cleared his throat and riffled through his notepad looking for his place.

"So Barry," Newsome asked, "the guy I called you about, Hiram Flanders, whatcha got on him?"

Barry motioned for them to follow him toward a set of three cubicles. He stopped at the first one, occupied by a female wearing a uniform. Barry asked her to pull up the Flanders report, then he ran his finger down her screen, his lips moving as he read silently. The woman glared at Barry while he leaned over her to read from her monitor, and when he straightened up to report his findings, the woman shook her head, then took a tissue and began wiping her screen.

"Flanders was a re- re- re- re- retired veterinarian, born in 1932, white male, five foot two, 170 p- p- p-pounds. Some kind of tattoo of a compass on his chest. Navy, I'd guess. You want me to get the photo?"

Bubba and Newsome both shook their heads.

"No, this guy didn't have any tattoos. And he wasn't near 170 pounds. Appreciate you looking though."

"Don't mention it."

Barry looked down at Bubba's notepad as he crossed through a line on his paper.

"How many you got left?"

"That was the last one."

Bubba counted several lines with his pen.

"Had one in Crawford County, one in Houston, eight in Bibb."

Barry nodded and said, "Yeah, that's about right. M-Must have been a slow week in M-Macon."

"Knocked all the others out in about an hour."

"Yeah, I reckon they all could e-muh, muh- muh- e-mail you the pictures."

"Yup, sure can," Harry said. "Your county is still in the Stone Age."

They chuckled together, shook hands, and departed.

Rocko watched them leave, and made another telephone call.

"Where to next?" Bubba asked.

Newsome took a breath as if to answer Bubba, but then he froze, staring at the Bronco. Bubba saw him freeze and looked in the same direction, then whispered, "Whatcha see? Is he getting out of the truck?"

"No, I was just thinking, wasn't Rocko the guy that entered that Country and Rock n Roll food festival in Comstock last year?"

"Dunno. Who cares?"

"Well, as I recall, he entered the contest with his own home ground sausage."

"OK. So?"

Newsome continued staring across the street. Bubba watched him a moment, then sat up in his seat.

"Wait a minute, what are you saying? Rocko did it? Because of some sausage?"

Newsome seemed to snap out of his fugue and started the car.

"I don't know, Bubba. Maybe the guy's just an expert on fancy meat."

Newsome reached for his car radio.

"Let's see what Rocko can tell us about MJ. Beats

waiting around for Maggie."

"Come on Harry, don't be so hard on your girlfriend."

"Ha."

Newsome pulled out of the parking lot, with the wheezing old truck zeroing in on them from across the street. He radioed the county's patrol division, and within ten minutes they were back in Gilbert County, and seconds after that they saw blue lights quickly approaching them from behind.

The marked Gilbert County squad car raced up to Rocko's Bronco, bumper locked it, then announced his presence with a short siren burst. Newsome kept his eye on his rearview mirror, watching the Bronco head toward the shoulder with the patrol car following close behind.

With Rocko boxed in between Newsome and the patrol car, the three vehicles coasted off the highway and up the ramp leading to State Route 96. They finally came to a stop a hundred feet down the off-ramp.

"You ain't going to stay parked in front of this guy are you?"

Newsome answered by pulling out onto the street again and making a U turn, passed the Bronco and the squad car, then made another U turn to park behind the squad car, waiting for the patrolmen to make their approach.

The first deputy emerged and slowly put on his tall gray campaign hat, followed by another deputy who left his hat off. *Hope there ain't no video going*, Newsome thought; the sheriff was a stickler for wearing your *full uniform* when dealing with the public.

The first deputy engaged Rocko in conversation while the second deputy stood on the passenger side to keep an eye on him. The first deputy motioned for Rocko to get out of the truck, and when he emerged, he towered over the deputy, strands of fake blonde hair flapping in the breeze. The second deputy jogged around the front of the truck to take a position behind Rocko. Just in case.

It started out amicably, but the cars whizzing by eventually blew off Rocko's wig. Rocko spun around to go after it, but the deputies ordered him to stand still. Furious, Rocko watched as the traffic blew the wig further and further down the street.

Rocko's agitation about the wig continued to grow, which in turn agitated the uniformed deputies. To Newsome's surprise, the situation devolved into a physical altercation. Rocko back pedaled right into the deputy standing behind him, causing him to flail wildly, one arm knocking the deputy in the shoulder. That was the last straw for the deputy facing him, who moved in to lay hands on Rocko. Rocko pushed the deputy away. The fight was on, and Newsome and Bubba jumped out to help the deputies.

As they approached, the deputies got Rocko down to his knees, but he was still struggling, tossing them around like rag dolls. Cars hurtled by just a few feet away; they had to end the fight before someone got killed.

One of the deputies reached for his can of pepper spray and yelled, "OC!" Bubba and Newsome stopped dead in their tracks when they heard him yell because they knew exactly what was about to happen.

The deputy sprayed Rocko in the face, a good three second burst, more than enough to shut down the fight. The other deputy turned away just in time, taking only some mist on the back of his neck. The strong breeze generated from the constant flow of traffic blew the rest of the spray away from them.

Rocko stopped struggling and clawed at his face.

"Eye, Eye! It burns!"

He was quickly subdued and handcuffed, screaming all the while about his eye. One of the uniform deputies searched Rocko carefully, then dragged him up to walk him toward the patrol car.

Afterwards, all four deputies stood around the passenger compartment of the white Bronco, hands in pockets, while Rocko wailed from the back seat of the squad car. Bubba occasionally turned to spit into the street.

"What was that about?" Newsome asked the deputy.

"Said he didn't have no license."

"On him?"

"Ever. Says he kept failing the test. I've actually seen him driving around town before. Didn't know he ain't never had no license. His ass is going to jail."

Newsome nodded, then motioned toward the truck, asked, "You gonna search it?"

The deputy was fiddling with his canister of OC spray but nodded back at Newsome.

"Damn right. Search incident to arrest. Look at all that crap in the back. If I don't do an inventory of it all, you know he's gonna say we stole something." Turning to his partner, he said, "hey, can you call the wrecker?"

Newsome nodded again, then took a step up to the door and peeked inside.

"You mind if I take a look at that phone there on the seat?"

"Go for it," said the deputy.

Newsome reached in and took the phone. It was an iPhone and it was locked. He glanced toward Rocko, now reduced to moaning and writhing in agony in the back of the patrol car, then turned back to the phone. He typed in all ones. Nothing happened. Then he tried 1234. It unlocked. Bubba rolled his eyes.

Newsome first checked the call history. There were numerous local calls to the same number throughout the day. The number looked familiar. Newsome took out his own cell phone and accessed the Internet, typed the number into a Google search, then chuckled at the results. He handed the phone over to the uniform deputy and thanked him.

"You taking him down to Central?"

The deputy looked over at his partner, then at Rocko still apoplectic in the back of his squad car, then let out his breath in a loud whoosh.

"Hell no. Sheriff sees I sprayed another guy, he's gonna have me working midnights in the jail."

"Stop by a gas station. There's a Shell one exit down."

"Forget it. Tried it last time. Someone saw me hosing the last perp down and ratted me out to the sheriff. I ain't taking any chances. His ass is going to Crawford County. Hose him down in private where ain't nobody gonna see."

"Crawford County? You kidding me? That's ten miles away!"

"I don't care. It's a straight shot down 96, be there in seven minutes."

Newsome sighed.

"OK, we will meet you over there."

"Stay off the radio!"

Newsome and Bubba returned to their car and once

they got inside and out of earshot of Rocko, Newsome said, "He's been talking to Geny all day."

⏚

Eight minutes later they arrived at the Crawford County Sheriff's Office. The deputy minding the electric fence recognized the uniform deputies and let them in with a nod; they let Bubba and Newsome in after checking their identification. They caravanned to the sally port and parked beside a coiled up hose connected to a spigot.

Rocko, still groaning and struggling in the cuffs, got out of the car with no coaxing, and when the uniform deputy started to hose Rocko in the face, his howls of pain immediately changed to groans of satisfaction.

As they stood around watching the deputy spray Rocko, a Crawford County patrol car passed by and parked at the gas pump about twenty yards away. The door opened, and Newsome and Bubba heard barking coming from inside. Bubba looked up, stared a moment, then looked down and muttered, "shit, shit, shit, don't look, just keep looking down, don't move, don't look over there."

Newsome made a face at Bubba and asked, "What the hell are you talking about?"

"It's TNT."

Newsome froze, then looked down just like Bubba. Bubba started holding his breath. The uniform deputy squirting Rocko glanced over at the overweight deputy pumping gas, then back at Newsome and Bubba. He started to smile.

"Hey, want me to bring him over? Hang on!"

The deputy took a deep breath as if about to yell. Newsome glared at him, then held out his phone and in an ice cold voice threatened, "How 'bout I video tape you with this genius here, and take it over to your sheriff?"

The smile melted off the deputy's face. Newsome glanced back over at TNT, then darted his head away when TNT turned to replace the nozzle. TNT turned back to the four deputies once, then again, and Bubba, still staring down at his feet, started chanting, "don't come over, don't come over."

The deputy turned off the hose and got Rocko up and back into the car, still handcuffed. Newsome and Bubba rushed to get back into their car before TNT approached, and breathed a sigh of relief when the uniforms finally headed toward the exit.

An hour later, they were back at the Gilbert County jail with Rocko safely ensconced in a small cell, morose but no longer howling in pain.

When Newsome walked into his cell, Rocko was staring at the floor clenching his fists. Bubba leaned against the wall, Gatorade bottle in hand.

"Hi, Rocko. You remember me?"

"Police man from police store."

"Precinct. Yes. Why were you following us?"

Rocko continued looking down, fascinated by his feet.

"Free country. Rocko drive where Rocko want."

"Yes, but you were following us. Now why would you want to do that?"

With a shrug, Rocko said, "Rocko has reasons."

"What's with the wig and the dark glasses?"

"Rocko reinventing himself. Experimenting with new look."

"The undertaker told you to follow us, didn't he?"

Rocko paused, looked up at Newsome out of the corner of his eye.

"Rocko don't know no undertaker. But if Rocko did, maybe Rocko was told policemen too stupid to catch killer." Rocko turned away from Newsome and muttered, "Veterans deserve better."

Newsome and Bubba glanced at each other; Bubba shrugged his shoulders.

"Veterans? What are you talking about?"

"Veteran murdered. Buried in wrong hole. Police never caught killer and even if police did, he just go to jail for few days. Rocko make sure justice served."

"Ah, so Geny doesn't think we are capable of catching the killer and even if we did, sending him to prison isn't good enough? Is that right?"

"Rocko doesn't know no undertaker man. Rocko innocent."

Bubba walked over and sat on the cot opposite Rocko.

"Hey Rocko, had your sausage at the food festival last summer. That sure was good stuff."

Rocko looked over at Bubba, and for just a moment, the corners of Rocko's lips curled up in a hint of a smile.

"Rocko made himself. Used grinder. Man hock grinder to me, now my grinder."

"Yup, sure was some good sausage. Listen, if I wanted to get some good pork sausage, I mean the good stuff, with the real casings and all, uncured all natural top shelf stuff, where should I go?"

Rocko sat up straight on his cot, puffed himself up a

bit and said, "No, Rocko can make. Rocko kill pig himself, grind him up with hands!"

As emphasis, Rocko held up his hands.

"Thanks, Rocko. I appreciate that. But where would anyone else go? Let's say I had to have it today. Being as you're kind of busy and all, where could someone get something like that today? Like right now?"

Rocko cocked his head to one side a moment, then closed his eyes. He mumbled to himself a few seconds, then his eyes opened.

"Guess you have to go way out past Fort Valley, out into the woods. Go shoot you a wild hog. But not with that," he said, pointing down to Bubba's empty holster. "That just make him mad. Get real gun. Go shoot one and bring him to me. I grind him up lickety split. Yum, yum."

Rocko rubbed his stomach.

"Sure do appreciate that, Rocko," Bubba said as he stood. "Why don't you let us see if we can get you out of here. How's that sound?"

"Yes, I do nothing wrong. Bad police man pull me over for no reason."

"Right. Other than following us around all day."

Rocko looked back down at his feet.

"Rocko do nothing wrong. Good Rocko."

As they prepared to leave, Bubba's phone rang. It was Maggie. Bubba listened, nodded his head a few times, then said, "Master Jeremy's? What kind of name is that?"

Bubba ended the call and looked over to Newsome and said, "I think we've got ourselves a butcher."

Newsome wrinkled his face and said, "What kind of name is Master Jeremy's?"

Still sitting on the cot looking at his feet, Rocko licked his lips again and said, "yum, yum."

╬

Bubba and Newsome sat in their car in the parking lot of the jail, staring out at the trees.

"Now what? Wanna go check out the butcher?"

Bubba rolled down the window, ran his finger across his gums to spit out his tobacco, then reached for the tin he kept in his back pocket to get another pinch.

"Not sure there's any point. I mean, we ain't got no prints, we ain't got no head, we ain't got nothing. Maybe some DNA, if he's a perp, but-"

Bubba closed his mouth, squinting, meditative. Newsome stared at him a moment.

"I've seen that look before. You got some hare-brained idea."

Bubba smiled, settled the dip behind his lip with his tongue, and chuckled.

"Oh, I've got an idea, and I think it's a good one, but you ain't gonna like it. Hell, I don't even like it."

"I don't like any of your ideas, why would this one be any different?"

"Funny, you already called me a genius once today for one of my great ideas."

"Funny, I don't recall you actually having any ideas today."

After a brief silence, Bubba said, "Well, you wanna hear my idea or not?"

"Shoot."

"TNT."

"What?"

"You know what I'm talking about. TNT."

Newsome stared at Bubba, then his eyes widened.

"Are you kidding me?"

"He's got the only K9 worth a damn in Middle Georgia."

"Didn't you just make us stare down at the ground so he didn't recognize us? Now you want to mix him up in this case?"

Bubba remained silent while Newsome began tapping his fingers against the steering wheel.

"Yeah, well, you can call him. I ain't calling him."

Thomas Nathan Thomas was a K9 handler and deputy sheriff employed by Crawford County, the same deputy that had filled his tank while they hosed down Rocko's good eye.

Because Crawford County was so small, Thomas was also the bomb disposal officer, the evidence supervisor, the training coordinator, and the quartermaster. Each was a part time assignment, but together minimized his interaction with the public; at least that was the sheriff's intention.

Thomas preferred for people to call him TNT, but most of the deputies started calling him Idi Amin after the sheriff saw him with all his patches, stripes, and medals, and grumbled that he looked like "that crazy African dictator."

Thomas filled the free space on his brown uniform like a developer plunking condos in a corn field, and according to the county attorney, there was nothing the sheriff could do about the artistic license TNT took because the department's uniform and appearance policy didn't expressly prohibit it.

The other deputies frequently complained about him, but the sheriff weathered the storm because although Thomas looked ridiculous, he actually was competent and took all his collateral assignments seriously.

The sheriff carefully chose his battles; he would never authorize Flowers to have lights and a siren, but gave Thomas enough freedom to festoon his uniform with flair.

Thomas acquired Nitro last year, after the dog bit his Macon PD handler. The dog was sent to be euthanized by the city's shelter, but Thomas somehow learned about the incident and intervened. The rumor was that he was having an affair with Bibb County's shelter supervisor, a brick warehouse of a woman, and he sweet talked her into forging the paperwork to show the dog was put down.

In fact, the story goes, she snuck the dog out one night and brought him to Thomas's waiting patrol car, parked under cover of darkness in direct violation of Crawford County's rule against driving take-home vehicles out of county.

Thomas laid low for a few weeks with the dog, formerly known as Wesson, until he thought all was forgotten, then, as quartermaster, he requisitioned a set of steel grates to be installed in his cruiser. The next day he introduced everyone to Crawford County's new (and only) K9, Nitro, who looked remarkably similar to another dog some had seen around.

The sheriff was livid and considered firing him, even went so far as to ask the county attorney for advice, but before he could start the paperwork, Thomas and his dog sniffed a drug mule off the interstate and seized eight hundred thousand in a spare tire. Under Georgia's criminal forfeiture statute, the sheriff's department kept 90% of the money. Thus was born the county's first K9 unit.

Some of the other officers, disappointed that TNT weaseled out of his own termination, scoffed that it was the largest bribe payment ever paid in state history. But even those officers kept their mouths shut when the sheriff handed them the keys to their brand new patrol cars, courtesy of TNT and his new dog.

Newsome and Bubba decided to flip a coin to determine who would have to call Thomas. Newsome lost. With a sigh, he scrolled through his contacts to I (for Idi) and pressed send.

"You have him in your phone?"

Newsome shrugged and said, "Well, he's an idiot but that damn dog has the nose of a bloodhound."

"TNT."

Newsome took a deep breath, rolled his eyes, and forced a smile.

"Hey Thomas, it's Newsome out of Gilbert County. How ya' doin?"

"Doing good Harry, been a long time. Hey, was that you I saw earlier over at my jail?"

"No, must be a case of mistaken identity."

"I reckon so. How's my girl Maggie?"

"She's just finer than frog's hair, really doing a good job here in dispatch."

Bubba mouthed, *"Maggie?"* and when Newsome nodded, Bubba made gagging motions, then made a fist, stuck out his thumb and pointed his index finger, and pointed it against his temple and clucked his tongue.

"So listen, I was wondering if you still had that dog of yours."

"Who Nitro? Yessir, still got him. He's right here. You got a car you need searched?"

"No, I got a cemetery."

There was a pause on the line before Thomas responded, a quiver in his voice.

"You shittin' me? A cemetery? You mean with a bunch of dead guys? Graves and shit?"

"Yes Thomas, it's a cemetery. There are dead people buried there."

"Well damn, Newsome, he ain't no cadaver dog. Even if he was, it's a cemetery, he'd just run around in circles barking at everything. Wait a minute. You think there's some drugs buried there?"

"No, Thomas. I think a murder victim was dumped in an open grave, and we don't know who he is. Somebody put him there, so I was thinking your dog could sniff around and see if it gets us any clues."

"Oh, gotcha. Well, he ain't a tracker, but we can give it a shot. But a cemetery? Ain't no zombies right? I saw this movie-"

"No, Thomas, there ain't no zombies." Then he muttered, "Jesus" and continued, "so, can you meet us down at Schmidt and Sons? Down here in Comstock?"

"Ain't that the one with that weirdo? The Russian Johnny Cash?"

Newsome stifled a laugh, said, "Yup, that's the one. Say 4 pm?"

"OK. Hey, you got something he can sniff first? That's how they do it, right? You got some clothing or something?"

"We will swing by the GBI and get something for him."

"10-4. I'll be there. But as soon as the sun starts to set, I'm out. Ain't taking no chances!"

╬

CHAPTER TWELVE

Yvgeny turned on the hydro aspirator and prepared to stab Maude just below the navel with his brand new trocar. He had engraved its handle in cursive with the word *Becky*, named after Becky Hemmingway, his Page Six muse, memorialized forever in his secret album.

Arterial embalming was the first step in the embalming process. It flushed the vascular system, then filled it with fluid. Unfortunately, the fluid could not reach any of the body's hollow organs; Yvgeny needed a special tool for that.

Enter the trocar. The purpose of this handy instrument was to puncture and aspirate those hollow organs, then fill them with his formaldehyde mixture.

Every time Yvgeny started the arterial embalming process on a client, he remembered his father explaining the procedure to him, comparing it to bleeding the brakes on a car, only in reverse.

You can't just suck the fluid out of the master cylinder and replace it, Yvgeny. That's only the first step. You have to bleed the brake lines, one line at a time, sucking out the old stuff, and sucking in the new stuff.

Yvgeny smiled with the memory. *Dear old Dad!*

Just as he started working on Maude, the phone rang.

"Sorry Maude, you just can't get a break!"

Leaving the trocar sticking out of her abdomen, he walked over to the phone, taking off one of his rubber gloves to answer it. It was Rocko.

"Rocko need money. And a ride back to truck."

"What are you talking about Rocko, where are you?"

"Rocko in jail. Truck in impound. Need money to get truck."

Yvgeny cursed under his breath. He was about to ask Rocko how much he told them, but then heard the beep on the line that warned him their conversation was being recorded. He chose his words carefully.

"I will be right there. How much is your bail?"

"Rocko doesn't have bail. Rocko standing at pay phone outside."

Yvgeny deflated.

No bail means no charges, and no charges means Rocko talked.

"I will be right there," Yvgeny said, then hung up. He turned off the hydro aspirator and lifted the rubber apron over his shoulders and re-hooked it on the wall. He left Maude on his table, unclothed, Becky still buried up to the hilt in her abdomen.

"Last interruption, Maude, I promise!"

When he walked out the door, he heard the sound of chopping and turned in the direction of the noise. He saw Alfred deep within the brambles beside his shed, hacking away with a small but exceedingly sharp hand axe. *Gertrude* was small, but its handle was long enough to support its longer name.

The invasive species had gained quite a bit of ground over the summer, and now that the woody vines had finally gone dormant, Alfred was reclaiming the space.

Yvgeny watched Gertrude flash in the bright sunshine a bit longer, then climbed into Cerberus and made his way down State Route 96. He considered making Rocko lie down in the casket as payback.

Yvgeny merged onto Interstate 75 northbound. At the same time, Newsome and Bubba parked at the GBI building to pick up the victim's clothing.

When Yvgeny arrived at the jail, Rocko was outside waiting for him. *Like a bad movie,* Yvgeny thought to himself. The top of his shirt seemed damp, and his good eye was inflamed and red.

Rocko folded himself into the front of the hearse after glancing toward the back as if expecting to see a body.

"What happened to you?"

"No dead people in here, right?" said Rocko.

"Of course not, Rocko, now shut the door."

As Rocko settled back, Yvgeny accelerated out of the parking lot, wanting to put as much distance as possible between himself and the jail. Once they were on the highway, Yvgeny glanced over at Rocko and asked, "So what did you tell them?"

"Nothing."

"I find that difficult to believe, Rocko. Nothing at all?"

Rocko balled his hands into big fists and pounded the dash of Cerberus. Yvgeny winced, hoping they didn't leave permanent impressions on the vinyl.

"Rocko never lie! Police stopped Rocko for no reason. They were rude to Rocko, so Rocko tried to punch them in their rude faces."

"You punched a police officer?"

"No. Rocko missed. Then police sprayed Rocko with mace for no good reason. It burned!"

"I see. Well, at least they let you out. Where's the impound yard?"

Rocko handed Yvgeny a yellow piece of paper with carbon etching all over it. He scanned the page until he found the address in the fine print. And the cost- $120. He muttered to himself. Rocko stared forward.

"Rocko hungry."

Yvgeny glanced over at him but said nothing.

"Rocko want sausage. Uncured pork sausage in all natural casings. Hand stuffed uncured pork sausage in all natural casings. Mmmmmm. Chunky."

Rocko emphasized his point by rubbing his stomach and licking his lips. Yvgeny tried not to stare at Rocko in disgust.

"Jesus Rocko. Awfully particular about your sausage, aren't you?"

"Rocko likes sausage. Rocko won second place in sausage contest last summer."

"Yes Rocko, I remember that. The whole town remembers that."

"Police remembered that, too."

Yvgeny glanced toward Rocko.

"You guys talked about sausage?"

210

"They were looking for good place to buy uncured pork sausage in all natural casings. For rude police people they know good sausage."

Yvgeny stared at Rocko so long he accidentally started floating into the next lane. The blare of a horn jolted his eyes back to the road and he swerved back into his lane. Rocko didn't flinch at all.

"So, Rocko, where the hell am I supposed to get you this sausage?"

"Master Jeremy's."

"Where?"

"Master Jeremy's."

"What kind of name is that? Where is it?"

"Dunno, they didn't say."

"Who didn't say?"

"Police."

Yvgeny glanced at Rocko again, who was staring forward through the windshield, a vacant expression on his face. Yvgeny considered, then pulled over and worked his iPhone until he figured out the location of Master Jeremy's. He set his iPhone to guide him there and leaned back and smiled at Rocko.

"So Rocko, how would you like to go get some of that great sausage?"

Rocko gave Yvgeny a quizzical look, then he smacked the dash hard with his palm and said, "Turn this meat wagon around, it's sausage time!"

Master Jeremy's was located in a warehouse district on the outskirts of Macon, in a dilapidated part of town through which both literal and figurative tracks crossed. Macon was truly a divided city, with blacks on one side of the tracks and whites on the other. Master Jeremy's happened to be on the black side.

Yvgeny's iPhone guided him through the collection of red brick buildings toward the far side. Master Jeremy's was easy enough to spot; the storefront was illuminated with neon piping and a flashing neon sign.

Inside, butchered animals hung from hooks. The swinging meat and the flashing red neon lights made the place look like a storefront in the red light district in Hell.

The parking lot was virtually deserted, with only two cars in the far corner. As they drove closer, however, they saw a group of around twelve black men huddling in the opposite corner. Yvgeny didn't pay them any attention until he parked and they opened their doors, at which time the raised voices and arguing became apparent. As they watched, two of the men started pushing each other, and the pushing became punching, and within seconds it became a true brawl.

Never one to miss a good fight, Yvgeny leaned against the side of Cerberus and crossed his arms. Rocko came around to stand beside him for a moment, then asked Yvgeny for some money. Yvgeny turned and asked Rocko, "what for?"

"For sausage!"

Yvgeny removed his wallet from the breast pocket of his suit and handed Rocko $20. The group was too busy arguing to notice their audience.

The argument grew more intense, then Yvgeny heard the sound of breaking glass. A moment later, one man fell to the pavement, and the group split up and fled in two different directions.

The bleeding man struggled to stand, then on wobbly legs looked around the lot, one hand clenching the bicep of his other arm. Blood poured from the wound and through his fingers. Then the man's eyes settled on Yvgeny.

The man homed in on the hearse, then his eyes darted across to the strange white man wearing the black suit. He seemed conflicted whether to go to him for help or to run away. Then he looked down at his wound and reached some kind of decision. He lurched toward Yvgeny, who was still leaning casually against Cerberus.

"Hey man, you gotta help me."

"And how would you propose I do that?"

"Take me to the hospital."

"The only items this vehicle transports are corpses. You aren't there. Yet."

The man looked in each direction, his face ashen.

"Come on man, I need help! I'm bleeding!"

Yvgeny glanced down at the man's arm, looked back toward the store, then hissed out his breath.

"Fine. Let me see the wound."

The man seemed unwilling to remove his hand, but Yvgeny pried away his fingers and looked. As soon as the pressure was removed, the wound bled freely. Yvgeny inspected it, then stepped back.

"Wait here."

Yvgeny walked over to the back of the hearse and opened the hatch. He had a cargo area, but to access it he had to pull out the coffin he had inside, a nice display model; *appearances were important!* It was clamped down on a wheeled frame so that it could be rolled in and out for convenience.

The man had leaned against Cerberus, which caused Yvgeny to stiffen, but the man was beyond noticing such subtle cues. Yvgeny shook his head, and reached into the back of the hearse to retrieve a large black tackle box. He rested it on the edge of the coffin, and began sorting through it.

"First aid kit?" asked the man, still clutching his arm.

"Well, more like a tackle box for corpses. One should always be prepared."

The man's ashen complexion lightened further. Yvgeny straightened up, holding some black thread and a long, curved needle. He carefully threaded the needle, then brandished it in the air.

"I don't have any antiseptic. And it's going to hurt."

"You ain't got nothing for the pain?"

"I work on dead people. They usually don't complain."

The man froze, then reached into his back pocket and pulled out a flask of whiskey. He used his teeth to open the bottle, spit the cap onto the pavement, then took a long pull. He offered the bottle to Yvgeny. Yvgeny took the bottle, peeled away the man's hand, then indiscriminately poured the whiskey over the wound, causing the man to howl.

Rocko approached the two of them, a bag in one hand, a sausage in the other, half eaten. He stopped beside Yvgeny, watching with interest. As the whiskey ran down the man's arm, mixing with the blood, Rocko stuffed the rest of the sausage into his mouth and turned to Yvgeny.

"Haman go hurt?"

Yvgeny could barely understand him with his mouth filled with food, but after so many years deciphering Alfred's grunts and clicks, he had grown fairly skilled at

214

translating.

"He got in a fight. He lost."

Yvgeny turned to the man and said, "Ready?"

The man had been staring fearfully at Rocko, but then returned his attention to Yvgeny and made a tentative nod. When Yvgeny tried to pry the man's fingers away from the wound again, the man weakly resisted. The loss of blood was beginning to make the man woozy, and he began to wobble on his feet.

Yvgeny paused, then looked back toward the coffin. He had an idea.

"Rocko, put down that bag and help me out. This man needs to lie down."

As Rocko complied, Yvgeny popped open the coffin lid and escorted the man toward the back of the hearse. When the man realized what he had in mind, he struggled.

"No way, man! I ain't gettin' in that thing. You crazy!"

"You want to bleed to death in this parking lot? Maybe Master Jeremy can grind you up and whip up a batch of idiot sausage. Throw in a little chicken to tamp down the gamey taste, spice it up for flavor, how does that sound, Rocko?"

With his mouth full, Rocko mumbled "mmmm, dark meat *and* white meat. Yum, yum."

Yvgeny reasoned with the injured man, who was now watching Rocko with a mixture of fear and revulsion.

"The second I stick this needle in your arm you're going to pass out. Nature's anesthetic. When that happens, you can either fall down and smack your head on the pavement, or you relax in a nice comfortable coffin."

The man equivocated, glancing down to the pavement, then over to the coffin.

"Look, think of it like a bed with a lid."

Finally, the man slumped forward, defeated. Yvgeny removed the fancy liner from the coffin and placed it safely to one side of the hearse, then threw in a couple of towels to soak up the blood. When he was ready, he wiped his hands on his jacket, stood, and turned to Rocko.

"Rocko?"

Rocko grabbed another sausage, placed it in the corner of his mouth like a cigar, then came behind the woozy man and lifted him up like a groom picking up his bride, then gently laid him into the coffin. Rocko was strong as an ox and made it seem effortless. The black man's complexion was so pale that by the time Rocko placed him in the coffin, he truly looked the part.

Yvgeny pushed the man onto one side to give him better access to the wound site. He held up the needle again and glanced at the now terrified man. Yvgeny smiled.

"Ah, just like a corpse. Well, more bloody, but other than that-"

After the first stitch, the man screamed, then lost consciousness as Yvgeny predicted. Yvgeny worked quickly and carefully, and a few minutes later the wound was completely closed. Yvgeny had no gauze or bandages, so he simply left the wound as is.

As Rocko and Yvgeny stood at the back of the hearse, the coffin still partially rolled out, Bubba and Newsome pulled into the parking lot. They were looking at the neon signs and did not, at first, notice the hearse.

"You gotta be kidding me," said Bubba. "Look who's here."

Newsome turned to look and saw the hearse. Then he saw the open coffin.

"What the hell?"

They pulled up beside the hearse, approached, then looked in the coffin to find what appeared to be a dead black man, bloody, a fresh wound on his arm. Yvgeny was still holding his needle and thread.

"Inspector. Fancy meeting you here."

"Who's the stiff?"

Yvgeny glanced into the coffin, then shrugged and said, "No idea. And he's not ready to be embalmed quite yet."

Rocko had a sullen look on his face when he saw the detectives, then suddenly he grew animated and pointed at Yvgeny.

"There was a big fight!" Rocko cried out, "then Geny man sewed up the black man, sewed him up just like a doctor. Geny man saved his life! Rocko saw it with his own eye."

Bubba stared at Rocko, his mouth open, then approached the coffin. He reached in, felt for a carotid pulse, then turned to Newsome and nodded.

Newsome said, "Bubba, why don't you call an ambulance," then after a sigh, turned to Rocko.

"Hey Rocko, loose lips sink ships."

"Rocko doesn't like boats."

As Newsome squared off with Yvgeny, the sound of a jingling bell distracted them. A short, fat man in a dark apron came rushing out of the butcher's shop. His arms seemed too short for his frame, and he waddled like a duck.

"What's going on here? You'd best get outta here before I call the cops!"

His announcement was punctuated by long wheezy gasps of air from the exertion of running across the lot.

Yvgeny turned to the man and said, simply, "Why didn't you call them twenty minutes ago when they were brawling in your parking lot?"

The man seemed to straighten up a bit, then took a closer look, saw the badges and guns, then stared a moment at Yvgeny, at his black suit, then the hearse, then noticed the coffin sticking out in back. He slowly walked around to the back of the coffin and looked inside, saw the man, and stumbled backwards.

"Jesus, you got a dead guy in my parking lot? I could lose my license!"

Rocko stepped forward, smiled at Yvgeny, then said to the man, "He's not dead yet!"

The butcher stepped backwards, then took another look at the badge around Bubba's neck and the one on Newsome's belt. Just as he started to relax, however, Yvgeny pointed at the man's apron and snorted.

"*Disposable* apron? Amateur! Rocko, I thought you said this place was the best!"

Rocko looked confused as he glanced at the man's apron.

"Any self-respecting dealer in cadavers knows rubber is the only proper material to use. Do you really think *that* will protect you from blood borne pathogens, or from getting soaked by squirting entrails or viscera? It will go right through that cheap paper. Have some self-respect, man!"

Yvgeny paused for dramatic effect, just like Holmes before one of his masterful deconstructions, then clasped his hands behind his back and stepped forward.

"Master Jeremy, I presume?"

The man nodded.

Newsome continued to stare at Yvgeny, but Bubba looked over at the man in the apron. Yvgeny cleared his throat before speaking.

"The inspectors here were about to ask you if you have a regular customer, an old man, maybe in his eighties or so, that likes to buy, what was it, Rocko? Oh yes, uncured pork sausage in genuine casings. Sound like a customer of yours?"

The man was still staring at the coffin, and when Yvgeny waved a hand in front of his face, the man startled and stepped backwards again.

Newsome also came alive and stepped between the butcher and the undertaker.

"We'll ask the questions here, Geny. And I got half a mind to arrest you right here for obstruction."

Before Yvgeny could reply, a siren pealed across the lot. Seconds later, an ambulance appeared.

Both doors opened at the same time and an EMT fell out on either side. The one behind the wheel ran around the front of the van and together they approached the group: a short, fat man with a green apron streaked with blood, a tall white man wearing all black, and two men wearing guns and badges. Then they saw one-eyed Rocko, dressed in coveralls and chewing on a sausage.

Finally, their eyes settled on the coffin and they slowly shuffled forward to look inside. One inched up and reached out two hesitant fingers to check for a carotid pulse. Just as his fingers touched the man's neck, the man's eyes opened and he screamed.

The two EMTs screamed in response and jumped backward in unison, knocking into each other. Both tumbled onto the pavement. An aluminum clipboard skittered across the pavement.

Master Jeremy also overreacted, backpedaling until he slipped on some loose gravel and fell flat on his back. Only the deputies, the undertaker, and Rocko were left standing.

The man in the coffin struggled into a sitting position, and Rocko helped him out and on his feet. He surveyed the scene, bewildered, then inspected his stitches. They were tight and perfectly measured out. He whistled.

"These look good, brother! And I didn't even have to go to no hospital! You saved my life! You saved my life!"

The man went over to Yvgeny and raised his hand to give him a high five, and when Yvgeny just stared at him with a bemused look on his face, he dropped his hand to waist level and held it out to shake. When Yvgeny grudgingly took the man's hand, he stepped in and gave Yvgeny a brief but fierce bear hug.

Yvgeny suffered through the spectacle, then shook his head slightly and said, "Ah, I forgot all about it!" and with a smile, ducked back under the rear gate of the hearse. He returned with a spray bottle and his stovepipe hat, which he placed on his head, then sprayed a mist over the man's arm. The man winced and took a step back and exclaimed, "Ow! That shit stings!"

As the injured man stepped backwards, Master Jeremy began the laborious process of pushing and pulling himself into a standing position, and, from there, seemed unable to decide whether to head toward the safety of his store, or to satisfy his curiosity as to what was happening in his parking lot.

Yvgeny smiled.

"Sani-sol 5. It's excellent for surface decontamination."

Tipping his hat to a rakish angle, he brandished the bottle and turned his attention to the two young EMTs, now back on their feet and staring at him, transfixed.

Still facing the EMTs, Yvgeny called out, "Bet you don't carry this in *your* tackle box, boys!" Then he turned to the black man and explained, "it's designed for corpses that have been decomposing for a while."

Yvgeny turned back to the EMTs, said, "You know that smell, boys, don't you? Like kitchen garbage left to rot in the sun, right?"

The two EMTs gathered their clipboard and slowly crept closer toward Newsome and Bubba as Yvgeny watched, a triumphant smile plastered across his face.

Finally, Yvgeny returned his attention to the black man, whose appreciative grin had faltered.

"Anyway, it's perfect for reducing the stench of death."

Yvgeny then stroked his chin and looked up to the sky, added, "Why, just the other day I got this client," Yvgeny winked conspiratorially at the injured man, and whispered, "you know, that's what I usually call my corpses," then resumed his professorial air.

"Yes, just the other day, I was with a client, he had been rotting in his living room for about three weeks. Nobody knew, at least not until they smelled him. Fire department had to wear their oxygen masks. You have to do that sometimes, don't you, my little emergency responders? When the Vicks just isn't enough for your little sensitive nostrils?"

Yvgeny glanced toward Newsome with an eye roll.

The EMTs stood in suspended animation just like

the injured man, unable to turn away from the spectacle Yvgeny had created. He had captivated them all with his special mixture of macabre showmanship and grotesque exposition, and they watched him, captivated, waiting for the grand finale like kids at the end of an Independence Day fireworks display.

"Anyway, a proper dousing of Sani-sol, and even a batch of rotten meat like that can smell no worse than, gee, I don't know," and then Yvgeny smacked his lips, pursed them, winked, and said, "well, probably no worse than moldy mushrooms."

"OK, Geny, time to move on," said Newsome, shaking his head. The spell broken, the black man shuffled away, backwards, then turned and ran, one arm clutching the other.

The EMTs watched the black man run away, then the clipboard wielding EMT flipped open the lid and scribbled onto a paper, and said to his friend, "Well, RMA it is. Let's go."

On their way back to the ambulance, Jeremy asked, "RMA?"

Bubba muttered, "refused medical attention."

Newsome just shook his head.

Rocko watched the EMTs race away from the parking lot, then reached into his bag for another sausage, unfazed by any of it.

Master Jeremy shifted from the undertaker to the detectives, then to Rocko eating his sausage. Bubba approached the man and spoke bluntly.

"You got any regular customers that come in here, maybe eighty years old, white, medium height and build?"

The man pulled at his apron, smearing the blood, his eyes not completely focused on Bubba. Bubba took a step closer and notched his voice up in volume.

"Hey, sport, you hear me? You got any regular customers? An old fart, eighty-ish? Likes your uncured pork?"

Yvgeny, still quite pleased with himself, turned and began to whistle an off key tune as he removed the bloody towels, replaced the guts of the coffin, then closed the lid and slid it back until it locked into place. He secured his go-bag and shut the rear gate. While busying himself with these tasks, he kept his ears tuned on the butcher.

"Um, well, sure. I mean, no. Wait, I got a lot of regular customers. A lot of geezers. Why?"

"Because one of them is dead."

The butcher began rubbing his cheek with one of his hands, unwittingly streaking some type of animal blood on his face.

"What's that got to do with me?"

Yvgeny came around the hearse to rejoin the group.

"We need to identify the man."

Newsome said, "We?"

The butcher looked from one face to the next, lingering on Rocko, who was stuffing his face with sausage and smiling at the meat as he chewed, oblivious to the conversation around him.

"Well, do you have a picture?"

Yvgeny stepped forward and interrupted with a long and theatrical "well...." Then he raised his hands up like a priest preparing to bless the head of an invalid, and said, "They can't really do that because when they found the corpse in my open grave, they-"

"Enough, Geny, I think we've all heard enough of

your bullshit for one day."

Newsome glared at the undertaker, and Yvgeny fell silent, still smirking. Newsome turned his attention to the butcher.

"Jeremy, right?"

The man nodded.

"How many old white men come in here each day? One or two? Or more like twenty?"

The man's lips moved as he seemed to calculate in his head, his eyelids fluttering.

"Maybe three or four."

"OK, good, three or four. Now Jeremy, how do they pay? You keep credit card receipts? You get copies of checks from your bank?"

He answered more quickly this time, as Newsome broke the spell Yvgeny had cast, and said, "Nope, cash only. No checks."

Newsome cursed under his breath.

"OK, you have any cameras here?"

The butcher looked around, astonishment on his face.

"Here? Somebody going to break in and steal half a cow? You know how much those things weigh?"

Newsome gave his best effort to remain patient and calm, but Bubba could see the placid waters beginning to ripple. Newsome reached up and began twirling on the tips of his thick mustache; Bubba knew the signs, and stepped closer to him.

Newsome stopped twirling his mustache and rested

his right hand on the top of his exposed sidearm.

"You know what? I've taken about all the crap I can take for one day. Now listen, you sumbitch, you know any of these geezers' damn names?"

The butcher was startled by Newsome's abrupt change in demeanor and shook his head violently, chanting, "No, no sir, no, I don't ask them for their names."

Newsome stared at the man until Bubba stepped between them and placed a hand on Jeremy's meaty shoulder. Bubba thought for a moment then asked, "Any of those customers Jews?"

Master Jeremy cocked his head and looked up in surprise, then confusion.

"I don't really know what Jews look like. They don't eat pork, right? Or is that a Muslim thing?"

"Both," said Yvgeny, but when Newsome snapped his head toward Yvgeny and glared, Yvgeny closed his mouth.

"But I don't think so. In fact, one of them, he really hates the Jews. I've heard him spout off all this crazy Nazi type shit."

Newsome asked, "What kind of Nazi type shit?"

"You know, the Jews take all the jobs, the Jews won't, how'd he say it, assimilate, or something like that. He got all pissed off one day about some Jew church, said it was right next to the grocery store. I thought he was crazy, I ain't never heard of no church next to a grocery store."

Yvgeny, Bubba, and Newsome all froze and stared at the butcher. The butcher, too absorbed in what he was saying to notice, continued.

"Yeah, I guess he got into some kind of argument over there, guess a couple of them whupped his ass. Boy, he was pissed that day."

His audience remained frozen, staring intently at the butcher, who took a step backward, nervous from the attention.

"What? Why y'all looking at me like that?"

The only sound was Rocko's mastication. He had plowed through almost $20 worth of sausage in less than ten minutes.

"Guess you don't know that guy's name, do you?"

"Like I said, I don't ask. They pay cash, I give them what they want."

"Well, you remember what that guy usually ordered?"

"Sure, the MJ Special."

"And that means?"

"Uncured pork, I use celery powder, no nitrates, much healthier. And real casings. I-" he paused, his shoulders slumping, "I make them myself, from the real thing."

Newsome turned from the butcher without a word, and approached Yvgeny, closer and closer, until he was only a couple inches from his face. Up close, Yvgeny could smell Newsome's cheap aftershave.

"Let me tell you one more time, Geny, and let me make it real clear this time. I catch you within a mile of me or that rabbi, I'm gonna lock your ass up, you hear? You know damn well where I'm about to go, and you'd best stay away from that place. Hell, stay off that exit. In fact, I'd say you get on the highway and go north, go all the way up to Atlanta for all I care. But I'm gonna send a

BOLO out over that police radio to every swingin' dick in this county. No, every county for fifty miles, and tell them to arrest the first Russian they find dressed like Dracula and driving a hearse. 'My making myself clear?"

Yvgeny stared back, unperturbed, and said, "Polish."

"What?"

"I'm Polish. Not Russian."

"Whatever."

"Also, according to the First Amendment, I have the freedom of association. So I can spend time with whomever I choose. According to my driver's license, I have the right to drive wherever I want. Thank God we live in a free country!"

"You done?"

"No. I also have the right to go shopping at my new favorite supermarket. And who knows, maybe I will go do some praying before I go shopping. Lord, give me the strength to pick only the ripest, freshest pineapples! Yes, I think the First Amendment gives me that freedom, too."

"I'm gonna shove that smug smile right up your-"

"OK, that's enough, everybody, that's enough. Harry, let's go. Geny knows better than to follow us around. Isn't that right, Geny?"

Bubba pushed on Newsome, trying to get him to turn away from Yvgeny, who remained standing facing Newsome, a smirk on his face. Newsome finally snapped out of it and started moving toward his car. To his side, Rocko began crumpling up his bag and dropped it beside the hearse and returned to the passenger side, opened the door, and sat down. He burped loudly, smacked his lips, then farted. Yvgeny cringed.

Newsome walked around his car and climbed into the passenger seat, then grabbed the lever beneath the seat and pushed back until he could stretch his legs fully. Bubba got behind the wheel with a shrug, taking the keys from Newsome.

"Crazy sumbitch. I swear to you, Bubba, I'm gonna throw his ass in jail the next time I see him. Him and that one-eyed retard."

Bubba started the car, then glanced at Newsome.

"Damn, Harry, calm down. Save it for TNT."

Newsome sneered, said, "TNT my ass. Name's Thomas." Newsome paused, then let out his breath with a whoosh.

"TNT. Why did God put idiots like him and that damn undertaker on this earth?"

Bubba smirked and reached for his Gatorade bottle, now half full, and muttered, "because it'd be a boring place without them."

Yvgeny watched them leave the parking lot, then returned to Cerberus.

"Come now, my dear Rocko, we have an investigation to complete."

∦

CHAPTER THIRTEEN

Newsome continued twirling his mustache and grimacing, mute; Bubba occasionally stole a glance in his direction but remained silent. He turned on the radio, found a good country station, and reached for his Gatorade bottle.

They made it back to the supermarket parking lot, parked in the fire lane outside the temple, then followed a middle-aged couple inside, where they joined a half dozen others sitting in the pews chatting softly.

The rabbi was in the corner speaking to an older man, but he stopped in mid-sentence when he saw them. He took a moment, then excused himself from the man and approached them with just enough speed to arouse the interest of some of the others. Oblivious to the stares, and before the deputies could speak, the rabbi lifted his arms and pushed lightly on them, attempting to usher them outside.

"Not here, detectives, not here. This is a house of God."

Both detectives bristled at the physical contact, but allowed him to usher them away. Once they were all outside, the rabbi pulled the door closed, then turned to face them.

"What brings you here, detectives, I've told you everything I know."

Newsome, still irritated by Yvgeny, growled, "You ain't told us anything. How about the old Jew hater one of your people here assaulted? I don't recall hearing nothing about that!"

The rabbi turned to glance briefly behind him at the temple door, and when he turned and spoke, his voice was thready, shaky. One of his eyes twitched.

"I didn't think it was relevant."

"Are you kidding me? How you figure that ain't relevant to a murder investigation? Of an old man?"

"A murder, detective, of an old man you found in Gilbert County. What makes you think it happened way up here?"

"Let's just call it a hunch. This ain't Atlanta, we don't have murders every day." Newsome took another step toward the rabbi, and added, in a low voice, "but I tell you what, if that's all you got, how about we wait out here and stop everyone walking in or out, and ask them a bunch of questions? Ask them about the fight. How about that?"

The rabbi paled, and shifted his weight from one foot to another, then asked, softly, "Look, let me finish my services here, then you can meet me at my home. I will give you my address. How about six thirty?"

Newsome glared at the rabbi, then agreed with a curt nod, adding, "Fine. But we're gonna need some answers this time." Newsome spun on a heel and returned to his car, leaving Bubba to get the address.

Newsome cursed the entire trip back to the highway.

He cursed about Yvgeny, about the butcher, the rabbi, even Rocko. Bubba knew to stay quiet and let the storm blow over.

Newsome fumed for another ten minutes, until they saw blue lights ahead on the highway. By habit, Bubba activated their rear strobes and pulled in behind the patrol car to make sure he was OK. The car belonged to the Crawford County Sheriff's Department, and was painted the universal Georgia brown preferred by most sheriff's departments. But as they got closer, they realized this car was different from all the others.

This car was emblazoned with especially large K9 emblems. Crawford County only had one K9 officer, so they knew who they had found.

The back deck lid bore a large airbrushed image of a German Shepherd with a message below it that read Nitro, 2014 - .

Georgia law required vehicles used primarily for traffic enforcement to have certain minimal emergency equipment and markings. These requirements were established to ease drivers' concerns about thugs and highwaymen masquerading as law enforcement and to increase the police presence on the roadways to minimize reckless driving and road rage incidents.

All Crawford County traffic enforcement vehicles adhered to the law, with reflective, brightly colored lettering, a light bar, and a siren. There was no question that each was an official government vehicle when they handled police business.

Thomas's patrol car, however, was in a class by itself. He had everything the other patrol cars had, plus side marker lights, pop up lights, and strobes in every window. His head lights had wig-wags. He had flashing brake lights. He even had directional flashers built into his light bar. It was like a rolling video arcade, and sometimes deputies tossed quarters into his car as a joke. TNT failed to see the humor.

Bubba pulled in behind him, angling the car away from traffic to protect his exit from the driver side. They emerged quickly and headed toward the shoulder, away from the speeding cars on the highway.

Thomas was busy speaking with the driver, his belly squashed against the door. It hung so far over his gun belt that his magazine pouches were invisible. He needed all the room on his belt, however, because he had more accessory pouches than the rest of the sheriff's department combined.

He carried three pairs of handcuffs, an Asp baton, pepper spray, a cell phone, his police radio, his Glock Model 22, a rubber glove pouch, a remote door release for his dog, who was barking like hell from inside the car, and a number of additional pouches neither Bubba nor Newsome could identify. Hanging from the back of his belt was a large ring of keys, lending to each step the *cha ching* of a cowboy in a spaghetti western.

Thomas was fully engaged with the driver and did not see them approach. They remained on the passenger side away from traffic, waiting for him to look up.

"Jesus, what's he got now?"

Newsome pointed to Thomas's uniform, toward the top, said, "Look at his shoulders."

Bubba stared, and then he saw it. He had epaulet covers that had something metallic affixed to them, glinting in the setting sun. The last time they saw him, his sleeves bore the standard departmental patch on each arm. This time, however, they sported rockers below each patch bearing writing too small to read. Thomas acquired uniform accouterments like an inmate acquired prison tattoos.

Suddenly, Thomas looked across and saw them. He grinned, returned to the driver, said something unintelligible, then disengaged. He waddled backwards toward his car, keeping his attention on the driver, demonstrating proper officer safety, but it made for a ridiculous visual for Newsome and Bubba as they watched the ring of keys attached to his belt swing to and fro.

After clearing the front of his own car, Thomas turned around. Newsome and Bubba used the opportunity to inspect Thomas's uniform more closely. He still wore the regulation uniform of a Crawford County deputy sheriff, the same badge, but that was where the similarities ended.

Closer inspection revealed the metallic objects on his shoulders were brass pins: the letters T, N, and T. The extra rocker panels they had seen from afar were emblems containing the words "K9 HANDLER." But there was so much more, and all Newsome and Bubba could do was stare.

Thomas had a braided golden lanyard that wrapped around his right shoulder, under his epaulet, and fastened beneath one of his shirt buttons. He hung a gold colored whistle from it.

Thomas had replaced his standard basket weave gun and utility belt with a patent leather rig just like a state trooper. Bubba and Newsome then looked down, transfixed by his final "improvement."

Thomas had added crimson stripes to his pants, and altered them in cavalry style, like a modern General Patton, with lots of loose fitting material on top, and the bottoms bloused and tucked into the tall, patent leather boots preferred by motorcycle officers.

Bubba turned toward the highway to stifle a laugh. Newsome turned red, but maintained a game face.

Deadpan, Newsome said, "Congratulations, Thomas, they finally promoted you to the rank of African dictator."

Thomas smiled at the ribbing and puffed himself up.

"I'm bringing style and class back to this backwater."

His accent was more pronounced than Bubba's, but different; Thomas had grown up even further south, in Moultrie, Georgia, and people from Moultrie tended to speak with what some confused as a British lilt.

He turned to Bubba and added, "Laugh it up, buttercup, you wish you could look this good in uniform."

Newsome cleared his throat.

"Look, Thomas, we got some clothing from the victim in the car."

Before Newsome could finish, Thomas said, "Great, let me finish up here, then we can both-"

"Well, actually, something came up, we have to make another stop."

"Where at?"

"Gotta go ask a rabbi some questions."

Thomas's eyes narrowed.

"Visit a what?"

"A rabbi."

"A Jewish guy? What for?"

"Long story. Let's just say he might know something about our dead guy."

"Where's he at?"

"A few miles up yonder, right off SR 18."

Thomas considered, then put his hands on his hips and said, "OK, let me finish up here, then we can all go together."

Bubba spit tobacco juice into the scrub on the shoulder, then turned back to Thomas and said, "We didn't say you needed to come with us. We're just saying we can't meet you at 6 pm."

Thomas squinted and pursed his lips in the universal expression of suspicion, then cocked his head at Bubba and said, "You crazy? If this rabbi is part of our case, then we're going together!"

"*Our* case?" Newsome and Bubba both exclaimed.

"*You* called *me*! Remember? Now hang on while I finish this here code 18. This kid's hinky. Your rabbi's gonna have to wait."

Bubba and Newsome exchanged a look, then Newsome said, "Whatever. But hurry up."

Newsome turned and walked back toward the passenger door of their unmarked car, but Bubba leaned against the hood to wait. Thomas smiled, then pressed the button on a device resembling a key fob for a car. There was a click, then the rear door cracked open. Nitro came jumping out of the car and Bubba opened his mouth in surprise.

Nitro was a golden Labrador, and Thomas had dressed him in a tan smock, and had somehow acquired a badge for his chest. The smock, to Bubba's dismay, had epaulets that matched Thomas's, and the dog's name in large Old English font.

Thomas grabbed Nitro's leash and walked back to the traffic violator's car with Nitro in tow. First, Thomas walked the dog around the outside of the car, occasionally tapping in various spots for Nitro to focus his attention. As he approached the rear of the car, Nitro started sniffing along the sheet metal, then suddenly sat down at attention at the trunk.

"Shit," said Bubba, shaking his head and turning toward Newsome and calling out to him, "He's got something!"

As they watched, Thomas opened the driver's door and ushered out a teenaged white male wearing a t-shirt and ripped jeans. Thomas cuffed him and walked him back to their car.

"Sorry guys, slight change of plans. Gotta stick him in your car for now. Nitro's hitting on something."

Newsome smacked the steering wheel. Bubba walked over to help Thomas place the young man in the back seat, rolling his eyes and shaking his head. Thomas returned to the man's car with Nitro, popped the trunk, poked around inside, and a moment later emerged with a package and placed it on the roof.

Thomas shoved his clipboard under one arm, then reached for his shoulder mike to update the dispatcher and request a wrecker.

"You gotta be kidding me," bellowed Newsome when he saw Thomas begin to inventory the contents of the car.

"We're investigating a murder, and this clown is making a dope arrest? Let's dump this perp and get the hell out of here."

Bubba let Newsome fume, then said, as mildly as he could, "We need that dog."

Newsome smacked the steering wheel, but after a few deep breaths he calmed down, muttering, "Dammit!"

Thomas completed his search, then returned to stand outside the rear passenger side window of Newsome's car to question his arrestee.

Newsome tried hard to maintain his composure, frequently looking at his watch and cursing under his breath. Finally, Thomas signaled to Bubba and Newsome to meet him out of earshot of the teenager. They converged at the rear of Newsome's car.

"Found at least a pound of marijuana. That's possession with intent to distribute, fellers."

"You're gonna bust him for a bag of weed? On the way to a murder investigation?"

Thomas's mouth opened in incredulous indignation.

"Are you kidding me? Marijuana is a gateway drug! What, you think I should let him go? Maybe give him a junior deputy sticker?"

They squared off for a moment, then Newsome muttered to Bubba, "Well, at least it means the damn dog might be worth something."

Newsome turned back to Thomas and said, "We don't have time to drive your perp to jail, we're interviewing that rabbi at 6 pm, and we need to get to the cemetery before dark."

"Damn right, we do!" Thomas said. He checked his watch, then looked out toward the highway, as if deep in thought. Finally, he tipped his head toward the man in their back seat and said, "Well, no big deal, let's just take him to the rabbi's place. Then he can go to jail."

"You're kidding me," said Bubba.

Thomas raised his eyebrows and shrugged.

"Who cares? You worried about a rabbi giving you a hard time? What's this guy gonna do?"

Thomas opened the rear door and called out to the subject handcuffed in the backseat.

"Sir, do you have any objection to us stopping at a rabbi's house on the way to jail?"

The bewildered subject squinted and said, "a what?"

"You know, a rabbi."

"A rabbi?" asked the handcuffed man. Then he looked over at Newsome's impassive face, then back to Thomas, and shrugged his shoulders.

"Great. Thanks," said Thomas, slamming the door.

"See? All handled. He's fine with it. Soon as that wrecker gets here, we can go."

Bubba spit, then asked Thomas, "Can't you just have one of your other uniforms come get him? Crawford County usually has at least five on shift."

Thomas adjusted his belt over his gut, then looked to the left, the right, up, down, anywhere but Bubba's eyes, suddenly unwilling to look at him.

"Well, we are kind of down today on the shift, I'd hate to take another guy off the road, and besides, they don't really like, well-" He paused, beginning to look like a dirty five year old just informed it was bath time, then added, "they don't really like taking my bad guys."

Thomas stood there, flapping like a battered flag in a stiff breeze. After a moment, Bubba shook his head and climbed back into the car without further comment. Newsome glared at Thomas, then muttered, "just don't scare this rabbi off with any of your bullshit."

Without waiting for a response, Newsome turned and got back into the car, behind the wheel. They both looked back at the handcuffed young man in their back seat, sitting next to the paper bag containing their victim's clothing. Newsome made a sound in his throat almost like a hiss. The man looked first at one deputy, then the other, then asked, "What's a rabbi?"

When the wrecker arrived, Thomas grabbed the package of marijuana from the roof of the car and stood to the side with his hands on his hips watching the man hook up the car. They argued over some paperwork, then Thomas finally walked off with two carbon copies of the inventory sheet and the weed.

Finally, they got back on the road. The arrestee pressed his cheek against the rear window to watch his car getting loaded onto the wrecker.

It only took a few minutes to get to the rabbi's house, and when they arrived, Bubba spit into his Gatorade bottle one more time, then screwed on the lid. The man in back leaned forward and said, "You know that stuff will kill you."

Bubba cocked his head to one side and responded, "Says the perp with a pound of dope?"

Bubba turned back forward and added, "Just sit there and shut up."

The man leaned back and pressed his cheek back against the window and muttered, "Popped by a friggin' fat bellhop and his monkey."

Newsome emerged and stood outside the car looking in each direction, back and forth. Bubba came around the car and approached him, watching him stare down each side of the street.

Newsome grumbled, "If I see that damn hearse, he's going to jail. Sumbitch."

Thomas pulled in behind them and they waited while he struggled to get out of his Crown Victoria. It was a laborious task; between his distended belly and the forty pounds of equipment wrapped around it, he first had to slide out his legs, then rock himself forward and back several times to generate the necessary momentum to emerge. Nitro paced in the back seat, barking in frustration, ready for a romp. Thomas finally stood, adjusted his belt, then opened the rear door.

Nitro jumped out immediately and sniffed around the area, made his way up to Newsome's car, and began to urinate on his tire. Newsome let loose a stream of expletives, and Thomas chuckled.

"Sorry Newsome. Bring it by the station later, I'll get one of the inmates to wash it for you."

Newsome grimaced and turned toward the house. The rabbi had opened the door and waited just inside the threshold. Newsome took one last look behind him at the dog, then unconsciously reached for his right shirt pocket, patted it, then sighed. He had quit smoking fifteen years earlier but he still reached for them when he was stressed. He put his thumbs in his pants pockets and headed toward the sidewalk.

"Hey Newsome," Thomas called out, "I'll stay out here with my perp. Why don't you gimme those clothes, I'll get Nitro all sniffed up for later."

Newsome chirped the alarm to unlock the doors without stopping or turning around. Bubba passed by Thomas just close enough to mutter, "Don't let him piss on the evidence," then followed Newsome.

Thomas brought out the brown paper sack and placed it on the hood. It was folded and stapled closed, with an evidence card still attached. Thomas turned the bag around, inspecting it, then tried to carefully bend back one of the staples without ripping the bag.

Bubba stopped just outside the rabbi's garage to spit into the crabgrass, and Nitro trotted over to sniff it. The dog sneezed, then returned to Thomas. When he saw the bag, Nitro began panting and repeatedly jumping, expecting treats inside.

Bubba watched Thomas fumble with the staples a while longer, then he sniffed, rolled his shoulders, walked over to Thomas, and with both hands ripped the bag open.

Thomas, open mouthed, watched Bubba walk away, then pulled out the old man's pants.

"Here boy, check it out, check it out!"

Bubba spit out his dip, ran a finger through his lower lip to clear it, then walked into the rabbi's house and shut the door.

Thomas held out the pants to Nitro, who sniffed them with fascination.

Newsome and Bubba followed the rabbi into his living room. When he turned to face them, he had his hands clenched together, knuckles white. He was pale. He looked first at Bubba, then Newsome, then toward a framed photograph of an old man with a long beard. His attention remained on that photograph. Finally, Newsome spoke.

"Rabbi, you know why we're here."

The rabbi let out his breath in a long whoosh, then nodded.

"I don't know his name."

"Well, tell me what you do know."

"He hated Jews. He's been harassing us ever since we moved in. At first, it was nothing; he would spit on the sidewalk as he passed. Or leave trash in our doorway. We are used to his kind. Name calling, too. Mostly under his breath, but we heard him just fine. Pigs, AMF, Nazi firewood, German candles, kikes, and others I will not repeat."

"AMF?"

The rabbi sighed. "*Arbeit Macht Frei*. Work will set you free. A cruel reference." Bubba squinted, still not understanding, and the rabbi raised an open hand, said,

"It doesn't matter."

The rabbi walked toward a rough tweed chair and took a seat. Behind him was a large window and sliding glass door that framed the back yard and the tree line beyond.

"Things started getting worse over the last few weeks. Someone started throwing things at our windows. Eggs. Tomatoes. The eggs were hard to clean. Even then, we did nothing."

"How do you know it was him?"

"Who else?"

Again, the rabbi sighed.

"I came to the *shul* early a few Saturdays ago. He was standing there in our breezeway, proselytizing his own brand of hate, announcing to whoever walked by that we were Christ killers, that we should be crucified. Most of my people ignored him, but some, some of the youngsters, they didn't truck his filth too well."

The old rabbi lapsed into a wet coughing spell, wiped his mouth with a white linen handkerchief, then swallowed.

"Go on."

The rabbi was quiet for a while, then started speaking softly, face angled toward his feet.

"We were just leaving Friday night services. It was a beautiful evening, warm for this time of year. A group of us remained on the sidewalk talking, enjoying the weather. All of the sudden, he was there. He tried pushing his way through us, as if he were in a hurry. Well, a few of us, they were just tired of the abuse. He pushed, he shoved, and this time they shoved back. He didn't get the message, so someone took a swing. Sent him to the pavement. He was livid.

Once he was down, someone else took a few kicks at him. He was so mad. Embarrassed, I suppose, but mad. He found me in the crowd, and he just stared at me, then he scurried off into the parking lot."

Newsome watched the rabbi carefully.

"Then what happened?"

"Then? Then we all went home. That was it."

Newsome did not move, still staring at the rabbi. The rabbi avoided his eyes. Newsome finally turned to Bubba, who was still standing in the corner of the room. Bubba then stepped forward and asked, "You tell any of this to the undertaker?"

╬

CHAPTER FOURTEEN

Yvgeny stopped Cerberus just outside the chain link fence surrounding the impound yard. He handed Rocko some cash, then Rocko got out of the hearse and disappeared into the low slung concrete block building.

As Yvgeny watched him leave, he noticed Rocko had left half a sausage in the armrest of the passenger door. Shaking his head, he reached over and tossed it outside, then drove away in a cloud of gravel and dust.

On the drive back to Schmidt and Sons, he waxed between confusion and irritation, anger and injured pride. Rocko's failures, the detective's rudeness, all just swirled around in his head; by the time he arrived home he was in a foul mood.

On his way inside, Yvgeny noticed fluorescent lights behind the mortuary. Curious, he padded around back toward Alfred's shed. Alfred was sitting in a wobbly wooden folding chair sharpening Gertrude with a long metal file. On the ground behind him was a huge pile of chopped brambles. Shaking his head, Yvgeny turned and headed back to the door.

Before he could open it, he saw headlights turning into his driveway from the street, and he muttered, "Now what?" *Those detectives again?* As he stood facing the headlights, they flicked off, and a door creaked open. His heart skipped a beat when he heard struggling and squeaking.

When he saw the bright cherry of a cigarette, he grinned. The cherry grew in intensity as she took her last drag, then he watched the cigarette butt arc through the air and land in the grass. His grin broadened.

As she approached in the near dusk, he noticed she was wearing her Golden Pantry smock. Her mobile phone was in her hand and the screen was lit.

"Brianna, what a pleasant surprise!"

In response, Brianna held out her mobile phone and said, "What in the freakin' hell is that?"

Yvgeny squinted at the screen and saw a close up photo of his opossum clutching the bouquet of flowers.

"It's an opossum. They are indigenous to the-"

"I know it's an opossum. But what's it doing?"

"Well, it's holding a bouquet of flowers. I'm not sure I understand-"

"What are you trying to do? Ricky's been staring at it all day, and it's freaking out all the customers. It's not real, is it?"

Brianna stared at him waiting for a response. His face remained passive, and after a moment she rolled her eyes and said, "Oh my God, you gotta be kidding me. You sent me a dead opossum?"

Yvgeny said, "Well, I-"

"And you threatened to steal his weed?"

"I thought you would like it. I found him on the side

of the road, and I gave him a second life."

She paused, fumbled in her Golden Pantry smock for her cigarettes, then lit one before he could reach out to assist her. She took a deep drag, then flicked the ash onto Yvgeny's stoop.

"So you didn't kill it or anything?"

"Of course not. I deplore killing. Life is too short, too impermanent."

He led her by an elbow a few feet further away from the open door to ensure Mama didn't wake up. As he turned to shut it, he said softly, "We're all just sand mandalas."

"What did you say?"

"Sand mandalas. Ritual art. The Buddhists in Tibet make these elaborate patterns out of colored sand, then destroy them."

"What the hell does that have to do with you leaving a dead opossum at my work?"

"It has everything to do with my gift for you. We exist, then we die. The Buddhists create their mandalas, then they destroy them. That's the whole point. Life is transitory."

"You're not making any sense."

Yvgeny took a step closer.

"We are all born, we live, then we die. Nothing is permanent. We are each nothing more than a sand mandala, we appear, we live briefly, then we turn to dust and are scattered to the wind."

Brianna flicked her cigarette into the bushes and took a step closer to Yvgeny.

"My gift exemplifies my beliefs. The flowers, they were alive until they were plucked from the earth. Now they're dead, and soon they will wither and dry up and you will throw them away and they will eventually return to the earth from which they came. Just like you and me."

Brianna took another step closer.

"The roses are beautiful now, but they'll only remain that way a few days. Like everything else, you must enjoy their fleeting beauty while they still possess it. You and I, together we are a bouquet, imperfect, temporary, but beautiful, and we should enjoy our short time together on this earth, while we still can."

Brianna moved up until her toes were pressed against his.

"But my opossum, well, *your* opossum, he was my creation. I have bestowed upon him the gift of eternal life. He died once, but will not die again. After the roses have returned to the earth, he will remain. He will not grow old. He will live forever, as long as someone cares for him. Loves him. Because love is the only true emotion, the only thing that matters, the only thing that survives even death."

Brianna shivered and set upon Yvgeny with a growl that sent shivers up his spine. She slammed him back against the side of the carport and snaked her tongue into his mouth, extinguishing his smirk. Her breath reeked of cigarettes, and her lips engulfed his mouth like a CPR mask, smashing his own lips against his teeth and taking his breath away; suddenly he was one of those sand mandalas that so fascinated him, and Brianna was the monk holding the broom.

Brianna spent him in that kiss, one grain of sand at a time, until there was nothing left.

Just as suddenly she pulled away, checked her watch and groaned, "Aw shit, I'm gonna be late."

She turned to leave, but not before smiling at him and saying, "That was so hot."

Then she was gone.

He stood motionless while she stuffed herself into her car, turned on her headlights, and sped away. He touched his lips with one of his hands, an evil grin slowly spreading across his face. Then he went inside, free of all the irritation that had taken root in his head.

Yvgeny's mind raced as if her kiss held caffeine, and he paced from one room to the next. He didn't care if his Mama heard him, he felt like a child who had twirled in circles until he got so dizzy he fell over.

Yvgeny continued pacing until he found himself in his work room standing over Maude, the trocar still sticking into her like a flag on a hill. He looked at his watch, then sighed as the drudgery of life set back in. He reconnected the tool to the hose, turned on the water to begin the hydro aspiration process, then donned his rubber apron.

As he worked on Maude, twisting the trocar around and listening to the gurgling of the water, his stomach began to growl. Yvgeny had missed supper.

His next thought was of Rocko standing beside Cerberus, wolfing down one sausage after another. Hunger combined with irritation, and within moments, his euphoria over Brianna's kiss was gone.

"Damn fool," he grumbled out loud, "plowed through twenty bucks' worth of sausage!"

Yvgeny adjusted the trocar, his mouth watering at the memories.

"Uncured, all natural pork sausage," he continued,

248

"and that crazy rabbi will never know what he's missing."

Yvgeny stopped suddenly, the trocar frozen in his hand. Then he stepped away from Maude and began to pace again.

"Hmm . . . ."

He mumbled to himself as he paced, his smirk slowly returning. He studied Maude, then checked his watch, then glanced at the telephone. He briskly walked over to his small bureau and riffled through a collection of papers all bearing his tiny handwriting until he found what he was looking for. He dialed the number.

"Pawn Shop."

"Reuben?"

"Yvgeny?"

"Reuben, that cousin of yours, is he still around?"

"Around? Of course he's still around, what, you think he joined the circus?"

"Reuben, can I meet him?"

"What do you want to meet an old rabbi for, Yvgeny? You thinking of converting? It's not really his department anymore, he's retired."

"I need to see him. It's important."

There was a pause before Reuben responded.

"You're serious? And what will be the purpose of this meeting?"

"Tell him a Jew may be in big trouble."

The pause was longer this time.

"Yvgeny, are you in some kind of trouble? I knew it! *Az farshiltn vakh*!"

"Of course not! It's a long story. I will tell you all about it in person. Now can you please contact him?"

"Tell you what, come by the store around six. I will have him stop by, we can talk in my back office."

"Thank you Reuben."

"And Yvgeny, that watch, leave it at home."

Yvgeny spent the time on the highway thinking about Brianna and her lips of steel. There was a little more traffic than he expected for a Wednesday night, and he arrived at the pawn shop a few minutes late.

There were plenty of open spots directly in front of the store, and he parked his hearse front and center. Three black men walked by on the sidewalk, took one look at him, then his hearse, then hurriedly crossed the street.

Reuben had already hung the CLOSED sign on the door, but had not yet locked it. Yvgeny entered, finding Reuben locking all the glass display cabinets with a key he wore around his neck.

"You're late!"

Yvgeny didn't respond.

"Well, lock the door will you?"

At first it appeared it was only the two of them in the store. Reuben continued walking around locking things while Yvgeny waited. Finally, he approached Yvgeny and shook his hand, looking down at Yvgeny's wrists.

"Ah, good, very good. Come, this way."

Reuben led Yvgeny behind the counter and into the back room, the same room Reuben had retreated into after seeing the watch. It was a small area with a tiny window set high up in the wall. There were cluttered bookshelves and a cheap table, the wood laminate peeling away from the corners.

Seated at the table was Reuben's cousin, Menachem Weinberg. He wore all black, like Yvgeny. Menachem stood slowly, stroking his long beard.

"So this is your friend, Yvgeny. *Yak spravy?*"

The old rabbi held out his hand, which Yvgeny took and briefly shook.

"I'm sorry, I don't speak Hebrew."

"Ha! I was speaking your language, Yvgeny. Apparently you don't remember the tongue of your parents."

"Remember? I never knew it."

"I see. Too bad! Well, what can I do for you?"

"Well, perhaps Reuben told you, I am an undertaker, and earlier this week someone dumped a body in an open grave on my premises."

The rabbi stood impassive, glanced at Reuben, then said, "Reuben said you were having some difficulties, but I wasn't expecting this. Please, continue."

"At first, I believed the man was a Jew, but for various reasons I am no longer so sure."

The old rabbi paced, still stroking his beard, then asked, "Why exactly are you asking these questions? Don't the police handle such matters?"

"They're supposed to, but I have a vested interest in making sure this murder is solved, and solved quickly."

"Naturally, young man. Not the sort of publicity that you desire."

Yvgeny nodded.

"But again, even if I was able to help, without seeing the body, I wouldn't know where to begin."

"His stomach contents included sausage."

"Pork?"

Yvgeny considered.

"I think so."

"Well, pork is not kosher, so if it was pork, he was probably not an observant Jew. What else do you have?"

Yvgeny glanced at Reuben.

"He was wearing a watch. An old German watch. With Hebrew writing on the back."

Reuben looked away and whispered, "*Ani l'dodi, v'dodi li.*"

Menachem pursed his lips, then after a brief pause, nodded with a shrug, and said, "well, possibly a Jew. What did he look like?"

"He had no head."

The old man stared at Yvgeny.

Yvgeny reached into his coat and said, "I have these."

Yvgeny withdrew several five by seven color photographs of the body, and handed them over. The retired rabbi took them and muttered something under his breath that sounded Hebrew. *Or Polish*, Yvgeny supposed.

Menachem flipped through the photographs, held one up close, scrutinized it, then returned the photographs to Yvgeny.

"An old man, a possible eater of *treif*, wearing a German watch with Hebrew writing, with a circumcision that looks to have been performed using a lawn mower?"

"That sounds about right," Yvgeny said.

"And no numbers?"

"What?"

"Numbers," Menachem said, "tattooed on his arm, or possibly his chest."

"Ah, right. No numbers."

"Well, seems to me this man was a Nazi. Or the son of one."

Yvgeny and Reuben's mouths both opened in unison.

"How do you figure that?" Yvgeny asked.

Reuben's breathing had become louder, and finally he coughed, and said, "*Oi vay!*"

Menachem turned and took his chair again, leaned back. Took off his hat. Yvgeny tried to remain patient, but began tapping his fingers against his legs.

"When the war ended, thousands of Nazis fled Germany. Many of them, the SS, especially, posed as Jewish refugees. They had exit strategies. Fake passports, traveling money, some even hired doctors to perform circumcisions, and not just for them. Their sons, too."

Menachem cleared his throat and continued.

"The officers maybe could afford a doctor. The rest, well, they did what they had to do. Tough surgery for an adult even in the best of circumstances. Think of the back alley abortions desperate pregnant women had before *Roe v. Wade.*

"So you have that, and of course, almost no Jew survived the War in Germany with any jewelry or money. The Nazis took it all. So, Yvgeny, all things considered, I bet that dead man was a Nazi, maybe SS, a prison guard masquerading as a Jew. Or one of his sons. May they rot in Hell."

"Prison guard?"

"They stripped the Jews of anything valuable. It's an assumption."

Yvgeny nodded.

"Of course. But why wouldn't they get a tattoo as well? To complete their disguise?"

"Well, who knows? Maybe you can explain away a circumcision, but the numbers only mean one thing. Nazis might have balked at a permanent symbol identifying them as a Jew."

"Yes, of course," Yvgeny said. "Thank you, Menachem, thank you."

"Yvgeny," Reuben called out, finally finding his voice, "that watch is cursed. You must get rid of it."

Yvgeny said, "I am beginning to agree with you, Reuben."

So that settled it. That was no Jew dumped in my hole, Yvgeny thought on his drive home. *It was the body of a murderer. Or the son of one. Either way, the inspectors will never figure it out, and even if they did, they'd just put the killer in prison.*

Yvgeny turned on his radio, found a good station.

If I find him first, I'll give him a medal! Yvgeny drove a few more minutes, then thought, *I have to find him first, before the deputies. Give him a head start.*

He let his mind wander as he drove, chewing on the mistake he made entrusting Rocko with anything important, on his conversation with Menachem and Reuben, on his troubles with the pesky inspectors, until he passed the exit for State Route 96, when thoughts of Rocko, and murderers, and inspectors, all disappeared, engulfed in the fire in his mind that was Brianna. He took the exit.

He parked across the street from the station, hoping

for a glimpse of her sweeping the parking lot, helping some customer at the pumps, taking out the trash, anything. He could still feel her soft lips crushed against his, her tongue a moist warrior fighting its way into his mouth. He considered surprising her, but convinced himself it was a bad idea. He knew the relationship must move forward on her terms.

He parked for a few minutes, then worked his way back home without returning to the highway, taking one surface street after another.

He passed by the decrepit office complex housing Dr. Flowers's medical practice. The digital clock on Cerberus's dash reported it was just after 8 pm, yet all the lights were on in his office. Yvgeny stopped in the middle of the intersection, staring at the place, until another driver honked their horn.

Yvgeny pulled off the street and into the parking lot, his mind racing. Maude might have to wait for a while. Again. Yvgeny had a new plan.

The office complex housing Flowers's practice was right off the main drag in downtown Comstock. Built in the 1960s, it looked more like a run-down motel. The doors all opened onto exposed and uncovered breezeways, the suite numbers marked with gold plastic stickers on a black background like those used on mailboxes.

Yvgeny took the stairs, then followed the suite numbers down to the last door which, Yvgeny was surprised to find, was painted a brilliant red, a close match for the color he chose for his van.

After the landlord threatened to evict him for painting the door (and refusing to return it to its original dark brown), Flowers went to the same lawyer Barry Jameson hired, and the lawyer wrote the landlord a letter convincing enough to make her back off her threats.

The suite was unlocked, and Yvgeny walked in without knocking. Flowers had an assistant, who Yvgeny found on the telephone chattering about personal matters while filing her long French manicured nails. She did not look up or acknowledge his approach.

Yvgeny stood at the counter a moment, watched her chattering, then held an index finger over the silver bell on the counter and deliberately slammed it down. The woman jumped in surprise, dropping the phone and the file. She cursed and looked up to launch a tirade at whoever caused her such a fright, but when she saw Yvgeny poised over her, all in black, a dour expression on his face, the words died in her throat.

"I'm here to see Dr. Flowers."

"You in a role?"

"Beg your pardon?"

"What's with the costume?"

Ignoring her question, Yvgeny took a step closer and leaned in to her, smelling her overpowering perfume.

"Please inform your master I am here."

The woman bristled, and said, "Oh no, you didn't!"

Yvgeny stood resolute, unmoving, the hint of a sneer on his face.

"It's after eight o'clock. We're closed!"

Yvgeny theatrically looked around the lobby, then leaned in and said, "Then why are *you* here?"

"It's billing day. He doesn't see patients at this hour."

"Good Lord, I wouldn't trust him with a paper cut, are you kidding me? This is a personal matter."

"And who are you?"

"The undertaker."

"The what?"

"Un-der-ta-ker. I can spell it out if you like."

They stared at each other, then she exhaled hard out of her nose and stood. She shuffled sideways toward a door, unwilling to turn her back on him, then stepped inside.

He didn't have to wait long, as Dr. Flowers came rushing out with his assistant in tow, his hair in shambles as if he had been sleeping, his tie crooked, his shirt partially un-tucked.

"Geny, what are you doing here?"

"I require your assistance. My vehicle is too conspicuous."

Flowers stared at him, his mouth open.

"Too conspicuous for what?"

"I will explain in the van."

"Geny, my van ain't exactly low profile either. What's going on here?"

Yvgeny did not respond, but turned and stared at the woman standing beside Flowers. There was silence for a good ten seconds before Flowers turned to follow his stare, looked at his assistant, then seemed to snap out of it.

"Right. Bonnie, give us a minute, would you?"

The woman stared at Yvgeny a moment, then left with a "humph!" and returned to her desk long enough to grab her Bic and her cigarettes. She pulled a cell phone from her back pocket as she headed toward the front door.

"That body you took up to Kincaid. It wasn't a Jew."

"So what?"

"The man had a circumcision that looked like a frog

in a high school dissection project."

"Thanks for the graphic details, but again, so what?"

"So I need to talk to the rabbi and I need you to take me there."

Flowers fiddled with his shirt sleeve to look at his watch, then stammered, "It's after eight! You want me to drive you to some rabbi's house now? You been huffing your formaldehyde?"

Yvgeny sniffed theatrically, then grimaced and yelled, "For Christ's sake Flowers, you smell like a brewery!"

"What do you care? I'm not seeing patients."

"Lucky for the patients. Look, Flowers, can't you just step up? It's important."

Flowers was still flushed and indignant, and Yvgeny held his breath and leaned closer and muttered, "You know, if you helped solve a murder before the half-wit detectives could figure it out, I bet you'd get a brand new ambulance."

Ten minutes later, Yvgeny was in the passenger seat looking behind him into the rear of Flowers's van. He had a collapsible gurney, but along the walls were rows of construction buckets containing tools. The buckets were secured to the shelves with bungee cords.

Flowers watched him inspecting the rear of the van and finally looked over at him and said, "What?"

"Nothing, Flowers, just admiring your decorating skills."

"Can it."

"Seriously, Flowers, you running a handy man

business on the side? What is all this junk?"

"Geny, one more crack out of you and I'll leave you on the side of the road. You can walk your sorry ass back to Comstock."

"Tsk, tisk, doctor, what kind of bedside manner is that?"

Flowers drove a minute longer, glancing sideways every few seconds, until he finally smacked the steering wheel.

"Well?"

"Well what?"

"Come on Geny, what are we going to this rabbi's for? And why do I have to drive you? At this hour?"

"Let's see. There's a dead old guy in Comstock. Ate pork. At the same time, some angry Nazi picks a fight with a bunch of Jews in Byron. What does that sound like to you?"

"Sounds like a whole bunch of none of my business. And a whole bunch of none of yours either! Sounds like the cops' problem!"

"The cops," Yvgeny said with a sneer. "They have enough problems of their own."

"Geny, if I told you I was going to start embalming people and burying them, do funerals in my living room, what would you say?"

"I'd say it might be a more suitable profession for you. You can't make the dead any deader."

"Very funny."

"I'd also say by the time you were done brutalizing them they'd look like a fresh batch of Frankenstein's monsters. I'd say the rest of the county would be up at night wondering whether the next lightning storm would bring back Grandma lurching back home on rotting feet."

Flowers turned and stared at Yvgeny with his mouth open until the van started leaving the roadway and began chattering on the warning grooves on the shoulder.

"Jesus, what's the matter with you? I'm just saying you should stay in your lane, undertaker."

Yvgeny glanced past Flowers and out his window, and muttered, "So should you."

╬

CHAPTER FIFTEEN

Nitro sniffed at the pants, then shoved his snout into the bag. He rooted around for a bit, then lifted his nose to the air, turned first in one direction, then another, then pressed his nose against the ground and with his tail pointed straight behind him, headed off to the side of the rabbi's house.

"Nitro! Come!"

The dog ignored Thomas and continued around the side of the house at a trot.

"Dammit!"

Thomas could not muster much more than a brisk walk, his equipment rattling like a Coke can full of coins. His right hand held up the gun side of his belt, while his left clutched at his radio. His ring of keys smacked against his rump, jingling like one of Santa's reindeer.

Inside the house, the rabbi looked up at Bubba and shook his head. Newsome walked over and took a chair facing Bubba, at a right angle to the rabbi, and began rubbing his hands against his thighs.

"The undertaker?" the rabbi asked, "what does he have to do with any of this?"

Before Bubba could respond, Newsome cut through.

"All this time, all this time you've been keeping this to yourself?"

"It has nothing to do with anything."

"How the hell is it not relevant to this here murder investigation?"

"Relevant? I am no policeman, so please tell me, how is an anti-Semite in a parking lot in Byron relevant to a dead body found in a grave in Gilbert County?"

Newsome leaned in closer to the rabbi and asked, "Any chance the body you saw at the morgue was the same person that's been harassing you?"

"Are you serious? How would I know? He had no head!"

As Newsome and the rabbi squared off, Bubba saw movement from outside the window and watched as Nitro trotted into view, his nose scraping the earth. About ten seconds later, Thomas came huffing around the corner, grabbing at his sagging belt, then stopped and put his hands on his knees and bent over to catch his breath. A moment later he resumed his labored lurch after his dog.

"Hey Newsome."

"Not now!" Newsome yelled, without turning away from the rabbi.

"An old man gets his ass beat at your temple, and a few days later we find an old man dead. Hell of a coincidence, ain't it? And I got news, rabbi, I know for a fact the dead man wasn't a Jew."

This time Bubba tapped him on the shoulder and said, "Newsome."

"Dammit, not now!"

The rabbi slowly stood up, his knee cracking with the effort.

"How do you know he wasn't a Jew?"

Newsome stood too, just in time to see Thomas's corpulent form disappearing into the trees. He turned to Bubba and raised his voice.

"Where the hell is he going?"

"He's going after his dog."

"Why didn't you tell me?"

Bubba just stared at Newsome.

"You've gotta be kidding me."

"You reckon we should go after him?" Bubba asked.

"Hell no, I ain't chasing after that damn dog! That whole thing was *your* idea, *you* go follow him. I'm staying here to finish this conversation."

Bubba pursed his lips, then gave Newsome a look as if to say *you got this?* and when Newsome whisked him away with a waving hand, Bubba left through the slider.

Bubba took the two steps down into the leaves, then jogged through the yard and into the tree line, walked for a while, jogged again, then walked the rest of the way. He stopped once to freshen the dip behind his lip. Occasionally he heard a bark, and homed in on the sound.

A few minutes later he stepped into a clearing and found Thomas standing still, sweat pouring down his face in rivulets. His whistle was dangling loose from its rope, and his shirt had come loose at the tail and was covering half the gear on his belt. He was still out of breath and helplessly watching his dog sniff around a tree stump. He held a Streamlight in one hand.

Bubba looked around in the failing light, seeing a dilapidated but tidy single wide about fifty feet away. A dirty old truck was parked beside the trailer on a gravel driveway. Bubba turned back to the dog, still sniffing around the stump.

Bubba smiled and announced, "Damn, T, looks like your dog cracked the case. Call the sheriff!"

Thomas remained quiet. He was pale, and didn't look up.

"You all right?"

Thomas lifted his shaking hand, turned on his Streamlight, and shined it on the tree stump. Bubba took a closer look, and his smile faded. Its flat, tan top was discolored by a dark, viscous substance.

"That look like blood to you?" Thomas asked.

"Yup."

"Looks like blood to me, too."

Thomas approached and leaned over the stump to study the black stains across the wood. Bubba looked over at the trailer, then dialed Newsome's number.

"Harry, you better get out here. Out back behind the rabbi's house. It's a good half a click away."

There was a pause, then Bubba moved the phone a few inches from his ear as Newsome griped, but Bubba cut him off.

"Trust me. You need to get out here. We got something."

Newsome's raging continued until Bubba interrupted him again. Thomas had started hopping around with his flashlight and pantomimed driving a car.

"Harry. Harry! Hang on a second. Thomas, what do

you want?"

"Tell him to bring me my kit bag. It's in the trunk. Should be unlocked. Black bag."

"Harry, you hear that?"

They waited on the line while Newsome went to Thomas's car. A minute or two later Bubba pressed his phone closer to his ear and listened.

"Thomas, he says your trunk's full of black bags. Which one is it?"

"Tell him it's the size of a lunch box. It's the only one in there that small."

A moment later Bubba ended the call. He looked at Thomas and said, "He's coming."

About ten minutes later Newsome arrived holding a black bag. His face was tight, his lips clamped together. The sun was quickly sinking behind the trees. Newsome glanced toward the trailer, then back at the stump. Thomas shined his light on the top, and Newsome crouched to inspect it.

"Looks like blood."

Everyone nodded at once.

"Hand me that bag, Newsome."

Newsome tossed the bag across to Thomas, who rooted around inside until he came out with a small bottle with an eye dropper. He shoved his hand back in and pulled out a Q-tip. He rubbed the Q-tip on the black substance and when he pulled it away it appeared reddish black. He dropped one drop from the dropper onto the Q-tip, then they all leaned in to watch the result. After about twenty seconds, Newsome looked up at Thomas.

"Phenolphthalin?"

Thomas nodded.

"You forgetting something?"

Thomas looked up blankly at Newsome, then it registered.

"Shit."

He held out the Q-tip to Bubba and rooted one more time through his bag and came out with a container of hydrogen peroxide. The cap held a dropper, and he added a drop to the end of the Q-tip. The dark red color fizzed and brightened into a pink color. Thomas looked up and the three of them stood quietly for a moment. Then Nitro started barking in the direction of the trailer.

"What the hell you doing on my property?"

Thomas shined his light in the direction of the voice, revealing an old man holding a shotgun and walking toward them. The shotgun was pointed down, but it wouldn't take long for him to lift it and pull the trigger. Newsome muttered softly, "Let me handle this."

Thomas looked over at Newsome and said, "This is my county, Newsome, I got this," but before Thomas could step forward, Newsome walked around the stump, his hands up, and called out, "sheriff's department! Stand down!"

The old man continued walking, but more slowly, and he squinted, looking down at Newsome's badge.

"I said sheriff's department! Drop that damn shotgun!"

Having gotten close enough to see the badges, the old man lowered the shotgun even further, but did not drop it.

"What's the sheriff's department doing in my yard? And where's your uniforms? None of ya'll look familiar." When he saw Thomas his face squinched together and he added, "Well, I've seen the fat cub scout before."

Thomas turned red, then shot a look at Bubba when he snorted.

"Gonna need you to let go of that there shotty," Newsome said.

The man took a few breaths, and Newsome kept his hand on the grip of his holstered Glock. Finally, the man pointed the shotgun down in the grass and crouched just enough so that it would not hit the ground too hard. Everyone relaxed.

"Whatcha been chopping out here?"

The old man looked over at the stump and looked back at Newsome in disbelief.

"Wood, what else?"

"Looks like you got a lot more than wood here."

The old man approached them, grumbling the entire time. He curled his thumbs around the braces of his well worn overalls and looked down at the stump, then back up at Newsome.

"Looks wet."

"Look again. Thomas?"

Thomas shined his light on the stump, and the old man's grumbling stopped when he looked down again. The Q-tip rested on the stump, the tip still bright red. The man stared a moment, then looked up at them.

"What is this?"

"It's blood, partner. I think maybe we should go have a chat at our place."

"I don't know nothin' 'bout no blood. I ain't been doing nothin' out here but chopping wood."

"Anybody else live here with you?"

"Nope."

"Come on, let's go have us a chat."

Thomas turned to Newsome and placed his hand on his shoulder, said, "Newsome, this is my county. He needs to come with me."

Nitro began to growl.

"With you? Where the hell is he gonna sit? We'll take him, and you can follow us."

"This is my jurisdiction guys, my case now."

Newsome rolled his neck, reached back and massaged the muscles, then patted at his shirt pocket again. He took a deep breath, then jerked his head toward the old man.

"Bubba, watch him. Thomas, over here."

Newsome forced Thomas away from the old man and spoke low, almost in a whisper, and said, "Look, Thomas, yes, it's your county. That means you have to get your crime scene team out here to work it. That also means you have to stay here and wait for them. That body was found in Comstock. There's blood here, sure, but you don't know if it's his, you don't even know if it's human blood, and hell, you don't know shit about the case yet."

"Yeah, but-"

"And how many murders you worked so far? Any? How about this; we will take him to your lockup, just let us do the talking."

"How about you leave Bubba here, and I go with you."

"Really? So your uniforms can pull up and find a Gilbert County deputy guarding your scene? And holding your dog? And ain't you the crime scene leader? Whatcha think your techs are going to say? Not to mention your sheriff!"

Thomas paused, his cheeks coloring.

"OK, then we all stay here until my crew arrives. Then we can figure it out."

"That could take hours, are you kidding me?"

Thomas stood, uncertain, weighing his options. Finally, after a long sigh, he said, "First, I'm gonna call my people and find out their ETA. If it's maybe thirty minutes, then we all wait. If it's too long, then fine, take him in. But you don't say one word to him until I get there. And if anyone asks, you tell them you're waiting for me!"

Newsome stared at Thomas, his lip trembling with frustration. Then he bit his lip, rolled his neck again, and said, "fine. Whatever. Call the damn crew and tell them to haul ass. But this old man needs to sit down, and I ain't making him sit in the grass for three hours."

Thomas nodded, then Newsome turned back to the old man and said, "Alright, partner, you got anything in your pockets, anything we need to know about?"

The old man absently felt his own pockets, then shook his head.

"You mind coming for a ride?"

"Well, I reckon you'll just arrest me if I say no, so what choice do I have?"

He took a few steps closer, then stopped.

"What about my shotgun?"

Newsome waited a moment for Thomas to react, then turned to him and asked, "Well?" Thomas stared blankly at the old man, then sprung into action. He crouched, grabbed the shotgun, then used it like a cane to bring himself back to a standing position. Newsome and Bubba cringed and took a step back.

Thomas walked to one side, turned away, and started racking the action to launch the shells out of the ejection port. He pocketed the shells, then re-joined the group.

They began escorting the man back into the woods, but he balked at the wood line.

"Where the hell y'all going?"

"Back to the cars."

"Through the woods?"'

"Yeah, we parked on the next street."

"That's over a half mile."

"So?"

The man looked from one face to another again, incredulous.

"I'm eighty goddamn seven years old! I got two bad knees, a bad hip, a bad back, and I haven't walked further than this tree stump since '98!"

Nitro, sensing the old man's aggravation, began to growl. Thomas reached down to pat him on his head, then looked up at Newsome.

"Well, there's no sense bringing my car over here, I ain't got no back seat."

Bubba spit, then held out his hand to Newsome, who tossed him the keys from his pocket. Then he snatched Thomas's flashlight out of his hand and traipsed off into the woods. The old man sighed and made as if to sit on the tree stump, but the minute he started, both remaining deputies yelled, "no!" and the man jumped back up, causing something in his leg to pop.

"Where's your axe?"

"I figured you took it. It was in the stump."

Around fifteen minutes later, Newsome's phone rang, and when he answered it he found an irate Bubba on the other line.

"What's that dude's damn address? I don't have a clue where that street is. And I sure as hell don't know what driveway is his."

They got what they needed from the old man, and right before Bubba hung up he said to Newsome, "Oh, and tell T his perp escaped."

⚜

"You mean he's listed in the phone book? You just looked him up? Just like that?"

Yvgeny looked over at Flowers as he pulled off the highway.

Yvgeny shrugged and said, mildly, "I am finding investigations aren't nearly as difficult as the police would have you believe. Turn left here."

They made several turns before finding the street. As Flowers made the turn onto the rabbi's street, Yvgeny saw a marked police car and Newsome's brown Taurus. Yvgeny sunk into his seat trying to disappear. He reached over and smacked Flowers on the arm several times.

"Keep going! Don't stop!"

"Why?"

"They beat us here."

Flowers chuckled and said, "Great. Let's go home."

"What? No, keep going. Over there," Yvgeny said as he pointed ahead. "Park over there, in front of that car."

"But you can barely see the house."

"Exactly. What do you propose we do, Flowers, pull in the driveway?"

"Well, that's usually what I do."

"Like I said, if the inspector sees me, that's it. I am not going to risk getting arrested by those hayseeds and end up getting my throat slit in a cell. We'll just have to wait them out. As soon as they leave, we can go have some words with the old man.

They were silent for a few seconds, but Yvgeny couldn't remain quiet, and blurted out, "But what the hell are they doing here at this hour?"

"I was about to ask the same question of us. Can't this wait until morning?"

Yvgeny rolled his eyes, and said, "Cops don't do anything at this hour but eat donuts and park under trees." Then he cast a baleful look in his side mirror and added, "except for these two, apparently."

"Irregardless, we can just come back in the morning, no harm, no foul."

"That's not a word, Flowers."

"What's not a word?"

"Irregardless. Doesn't even make any sense. You sure you're an actual doctor?"

Flowers sat quietly a moment, then said, "I can't believe I actually let you talk me into this."

"Trust me, Flowers, we're doing God's work here."

Flowers reached under his seat and came up with a bottle of some kind of liquor.

"You're a strange duck, Geny."

The doctor then crouched forward and slid out of his seat and climbed over the center console and into the back.

"What the hell are you doing?"

"This is your project, not mine. I'm having a snort and a nap."

Flowers heaved and grunted himself into the collapsible gurney, took a long pull from the bottle, then settled back. Yvgeny watched him in disgust, then turned his attention to his side view mirror. *Perfect,* Yvgeny thought, *what are they doing? Surely Reuben didn't call them!*

Yvgeny let his mind wander as he kept his eye on the mirror, watching the rabbi's house, conveniently illuminated by a street light that occasionally switched off and on for no apparent reason. Then he saw movement.

"Flowers, get up."

"Why?"

"Someone's coming!"

Flowers struggled to get up from the gurney but succeeded only in knocking over his bottle and rocking the van. Yvgeny exhaled in a hiss of frustration and kept his eyes peeled on the mirror. Seconds later, he made out the silhouette of a man running directly toward them, his hands behind his back. Flowers finally forced himself into a seated position, barely able to see out of one of the square rear windows.

Just before reaching them, the man darted to the left and down the street and into the shadows. As he passed, both of them saw the glint of the handcuffs.

A few minutes later they saw someone walking out of the woods with a flashlight, get into the brown Taurus, and then drive away. The marked patrol car remained.

╬

CHAPTER SIXTEEN

Neither Newsome nor Bubba spoke the entire trip to the Crawford County Sheriff's Department. The old man in back looked out the window, also silent. They placed him in a holding cell and kept their promise. Thomas showed up about an hour later, red faced and cursing.

"Hellfire, I can't believe that damn perp escaped!"

Bubba chuckled.

"Maybe Flowers saw him."

Newsome and Thomas both looked at Bubba.

"What do you mean?"

"Y'all didn't see him parked? He was the next street over. You can see that van from a mile away. Must have been picking up a stiff."

Thomas stopped cursing and cocked his head at Bubba.

"No, my sheriff hates that guy, he ain't got no contract to pick up stiffs in my county."

After a moment of silence from all three, Newsome let loose a torrent of foul language, pumping one balled fist into his open hand. A work-release inmate in a white jumpsuit turned to follow the sound, then quickly left the area.

Newsome turned to Bubba and growled, "You didn't

think that was maybe something to tell us a little earlier?"

Before Bubba could respond, Newsome looked over at Thomas and barked, "Tell your guys working the crime scene to run up there and look for those fools."

Newsome turned to leave as Thomas reached for his shoulder mike, then he stopped and focused on Bubba again and said, "And send someone over to the funeral home. Flowers's place, too. If that hearse is there, tow it."

"What if they're at the rabbi's?"

"Gee, I don't know Bubba, maybe take them out for pancakes and ice cream. Or, better yet, lock their asses up!"

"What for?"

"How about obstruction? Damn, Bubba, who cares? Make something up!"

Then he turned to Thomas and said, "Come on."

They walked into the holding cell with the old man and as soon as Newsome closed the door, Thomas pushed past Newsome and approached the old man.

"Rudy Sanders, right?"

"Yup."

"You know why we brought you in here?"

The old man stared at Thomas, rhythmically pursing his lips in the manner of the elderly, his expression reminiscent of one who had just bit into something sour.

"Dunno. Maybe you missed your quota."

Thomas leaned back, the picture of affront.

"That was blood we found on that stump."

"So what?"

"So we are going to test that blood and see if it

matches a dead guy we found. If it matches, you're gonna get the chair!"

The old man seemed nonplussed by this revelation, and hunkered down into the cot, crossing his arms over the bib of his overalls.

"I didn't kill nobody."

"We gonna find blood in your truck?"

"Being that somebody got smoked on my property, maybe you will, maybe you won't."

Thomas leaned forward and said, "You sure are confident, old man. Where'd you hide the murder weapon?"

Newsome glanced at Thomas and grimaced.

"Thomas, I got this."

"Look here, fat boy, I'm confident because I didn't do anything wrong. Now why don't you get me some coffee if you're going to make me sit here all night!"

Newsome raised his eyebrows at Thomas, who took a step back while violently shaking his head.

"I ain't getting him any coffee, not after what he just said."

"Thomas, this ain't my jail. I don't even know where you keep the coffee. You think your deputies are going to get it for me?"

"Hell, no!"

"OK then. Why don't you get me one, too."

Grumbling, Thomas hoisted himself up and left the cell. The old man watched him leave then shook his head and muttered, "Idiot."

"Mr. Sanders, You ever see anyone else traipsing around your property?"

The old man considered, then said, "other than you two and that chubby cub scout?" Nope, not that I can recall. Don't get too many visitors."

Newsome nodded.

"Hey, you know who he reminds me of? Who was that colored king in Africa, the one that wore all those medals on his uniform?"

"Idi Amin?"

"Yup, that's who he reminds me of!" said the old man, then he leaned back with a satisfied grin. A moment later he asked, "Where'd y'all come from, anyway? That rabbi's house?"

Newsome's ears perked up and he leaned forward.

"What would make you think that?"

The old man smiled, revealing brown, crooked teeth.

"Well, you came out of the tree line, and the rabbi's the next house back there. Seems logical to me."

Newsome didn't answer.

"So what happened, that Jew tell you I was making noise? Is he sayin' I killed somebody?"

"I can't say."

"Yeah, I bet you can't."

The circular conversation continued until Thomas returned with two cups of coffee and a scowl across his face. Bubba came in right after, and all eyes settled on him.

"Just towed the hearse. Flowers's girl says him and Geny left in his van."

Newsome turned a shade darker and before he could check himself, a slew of expletives burst forth.

"Thomas, did one of your guys go over to the rabbi's?"

"Yeah, you heard me call out over the radio. You seriously want us to arrest that undertaker dude?"

Newsome just stared at Thomas until he reached for his shoulder mike. Newsome turned back to the old man.

"You have a problem with us searching your house?"

The old man stared at Newsome a moment, then he sighed and stuck a finger into his ear, dug around, then wiped his hands on his pants.

"Well, I figure you're gonna get a warrant if I say no, aintcha? So you go do what you gotta do. But I might be finding me a lawyer when this here's all done."

Newsome nodded his head and turned to Thomas and asked, "You guys got consent forms here? Can you give me one?"

"Yeah, Newsome, but this is Crawford County business. I'll go get my guys to toss the place."

Newsome stood and turned his back on the old man.

"That's fine. Tell you what; you handle that scene, and run that blood, and get a sample up to Macon for Kincaid to match."

Thomas's eyes widened and he exclaimed, "Rufus Kincaid? He's still alive?"

Newsome smiled.

"Yup, still alive, and crazier than ever."

Thomas chuckled and nodded his head, said, "Sure,

I'll take the sample up there myself. Haven't seen him in years."

Newsome thanked Thomas, then approached Bubba.

"Let's go back to Eldred's. I'm gonna sit there until his dumb ass shows up."

Bubba followed Newsome down the hall, lips pressed together tight. Finally he stopped, hands on his hips.

"Then what are you going to do?" asked Bubba.

Newsome glared at him.

Bubba glanced down the hall toward Thomas, who had stopped to adjust his gun belt, then leaned in to whisper, "Harry, all you can prove is that he was up the street from the rabbi's house. That ain't enough to arrest him."

"I don't care. It's enough to bring him in and question him. Witness tampering, obstruction, and the more he meddles in this thing, the more I'm thinking maybe murder, too."

They resumed walking toward the parking lot.

"You really think he's got the stones for that?"

Newsome fumbled in his pocket for his car keys, and shrugged. "I don't know, but think about it. He says he found the body, and it was in one of his open graves. At least that's what he said. If that's the case, why did he take the body out? Why'd he remove the clothes?"

Newsome started pacing, absently patting his shirt pocket.

"Then he drives out to the precinct to tell me the vic was a Jew. I'm starting to wonder if he's just trying to throw me off the scent."

Bubba listened carefully, nodding and pursing his

lips. Newsome took a breath and continued.

"He sent the village idiot out to follow us around, went hunting around the temple to see the rabbi, and now I hear he was parked right up the street from the rabbi's house. You tell me, is that stuff a witness would do?"

Bubba looked out into the horizon, silent, unmoving, until Newsome chirped the remote key fob. As he got into the passenger seat he responded, "hard to say, it sure ain't regular behavior. Then again, look at the guy, Harry, he's half nuts anyway."

"Well I don't like it, and I don't trust him. Either he killed him, or he knows something."

╬

Yvgeny watched the man run by and chuckled.

"The plot thickens. Let's go pay our friend a visit."

Flowers climbed back up to the driver's seat but made no move to start the van. He picked at his long sideburns, a nervous gesture, and after a moment, Yvgeny turned back to him and said, "Come on, let's go!"

"I don't like this, Geny, I got a bad feeling. Escaped prisoners running around, you hiding from the cops, I don't like it. Don't like it at all."

"Forget about it! This is Crawford County, they got nothing to do with any of this, they obviously can't keep a hold on their own prisoners, let alone unravel some crime. They're clueless, so what are you worried about?"

"It smells, Geny, and I ain't getting involved."

"That rabbi knows something, and I wanna know what it is!"

Flowers began coiling and twisting in his seat. He moved on from his sideburns to the center of his chest, which he kept scratching over his shirt by bunching up the material and digging in with his nails. Finally he stopped, nodded his head to himself, and started the van.

"Sorry Geny, I ain't sticking my nose in this."

He began pulling out and away from the rabbi's street. Yvgeny smacked the dashboard with a loud objection, but before he could say his piece, Flowers slammed on the brakes, sending Yvgeny slamming against the dash.

"You wanna go talk to him, get out and walk over there yourself. But I ain't getting involved! None of this has anything to do with me. I only went this far 'cause I was pissed off they didn't let me dice the guy. They obviously got something against me, but I ain't handing them the rope to hang me. I'm going back to the office and if I was you, I'd do the same thing."

Flowers waited with his foot on the brake staring at an indignant Yvgeny, who twisted in his seat a moment, then settled in and crossed his arms over his chest like an angry child. Flowers nodded his head, looked in the rear view mirror and accelerated again, and muttered, "besides, I don't know why you're so hot and heavy about catching this guy before the police."

Yvgeny looked at him, astonished.

"Catching him? That's what you think I'm trying to do? I'm trying to save him before those cops arrest him!"

"What do you care? Didn't you tell me once that you liked dead people more than the living?"

Yvgeny shifted in his seat, adjusted his cravat.

"I do. But this is different. If that cadaver was a

Nazi, then the man who killed him is guilty of nothing."

"How do you know?"

His recurring dream of a twisted Atlanta filled with Nazi policemen bubbled up into his conscious.

"He was a Nazi. It doesn't matter how he got dead. He deserved what he got."

For a couple minutes the only sound was the vibration of the tires on the asphalt. Then Flowers glanced at the undertaker and said, "Geny, just let the criminal justice system handle it. If he's guilty, he's guilty. If he ain't, he ain't."

Yvgeny rolled his eyes.

"Of all the people in this town, you're the last person I would figure for a supporter of law enforcement."

Yvgeny rubbed his face with his palms, stretched his neck one way, then the other, then added, "I don't know what they're up to, but if they were there to arrest him, we would've seen him led out in cuffs. If I can get to him before they get a warrant, maybe I can give him a head start."

"Jesus, Yvgeny, you're going to get arrested, they're gonna throw away the key, and for what? To help a murderer escape?"

Flowers fumed and sputtered. The sour smell of a body metabolizing alcohol oozed from his pores. Yvgeny turned forward and leaned his temple against the cool glass.

When they arrived in Flowers's parking lot, Yvgeny sat up straight, looked around, and cursed.

"Forget where you parked?"

"Of course not. I know exactly where I parked. It isn't there."

"Who would steal a hearse?"

"I suspect it wasn't a thief, Flowers. See what I mean? Instead of looking for the killer, they are harassing a local businessman just trying to earn a living and do his civic duty."

Yvgeny leaned back, re-crossed his arms across his chest and announced, "I will require transport home."

"You require transport home? Where in the hell did you learn English anyway, Geny?"

Yvgeny didn't answer.

Flowers and Yvgeny both made certain not to look at each other for the remainder of the trip, both brooding and unhappy. Yvgeny watched the trees blur into a vomit of browns and greens, the mixture reminding him of camouflage, which reminded him of the uniform wearing twisted Nazi cops of his dreams, which finally circled him back to the dead man he found.

His death was one to celebrate, not mourn! Yvgeny thought. But, of course, it wasn't so simple. The police wouldn't care a bit about it. Yvgeny could already imagine the arguments lodged by the district attorney's office, could hear some self-important boob spouting off to a jury about vigilante justice. *No, they won't be happy until the criminal justice system convicts an innocent old man of murder, and sends him off not with a medal, but with a life sentence.*

"Geny!" Flowers yelled.

Yvgeny startled out of his funk and yelled back, "Jesus, Flowers, what do you want?"

"We're back. And you've got company."

╫

CHAPTER SEVENTEEN

"How long you figure on keeping him?"

"I don't know Bubba, probably can't keep him much longer. Thomas find anything at the house?"

"Like I said, nothing yet. His team just got there, they're probably still setting up."

"No axe?"

"Nope."

Newsome rolled his neck until it cracked, glanced at his watch, then crossed his arms and leaned back in his seat. He allowed Bubba to drive, which, Bubba knew, meant he was too distracted to pay attention.

Bubba drove quietly for several miles, then turned toward Newsome.

"Harry, you still dead set on locking him up? I ain't got no charges on the guy. Do you?"

With his eyes fixed on a point outside the side window, he replied in a cool voice, "Didn't I already run down the list? I'm telling you, he's either a murderer or a liar. Or both."

Bubba considered, then said, "or he's just crazy. I mean, just look at him!"

"He's weird, Bubba. But he ain't crazy. Big difference."

"You think?"

"Hell yes. *Crazy* gets you three squares and a cot in the loony bin. *Weird* gets you life in prison or a needle in your arm."

Bubba turned away, silent for a while. But then he turned back to Newsome.

"Thing is, if you think it's the undertaker, then why are we keeping that old fart in a cell?"

Newsome was quiet for a mile or two, and Bubba began to feel the urge for another dip and reached into his back pocket. He managed to get the tin open and get a fresh dip while controlling the wheel with his knees. Finally, Newsome changed position in his seat and cleared his throat.

"There's blood on that stump. And I bet you it matches the victim."

"OK. But if you think it's the old man, then why are you so stoked about the undertaker?"

"I don't know!" Newsome yelled. He rolled his neck again, feeling one of his vertebra pop, then said, "It's gotta be one or the other. Who else? Maybe both of them together. I mean, what, you gonna tell me you think that rabbi did it? That old man ain't strong enough to lift an axe, let alone chop off someone's head!"

"What about Rocko?"

Newsome considered for a moment.

"Hell, he can't even spell his own name. No, my

money's on that undertaker. I mean, who's left? You?"

Bubba raised an eyebrow but didn't speak. He took the Comstock exit, en route to the mortuary. At that late hour, the streets were empty. As they entered the city limits, Newsome's phone rang. It was Thomas.

"Nothing in that house, at least not yet. Gave the blood samples to Dr. Kincaid. Man! What is he, like 100? I asked him how long it might take. He told me to tell you not to hold your breath."

Thomas chuckled but quickly realized Newsome wasn't in the mood.

"Listen, the sheriff wants me to cut that old man loose, says he's been crabbing about suing all of us. He also said it looks bad."

"Do whatcha gotta do, Thomas. We're already back in Comstock."

"You gonna go after that undertaker? Wait, you said I was gonna be a part of that."

"Appreciate it Thomas, but we got it from here."

"*You got it from here*? No you don't! We've been working this together from the beginning, you can't just cut me loose."

He paused, then quickly added, "I'm coming down there."

"No, that ain't necessary. We don't even know if he's here!"

"Don't matter, I will head that way. That was the whole point from the beginning, wasn't it? You wanted Nitro to sniff around that grave site."

"Thomas, it's full dark outside. How you gonna run

286

your dog in the dark?"

"We got flashlights, don't we?"

Newsome sighed, then glanced at the digital clock in his dash. Then he had another idea.

"Thomas, it's after eleven, by the time you get here it will be almost midnight. You really want to go to a cemetery at midnight?"

Thomas breathed loudly into the phone but didn't speak.

"Look, Thomas, for all we know that old man slaughtered a damn hog on that stump. We got nothing. Just because that dog can smell a bag of weed don't mean he's a damn bloodhound. I'm telling you Idi- Thomas, that dog's just going to get in the way."

"Wait a minute, I see what's going on here. You don't need Nitro because you ain't going to do a search. You're going to do an arrest!"

"Listen, that ain't-"

"You think the undertaker did it! You're trying to cut me out! I'm stuck doing all the leg work and you're going to go get you a confession!"

"Thomas, are you nuts?"

"Harry, I'm heading down there and that's final. I don't care if there's zombies and vampire bats or whatever. And I'm bringing Nitro!"

Thomas ended the call, leaving Newsome cursing into his phone. Then he smacked it against the dashboard several times, then dropped it into the floorboard and leaned back. He began to rub his temples.

Bubba's eyes flicked toward Newsome, then back to the road, and he asked, "So it's gonna be a party?"

Newsome just closed his eyes and muttered, "Damn idiot."

A few minutes later they pulled into the carport at Schmidt and Sons.

Bubba got out of the car, stretched, then checked the door leading inside. Locked. He peered through a couple of the windows, then looked at Newsome, still in the car, and shook his head.

Just then, Bubba heard the throaty rumble of Flowers's bright red van. He smiled at Newsome, who hopped out of the car and stood beside Bubba, watching the van come to a stop in the street by the mortuary sign. The moment Yvgeny emerged from the van, Flowers accelerated in a tight 180 degree turn and departed with a squeal of tires. Newsome and Bubba walked down the driveway to meet him.

"Inspectors, to what do I owe this unexpected visit?"

"Can it, Geny, I'm just looking for a reason to throw your ass in the back seat and take you to jail."

Yvgeny feigned surprise, then placed his hands on his hips and announced, "and whatever for? What have I done? Oh, and by the way, where is Cerberus? I don't recall parking in a fire lane. And I am quite certain my registration was current. That's theft, inspector, an unlawful taking by the government without due process. Perhaps I should contact my attorney?"

"Cerberus?"

"My hearse."

Bubba and Newsome exchanged a glance, then Newsome shook it off and took a step toward Yvgeny.

"I've had about all the crap I can take for one day, sport, so why don't we go inside and you can start shooting straight with me or that's it, I will haul your ass off to jail just for fun. You *and* Cerberus. *And* your one eyed retard!"

"Tsk tsk, inspector, such an attitude, I'm not inclined to let you into my home after such threats. And I believe it would be prudent for me to exercise my right to remain silent."

"Go for it, Geny, exercise whatever you want. And sure, call a lawyer too, maybe your friend Flowers has some hippy loser you can hire to guarantee a conviction."

Newsome moved closer and snarled, "and yes, why don't you kick us off your property. I will go straight down to Judge Mahoney and swear out a warrant for this place, and come back with a damn backhoe and dig up every casket you got, line 'em all up in the front yard and tear them apart."

Newsome started pacing around Yvgeny as he talked.

"First one's gonna be that fat bastard Dunlap himself, roll him out of his box and take a good look inside. Just in case we missed something."

Newsome turned to Bubba and called out, "Hey, Bubba, you still know that reporter for Channel Seven? Maybe you can give her a call, tell her there's gonna be a show out here at Geny's place, and she ain't gonna want to miss it!"

Newsome turned back to Yvgeny and clapped him hard on the back.

"Ah, Geny, the good people of Comstock will be talking about that for months."

Yvgeny frowned and glanced furtively around to make sure nobody could hear the exchange.

"Surely you jest."

Newsome stared at Yvgeny, deadpan, and said, "Try me."

Yvgeny sputtered but did not respond, and Newsome took another step closer, just inches from Yvgeny's face, and whispered, "Oh yeah, don't think we don't know about your supplemental income. Bet you didn't know this, but we got two detectives that work the pawn shop beat. All they do all day long is go to pawn shops and keep track of who is hocking what. They got a whole ledger on you."

Newsome paced around Yvgeny, a predatory smile on his face.

"So chew on that for a while, champ. If I start digging up bodies, I bet there's a whole mess of them out there missing all their jewelry, and all their teeth. So let me ask you, you really want to play with me?"

They stared at each other for a while before Yvgeny finally deflated.

"I do believe you are half embalmed already, inspector."

They followed Yvgeny into his study, where he turned to face them. He did not offer them a seat.

"So what do you want?"

"I don't know, Geny, how about the truth?"

"Sorry, inspector, but I am much better at reading the minds of dead people."

"Well, for starters, did you kill that guy?"

"Of course not. I don't need the extra business that badly."

"Seems to me, you've been trying to throw us off the scent the whole time. You moved the body, and as if that ain't enough, you stripped him down. What the hell for?

Then you come around with that story about him being a Jew, just because he's circumcised."

"Well, inspector, I-"

"Then," Newsome continued, "you go talking to some rabbi. That don't make no sense, neither. I figure that was just some more of your misdirection. Am I on the right track?"

Before Yvgeny could respond, Newsome continued.

"But then that wasn't good enough, was it? Then you had to start *really* getting in the way. Sending that army surplus retard after us, then showing up with him at the butcher's."

"Jesus, Geny. Rocko and Flowers, you drafted the two biggest morons in Comstock, sucked them both into all your bullshit. What's really going on here, Geny? Huh?"

While Newsome raged, Yvgeny repeatedly turned to look up the stairs. Newsome waited for a response, hands on his hips, then cocked his head.

"You know, I've been giving this a lot of thought. Seems to me, maybe *you* were the one that chopped the poor bastard up, did it yourself. After all, you gotta be the least squeamish dude in the whole county. Got that right? Was it you? Am I gonna find your prints in the blood on that stump?"

Bubba stared open mouthed at Yvgeny, waiting for his response. Yvgeny stood motionless, swallowed hard, and whispered, "stump?"

"In court," Newsome whispered back, "the DA would say something like 'objection, non-responsive.' I reckon that's what he'd say. So tell me, Geny, did you kill him? Did you chop him up? You still got that axe?"

Yvgeny looked up the stairs again, and Newsome said, "What's wrong, Geny, are you worried Mommy might hear your confession?"

Newsome's reference to an axe caused Yvgeny to flash back to the previous evening, watching Alfred and Gertrude chopping the brambles. For a moment, Yvgeny forgot all about the inspectors.

My dear Alfred, what have you done?

It made perfect sense. That's why he and Flowers didn't see the rabbi led out of his house in handcuffs. Yvgeny's mind raced as he connected all the dots.

Oh, Alfred! You poor righteous fool!

Yvgeny knew what he had to do.

"Inspector, I will not dignify your baseless accusations with a response, and even if I did respond, it would only be to invoke my constitutional right not to answer your questions."

"Bubba, cuff this piece of crap."

As Bubba moved forward to handcuff the undertaker, they heard a siren in the distance, quickly increasing in volume, and seconds later, a marked Crawford County patrol car slid to a halt in the street. Blue and red lights flashed from every window, every corner, like an angry Christmas tree on wheels.

As they watched, Thomas half fell out of the car and began jogging toward the door, one hand on each side clutching his gun belt. His cheeks were red from the effort and he huffed like a steam engine.

Nitro must have crawled through the cage separating the front of the car from the back, because he came bounding out behind Thomas and disappeared around the side of the funeral home barking constantly as if he was rabid.

Thomas burst through the open front doorway and

froze, looking from one to the other, his eyes settling on Bubba's handcuffs. Thomas quickly moved between Bubba and Yvgeny.

"No way, hoss, this is my collar."

Bubba turned to Newsome.

"Back off, Thomas, we ain't arresting him for murder."

"Then what the hell you arresting him for?"

"Obstruction. Witness tampering. Being an asshole."

Bubba pushed Thomas to one side and moved in to make the arrest. Thomas stared at Newsome, who smiled and added, "and he committed it all right here in Gilbert County."

Bubba noticed flood lights clicking on outside, and looked out the back windows just in time to see Nitro running across and through the headstones, his nose down following a scent.

"You gotta be kidding me."

"What is it, Bubba?" Newsome asked.

"That damn dog again."

Thomas shot a look at Bubba, followed his gaze, then glanced down at the handcuffs in Bubba's hand. He turned to Yvgeny one more time, then with a curse, Thomas left through the back door yelling, "Nitro, come here, boy!"

Newsome stared at Bubba, still frozen, then with a grunt he took his own cuffs and stepped toward Yvgeny.

"Turn around, Geny, you're going for a ride."

Yvgeny closed his eyes and thought to himself, *This is for you, Alfred.*

Newsome grabbed Yvgeny's right wrist and snicked a cuff over it, then twisted his other hand back to meet it.

After he handcuffed him he patted him down thoroughly. From his inside coat pocket he pulled out a collection of photographs.

"Jesus, Geny, what kind of whack job are you?" said Newsome, then handed the photographs to Bubba.

"Is this what I-"

"Yup. He's carrying photographs of the dead guy. And his junk."

Bubba stared at the photographs, shuddered, then reached for the tin in his back pocket.

Newsome continued searching Yvgeny. Next, his hand scraped across Yvgeny's front pants pocket, lingered, squeezed, then removed his hand.

"Do I even want to know what that is, Geny?"

Yvgeny smirked and said, "Ah, just my good luck charm."

Newsome muttered, "It don't feel like no rabbit's foot."

Yvgeny's smirk turned into a full smile.

"No, but it's close."

Newsome reached into the pocket and withdrew a darkened and desiccated index finger.

"What the-"

"Dear old Dad," Yvgeny sang in an eerie, high voice. "When he was unhappy with me, he used to give me the finger. So when he died, well, I took it for myself!"

Newsome just stared at the handcuffed undertaker, his mouth open. Outside, Thomas slowed from a jog to a crawl as he maneuvered around the headstones. The bright security lights illuminated almost the entire cemetery in a harsh, unnatural light, making it appear as if Thomas was traipsing across a movie set, wandering through fake headstones, calling out for Nitro.

Thomas grew increasingly unsettled as he imagined decomposing hands reaching up from the earth to snatch Nitro and pull him beneath the surface. He muttered to no-one in particular, "damn zombies got him."

Panic began to descend, and Thomas tried to remember whether someone bitten by a zombie would become one. *Did they eat people? Or just bite them?*

He approached a small shed beside a pile of chopped brambles stacked waist high. Then, suddenly, a dark figure appeared from the shadows behind the shed. The shadow stopped when it saw Thomas, then started moaning and calling out to him, "ng! nnng ng ng!"

Thomas screamed and reached for his gun and in a high pitched voice squealed, "zombie! Zombie!"

Thomas cracked off a round toward the figure, and it uttered a strangled and hoarse cry and collapsed to the ground. Thomas screamed, "Newsome! Newsome! Zombies!" Then he started spinning in circles, waving his gun, a look of sheer terror on his face.

Thomas saw glinting green eyes within the brambles and was overcome by terror, firing off several more rounds. The eyes disappeared, and he saw something small and furry streak across the ground.

The back door of the funeral home shot open and Bubba and Newsome came running out, guns in hand. Behind them shuffled Yvgeny, still handcuffed. Thomas continued whirling around brandishing his weapon, eyes constantly flitting back to the prone figure. The deputies approached Thomas with caution, Yvgeny creeping right behind them, his face ashen.

From the ground, Alfred wailed, "nnngh! Nnngh

ngh!"

Newsome and Bubba stopped about ten feet from Thomas and Newsome called out, "Thomas! Put away your gun!"

"Alfred!" Yvgeny called out.

Yvgeny ran past the detectives and straight toward Alfred, who was on his stomach rolling one way and another, running his hands over his body, looking for extra holes.

Yvgeny fell to his knees, and inspected the manic form of his gravedigger. His hands were still cuffed behind him, and all he could do was look on with concern.

"Are you hurt? Did he get you? Alfred? Alfred!"

Eventually, Alfred calmed down, turned onto his back and stared up into the heavens.

Yvgeny inspected Alfred closely and, satisfied he was not injured, struggled to his feet and called out, "Congratulations, constable, you almost killed my gravedigger."

In a frantic voice, Thomas responded, "your what?"

The cat that had been hiding in the brambles raced toward Alfred and posted beside him. He hissed at Thomas.

"Gravedigger. One who digs graves."

Yvgeny stared balefully at Thomas, then turned to Alfred with a smile and said, "Don't be rude, say hello to our new friend."

Alfred fearfully watched Thomas holster his weapon, then carefully hauled himself up from the ground. A wave of foul odor wafted across the cemetery as he stood.

296

Thomas sniffed, buried his face into the crook of his arm, and asked in a muffled voice, "You sure he ain't a zombie?"

Just then, Nitro came trotting out of Alfred's shed with something in his mouth. He navigated around Alfred, who was still absently feeling around his body checking for holes.

The dog proudly paraded his treat in a circle around Thomas, tail wagging. All eyes were on Nitro as he wrenched his neck in violent circles as dogs like to do with a new toy. Then he uttered one play growl and laid down at Thomas's feet and began to gnaw on the object.

"New-some?" Thomas said, uttering each syllable separately as if each was its own word, and speaking his name as if it was a question. "Is that a . . . ."

Yvgeny squinted at the object, then looked over at Alfred and opened his eyes wide in surprise and said, "Alfred!"

Alfred looked aghast and started backpedaling as the dog chewed on the greenish rotting hand. Bubba and Newsome stared at the hand for a moment, then all eyes left Nitro's prize and converged on a panic stricken Alfred.

"Nnngh! Nngh! Ngh!"

Alfred raised his hands and took another step back, bumping into the side of his shed. Newsome held out a hand toward Alfred, palm down.

"Alfred, calm down, we can work this out. Don't do anything stupid. Come on, Alfred, be cool."

Newsome continued talking in a smooth, calm voice, slowly angling away from everyone to keep Alfred's attention from Bubba. While Newsome talked, Bubba slowly flanked Alfred, and a few seconds later, he was close enough to grab him.

Alfred stiffened when he felt Bubba's hands, but

Bubba subdued him quickly and handcuffed him without a struggle. In such close quarters, Alfred's scent was unbearable, and Bubba began to gag. He buried his mouth and nose in the crook of his free arm.

"Alfred, um," Bubba called out to Yvgeny, "what's his last name?"

Yvgeny shrugged and said, "I'm not even sure he has one."

Bubba muttered, "of course not," then called out, "Alfred the gravedigger, you are under arrest!"

Newsome turned around to find Thomas squinting at Alfred as if still not sure he was human.

"Hey Thomas, you mind grabbing that evidence before your dog finishes eating it?"

Thomas reached down, hesitated, then took his asp baton from his belt, flicked it open, then tapped it away from Nitro, who growled and tried to get it back. Thomas looked around desperately for something to pick it up with, then remembered his basket weave container attached to his belt near the small of his back. It took some minor contortions to get his hand close enough to reach inside, but eventually he made it and removed a pair of bright blue rubber gloves.

Newsome glanced at Bubba and said, "Watch them," then stepped into the shed. A couple minutes later, he came out with a white bucket and an axe.

Bubba had placed a handcuffed Alfred into a seated position on the ground, where he groveled and moaned as if suffering from some terrible disease. When he saw the bucket, he started to make strange, guttural noises deep in his throat. Thomas watched Alfred with growing alarm.

Newsome placed the bucket on the ground, and everyone moved closer to get a look inside. Neither Bubba nor Newsome stopped Yvgeny as he leaned forward and looked down into the bucket. He stared a moment, then looked over at Alfred, his face contorted in a mixture of pride and disappointment.

"Oh Alfred, why'd you have to keep souvenirs?"

╬

CHAPTER EIGHTEEN

Newsome and Bubba stuffed Alfred and Yvgeny into the back of their car, then rolled down all four windows. Yvgeny griped for most of the ride, complaining about the handcuffs, about the smell, about the egregious violations of his constitutional rights, while Alfred silently stared out the window, his eyes unfocused and watery.

Thomas had followed closely behind, but then suddenly turned off to head down another street. Newsome glanced in his rearview mirror when Thomas's headlights disappeared, and Bubba turned around in his seat and looked behind him.

"Where's he going?"

"Who cares?"

Newsome continued toward the jail without another word.

The streets were deserted at that late hour, allowing them to race through town to the jail in only a few minutes. They passed through the two sets of chain link fence, razor wire over the tops, and parked in the sally port.

After they parked, they secured their weapons in the trunk of their car, then walked Alfred and Yvgeny into the intake area and toward the counter, where two uniformed city policemen were hunched over scribbling out paperwork stacked on their aluminum clipboards.

The sergeant on duty glanced over at Newsome and Bubba, did a once over of their quarry, then made a face when he smelled Alfred.

"Jesus, Mary, and Joseph, Harry! What the hell did you bring me? Get him outta here!"

"Sorry Gunny, you gotta take this one."

"The hell I do! He's stinking up the whole damn pod! Whatcha catch him doing, sleeping on a park bench? Cut him loose with a ticket, he ain't staying here!"

"I got him for murder, Clay, he ain't going anywhere."

Sergeant Clayton Howell was a rigid former Marine with a flat top and no sense of humor. He froze a moment, then asked, softly, "He's the one that offed the old man?"

Newsome nodded.

Clay Howell nodded back at Newsome, then turned toward a group of young jailers huddled around a small television and yelled, "Hey kids, take this one to the showers. Scrub him down before we all go blind!"

As the jailers scrambled to take Alfred away, Howell turned to Yvgeny.

"And this one! Good Lord, Harry, you bust a costume party?"

Yvgeny puffed up with indignation and called out, "On the contrary, constable, I am a-"

"Can it, Dracula," Howell replied curtly, then turned back to Newsome.

"What's the story with *this* clown?"

Yvgeny turned red and struggled in his cuffs, while Newsome sighed and responded softly, "He's an accomplice."

Howell grinned at everyone and called out, "hot damn, boys, two killers right here in booking. Haven't had this much excitement since Rusty brought in that tranny from Atlanta!"

Newsome grabbed a clipboard from the counter with the necessary booking paperwork and turned to Yvgeny. A pen was tied to the clipboard with a string and swung back and forth like a pendulum.

One of the young jailers Howell had summoned came around from behind the counter, a pair of gloves in one hand. He motioned for Newsome to bring Yvgeny over to an area beside the counter, the floor marked with two large red footprint stickers.

"Right here, sir."

Yvgeny stood over the stickers, grumbling, while he waited for the jailer to remove his handcuffs. As the jailer began the search process, Newsome muttered, "Damn!"

"What's wrong?"

Newsome turned to Bubba and whispered, "Just remembered, that freak has a finger in his pocket."

Bubba stared at Newsome a moment, then said, "a what?"

"A finger. He cut it off his father when he died."

Bubba stared at Newsome, pokerfaced, then chuckled and turned toward the jailer performing the search. As they watched, the jailer worked his way to Yvgeny's front pants pocket, felt the lump, pinched it, manipulated it, then slowly reached in, closing his eyes.

"What the-!"

The jailer tossed it on the counter and screamed. Two more jailers came running, saw the finger, and froze.

Just then, the sound of a buzzer caused Newsome and Bubba to turn toward the door. Thomas stood within the sally port, and with another buzz, the inner door opened and Thomas waddled over to them. He looked on as several jailers huddled over the finger, now laying on its side on the counter. Yvgeny looked on with a smile.

"Well look what the wind blew in," Newsome muttered. Then in a louder voice, added, "Nice of you to join us. You get lost?"

Thomas ignored the jab with a sheepish smirk and took a spot against the counter to watch Yvgeny get searched.

"What's with them?" Thomas asked, as one jailer poked the finger with his pen.

"Long story."

The jailers all stared at the finger as if waiting for it to start crawling across the counter. The jailer who had found it was still shivering in disgust over having to touch it.

Howell watched his jailers with his own expression of disgust, then walked over, scooped up the finger with an ungloved hand, then dropped it into a large, clear plastic bag already containing Yvgeny's wallet, watch, and personal effects.

As the jailers watched in horror, Howell bore down on the property sheet with his pen and dictated out loud as he wrote, "one human finger, grayish-white in color." Then he turned to Newsome and called out, "He's all yours."

Newsome and Bubba walked Yvgeny toward an open holding cell and directed him to sit on the cot.

"Good as new!" They heard someone yell, then a moment later a smiling jailer paraded a wet, matted, but clean Alfred past Yvgeny's cell and into an adjoining one. Alfred was dressed in a dark green jumpsuit. On the back, in large white letters, were the words GILBERT COUNTY JAIL.

When Thomas saw Alfred, he shuffled backwards toward the far corner of Yvgeny's cell and reached into one of his pockets. A moment later, Newsome looked around and said, "You smell that?"

Bubba asked, "smell what?"

Newsome continued to sniff, then Bubba crinkled his nose and turned toward Newsome, an inquisitive look on his face. Yvgeny smelled it too, and eventually all three looked toward Thomas, who had shrunk into the corner.

"What did you do, Thomas, stop for Italian food?"

Bubba walked toward Thomas, sniffing periodically.

"I know that smell."

Thomas removed his hand from his pocket, revealing several head of garlic. He cast a sheepish glance toward them, then got defensive.

"Well, look at him! He's a zombie! I don't care what y'all think, I ain't taking no chances!"

Thomas continued squeezing the garlic, his manipulations filling the room with the pungent smell. Newsome closed his eyes and sighed, then announced, "Thomas, you idiot, garlic is for vampires. It don't work on zombies. Now go toss that crap in the trash and make yourself useful. Keep an eye on Yvgeny here while we go talk to your zombie."

Thomas put the garlic back in his pocket and

turned to face Yvgeny. As Thomas turned, Newsome saw something flash on Thomas's chest, and he took a step closer to confirm Thomas was wearing a crucifix on a chain around his neck, exposed on the outside of his uniform.

Newsome shook his head and said, "nope. Only vampires. Not zombies." Then Newsome turned and walked out of the cell, Bubba following him with a chuckle. Thomas squeezed the crucifix in his hands, eyes darting around in fear.

When they walked into Alfred's cell, he watched them intently, the pupils of his cloudy blue eyes large as saucers. Newsome held up his hands, palms toward Alfred, and tried to speak in a soothing voice.

"Woah, calm down, you look like a rubber band twisted all up. Cool your jets, we just want to talk."

Bubba kept his eyes on Alfred but whispered to Newsome, "more like a meth addict than a zombie, if you ask me."

The old gravedigger's Adam's apple began to bounce as if it was preparing to burst from his neck. One hand was handcuffed to a rail bolted into the wall, and the other was scrabbling at the mattress. He stared intently at each of them, one at a time, then everywhere else but them, as if looking for an escape route.

"Alfred, Geny says you can't talk. Is that true?"

Alfred, refusing to look at Newsome, did not react.

"Alfred, come on now, can you talk?"

Bubba leaned in to Newsome and whispered, "He's deaf. Pretty sure he reads lips."

Newsome stared at Alfred a moment, then leaned in and waved his hand so Alfred would see him. He looked up, stared at Newsome, frozen as if in *rigor mortis*. Newsome repeated his question, and Alfred nodded curtly.

"I see. Well, Alfred, did you chop that man's head off?"

Alfred vehemently shook his head. A grunt of sorts escaped from his throat, ending with a phlegmy accent.

Bubba leaned in toward Newsome and whispered, "Don't you need to read him his rights?"

Newsome smacked his knee and said, "Thanks, Bubba."

Newsome recited Miranda to Alfred, knowing the words by heart. Alfred stared at Newsome, motionless. Newsome shrugged.

"Anyway, Alfred, if you didn't do it, why'd you have some dead guy's head and hands in a bucket? Is that something you normally do?

Again, the old man shook his head so violently, something in his neck cracked.

"Maybe Geny did it. Did Geny chop him up?"

Shaking head.

"Did he use that axe we found?"

Shaking head.

"Well come on now, Alfred, if you didn't do it, and Yvgeny didn't do it, who did? Leprechauns? They were right there in your shed, in that bucket, ain't no way you didn't know they were there. So what's going on? Want me to get you a pencil? Maybe you can write it all down for me, explain to me what happened."

Alfred looked down, shook his head slowly, then raised one hand in a mixture of supplication and, *what else*, Newsome wondered. Then he figured it out. *Abjection.*

"You can't read or write, can you?"

Shaking head.

Newsome turned to Bubba, said, "Got any ideas?"

Bubba squinted and cocked his head at Alfred.

"Can Geny understand you?"

Alfred smiled and nodded his head vigorously. Something else cracked in his neck. His arm tugged on the handcuff which jangled against the eye hook bolted into the wall.

"You sure that's a good idea, Bubba? Ain't our theory that they're co-conspirators?"

Bubba shrugged and said, "Maybe they are, but this is some Helen Keller type shit here, so I don't reckon we got much of a choice."

Newsome held his pen in his thumb and index finger and tapped it rhythmically against the scarred wooden table beside the cot. He yawned, looked at his watch, then grunted and said, "fine," as he stood. Thomas, overcome by curiosity, had slowly wandered up to Alfred's cell and tentatively peeked around the cinder blocks, a pudgy hand grabbing one of the bars.

"Thomas, can you grab Geny?"

Thomas sighed and opened Yvgeny's cell door and beckoned for him to follow him. Thomas remained outside Alfred's cell, one hand in his pocket, the other fingering the cross around his neck. When Yvgeny arrived, Thomas motioned toward Alfred's cell with a neck snap, keeping his hands around his crucifix and his garlic. Thomas remained outside the cell.

When Yvgeny stepped into Alfred's cell, Newsome said, "Okay Geny, I don't like this at all, but it seems you're the only one that understands the guy. That true?"

Yvgeny ignored the deputies and scrutinized Alfred closely.

"Why, Alfred?"

"Nng, nnnghh! Ng, ng."

Alfred started yanking his handcuffed hand to and fro, struggling to move, until Newsome finally stood, reached over, and un-cuffed him. Thomas cringed and took a step back from the cell door and whispered, in a shrill, thready voice, "Newsome, are you crazy?"

"Nnngh! Ngh nnn ngggg!"

As soon as his hand was free, Alfred shook it out, rubbed his wrist, then stood. He started to wind mill his hands and made digging motions, then a series of pantomimes and grunts ensued. Yvgeny paid close attention, getting more irritated as Alfred motioned and grunted. Finally Yvgeny threw his hands in the air and yelled, "All this time? Alfred!"

"What's he saying?" Bubba interjected.

Yvgeny continued glaring at Alfred, who withered under the scrutiny.

"It appears he saw someone bury a bag with the hands and the head inside. In *my* cemetery. He waited for them to leave, then dug them up. With one of *my* shovels. Without even bothering to let *me* in on his big secret."

"Someone? Did he see who it was?"

Yvgeny, still glaring at Alfred, raised his eyebrows and said, "Well?" Alfred swallowed, then made another series of gestures.

"Nope. He only knows there were three of them."

Newsome and Bubba exchanged glances.

Yvgeny continued to stare at Alfred, then his face opened in surprise.

"Alfred, you stole that bottle of juice, didn't you?"

Alfred looked down at the table.

"For this?"

Alfred sat, frozen, then almost imperceptibly slumped and nodded his head.

"Oh, Alfred, do you know how hard it is to embalm a head?"

Alfred slumped further into the chair. Yvgeny turned to Newsome.

"So it appears my amateur undertaker here saw three people wandering through the headstones late the night before we found the body. He watched them dig a hole and bury something. Alfred waited for them to leave, then grabbed his shovel, without, I might add, informing me. When he realized the pieces were starting to rot, he tried to preserve them."

Newsome glanced at Alfred, who had started smacking the side of his head against the concrete block walls of the cell.

"And the body, what about that?"

Yvgeny dejectedly watched Alfred's response and nodded.

"Alfred, Alfred, Alfred, here I was quietly applauding your courage, your selfless act of vengeance. When they found those parts, I was so impressed! But no, the fact is, you were as surprised as me when you saw that body, weren't you?"

Alfred just smashed his head into the cinder blocks harder.

Yvgeny then stood and turned to Newsome. Straightening his morning coat, he said, "Well, inspector, no need to thank me, just kindly show me the door and I will take my leave."

"Are you kidding me?"

Aghast, Yvgeny cried, "I obviously had nothing to do with this."

"Obviously? How do I know you didn't kill him yourself?"

"Alfred just told you-"

"Alfred didn't tell me anything! You were the one doing all the talking."

"But-"

"Tell me about that axe, Yvgeny? Is it going to match the cuts on those parts?"

"You heard Alfred, he said-"

"No, all I heard was a bunch of grunts. The only person I heard talking was you!"

Newsome turned to Bubba and said, "Those parts need to get up to Kincaid. And that axe, too!"

Newsome and Bubba filed out of the cell. Yvgeny's mouth opened in surprise.

"You can't hold me! You have no evidence!"

Newsome spun around and shot, "the hell I don't! The body was in your cemetery, and the parts were in your friend's shed!"

"He's not my-"

"And you've been meddling in this investigation since the beginning!"

"I have not-"

"And besides, I can hold you for 48 hours without charges. I'd say loosen up, buttercup, you're gonna be here a while."

As the lawmen filed out of the cell, they heard Yvgeny say, "Good Lord, Alfred, this is the best you've smelled in twenty years."

Bubba waited a moment, then said in almost a whisper, "None of this makes any sense, Harry."

Newsome nodded, looked away, said, "I know," then added in a hiss, "but they're all full of crap, especially that damn undertaker."

"Yeah, but you think he killed the guy?"

"No, not really."

Thomas fidgeted, looking back at Alfred through the cell every few seconds.

"What about the old man?" Bubba asked.

Newsome shrugged his shoulders and said, "Not sure. What's his motive?"

"Hell if I know. Might help if we knew who the victim was."

"The techs should be on their way to Kincaid by now. Maybe we'll get lucky and get a hit on those prints. Maybe the axe will be a match, too."

All three nodded. Then Newsome looked at Bubba and asked, "you get some good pictures of that head? Maybe the rabbi can identify him."

"Not sure anyone would recognize him now."

Newsome looked at his watch, then glanced at Bubba and said, "Let's go."

Thomas tore his eyes away from Alfred and pushed off the bars and said, "I'm coming too."

"What for? All we're going to do is show the rabbi the picture."

"That church is in my county, not yours. You need

me."

"We really gonna do this again, Thomas?"

From down the hall, Yvgeny yelled, "It's a synagogue, not a church!"

A vein in Newsome's forehead that Bubba never noticed before began to pulsate. Without a word, Newsome stormed toward the double doors that led out to the sally port. Thomas and Bubba followed silently.

Newsome had started rubbing his stiff neck, and when they caught up to him, he rolled his eyes.

"It's late, I'm tired, and I'm going home and getting some rest. We can hit it again in the morning, starting with that rabbi. Thomas, look, we need someone to go to that strip mall where the synagogue is and show around that head shot, maybe somebody will recognize him."

Thomas squinted at Bubba and Newsome, one at a time, as if searching for a trick, then nodded slowly.

"Fine. Text me the pic. But if that perp starts talking, you tell me immediately. Deal?"

"Sure, Thomas, deal."

╬

The next morning, Newsome and Bubba visited the rabbi at his home around 8:00. He was still dressed in his bathrobe when he opened the door. When he saw Newsome he closed his eyes and muttered, "*oi vay.*"

"You mind if we come in?"

"I just woke up. Haven't we had enough excitement

for one lifetime?"

"It's important."

"Forgive me deputy, but I believe I have said all that I need to say."

"Rabbi, we just need for you to look at a picture. Tell me if he looks familiar."

The rabbi paused, then breathed, "very well." He waited while Bubba thumbed through his phone, then zoomed in on the photograph. He held it out to the rabbi, who craned his neck forward to look. He grimaced and turned away.

"*Gevalt! Y*es, that's him. That is the man that was harassing us."

"You know his name?"

"No idea. Now if you please, I would like to shut this door."

They let the rabbi shut the door, then returned to their car.

"Now what?"

Newsome smiled, leaned back in the seat, and said, "Now we are going to start making some progress. I can feel it!"

Bubba rubbed his eyes, reached for the tin in his back pocket and shrugged, said, "You ever think maybe the rabbi did it? I mean, all that blood back there, the dog and all."

Newsome snorted, glanced over at Bubba with a grin and said, "sure, why not? Maybe it was a battle for turf. Or a fight over a prostitute."

Still smiling, Newsome felt his phone vibrating and checked it. It was a text message, and as he read it, he muttered an expletive.

"The Crawford County Sheriff just cut the old man

loose."

Bubba nodded, but remained silent. As Newsome replaced his phone on his belt it vibrated again.

"And the captain just cut Yvgeny loose, said we didn't have anything on him. Alfred too!"

Newsome stared straight ahead, then smacked the steering wheel with a curse. He looked over at Bubba and said, "That idiot had the guy's head in a damn bucket!" He paused, then blew out his breath in a rush and said, "All the sheriff cares about is how much it's going to cost to keep these perps in a cell."

Bubba waited a moment while Newsome tried to calm himself.

"What now?"

Newsome looked at his watch, started the car.

"Now we get some coffee. Then we go to Macon. Kick Kincaid in the ass, make sure he doesn't dawdle."

"Can't we just call him on the phone?"

"Sure, but you know how he is."

╬

Yvgeny had a taxi take them to the impound yard so he could get Cerberus back. He directed Alfred to sit up front with the driver, an elderly man with a crew cut and a scar over one eye. He didn't blink when they got into the car; his expression made it clear there was no longer anything on earth that could surprise him.

On the way, his mother called him on his mobile

phone to nag him about his preparations for Maude. He let her rant, then promised her everything would be perfect. He checked his watch again. And everything *would* be perfect. He had set in motion a funeral that would become the yardstick by which all future funerals would be measured.

He debated calling Channel 7 for the scoop, but in the end decided some might find it in poor taste. And, as an added treat, Brianna would be there by his side. It was going to be the greatest moment of his life.

Despite everything that had happened in the previous couple days, Yvgeny couldn't help but smile as he gazed out the window and thought about the days to come.

He tried to maintain his sunny disposition when he emerged from the cab and stepped on a piece of Rocko's day old sausage. He even took a deep breath and maintained his smile when the solid woman behind the desk of the impound office looked up at him and cried out, "Damn, is it Halloween already? Seems like it gets earlier every year."

While Alfred shuffled back and forth outside, the woman began to scribble on some yellow carbon copy paperwork. Yvgeny took a deep breath, grinding his teeth behind his smile.

Yvgeny even managed to remain silent when, in the process of compiling the huge stack of useless papers, the woman looked back up and added, "and a hearse, too, man, you go all out. I had no idea you could rent them! Must be a hell of a party."

Yvgeny handed her his car keys, snatched the papers, and marched out of the office to wait until someone brought Cerberus outside the fence. As he and Alfred got inside, Yvgeny turned to him and said, "Whoever said 'let a smile be your umbrella' was a damn fool."

When Yvgeny returned home he found his mother waiting for him in the doorway. Alfred saw her waiting, glanced at Yvgeny, then scurried away through the carport and into the back yard toward his shed. Yvgeny took a deep breath.

"My son, the convict."

"Mama, it was a false arrest."

"Sure, the police meant to arrest some other undertaker."

"They had no evidence."

"No evidence? That's the response of a guilty man. What did you do?"

"I did nothing."

"Hmph."

"I'm the victim of an overzealous inspector."

They stared at each other a moment, then she changed the subject.

"Maude's been on ice too long. And you left your trocar stuck in her. Have some respect for the dead."

"She's dead. What does she care?"

"Ach! Your father, God rest his soul, he never would leave a tool sticking in someone. It's not right."

Yvgeny had used up all his patience at the impound yard; he had nothing left for his mother.

"Mama, do you want me to finish her, or argue about her? Relax, everything be perfect." Then he added, with a smirk, "It's going to be a very special event."

His mother squinted at him and said in a low voice, "and why is it going to be so special? What are you not telling me?"

Yvgeny just smiled at her, so she turned and stormed off, her cane clacking on the floor. As she took the stairs, Yvgeny heard pounding from outside, and followed his ears into the yard and over to Alfred's shed, where he found the old gravedigger pacing and occasionally stopping to pound his head against the tin walls. To Yvgeny's surprise, Alfred's scent was already starting to blossom again.

"Alfred, what in the world are you doing?"

Alfred continued to pace, stopping only to cast an angry glance toward Yvgeny.

"I don't know what's gotten into you, but your little stunt made us both suspects in a murder. Why would you hang on to the head? And the hands? Are you nuts?"

Alfred put his hands on his hips, defiant.

"And they took Gertrude!"

Alfred watched Yvgeny's lips as he spoke. Then he grunted loudly and motioned to Yvgeny, mimicking someone unbuttoning and removing a shirt. Then he gave Yvgeny another hard look, and motioned with one hand to the other wrist, circling his fingers around the wrist, pretending to remove something, then held it up to his ear. Then, with a toothy smile, Alfred mimicked placing the invisible watch back on his wrist.

"I see. I suppose we have both been less than forthcoming."

Alfred crossed his arms over his chest again, smirking and raising his eyebrows.

"Were you telling the truth about three people burying those parts?"

Alfred nodded.

"You couldn't see them at all?"

Alfred pursed his lips but did not otherwise dignify the question with a response.

Yvgeny left the shed and began to pace up and down his driveway, trying to sort out the events of the previous couple days. Alfred wandered out of the shed after Yvgeny, then stood watching him pace.

Surely Alfred didn't have the wherewithal to kill a man. And he certainly didn't have enough sense to lie about it!

Three people, Yvgeny thought, *three people and a righteous killing.* But for Yvgeny, it didn't change anything. He had to find the killers before the police and warn them, give them at least a chance. The question was, *who were they?*

Yvgeny finally stopped pacing and checked his watch. With a sigh, he turned back to Alfred.

"Well, Alfred, I suppose that's all for now. Promise me the next time you find body parts that aren't in the right place, you will tell me *first*, yes?"

Yvgeny wandered the house, eventually returning to his workroom. He shut the door quietly, then locked it. Maude was in the corner where he left her, and he sighed. *Duty calls.* He grasped his trocar and finished her, but he was distracted, his body doing the work while his mind crunched on the body in the hole, the three suspects, the police.

He corked her and checked for leaks, only vaguely registering that she appeared water tight. He still had to dress her and put on a little makeup, but that could wait until morning.

He realized suddenly, *it was almost Friday!*

Brianna had hesitated when he first made his pitch, but he wore her down with his persistence, overcoming every roadblock she placed in front of him like Clarence Darrow in court.

"I don't want to see Ms. Oliver like this," she had said.

"Like what? Wait until you see her. You'll think you've gone back in time!"

"But what will the family think?" Brianna had countered.

"My dear Brianna, the family will think you are an excellent usher and a lovely addition to the staff."

"But what about your mother?"

"What about Mama? She will complain and criticize as always, but that's just her way of expressing approval. Just tell her you plan on keeping an eye on the caterers. That will cinch it."

"But what if they think it's a date?" she asked, one eye raised, in her final challenge.

"Why would they think that? Nobody will have a clue unless you got frisky with the master of ceremonies! Is that what you have planned?" Yvgeny said with a sly grin.

Brianna punched him in the shoulder, hard, and his arm throbbed for an hour afterwards.

The truth was, of course, nobody would be paying any attention to her, because they will all be too busy *staring at my handiwork.*

Ah, Maude, my Mona Lisa. You look twenty years younger, even better than you looked when you were alive!

✠

CHAPTER NINETEEN

Newsome rounded the corner to find Rosy sipping something out of a silver flask. When she saw him, she tried to hide the flask, fumbling to replace the cap. In her haste, the cap flew from her grasping fingers, rolled across the desk and bounced to the floor with a *tink* at Newsome's feet.

"Damn, Rosy, it's barely 10 am."

Rosy blushed, then snapped, "You try working here with *him* all day."

Just then, Bubba rounded the corner to stand beside Newsome, and found the two of them staring at each other in what appeared to be suspended animation. Bubba saw the cap at Newsome's feet, crouched to pick it up and place it on the desk, then he cleared his throat and turned to Newsome.

"Um, Harry, is Kincaid here?"

Without looking at Bubba, Newsome said, "I don't know, let's ask Rosy. Rosy, is Kincaid here?"

Rosy finally broke her stare and looked down.

"He's with a customer. Client. Patient. Whatever."

"Mind if we pay him a visit?"

Rosy shrugged and pointed down the hall with a thumb, saying, "OR 2. On the right."

They followed her finger down the hall for about twenty feet, then pushed in the swinging doors just in time to see the old doctor holding up a liver, raising and lowering his hand rapidly while looking up to the ceiling. Then he unceremoniously plopped it onto the scale, where it landed with a wet thud. He squinted at the scale, then shook his fist in the air and yelled, "Yes!" then pressed his mouth against the microphone hanging down over the body. It swung away from his mouth, then bounced against it several times. He waited for it to come to rest against his lips, then announced, "liver is. . . . about 3.6 pounds."

He reached into the body again, and fished around for something else. Bubba turned somewhat pale, but Newsome looked on, stone faced, then walked in, his shoes squeaking on the linoleum. Kincaid started talking without looking up.

"Did you hear that Rosy? I guessed three and a half. I was close! Hey listen, Rosy, I need you to go get me something to drink. I like those Mr. Pibbs in the machine."

The doctor began smacking his lips as he continued digging into the abdomen of the body on his table, then cleared his throat and added, "Yes, a Mr. Pibb, I have some money here in my pocket, why don't you just come stick your hand in and find it. Come on, I have blood all over me, don't be shy."

"I ain't sticking my hand in there, Kincaid."

The old doctor jumped backwards at Newsome's voice, his hand still clutching one end of the cadaver's intestines. The organ began unraveling from the body as he glared at Newsome, and finally reached the end and slopped onto the floor.

"Jesus, Newsome, look what you made me do."

Kincaid stared at the heap of intestines on the floor and sighed. He walked over to the corner of the room and retrieved what appeared to be an aluminum cane with a pistol grip on one end and a claw on the bottom. The words *EZ Grabber* were painted in large black letters up its side. Someone had fixed a rubber glove around the four ends of the claw, which left the thumb hanging from the side like an udder.

Returning with his EZ Grabber, he clamped down on a section of intestine, then carefully lifted it to waist level. He grabbed the loose end, then gathered up the rest, hand over hand, shoving it back into the body.

When he finished, Kincaid pulled off his rubber gloves, grabbed his EZ Grabber, and walked stiffly past them toward the hallway, grumbling to himself. As they followed him into the hall, Kincaid asked, "So why are you here? Don't tell me you got another body. Just send it to Atlanta. I'm goin' fishin' right after lunch."

"Nope, we're still waiting on a report on those body parts we sent up here. Figured we'd come check on them."

The doctor stared at Newsome, uncomprehending. A few seconds later he nodded in recognition, and lifted his claw, pointing it at Newsome as if it was a shotgun.

"Let me get this straight. You send some cop up here in the middle of the night with a damn head in a bucket, make me drive my old black ass up here to throw it in the freezer, and here you are the next morning asking me if I've had a chance to make a report?"

Kincaid started squeezing the handle of the claw,

emphasizing his words by snapping the plastic grabbers together at Newsome.

"Hell no, I ain't looked at them. They killed two more since you sent that damn bucket up here, and do you see anyone else around here to chop 'em up? Your old man is old news!"

"Damn, Kincaid, you're a real gem this morning."

They followed Kincaid back to the cold storage room where he began opening lockers, looking inside, then slamming them shut.

"You forget where you put them again?"

Kincaid only grumbled in response.

Finally, he opened a locker and grunted in satisfaction. He pulled out the tray and grabbed one of the hands with his own bare hand, inspected the fingers, then sniffed it.

"Formaldehyde? Someone pickled this thing."

He looked back down at the fingers again, more carefully this time, running a finger along the pads.

"Yeah, they're still good. I'll roll them and send them off. Should be back within the week."

"A week? You gotta put a rush on them. I got three suspects and they've all been cut loose from jail. They could be in Tijuana by then!"

"They could be in Tijuana already, cowboy."

Kincaid looked back down at the amputated hand, biting his lower lip, then said, "Well, if it means that much to you I can put a rush on them. Sometimes they can run them in a few hours."

The doctor tossed the hand back on the table, rummaged through the locker, then called out, "Jesus, Newsome, somebody tried to embalm the head! You know how hard that is?"

"Long story."

Kincaid slid the head closer, then rolled it over to pry open the mouth and peer inside. Then he whistled and said, "Look at all that dental work. Some dentist got a new BMW out of this guy's mouth."

"So a few hours?"

Without looking up from the head, the doctor said, "Maybe so. Go relax. Eat a donut, or whatever it is you cops do when you ain't harassing poor old pathologists."

‡

Yvgeny approached the coffin, secured to a special frame shrouded behind purple velvet. He crouched down to check the special equipment hidden beneath. Everything appeared in order. He overcame his urge to test it all one more time, then paced back and forth, rubbing his knuckles.

There was much on his mind. First, he was filled with righteous indignation; he felt a moral obligation to find the killers and warn them the posse was coming. The facts all pointed to one conclusion: it was a righteous slaying, a biblically defensible death. He had to identify the killers before the inspectors and give them a head start from the cops.

He also was anxious about the Maude Oliver job. It was probably the biggest funeral he'd sponsored in years, bigger than any of the Dunlaps, and with the special surprise he had prepared, it would make the newspapers. Maybe the Macon Telegraph. Perhaps even the Atlanta Daily Journal! People will be lining up outside with their bodies to have the same treatment! He will have to hire extra hearse drivers.

I could leave flyers taped to the doors of every pizza delivery joint in Gilbert County. Who wouldn't jump at the opportunity! He began to consider names for the new hearses. *Charon* would be grand! *Tartarus* would also be a winner.

Finally, he was anxious about Brianna being there, by his side. The lovely Brianna, his muse, his Irene Adler. *Yes, everything must be perfect!*

He sighed as he realized that for now, the killer would have to wait. He needed all his attention and efforts focused on Maude's funeral. The whole town would be there. *Maybe even the killers themselves!"*

He checked his watch again, then went out to Alfred's shed, where he found him sitting in his ratty lawn chair picking at his nails with the sharp end of a spade. Alfred glanced up when he noticed the shadow Yvgeny cast in the doorway.

"Alfred, we only have an hour before guests start arriving. Let's set Maude up in the viewing area, then start placing the chairs. And remember, Maude needs to be near the outlet in the corner. And be careful with her!"

Alfred just stared at him, spade in hand, then returned to digging at his nails. Yvgeny flexed at the waist and waved a hand in front of Alfred's face to get his attention again.

"And while you're at it, Alfred, why don't you get some soap and get cleaned up. Half the damn town will be here."

Alfred pursed his lips, then returned to his nails. Yvgeny watched him a moment longer, took a breath to scold him, then changed his mind and left with an eye roll.

He returned just in time to hear his mother yelling

for him.

"*Tygrysek,* where have you been? The caterers just pulled up, and where the hell are the chairs? Guests will be coming in an hour, and look at you! Half the town is going to be here. Are you wearing *that?*"

Yvgeny stepped around her and inside.

"Everything's fine, Mama. Alfred is on it."

"Alfred? Your father would never. . . ."

Yvgeny kept walking as his mother continued to rail, and shut the door to his study to tune her out.

Thirty minutes later he emerged, scrubbed, dressed in his best Victorian finery, and navigated around six caterers in the kitchen to get into the main room. He stopped suddenly, then returned to the kitchen and grabbed his special cans. *Need to put them somewhere safe.*

After hiding the cans, he returned to the main room, where the flowers had all been arranged by the windows, and Alfred, despite his cavalier attitude, had begun setting up the chairs. He was chagrined to notice Alfred had not made any effort to clean himself up.

Maude was parked in a moderately priced split-lid poplar affair made by Navajo Caskets in Florida. The owner gave him a discount; meeting him was the only positive highlight of his attendance at the mortician's conference in Atlanta.

He kept the lid closed during set up, as exposure to air sped up bacteria growth and he didn't want to take any unnecessary risks. Maude had lots of friends of a similar vintage, and he had a stack of business cards in his pocket he intended to pass out to all those future clients before they left.

Yvgeny checked his watch, then checked it again. One hour to go. *Brianna would arrive any minute.* He zipped from one corner of the room to the other, checking the layout of the chairs, adjusting the bouquets of flowers, then stopping to check his hair in the mirror. Behind him, in the reflection, his mother appeared with her usual dour expression.

"What is *she* doing here?"

His heart jumped in his chest. *She's here!* He turned to see Brianna hoisting herself out of her little coffin on wheels, cigarette sticking out of the corner of her mouth. His jaw dropped as he examined her skin tight black sheath dress, her curves reminding him of a windy dark road, or, no, he thought, like a wiggly roller coaster! She took one more long drag on her cigarette, then chucked it out into the lawn.

"Ugh! That trollop's not coming in here looking like *that*!"

"Yes, Mama, yes she is. There's going to be eighty guests here. Are *you* going to greet 'em and seat 'em?"

"Yvgeny, you know I don't-"

"That's what I thought. And remember when I asked about hiring two ushers?"

"You know that's a waste of money, and we can't afford-"

"Exactly. So unless you want to bring over your canasta playing grannies to usher people to their seats, I suggest you re-evaluate the necessity of having her here."

Yvgeny didn't wait for a response, but jogged past her to the door, opening it just in time.

"Ravishing, Brianna, simply ravishing. Your grandfather would be proud."

Brianna looked past Yvgeny at all the chairs, then

over at the flowers.

"I can't believe you call this a date."

Yvgeny took the bait.

"Would you prefer something dull and pedestrian, perhaps some crummy restaurant and a crappy glass of wine? Or wait, what about a quiet evening at home where I make you spaghetti and rent a movie?"

Yvgeny spread his arms wide, turned in a circle, and announced, "or would you like to be the center of attention surrounded by people captivated by your date as he brings the dead back to life?"

Brianna watched him with her mouth open, then stepped inside, clutching her bag in both hands.

"You are one weird dude. I'm only here because Ms. Oliver was my fifth grade teacher and I liked her."

Yvgeny, feeling frisky, whispered, "and you like me."

Brianna struggled to hide her smile, but he saw it.

"Maybe I'm just curious to see you in action."

"Wait until you see my work."

He imagined her in his Goliath Galaxy, in that black dress, with him snuggled at her side.

"Aren't you going to introduce us, *tygrysek*?"

Yvgeny pressed his lips together in irritation.

"Who?" Brianna asked.

His mother's mouth opened in a pointy toothed smile.

"My *tygrysek*, my little tiger! He used to love it when I called him that, didn't you sweetheart?"

Yvgeny steeled himself.

"Brianna, this is my Mother."

"Pleased to meet you."

"Of course you are. Now right this way, Yvgeny tells me you will be helping out, so I need you over here . . . ."

His mother spirited her away, but not before turning to give him one more angry glare. Yvgeny watched them leave; well, mostly he watched Brianna leave, her body rolling and rocking like high tide in a fleshy ocean.

Everything is going to be just perfect, Yvgeny thought to himself.

Guests started arriving soon after. Brianna remained near the door, offering her arm to the elderly men before seating them, and Mark Oliver, Maude's adult grandson, took care of the women.

Yvgeny watched the place fill up while guarding Maude, his hand resting on the lid to make sure nobody got curious. He fingered the remote, having memorized each button and their purpose, then dropped it into his pocket.

Yvgeny glanced at Mama standing in the hall, catching her staring at Brianna with a sneer of contempt. Her stare was broken only when her eyes were pulled away by the raucous din of the caterers in the kitchen.

Some guests, never having been to Schmidt and Sons before, never having seen Yvgeny before, froze when they entered. Yvgeny smiled at them, his top hat slanted at a rakish angle.

Yvgeny checked the time again. Fifteen minutes. He fished around in his pocket, pushed his father's mummified finger out of the way, then with a sly smile pressed the big button without removing the remote from his pocket. The sound of gentle piano music emerged from speakers recessed into the ceiling.

Brianna left her post by the door to take a smoke, and Yvgeny's mother watched her leave, then turned to glare at Yvgeny with her hands on her hips. As he stared outside at Brianna with her cigarette, he saw behind her an old man walking toward the door accompanied by three teenagers. It was the rabbi. *Why is he here?*

Yvgeny hurried across the room and met them at the door as they arrived. The rabbi saw the confused expression on Yvgeny's face, and motioned for the teenagers accompanying him to find seats. Yvgeny glanced at them as they passed, then turned to the rabbi. The rabbi spoke first.

"Maude used to give piano lessons. I drove my grandson down once a week, with his friend there," he added, nodding toward one of the other teens. "Nice lady."

"I see."

"I've never been to a *goy*; sorry, a Christian funeral. I trust it will be a tasteful affair?" the rabbi asked, then stole a quick glance up at Yvgeny's top hat.

"Of course. It will be a mixture of old world charm and modern science. Wait until you see her."

"Viewings are not one of our traditions."

Yvgeny grinned and said, "Ah, then you're in for a real treat!"

Yvgeny looked down at his watch, then puffed up and said, "Well, duty calls!"

Brianna returned, and Yvgeny winked at her, then walked across the room to reclaim his post beside Maude. Maude's great granddaughter was picking flowers from one of the bouquets, and Yvgeny nudged her with his foot. She turned to look up at him, then over at the casket.

"Hey, what's in the box?"

Yvgeny looked around in each direction, then looked down at her and whispered, "your great grandmother."

The little girl screamed and ran back to her chair. Yvgeny fixed a Cheshire cat smile on his face and held up his hands.

"Let us begin."

☩

"You ever seen this guy?"

Thomas stood on the sidewalk beside the synagogue's door, accosting each passerby, flashing his mobile phone and demanding they take a look. He left his car parked in the fire lane, with Nitro punctuating every conversation with frustrated barks.

Thomas stood in the center of the sidewalk, effectively obstructing all foot traffic; there was little chance for anyone to avoid seeing his digital photograph of the decapitated and partially embalmed head.

While shoving his phone into the faces of two cringing teenagers, the photograph disappeared and a large icon of a telephone replaced it.

"Thomas?"

"Hi Amanda. You sound particularly lovely today."

"Up yours, T-Bone."

"Come on Mandy, you know I'm your favorite."

There was a moment of silence, which Thomas took for agreement.

"That's why you called me on the phone instead of over the radio. You know, after work we should-"

"Jesus Thomas, keep it in your pants, I used the phone because you didn't respond on your damn radio. I've been trying to raise you for ten minutes."

Thomas reached down and fumbled with the knobs on his portable radio and was surprised to find it was off.

"Listen, they found something, and they want you to bring that dog back."

"Really? What did they find?"

"How the hell would I know? I'm sitting here in Dispatch."

"Ah, Dispatch, I will stop by later, Mandy, I can take a hint."

Mandy let out a growl of frustration, then hung up the phone. Thomas smiled, then hustled back to his patrol car, holding up his gun belt with both hands as he jogged.

╫

CHAPTER TWENTY

During their drive back to Gilbert County, Newsome received a text message. Newsome squinted to try to read it, cursed, then handed the phone to Bubba.

"Bubba, I can't read this without my glasses. What's it say?"

"Let's see here, Grandpa," Bubba said, then scanned the text and snorted.

"'T got called back to the old man's house, they're actually using that dog again. They got a blood trail.'"

"What took them so long?"

Newsome and Bubba headed straight for the old man's house and pulled into the gravel driveway, walked past the trailer, across the weed covered back yard, and joined Thomas standing beside the stump, accompanied by several crime scene techs. The old man who lived there had settled into a dingy lawn chair a few yards away, beer in hand. Thomas smiled sheepishly when he saw them glance in the old man's direction.

"He's fine. My sheriff smoothed it all over. But we're gonna hold on to his shotgun until we're done."

Newsome nodded.

"Great crew you got here. Took them all night to find a blood trail?"

"Well, the on-duty magistrate was drunk, so it took them a while to find someone else to sign the warrant."

"You got a search warrant for a tree stump?"

"Sarge said it's within the curtilage, so we needed to make it legit."

"The guy gave consent."

"Yeah. He revoked it when his hip started hurting at the jail and the nurse wouldn't give him an aspirin."

Newsome sighed.

"So what's the story?"

"After we got the warrant, they sprayed Hemaglow around the stump, found a few drops leading off to the south, but they couldn't find any more. They waited for daylight, then called me to see if Nitro could come back."

"I let him sniff the blood they found, then we let him go. Anywhere he sniffed, they sprayed. Found a trail of blood leading right back to the street outside the rabbi's house."

"Does it match the blood on the stump?"

"Dunno. Once you spray it, you can't type it anymore."

"You go talk to him yet?"

"Nope."

"Does he know you were there?"

"I don't think anyone's home."

Newsome turned to Bubba and said, "What do you

think? Do we get a warrant now, or go find him first?"

Bubba turned to Thomas and asked, "Who is the magistrate on duty today? You know him?"

Thomas checked his watch, then looked up into the air, counted with the fingers of one hand.

"Um, I think it's Welch."

"What's he like?"

"We call him Welch the Squelch."

Newsome gave a curt nod and said, "Well, that settles it. Let's go."

Thomas whistled for Nitro and followed Newsome and Bubba back toward the gravel driveway. Newsome turned toward Thomas with a raised hand, then instead looked at Bubba, resignation on his face. Bubba nodded.

"It *is* his county, Harry."

╫

"Let us begin."

As the guests found their seats, Yvgeny stood smiling, hands clasped behind his back, his right hand clenching the remote that would launch Schmidt and Sons into the stratosphere.

Visions of book deals and news exclusives danced before his eyes. *Perhaps a made for television movie. No! A cable TV series!*

He glanced at Brianna, and swelled with pride as he watched her escort an old man to his seat. She placed him beside the rabbi and three teenagers.

He imagined them together in Hollywood, waving to his adoring fans at the release of the pilot episode of his cable TV series. He already had the perfect title: *His and*

Hearse.

Everything was coming together, and he felt the need to pinch himself to return to earth.

As he waited for everyone to take their seats, he caught flashes of his mother still policing the caterers from the hallway.

Yvgeny took a quick head count, then calculated the cost of the affair, factored in the fee he charged for his services, then tried to estimate the profit. He started in the front row and worked his way back, ending with the rabbi and his three teenagers.

Yvgeny squinted, staring at the boys in their chairs. Something nagged at him, like that feeling one gets when they leave home and wonder whether they left the oven on. He lost his count, and started over.

Just then, the front door swung open with too much force, smashing the doorknob into the wall. It sounded like a pistol blast, and several of the elderly guests reflexively shot their arms up to cover their faces.

Rocko lurched inside, his eye wide open, as if the door scared him, too, then he hurried to close it. He wore military fatigues with a faded blue oxford and plaid bow tie that lay crooked at his neck. He wore muddy combat boots. He scanned the crowd, his cheeks red with embarrassment, then shimmied through the seated guests toward the back of the room.

As master of ceremonies and the emcee, it was time for Yvgeny to start the show.

"Family, friends, students, neighbors, thank you all for coming. We have a great show for you this afternoon, all in memory of Maude Oliver, mother, wife, grandmother, great-grandmother, teacher, and friend."

Yvgeny turned toward the opposite corner, where he had arranged for five of Comstock Middle School's greatest musicians to perform a few tasteful and appropriate songs.

Yvgeny's first choice was Frank Sinatra's *My Way*. The boys and girls brought up their instruments: two flutes, a trumpet, clarinet, and a trombone, and in unison they took deep breaths and began playing.

One of the flutes was slightly out of tune, and the trombone player wasn't sure of some of the notes, but Yvgeny maintained his smile and evaluated the audience. It appeared they tolerated it, causing Yvgeny's smile to broaden even further.

That little great idea saved me over $800!

He panned over to Brianna, who shifted in her seat to get more comfortable. The chair beside her was empty. *His* chair.

He heard a snort come from the back of the room; the old man he had watched Brianna escort had fallen asleep, his head canted back as if he was staring at the ceiling. All three of the teenagers beside him turned as one to look at the snoring old man.

Yvgeny turned back toward Maude's coffin. It wasn't just an ordinary split lid affair; it was special. As Sinatra played on, Yvgeny unlocked the head piece of the coffin and lifted it up and over, removing the top half like the t-tops of an old Camaro.

He placed the lid against the wall and positioned the coffin so Maude's feet were facing the crowd. Upon exposing her to the air, Yvgeny risked a quick visual inspection of her face- she looked perfect.

Beneath the lower section of the lid and away from prying eyes, Maude was securely strapped in for the last ride of her life.

With a smile, he turned to face the crowd, then

nodded toward the back, where the local pastor had been waiting with his mother. The pastor, however, was busy whispering in his mother's ear.

As Yvgeny watched, whatever the pastor whispered caused her to blush. She was completely oblivious to the caterers and everything else around her.

Yvgeny hadn't seen her smile that way since before he lost his father, and as the song came to an end, all Yvgeny could do was stare. After a few seconds of silence, with all eyes on Yvgeny, he stammered out, "and now, a few words from Pastor Michaelson. Pastor?"

The pastor's head shot up and around toward the crowd as they all craned their necks to see him approach. His mother abruptly started smoothing out her dress with one hand, the other clutching her cane.

The pastor approached Yvgeny, shook his hand, then turned to the crowd. Yvgeny gave him the floor, and strolled over to his rightful place beside his muse, who leaned in to whisper in his ear.

"Jesus, if I don't get a cigarette soon I'm going to kill someone."

Yvgeny patted her hand and said, "That's lovely, dear, we can always use more business."

Still smiling, Yvgeny scanned the crowd, lingering again on the rabbi and his entourage. Something continued to bug him about the kids, but he couldn't place it, especially given his preoccupation with making Maude's event perfect.

What am I missing?

╫

Thomas knocked on the door several times while the detectives stood to one side. Nitro sniffed around the stoop, then lay down with his chin on his paws, bored. When nobody answered the door, Bubba walked around the perimeter, looking into all the windows, then came back and shook his head at Newsome.

Newsome cursed and said, "Forget it. We're gonna have to get that damn warrant."

Thomas shrugged and said, "how about exigent circumstances?"

"Nah, the guy's dead already."

"Well, we can wait a while, maybe he's just gone grocery shopping."

But Newsome was already shaking his head.

"No, no, we still need the warrant. You really think he's going to consent to us tearing up his house?"

Bubba pushed on his dip with his tongue, then shrugged and turned toward the car. While Thomas tried to coax Nitro off the stoop, Bubba elbowed Newsome in the side, and winked.

Newsome followed Bubba away from the stoop, then whispered, "Whatever you're thinking, I don't like it."

Bubba just smiled in response, then walked back toward Thomas.

Bubba, hands in pockets, sniffed and said, "OK, Thomas, I guess let us know when you get that warrant. Welch, right? Better make sure you give him all the details, you know, start at the beginning, tell him everything Kincaid found, OK? Don't give him the chance to kill it!"

Thomas's eyes darted between Newsome and Bubba, suddenly frantic.

"Wait, what? Wait a minute, me? I can't write that!"

Bubba cocked his head in feigned confusion.

"What do you mean, Thomas? This is *your* county, not *ours*! How you expect us to do it?"

"Well, I don't know, but, no, wait, I can't write it, it's, it's, well, you have to do it!"

Bubba glanced over at Newsome, who was smiling and shaking his head. Bubba adopted a serious and concerned expression and kicked at the dirt with a toe.

"Well, I guess we could go try to do it, then tell you what happens?"

Thomas, suddenly agreeable, nodded vigorously, and said, "Yes, yes, that's a much better idea, seeing as you have all the facts and stuff. Yes, let's do that. I will tell you where he sits."

"And meanwhile, maybe you can gather the posse to handle the search?"

"Of course! Consider it done!"

After they returned to the car and shut the doors, Newsome turned to Bubba and said, "See? I told ya you were a damn genius."

╬

Welch the Squelch was a short, hairy, balding man who looked more like a troll than a human. He sat behind a 1990s era clear plastic desk with black legs. Hanging behind him was a silver bamboo-style framed Nagel print.

The man wore a turtle-neck that accentuated his

chins and large gut, and a corduroy blazer, threadbare around the cuffs. One of the imitation leather elbow pads had lost part of its stitching and was hanging open, revealing an oval section of corduroy three shades darker than the rest of the blazer.

The first few minutes were spent convincing Welch they had standing to swear out a warrant outside their own county, and it went downhill from there.

"You want to search what? A rabbi's house? Are you crazy?"

"There's a trail of human blood leading to his house."

"But that could mean anything!"

"Really? What does a trail of human blood mean to you?"

Welch flipped through the pages, then his eyes widened.

"Yvgeny? The undertaker? That's Aneta's boy!"

Newsome and Bubba exchanged a glance, then Newsome cleared his throat and said, "Aneta?"

Welch's cheeks colored, and he stammered out an unintelligible response. Then he picked up the affidavit and thumbed through the pages, this time more slowly. While doing so, he rhythmically shook his head as if he could, with the movement alone, automatically and prospectively deny any request made of him.

"I don't know. I really don't see enough here for probable cause."

Still shaking his head, he squared the affidavit in the middle of his desk with his hands.

"Well, usually judges actually *read* an affidavit before they deny it. Isn't that what judges do?"

The magistrate stopped shaking his head and

looked up.

"Don't get smart with me, young man."

He stared at Bubba a moment longer, then turned to Newsome.

"Give me an hour to review it. Then come back."

╬

The pastor finished his sermon, then, after getting a confirmatory nod from his mother, Yvgeny began the viewing ceremony.

"Ladies and gentlemen, friends and family, guests," *and future clients,* Yvgeny thought, "we will now begin the viewing. I recommend you approach one row at a time, but please, if you will indulge me for one moment, I have arranged something special for you, something unique, something you will only find here at Schmidt and Sons, Middle Georgia's premier mortuary, where you're not just a corpse, you're a client!"

In his excitement, Yvgeny pressed the wrong button and the music started again. *No problem,* Yvgeny thought. He turned off the music, then he pressed and held the *other* button.

With a low hum of hydraulics, Maude's coffin began to lift as if by magic, then swivel forward, effectively moving Maude toward a standing position.

Maude's granddaughter jumped out of her chair, screaming, and hid behind her mother. Yvgeny glanced behind him to gauge the angle, and released the button when she was almost vertical. The straps held, keeping her securely ensconced in her Navajo Casket coffin.

With a smile, Yvgeny turned back toward the crowd. Eighty pairs of eyes stared not at him, but at Maude, slack jawed, Brianna included. His mother fell back into a chair, and the pastor rushed to tend to her. The entire room had gone completely silent.

Magical. Simply magical. Visions of Yvgeny and Brianna bobble heads danced across his vision. *T-shirts, PEZ dispensers, coffee mugs, hats, not to mention a Victorian fashion craze. A whole world of flair. We can open an online store, Alfred can handle order fulfillment!*

Yvgeny's mind raced with possibilities. He looked down the hall and thought, *we can put the gift shop over there!*

He would have Reuben help him with pricing and inventory. Maybe Rocko would be able to feature his line of products at his shop.

Yvgeny floated within his fantasies, soaring above his little version of heaven.

I wonder who will call first? CNN? Discovery Channel?

Suddenly he had a revelation and whispered, involuntarily, "No!"

Not just a news report! A cable series! No, a reality show cable series! His and Hearse, featuring Yvgeny and Brianna Jedynak! Oh, this is too much, it's just too much!

Yvgeny pinched himself on his arm.

After the moment passed, the crowd overcame their shock and looked around at each other. Sensing it was time, Yvgeny nodded at the ensemble of twelve year olds, and when they did not immediately respond, he cleared his throat and bulged his eyes at them. Finally they clutched their instruments and launched back into song. *The Wind Beneath My Wings*, by Bette Midler.

As the music started and people began to mill about, Louise Humperdink rose from the back row, clapping her hands and yelling, "Bravo! Bravo!" Yvgeny took a formal bow to her, his stovepipe hat in his hand, then stepped back to officiate over the viewing. Louise stuck her pinkies into the corners of her mouth and whistled loudly.

A few intrepid guests finally started to approach the casket, but the majority remained in their seats, bewildered. In back, the pastor began fanning his mother with a hymnal.

Look at them all, they are in awe! Yvgeny reveled in the stares of his guests. He wallowed in the mushy emotion springing forth from those gathered, his dear, future clients. He relished the feeling, savored the moment.

Pack your bags, Lenny Updike, you're finished!

As the guests took their first tentative steps toward the coffin, Yvgeny shuffled backwards to make room and almost knocked over the monstrous flower arrangement provided by *Jumpie's, Inc.* of Macon; per their agreement, the huge display was placed exactly two feet from Maude, and included a prominent sleeve filled with business cards featuring a mock up of a 1977 Monte Carlo with a huge lift kit.

Yvgeny stabilized the arrangement, and when he turned back to the crowd, he saw Alfred shuffling in from the back of the room, pulling a low cart bearing several stacked tables. As Yvgeny watched him, something clicked.

Suddenly, like a lightning bolt, he knew what happened. Everything fell into place. He smacked his

344

hands together, louder than he intended, causing several people to jump.

How did I miss it? How could I be so stupid?

He turned and searched through the crowd for the rabbi, but he was nowhere to be found. The three teenagers were also gone. He cursed to himself and looked out the window in time to see a small Toyota back up into the street and accelerate away. He couldn't see the occupants.

"What's wrong?"

Brianna had approached, and was watching him with interest as he looked out the window. Yvgeny sighed and tried to force a smile.

"Oh, nothing, just making sure everything is perfect."

Brianna glanced over at Maude.

"A remote control coffin? Are you serious?"

Yvgeny smiled and said, "I know, it's really going to put us on the map. You'll see!

Brianna didn't respond, but reached into her bag for her smokes and whispered, "be right back."

He turned away and found his mother right beside him, watching Brianna leave.

"Ugh. Smoking. Better save a hole for her out back."

"Mama!"

"A big hole. Cost extra."

She shrugged her shoulders and then glanced behind her.

"Guess I'll have to watch those caterers myself, while your trusty usher slowly kills herself."

His grand dream of saving the day and winning the girl was slipping away before his eyes. He checked his watch, then looked back out the window. He had to reach the killers before it was too late. But he couldn't leave.

The music fell apart when the trombone player saw a caterer deliver a plate of brownies to the buffet. Trombone in hand, he hurriedly weaved through the crowd to grab one from the tray, shoved it into his mouth in one bite, then returned to his chair, chewing quickly while his colleagues looked on with dismay.

A line had finally begun to form before Maude's casket, some making the sign of the cross, some dropping little items inside. Some cried, some smiled. Yvgeny could not stop glancing down at his watch, anxious for the festivities to reach a point where he could escape.

Brianna returned to his side, and he took a deep breath, taking in the mixture of floral perfume and burnt tobacco. *Delicious.*

In his head, he ticked off what was left: finish the viewing, then snacks while they cart her out to the cemetery, then the pastor does his thing again, *ashes to ashes and all that crap*, lower her into the ground, then stand by the door as Mama steers everyone out.

At least two more hours.

He let out his breath in an exasperated whoosh.

Brianna took his hand and squeezed, sending a glorious sizzle up his arm and making him forget everything else. At least for a while. She was his prisoner for a couple more hours.

He was disappointed about the direction the afternoon had gone. He intended the funeral to sweep her off her feet, to lure her completely into his net, but he was too distracted, and now he had to see the rabbi and those kids, to warn them, to get to them before the cops did.

Yvgeny froze. An idea formed in his head even better than the one that brought Brianna to the funeral.

Sometimes I even impress myself!

Imagine if Holmes could have taken his Irene Adler to the scene of every crime he solved!

If Brianna could see him in action, watch it all unfold as he saved those kids from almost certain arrest and a death sentence, it would be the *pièce de résistance!*

He tried to relax, but couldn't help teasing Brianna just a little by whispering in her ear, "If you think this is grand, wait until you see what I have planned next!"

Brianna closed her eyes a moment, then leaned in to him and whispered back, "If it's another dead animal, keep it."

⚏

The detectives left the courthouse without speaking, and when they got outside, Newsome started to pace. Occasionally he cursed under his breath. Bubba leaned against the wall of the courthouse and took out his tin of Copenhagen. Newsome eventually stopped pacing and turned to Bubba.

"Where the hell is Kincaid with those prints?"

Bubba checked the time on his phone, then shrugged and mumbled, "Well, he said it would be a few hours."

Newsome grunted something unintelligible and resumed pacing. Then he stopped again and faced Bubba.

"Where the hell is Thomas? He insisted on being a part of all this, then disappears when we need him the most. I bet he's back out there writing speeding tickets." He paused, then called out, "Dammit!"

Bubba opened his mouth to speak, then stopped, pressed his tongue against his dip. There was no point.

"You think he's even bothered to gather anyone to help with the search warrant? You think he's getting things ready? You think those Crawford County crime scene techs are worth a damn?"

"Well, they found the blood, tracked it back to the house," Bubba replied, trying to sound amiable, then he smiled and added, "I believe Thomas is in charge of *them*, too."

Newsome slapped his hand against his forehead and groaned, "Of course."

"You don't think Welch and Geny's mother-"

Bubba covered his ears and chanted, "la la la la," then he shuddered.

Newsome stopped pacing and leaned against the wall next to Bubba, then patted on his shirt pocket, mumbled, "I need a damn cigarette," then turned to Bubba and said, "You think Thomas has the sense to post someone on the house?" Newsome asked.

They both stood in silence a moment, then Bubba reached for his phone and sent a text to Thomas.

When they returned to Welch's office an hour later, they spent another thirty minutes convincing him to sign it, which he grudgingly did only after numerous caveats, edits, and provisos were scribbled in by the man in a choppy blue inked scrawl. It took the secretary another twenty minutes to edit the changes in the electronic copy they had to email her. By the time they left, it was almost five o'clock.

When Welch finally returned with their warrant,

Newsome had to yank it out of his grip, Welch's knuckles white as he clenched it, unwilling to let it go.

╬

Yvgeny waved his last goodbye, then grabbed Brianna's sweaty hand and said, "Come on, we have work to do."

"What are you talking about?"

"I will explain in Cerb . . . damn!"

Yvgeny had dragged Brianna outside, then noticed the catering truck was parked in the driveway, blocking Cerberus.

"What's the big deal? I'll drive. I'd rather not get into that meat wagon again anyway."

Yvgeny glanced between Brianna's tiny car and Cerberus, then sighed. She chirped the alarm and Yvgeny hopped into the passenger seat while Brianna squeezed behind the wheel. Then she turned to him and asked, "Where are we going?"

"We're going to see a rabbi."

Brianna glared at him, a cigarette dangling from one corner of her mouth, then she shut her eyes and exhaled forcefully with frustration.

"What in the hell are we going to see a rabbi for?" Her eyes narrowed, and she added, in a menacing voice, "I ain't getting married again."

"What?" Then recognition set in and Yvgeny raised his hands and hurriedly said, "no, no, nothing like that. Look, can you start driving? I'll explain on the way. Head east."

Brianna took one more look at Yvgeny, then started pulling out of the driveway. Yvgeny took a deep breath and said, "OK, look, you know about the body they found at the cemetery, right?"

"Um, isn't that kind of the point of having a cemetery?"

"No, I mean the body that didn't belong."

"What?"

"I found a body in one of my holes."

"You're starting to sound like a freak again."

Yvgeny sighed.

"I was burying a guy in that hole. The night before, somebody dumped another body in it. Tried to hide it. Some old man."

"Oh. So what's that got to do with us going to some rabbi's place?"

"Because I think his grandkids did it."

"Grandkids? Are you nuts?"

"It's complicated."

"You're taking me to a rabbi's house to find a bunch of murdering kids? And you're calling it a date? You *are* a freak! Get out of my car!"

Brianna slammed on the brakes and swerved to the shoulder.

"Listen, it was a righteous killing. The old guy deserved it. He was a Nazi."

Brianna took her last drag from her cigarette, flicked it out the window, then started fumbling in her bag, pulled out another cigarette, then twisted off the filter and threw it onto the floorboard. Her hands shook. She began to mutter as she fished for her matches, then punched the cigar lighter on the dash.

"My father was right, I always pick the whack jobs. Jesus Christ, I've gotta move away from here. Go somewhere where people aren't CRAZY!" She turned to Yvgeny and screeched the last word so loud Yvgeny jumped in his seat.

"Brianna, the authorities are going to figure it out any day now, maybe they have already. We have to warn this guy, give him a chance to get those kids away before they send them off to prison."

"You said it was a righteous killing."

"It was, but those inspectors don't have enough sense to tell the difference."

Brianna lit the cigarette, took a drag, coughed, then took another. Then she rolled the window back down and coughed up some phlegm, spit it out, then rolled the window back up.

She sat, pensive, then muttered, "How the hell do I get myself into these things?" Then she cast him a sidelong glance and added, "an undertaker, taking me on a date to talk to some killers. With a freakin' rabbi. Grandpa Schtumpf must be doing cartwheels."

Brianna tried to smoke the cigarette but got so annoyed by stray pieces of tobacco, she finally dropped it out of her car door.

"Where does this rabbi live?"

"Not far, Crawford County."

"You sure know how to show a girl a good time."

Yvgeny smiled as she pulled back out onto the street.

Brianna saw his smile and growled, "I was being sarcastic. Freak!"

⊥⊦
⊤⊦

CHAPTER TWENTY ONE

Brianna pulled into the rabbi's driveway, then turned to Yvgeny and said, "now what?"

Yvgeny took her shoulder and with a toothy smile declared, "just watch."

They emerged from the car and Yvgeny crossed the driveway in long, confident strides, channeling his inner Holmes, trailed by a less confident Brianna. He knocked on the door, once, twice, then stood straight with his hands clasped behind him, his chin out, the epitome of a Victorian era gentleman. Finally the door opened. It was one of the teenagers he saw at Maude's funeral.

The teen studied Yvgeny, then smirked. "Nice outfit."

"Thank you, dear boy. Where is your, um, grandfather?"

Yvgeny stared at him, expressionless, and after a moment, the teen walked away leaving the door open.

"Grandpa, that weirdo with the big hat from the

funeral is at the door, wants to talk to you!"

Yvgeny glanced back at Brianna, who was leaning against the exterior wall smoking, her eyes on the street as if she was the lookout in a burglary.

Inside, on the couch, the other two teens sat, bearing an uncanny resemblance to each other. Before Yvgeny could study them, the teen that answered the door returned with the old rabbi.

"*Oi vay.* Mr. Jedynak, why are you here?"

"Rabbi, we need to talk. We don't have a lot of time."

Just then, Brianna peered around the corner and took a look at the rabbi, whose eyes widened upon seeing her. He glanced behind him, then walked out onto the stoop and shut the front door.

"Young man, I told you, I have nothing to discuss with you. Go home. Let the police do their job."

Yvgeny smirked, and whispered, "I know who killed that Nazi."

The old man froze, then turned pale, nervous. He involuntarily glanced behind him again. For a long moment the old man stared at Yvgeny. Then he whispered, "What do you want?"

"To warn you. The authorities are close to figuring this out. Then they will come here. They could already be on their way." Yvgeny gestured toward the door with his chin and said, "they still have their lives to live. I'd hate to see them spend them behind bars." The old man winced, but Yvgeny did not let up, adding, "you need to get them out of here. Now."

"Are you crazy?"

"No, just trying to help."

"They didn't do anything wrong. That man showed up at my house with a gun, tried to kill me. What was I supposed to do?"

Yvgeny stared at the old man, confused.

"*You* killed him?"

The rabbi did not respond.

"And you got your grandson and his friends to hide the body?"

"No! Well, yes, they hid the body, but I didn't know they were going to do that. I intended to report it, but, well . . . ." the rabbi trailed off.

"What do you mean?"

"I was in shock. They found me on the floor next to the body. By the time I snapped out of it, the body was gone, along with my grandson." He paused, then said, in a tiny voice, "they told me later."

"Each day, I have told myself I would call the police. I even picked up the phone a few times, but, I just couldn't. I don't care about myself, but I worry about them, especially my grandson."

"Rabbi, you have to get out of here. And take them with you!"

"No! We did nothing wrong. He came here to kill me. What was I supposed to do?"

Yvgeny adopted a magnanimous smile and said, "I totally agree, rabbi, but I fear the cops won't understand the whole story like I do. That's why you have to leave, now, while you can. And take them with you." He nodded toward the door. Just then, the front door swung open. It was his grandson.

"Grandpa, what's this guy doing here? Want me to get rid of him?"

"No Jake, that's OK. He knows."

"Knows what?"

"All of it."

The rabbi brushed by the teen as he went back inside, with Yvgeny in tow. Yvgeny took a few steps toward the couch and took a better look at Isaac and Albert Cohen, and also the rabbi's grandson, Jacob. Brianna trailed in behind Yvgeny and tried to disappear into the shadows.

Yvgeny watched the rabbi schlep toward an old olive colored chair and take a seat. Exasperated, Yvgeny raised his voice and called out, "Rabbi, you don't have a lot of time," then turned to the kids on the couch and added, "neither do you three."

The rabbi sighed and said, "We aren't going anywhere. I have lived with this burden too long. We will turn ourselves in."

Yvgeny's mouth stood agape.

"Are you insane? These bumpkins will send you to the chair for murder! Do you know what a Gilbert County jury looks like? Twelve illiterate farmers who probably think Jews have tails."

"It happened here in Crawford County."

"Do you really think the outcome will be any different? Wait. What? It happened in Crawford County?"

The rabbi glanced over at Jacob, and slowly nodded his head. Jacob winced and made an expression that seemed to ask his grandfather, *are you sure?*

"It's OK, my boy, show him."

Jacob stood and walked past his grandfather and Yvgeny, toward the wall where Brianna had posted herself. Beside her, there was a large tapestry hanging from the wall. As the boy approached the tapestry, Brianna slithered along the wall toward the door. The tapestry depicted a forest, in all greens and browns. The teenager removed the tapestry and stood back.

The tapestry had been covering up a pink stain on the wall, around two feet up from the carpet. The teenager used a foot and slid over a wooden chest that had been leaning against the wall beneath the tapestry. The stain in the carpet was darker.

"Here?"

The old man sighed.

"He followed me home the evening after Albert pushed him to the ground."

Yvgeny looked over at the couch, asked, "Which one of you is Albert?"

The skinnier of the two looked away, thus identifying himself. He had mousy brown hair, a complexion riddled with acne, and a generally fidgety demeanor. Yvgeny nodded, then turned back to the rabbi.

"So you shot him?"

"It was an accident. He showed up at my door and rang the bell. It's Crawford County, I didn't even look through the peep hole. I couldn't believe it was him. He didn't say a word, he just pulled a revolver out and pointed it at me, pushed me backwards and forced himself inside."

Jacob walked over and stood beside his Grandpa.

"He started complaining about the Jews, said his father was an SS officer during the war. He said his father taught him everything he needed to know about Jews. He said he would make me pay for embarrassing him."

The old man's hands were shaking as he spoke.

"I didn't know what to do. He got angrier and

356

angrier. I tried to talk him off the ledge but he kept telling me to shut up. Said that he was going to fix everything. He got closer and closer, pushed me up against the wall. I had nowhere to go. I grabbed the barrel of the revolver, tried to twist it away."

The rabbi shook his head, muttered, "two old men, fighting over a gun."

Then he looked back up at Yvgeny.

"We fell to the ground, still locked together. He kneeled on top of me, and we were still fighting over the gun. Somehow, during the struggle it went off."

"Head shot?"

The rabbi nodded.

Yvgeny looked over at the three teenagers.

"And you three tried to help him."

They nodded.

"Which one of you came up with the idea?"

The three sat like concrete lawn ornaments until finally, Albert glanced toward the others, then said, in a small voice, "I did."

Yvgeny took a few steps closer to the couch, and with great interest, asked, "Tell me."

Albert gulped air, and spoke.

"I remembered the old man that lived in the woods, he had an axe, he chopped wood on a stump. I figured we could take the head and hands off, then nobody could identify him, at least not for a while."

The rabbi shuddered.

"Yes, go on."

"Well, Jake's Grandpa, he gets the newspaper, and I like to read it when I'm here. I, well, I . . . ."

The boy nervously looked across at his friend on one side, his brother on the other, and blushed.

"I like to read the obituaries. I don't know why. But I remembered something about a funeral for somebody the next day. I kind of figured, well, maybe they dig the hole the day before, so that was my plan. Go bury the body in the hole, cover it up, then the next day they drop a coffin in and that's it."

Yvgeny had been nodding his head, and turned to check on Brianna, who was paying rapt attention to the boy's words.

"What about the head and the hands?"

"Took them to another grave that still had flowers on it. We wanted one with flowers because I figured it would be freshly dug. Makes it easier to dig it up again, loose earth. And nobody would know if we dug it up again. Nobody would think anything was out of the ordinary."

Yvgeny nodded and goaded him on, exclaiming, "Fascinating! Yes, of course. Please, continue."

Yvgeny's face took on a gleam as he listened to the boy, like a proud father watching his son hit his first home run.

"Well, we loaded him up in Grandpa Shachter's wheelbarrow and wheeled him over to the stump."

He glanced over at his friends and, with a suddenly irritated expression, added, "Well, it was mostly *me* that loaded him up. Some of us claimed to be too '*queasy*.'" Albert emphasized the last word and the two other kids looked away.

"We got him up on the stump and I took care of it. One of us," Albert said, with another sidelong glance of contempt, "had to go throw up."

Yvgeny could barely hide his glee at the story. He waved his hand in a circular motion, to ask for more. Albert, energized by Yvgeny's satisfaction, began to sensationalize it.

"We wheeled him back to the house and stuffed him into the trunk of his own car. I took a pillowcase and put the parts inside. Then we took off."

"To my cemetery."

Albert looked him in the eye and nodded.

"Yup."

"We took the wheelbarrow. And a broom. Shovel, too. Oh yeah, and a rake. It was kind of hard to wheel him into that grave, and we tried to be careful about leaving marks in the dirt. I had my brother use the rake to try to smooth out our tracks. Didn't work great, but then it started raining. Made it a lot easier. Then we found that other grave with the flowers, and buried the pieces there."

With a smile, Yvgeny asked, "the car?"

"Dumped in a lake back there," he said, pointing toward the large window overlooking the back yard.

"The axe?"

"In the trunk."

Yvgeny clapped his hands together.

"Bravo!"

Yvgeny turned to the old rabbi and said, "I must admit, sir, I had my doubts about you, but this was excellent planning. I wouldn't have pegged you for one capable of participating in such a conspiracy."

"Are you kidding me? After I found out what they did, I took two of my painkillers and knocked myself out."

Yvgeny turned back to Albert, awe on his face, and

said, "So this was all your doing? You planned it all?"

Albert looked around the room, then shrugged.

"Ah, such a *tygrysek*!" Yvgeny exclaimed, then he stepped up to tousle the boy's hair.

Brianna interrupted, calling out, "We've got company."

Everyone jumped when the doorbell rang, then Newsome bellowed, "Geny, you better get your ass out here, before I come take it out in pieces!"

"Ah, my ride is here. Albert, before I go, how would you like a job with me as my apprentice? I need someone with your abilities."

"I got a scholarship to UGA."

"Too bad."

"But I could come in on the weekends. And summers?"

Again, Yvgeny smiled like a proud father.

Yvgeny walked up to Brianna, took her in a rough embrace, and kissed her, hard, shoving his tongue past her teeth. She smacked her palms against his chest once, twice, then relented and wrapped her arms around him.

The rabbi turned away and coughed, and Isaac and Jake made puking sounds. Albert watched, intently, with the detached fascination of a wildlife biologist. Finally, Yvgeny pushed her away and headed toward the door without looking back.

Yvgeny walked out into the sunlight, beaming, like a famous actor at the release of his latest movie. Newsome and Bubba stood on the grass, flanked by Thomas and a handful of uniformed officers and crime scene techs. Nitro started barking from inside one of the cars. Yvgeny glanced around at everyone and chuckled.

"Aww, all this, for me? You shouldn't have!"

Newsome's cheeks turned beet red and he began cracking his knuckles. His eyes flicked behind Yvgeny when he saw Brianna emerge. She saw all the uniforms and with shaking hands reached into her purse.

"No! Drop the purse!"

Thomas drew his weapon and pointed it at Brianna, who screamed and dropped her purse. Yvgeny took a step in front of Brianna and held up his hands and yelled, "Don't shoot!"

Newsome and Bubba both reached out toward Thomas and pushed down on his arm, then stepped forward to retrieve the purse. Newsome asked a terrified Brianna, "Anything in here we should know about?"

Brianna seemed not to comprehend him, then nodded and said, "pepper spray. And my cigarettes. I really need the cigarettes."

Newsome fished around inside and found the pack, with a lighter shoved inside the box. He stared at them a while, deep in thought, then slowly opened the pack. He looked around furtively, then leaned in and whispered, "You mind if I have one?"

Brianna shrugged, and Newsome took a cigarette, lit it, then took a drag. He shut his eyes and let the smoke curl out of his nostrils, then he sighed. He stepped up and handed her the cigarettes. Bubba watched, shaking his head.

Yvgeny cleared his throat to get everyone's attention.

"Not bad, inspectors, you're only about an hour behind me. I am impressed! I figured it would be days before you figured it all out."

Newsome flicked the ashes from his cigarette, his

eyes black. Bubba cast him a worried look, then was distracted by his phone, vibrating on his belt. He looked at the number, then answered.

"Talk to me."

Newsome, staring at Yvgeny, took a step forward and said, "Undertaker, I don't even know where to begin. I'm going to ask the sheriff if we got any space *beneath* the jail to stick your ass."

Yvgeny adopted a surprised expression and called out, "Inspector, there are children inside, watch your language!"

"Let me tell you something you sick-"

"Harry."

"What?"

"It's Kincaid. They got an ID. Franz Rolf, born in 1938, emigrated from Germany. Got a criminal record a mile long. Did twenty for manslaughter in the seventies. He's the real deal."

"What else?"

Bubba replaced his phone on his belt.

"Blood on the stump matches the guy."

Newsome nodded his head and took another drag.

"And Kincaid says the cause of death was a GSW to the head. Upward angle. Shooter was beneath the guy."

Newsome put his hands on his hips and appraised Yvgeny.

"So all we need now is a confession, Geny. You ready to step up?"

"One confession, coming right up!"

Yvgeny opened the front door to the rabbi's home with a flourish, and the rabbi stepped outside, white as a sheet, shaking.

"Rabbi, the good inspector here would love to hear everything you told me. Inspector, you will find he acted in self defense. His grandson and friends did what they had to do. There has been no crime here."

"Last I checked, it's a crime to practice law without a license. And I'm just looking for an excuse."

Newsome turned to the rabbi and asked, "any of that true, rabbi?"

"Unfortunately, yes, that man showed up at my house and tried to kill me."

Jacob Shachter then emerged from the house, stood by his grandfather.

"He didn't do anything wrong."

"Well, OK, maybe the forensics back it up, and maybe they don't. Maybe he *was* defending himself."

The rabbi sighed, nodded slowly.

"But then he chopped up the body and hid it in a cemetery. That's a problem."

"It wasn't him. It was us."

As if choreographed, Albert and Isaac came out of the house to stand beside Jake. Newsome and Bubba both stared, and Bubba muttered, "I'll be damned. That old gravedigger was telling the truth."

Newsome took one more drag on his cigarette, dropped it, then squished it with a foot. Then he stood looking at the teens with his hands on his hips, shaking his head. Thomas, meanwhile, swiveled his neck between Newsome and Yvgeny, confusion on his face.

"Still a lot of crimes here, folks," Newsome replied, "improper disposal of a body, for one. Felony."

Yvgeny waved his hand dismissively and called out, "You can't charge them, they're still kids! Even if you took them to juvie, they'd get probation."

"Criminal trespass, for hacking up the body on that old man's property."

"Pshaw! Misdemeanor. Slap on the wrist. They pay a fine, pick up trash on the highway."

Yvgeny smiled at Brianna and rolled his eyes.

"How about burglary, trespassing at the cemetery to commit a felony therein."

Yvgeny nodded sagely, then his smile returned, broadened.

"The owner of the property would testify that these young men were authorized to be there. Personally. By me."

Yvgeny then pointed at Albert and added, "He's my newest understudy, and has free access to my grounds. Try again, inspector."

Newsome turned red, exhaled in a whoosh. Bubba took a step closer to him, just in case. Then Newsome turned back to Yvgeny.

"How about obstruction of justice, Geny? Conspiracy? Maybe party to a crime?"

"Misdemeanors."

"Yup. True enough. But I could have a chat with the judge. You ever heard of stacking charges, hoss? Three misdemeanors could mean three years. Consecutive sentence. Try that on for size."

While Newsome stared at Yvgeny, Bubba approached and put his hand on Newsome's shoulder and whispered, "He ain't worth it, Harry."

Newsome made a prune face, then turned to Thomas.

"Thomas, get your team in there to process this scene. Where's your photographer? Get him in there first. I want it done by the book."

Thomas turned to an older man standing nearby, black satchels under each arm, and said, "You heard the man, Junior, let's get started."

As the man crouched and started to rummage through his bags, Yvgeny made a beeline toward him, dragging Brianna along behind him.

"This is perfect! Can you get a shot of me and my lovely assistant? And Newsome, oh Newsome, why don't you join us? Come on, don't by bashful!"

Newsome turned to Bubba, said, "Bubba, I'm gonna shoot him. I ain't gonna kill him, maybe just tag him in the leg. But I'm gonna shoot him."

As the photographer tried to get past Yvgeny, Newsome addressed the rabbi.

"Rabbi, we're going to present this to the district attorney, see what he says. I'd like you all to come into the office, give us a statement. Maybe testify at the grand jury. I ain't promising nothing, but if what our armchair detective here says is true, this probably ain't no murder."

The rabbi leaned heavily on Jacob, suddenly too exhausted to stand without help.

⊥⊥
⊤⊤

CHAPTER TWENTY TWO

Yvgeny sat in the passenger seat of Brianna's car as Thomas's team processed the scene. He fiddled with his watch, taking it off, squinting at the tiny letters on the back, then curling the band around his wrist again.

He held it up to his ear to hear the ticking, then sighed and looked out the window. Brianna was outside smoking another cigarette with Newsome, who occasionally turned to glare at him.

Newsome's head shot up, then, and a moment later Yvgeny heard the throaty rumble of a V8 with glasspacks in the distance, approaching fast. He craned his neck around to look down the street in time to see a fire engine red van skid around the corner and accelerate toward the house. It was Flowers, with Yvgeny's mother in the passenger seat.

His mother scrambled out of the van before it completely stopped, then reached in and grabbed her cane. She hobbled through a throng of uniforms and went straight for Newsome.

"What's going on here? What are you doing with my son?"

Newsome glanced toward Yvgeny in the car, then back at his mother.

"I'm not doing anything with your son. But she is!"

Newsome pointed his thumb at Brianna, who blushed but looked her in the eye.

"Your son," Brianna said, flicking her cigarette butt into the grass, "came all the way out here out of the goodness of his heart to warn this old guy and his grandkids that the cops were after them. That's some kind of son you have there."

The old woman sputtered a moment, tottering on her cane, glancing from Brianna to Newsome, then looked inside the car at her son, who finally opened the door and emerged.

"Mama, how did you know?"

"You kidding me? Mike called me as soon as he signed that warrant."

"Mike Welch? Welch the Squelch?" asked Newsome.

"He hates it when you cops call him that."

"He told you?"

"We are close."

His mother looked down and kicked at the asphalt.

Yvgeny made gagging sounds and looked away.

Yvgeny looked over at Flowers, who was slumping behind his steering wheel trying to hide. Newsome also noticed him, and yelled out, "You might as well join the party, Flowers. The rest of Comstock's already here."

"So what's gonna happen to my son?"

"Well, I'd like to toss him in a cell for a year or two on general principle. But most likely, nothing."

"You mean you're not arresting him?"

"As much as I'd like to-"

"So he's not a criminal?"

"Well, I didn't say that."

The old woman stared at Newsome a moment, processing the information. Then her eyes narrowed.

"You should give him a medal."

Bubba snorted and reached for his Copenhagen.

On the way back to Schmidt's, Yvgeny couldn't stop fiddling with his watch and finally Brianna grabbed his wrist and asked him, "What is it with this watch, you've been screwing around with it all afternoon."

"This watch-"

"Came from some dead guy, right?" Brianna replied, "and now you're wearing it. Fabulous."

Yvgeny thought a moment, then said, "Yes, it came from someone who no longer cares what time it is. So what?"

"Like I said," Brianna responded, "that's just gross."

"Gross? When Grandpa Schtumpf died, did you burn down his house? Of course not! You moved in. You eat on his plates. A *dead guy's* plates."

"Still gross."

Yvgeny took a breath, then continued, more softly.

"The ground you walk on, the air you breathe, the cells that came together to make all the lovely pieces of you, they're all made from little tiny bits of everyone else that used to live on this earth, long before we got here."

Brianna kept turning toward him as he vented, her cheeks flushing. She began to slow down, and other cars passed her, blaring their horns.

"The gasoline fueling your lovely little chariot was once the blood and flesh of long extinct creatures that were born, grew up, and died right here, beneath the asphalt. Look around you. Every single thing you see is made up of pieces of every single thing that lived before it. Life from death, my lovely Brianna. It's the cycle. It's everything."

He grabbed her hand and leaned in, whispered, "You are a beautiful sand mandala. Recycled carbon from every heart that ever beat."

With her cheeks a flaming red, Brianna yanked the steering wheel and screeched to a halt on the shoulder, horns blasting behind her. She twisted sideways and grabbed Yvgeny by the cheeks and brought him half out of his seat and attacked him with a fury. Yvgeny was in heaven. Again.

When she finally let him go, he caught his breath, then checked his watch.

"Ready for our second date?"

She cast him a sidelong glance.

"Think it will top the first?"

"Oh," Yvgeny responded, "definitely. A black bag job under cover of darkness."

"What? A burglary? Are you crazy? I'm no criminal!"

"No, we are stealing trash."

Brianna glanced over at him again, quizzically, and smacked his leg with her fist.

"You're kidding me. Whose trash?"

"Barber shop. I will explain later."

JONATHAN B. ZEITLIN

THE END

<<<<>>>

Additional

Material

I sincerely hope you enjoyed my book, The Body in the Hole. As a special treat, I am including here the first three chapters of Book Two, tentatively titled The Gummer and His Ghost. But first, please indulge me as I make a few final comments.

I would very much appreciate your honest reviews. If you're like me, when you're shopping for a book, you rely on reviews. Well, when you write books, reviews are currency. Reviews are gold. Please consider writing one. Even a short one! You can write one on any of the big websites where books are sold.

If you are one of my pre-order friends, just indicate in your review that you purchased your copy as part of a pre-order. That way, they know you are a real reader and not someone I paid for a fake review.

If you have questions, or just want to chat, you can reach me at zeitlinfiction@gmail.com, or find me on Goodreads at:

www.goodreads.com/author/show/17220658.Jonathan_Zeitlin.

Best,

JZ

An Excerpt from
The Gummer and His Ghost

Book Two of the Undertaker Series,

Chapters One, Two, and Three

CHAPTER ONE

Cars began swerving toward the curb as the sound of sirens grew. Yvgeny slowed Cerberus, his late model Cadillac hearse, and looked into his rear view mirror, his eyes wide and a smile on his face. Brianna, his new girlfriend, eyed him with disgust.

"Seriously? Someone could be dying!"

Yvgeny continued looking into his mirror, rubbing his hands together, then gushed, "we can only hope!"

Finally, the ambulance came into view, and Yvgeny rolled forward a few feet, angling his hearse for a quick getaway. As the ambulance passed, Yvgeny accelerated and fell behind it.

"What are you doing?"

"The early bird gets the corpse!"

Brianna stuffed another piece of nicotine gum into her mouth and tried to hide her face as they passed the other drivers, still perched on the shoulder. Cerberus garnered quite a bit of attention, especially when tail gaiting an ambulance.

It wasn't long before the ambulance turned onto a side street very familiar to Yvgeny. He slowed, and when the ambulance pulled into the circular driveway, Yvgeny raised a balled fist and let out a "cha ching!"

Brianna glared at him, chomping and smacking her nicotine gum.

"Now what? Are you going to run inside and hand out business cards while some poor guy is dead in the hall?"

Yvgeny leaned back in his seat, a satisfied smile on his face.

"Not necessary. This is our turf! Mama has a deal with the manager of Sunset Manor. We pay for her beautician once a month for a touch up, and she lets us stack our brochures and cards on the front desk. And she puts in a plug for us whenever someone konks."

Brianna turned and looked out the window, muttering, "Heartwarming."

Yvgeny pressed a button on his steering wheel and after the beep slowly uttered, "Call Mama."

The Bluetooth system connected him with the landline at Schmidt and Sons Mortuary, where he and his mother lived. Yvgeny took over the family business from his father, who had taken it from the last surviving Schmidt. Yvgeny spent most of his formative years in and around the place, making him an unusual and unpopular child in his neighborhood.

The phone rang several times before his mother picked up the phone.

"Mama, there's fresh meat at Sunset Manor."

Brianna's mouth fell open and she turned away again with an eye roll.

His mother chuckled and said, "Excellent! I will give Beatrice a call. Oh, and there's still a few bouquets from the Hiram funeral, I will pluck out whatever still looks pretty and put together a nice wreath for you to bring over a little later."

"Perfect Mama. Toodles!"

Yvgeny pressed the red button and ended the call.

"How can you be so sure someone's dead? Maybe they just fell, or they're having a heart attack."

Yvgeny shook his head vigorously, smiling.

"Nope. Look around. No fire truck. No cop car. When it's just one ambulance, he's worm food."

Yvgeny let a self satisfied smile escape, then he motioned with his chin toward the commotion.

"Just look at those guys. They're still screwing around with their radio. And do you see anyone running out the front door yelling and screaming? Nope. Trust me. He's DRT."

"Do I even want to know?"

"Dead right there."

Brianna just sighed and looked back out the window.

As the paramedics finally brought out the collapsible gurney from the back of the ambulance, Yvgeny turned to Brianna and asked, "Ready for some pizza?"

⁜

When they returned to Schmidt and Sons, his mother was waiting for them in the main receiving room.

On the table was a large wreath made from week old flowers his mother cobbled together from bouquets left over from the Hiram funeral. She sat proudly beside her handiwork, her walking cane standing beside her on its four rubber pads.

Yvgeny inspected the wreath with a smile. Brianna remained outside, smoking a cigarette. When his mother glanced over Yvgeny's shoulder and saw her, her smile faltered.

"Still with the *wieloryb*. And the cigarettes."

"Focus, Mama. What did Beatrice say?"

His mother glanced back at Brianna one more time, pursed her lips, and looked away with a strangled sound.

"Earnest Ledbetter. He was on hospice. Kicked the bucket this morning. Family's in Atlanta. The cops will handle the notification. The family only visited the guy a couple times over the last year, so she doesn't think they're close."

"Great." Yvgeny said, dejection in his voice.

There was always more money to be made when a family lost a loved one they actually loved. If the survivors were estranged from the decedent, Yvgeny knew he would be looking at far fewer dollars in his pocket.

"Don't forget to take care of Beatrice."

"Of course, Mama."

Usually Yvgeny brought over an Amazon gift card. However, last time, he arrived to find Beatrice watching television on a forty two inch plasma screen on the wall in the lobby, installed personally by Lenny Updike, the owner of Updike's Funeral Home in Warner Robins. Ever since, he and his Mama had to up their game. The beautician appointments just weren't enough. Competition was fierce, especially as life spans were growing longer. It was a dog-eat-dog business.

"When you bring the bouquet, you can ask about setting something up."

"As I always do, Mama."

He stood, and she sat, both silent. Yvgeny knew something was on his mother's mind, and he waited, somewhat impatiently, for her to come out with it. He knew from experience that when she carried that pensive expression, something distasteful was on its way. He checked his watch, an old Laco, a gift from a former client, then glanced outside toward Brianna.

"Your father, may his memory be a blessing, he wouldn't have me working my fingers to the bone creating wreaths and hawking our wares like some door to door Amway salesman. So much for my golden years."

Yvgeny grimaced.

"Of course, Mama. My goal is to make you suffer."

"That's right, Yvgeny, take my suffering, take my despair over losing your dear father, make a joke of it. All I have left is you, and all you can offer is sarcasm. I blame myself. Where did I go wrong?"

Grabbing her cane, his mother struggled to her feet and stormed away, smacking her cane on the heart of pine floors. Yvgeny watched her slowly take the stairs to her room, shrugged his shoulders, scooped up the wreath and left. Passing Brianna on the sidewalk, he muttered, "Got it," and headed back toward Cerberus.

The Sunset Manor Assisted Living Center occupied a lovely corner in downtown Comstock, at the intersection of Main and Elm. Its façade was modeled after a southern plantation house, with an ample wraparound and columned porch with potted ferns hung at regular intervals. The rocking chairs were all filled with old men and women watching traffic and reminiscing.

As Yvgeny parked Cerberus outside, Yvgeny muttered, "ah, fruit of the womb. You may only see toothless geriatrics, but I see wrinkly stacks of benjamins!"

Brianna served him with another look of disgust, then shook her head. She reached into her purse and this time withdrew her electronic cigarette, took a deep drag, then exhaled. She glanced at him one more time and said, "You're a mess."

Yvgeny just smiled, collected his wreath from the back seat, and emerged from Cerberus. He placed his stovepipe hat upon his head, canted it just enough to capture the rakish look of a true gentleman, then straightened his morning coat. Looking in his reflection captured in the tinted windows of the hearse, he ensured his Victorian finery was impeccable.

Yvgeny was much younger when he came upon old man Schmidt's steamer trunks, hidden away in a musty corner of the attic. He was delighted to find them full of ancient formal wear, all in impeccable condition, having survived the ages. *Modern suits simply had no class*, Yvgeny believed.

He turned, checked his profile, adjusted his crimson cravat, then with a smile and nod, he made for the door. Brianna took another drag from her e-cigarette, then oozed out of the car. She had to grab the lip of the roof with one hand, and push off the dash with the other. She usually had to rock back and forth several times to generate enough momentum to get out.

By the time she emerged, Yvgeny was already at the door waiting. Two old men nearest to the door stopped rocking and watched him carefully. One of them finally gathered up the courage, and called out in a cracking voice, "pickup?"

Yvgeny brandished the wreath and called out, "and

delivery!"

Beatrice must have been waiting for him, because he didn't have to knock before she came stumbling out, her hair a mess, wearing a dress that hadn't been in style since Jimmy Carter was president. At seventy, she was one of the youngest occupants at Sunrise Manor, and as proprietor, she took her job seriously.

"Ah, Yvgeny, you're here." Looking down at the wreath, she cocked her head and smiled, adding, "Aww, you're so sweet, so kind. Such a good boy!"

Beatrice squeezed his arm and ushered them both inside. The foyer was as cold as a meat locker. Brianna immediately shivered and clutched her sides. Beatrice motioned for them to follow her up the stairs and down first one hallway, then another. The second story had the feel of a hotel, and finally they stopped outside one of the doors. She opened the door, waiting for them to enter, then said "OK, come on down when you are finished!"

Once the door was shut, Brianna reached into her purse and produced her e-cigarette. Yvgeny raised an eyebrow, but said nothing, turning toward his client. Brianna pressed herself against the furthest wall, trying not to look, but unable to turn away. Yvgeny turned to the body.

He was in his pajamas, his lips bluish. His arms were folded over his chest, which Yvgeny assumed was a pose initiated by a good-intentioned friend and resident of the place.

On his nightstand was a clock radio, a collection of prescription bottles, and a mug of coffee, half full. Yvgeny stuck his finger into the coffee, then put his finger in his mouth.

Still warm. And too sweet.

Lifting the sheets, Yvgeny peeked beneath and saw nothing amiss. Beatrice helpfully placed a copy of the hospice agreement at the foot of the bed, which Yvgeny glanced at. He smiled and turned to Brianna.

"Confirmed hospice. No coroner required! My lucky day!"

Brianna turned slightly green and looked out the window while Yvgeny produced his iPhone and started photographing the body.

Yvgeny took a second glance at some of the prescription bottles, looked around one more time, then clapped his hands together.

"Come on!"

Brianna waddled behind Yvgeny as he left the room, hospice agreement in hand. Beatrice had tactfully placed herself in a Queen Anne upholstered chair at the end of the hall, clearly in an attempt to prevent any of her residents from getting too close.

"Is everything OK?" Beatrice asked, her smile a mask.

"Sure is, I have the hospice order here, I just need next of kin contact information and of course I need to collect the m- m- the, uh," Yvgeny looked down at the order, scanned the first few lines, then nodded, "Mr. Ledbetter."

"Of course." Beatrice looked at her watch. "Actually, if you don't mind waiting a few minutes, Madame Jezelda should be here around 3 pm to do readings. The whole place lines up for her! You could handle your business and nobody would even notice."

"Jezelda? The psychic on Seventh Street?"

"Ah, you know her?"

Yvgeny snickered. "Who doesn't? Her picture is on

every bus stop bench in town!" He looked around, then muttered, "pure quackery."

Beatrice raised her eyebrows. "Quackery? I've seen her in action. She's the real thing. She talks to the dead!"

With significant effort, Yvgeny restrained himself from responding, turning slightly purple.

"What's she charge?"

"Twenty bucks," Brianna blurted out, and when Yvgeny twirled around to glare at her, she raised her voice. "So what? It's my money. And hey, she told me I should give you a chance!"

Yvgeny's glare softened and he muttered, "Well, maybe she's not a complete quack."

He checked his watch, then nodded.

"OK Beatrice, that's only ten minutes away. I will make all the preparations and return with a gurney at, say, 3:15?"

Beatrice stood and with a clap, said, "Perfect!"

They filed out behind Beatrice as she went down the circular stairs and back out onto the porch. Beatrice pulled a card from her pocket and handed it over to Brianna, and said, "Jeanine Ledbetter, his daughter. His son's information is on the back."

Yvgeny nodded and he and Brianna returned to Cerberus. He could feel the uneasy looks from the old people in their rocking chairs.

"What were you going to call him?"

"What are you talking about?"

"You told Beatrice you were going to collect the mm- Mr. Ledbetter. What were you going to say?"

Yvgeny opened his mouth, then closed it.

"You were going to call him meat, weren't you? Collect the meat? Are you serious?"

Yvgeny shrugged.

"Fruit of the womb, my dear, that's all we are. Meat in motion. And when we die, we're just meat."

Brianna stared at him in amazement as he turned and fiddled with the rear gate of Cerberus. Then he sat against the gate and called the next of kin to close the deal. There was no answer, so he left a message, then tried the son, with the same result.

He sighed, then shrugged. The body had to go somewhere, and usually the man with the meat was the man with the deal. Yvgeny slid out the collapsible gurney he kept in back for just such an occasion.

Promptly at 3 pm, Jezelda pulled up in the street in her BMW five-series sedan. She claimed to be a Haitian voodoo priestess, but Yvgeny knew better. Her multi colored flowing skirts and head kerchief was nothing more than a costume. She marched up the driveway and when she saw Yvgeny and Brianna, she headed their way. Yvgeny turned and pretended to be busy with a corner of the gurney.

"Brianna, my *bèl ti fi*, how you doing?"

Brianna smiled, and then Jezelda looked over at Yvgeny. Yvgeny did not look up until Brianna's elbow connected with his ribs. He forced a smile and then, with his arms crossed, motioned with his head toward her car and asked, "Nice car, how many stories did you have to make up to afford it?"

Jezelda stared at him, then motioned to his hearse, asked, "and how many ditches you dig for *dat korbiyar*?"

She looked at her watch, then announced, "I'm late,"

kissed Brianna on the cheek, then pushed past Yvgeny and headed toward the front door of Sunset Manor.

"Do you always have to be such a jerk?"

"Of course not. I *choose* to be such a jerk!"

A few minutes later, the front door flew open and Jezelda came stumbling out, wailing. She took several steps away from the door, fell onto her knees in the grass, then pressed her face against the ground as if in prayer.

Brianna ran toward her, and Yvgeny started at the sound of the door, bumping his head on the top of his hearse. When he saw Jezelda on the grass he also headed in her direction, a smirk on his face. Jezelda had been trailed by Beatrice and several of Sunset Manor's elderly guests. One of them emerged with her smartphone, recording the show for posterity.

Brianna got to Jezelda first. She put her hand on Jezelda's back and asked, "What's wrong? What happened?"

"Death! Murder! It's here, I can feel it! *Ghede Nibo* tell me! He tell me through his *chevals*, they speak with the voice of the murdered, and they speaking to me, they says he be killed!"

Yvgeny's smirk broadened into a smile as he listened to her hysterical tirade. Beatrice came up and perched beside Brianna.

"Jezelda, whatever is the matter?"

Jezelda just wailed and buried her face further into the grass. Beatrice looked over at Brianna and Yvgeny, and paused a moment when it registered that Yvgeny was smiling.

"She was saying something about murder."

384

Beatrice's eyes narrowed and she glanced back down with a sympathetic expression. "Poor dear, she didn't even make it past the lobby, she just looked around as if she heard something, then she just went crazy."

Jezelda looked up, turned back toward the house, nodded her head, and, with tears streaming down her face, turned to Beatrice and said, "Death! There's death inside!"

Beatrice put a soft hand on her shoulder and said, "Yes, Jezelda, a man died late last night. He's still upstairs. Yvgeny is here to pick him up. He was very sick, Jezelda, he wasn't murdered."

"Murder! Cold blooded murder, *Ghede Nibo*, he used his *chevals*, his *chevals* spoke to me in his voice, the voice of the dead, the murdered man!"

Jezelda wailed again, but started to climb to her feet. She turned to Yvgeny and pointed a dark finger at him. "Don't you take dat body, you go fetch da police. This is a murder!"

"Right. I will go call the police right now and tell them some dead guy told you he was killed. Why don't you just tell the dead guy to go file the report himself?"

Jezelda fell out of character for a moment, and she muttered, "They don't take my calls." Then she pointed at him again and cried, "but you, they will listen to you!" Then she looked into the sky and in an ominous low voice, chanted, "Scorn your lover, pay the price, Darkness hides your biggest vice. Jealousy vexes everyone, eats your soul until you're done. Evil hexes you to kill, force your hand, destroy your will."

Jezelda turned in a circle, looking at the three of them, then lurched across the grass toward her car.

"Jezelda, but you aren't finished yet!" Beatrice called out to her, waving a wad of money in her hand.

Without turning around, Jezelda raised a hand and

yelled, "Must get to my house, the *Loa* need a sacrifice!" And a moment later she was gone, leaving only some greasy skids in the street from her rapid acceleration away from the crime scene. Yvgeny turned to Beatrice and said, "Well, that was fun!"

Yvgeny returned to his hearse to get his gurney, leaving Brianna and Beatrice on the lawn, their faces full of pity and indecision. Yvgeny wheeled his gurney up the sidewalk, humming a breathy tune, then stopped to look at them both.

"Oh come on, are you serious? She's a lunatic! Brianna- you going to help me with this?"

Both ladies just stared at him in horror.

"Fine, I'll do it myself."

He kicked the front wheels over the threshold and wheeled the gurney inside. Instead of being unobtrusive and unnoticed, as was the plan, he wheeled it toward the staircase through a throng of elderly people, some with canes, some crutches, some wheel chairs. As they milled about, Yvgeny began calling out, "step aside, meat wagon coming through!"

Some crossed their heart. Others stared at the wall, oblivious to everything. He navigated to the first step then kicked a pedal beside one of the wheels and the gurney collapsed. It was very light, and easy enough to break down to carry up the stairs. However, he would probably need Brianna to help him get it back down once the old man was strapped in.

As he broke it down, one voice carried over the generally soft murmur of the ancient voices.

"Better call the coroner!"

Yvgeny turned toward the voice, but saw nothing but a sea of elderly white faces.

"Who said that?"

"Over here, sport!"

Yvgeny scanned the crowd, and after a moment, he saw a commotion toward the back of the atrium, and some muffled curses as an old man pushed his way through the geriatric masses. The man that stepped clear of the group was clearly in his eighties, wearing a plaid flannel shirt and jeans. He was a little stooped but didn't have a cane. He wore his gray hair in a flat top and had a well-trimmed mustache.

"Luther P. Telfair, at your service!"

Yvgeny smiled and said, "Well, Luther, a coroner notification is standard procedure for a nursing home like this-"

"This ain't no nursing home, sport, this here's an assisted living center. Look around, we ain't a bunch of damn gummers."

"OK, whatever it is, I'm sure Beatrice already notified the coroner."

"Coroner's going to have to call the GBI, you got a witness saying this here's a murder!"

Yvgeny sighed.

"A witness? Jezelda's nuts, that guy was on hospice, he was on his way out already."

"Don't matter, sport. Murder's murder. Guy jumps off a cliff, and you shoot him in the head on his way down, it's still murder, and you're going to jail."

Yvgeny took a deep breath, stuck an index finger in his ear and scratched.

"What are you, some kind of expert?"

The whispers and murmurs suddenly stopped as all

eyes turned to Luther P. Telfair. One of the women standing nearby turned to Yvgeny and asked, incredulous, "you don't know Chief Telfair?"

"Doesn't ring a bell. Should it?" Yvgeny asked, inspecting his finger, then switching ears.

The old woman cleared her throat and recited, "Cobb County Police Department's longest serving officer ever, fifty seven years!"

A collective croon of respect washed over the group. The recipient blushed slightly, then straightened his back.

"Hash marks all the way past my elbow."

"Huh?"

"Hash marks. Where you been, sonny boy? Under a rock? You get a hash mark on your sleeve for every four years' service. I had 'em up past my elbow."

"I see. Congratulations. Now if you'll excuse me, I have a client to tend to."

Luther shuffled a little closer, and, after a conspiratorial glance over each shoulder, leaned in and whispered, still loud enough for the entire room to hear him, "You and me need to talk."

Yvgeny shrugged, then rubbed his index fingers on his pants. He noticed hearing aids in each ear as the old man turned left, then right.

"OK, follow me upstairs."

"I don't do stairs. I'll take the elevator."

Yvgeny cursed under his breath.

"You have an elevator?"

CHAPTER TWO

⥮

"So what is it we need to talk about?"

Luther walked ahead toward Earnest's room while Yvgeny followed behind him with the cart. Brianna remained with Beatrice on the lawn.

Luther stopped outside Earnest's closed door and leaned across the gurney separating him from Yvgeny.

"Motive, sport, if you have a motive, you might have a murder."

"That's great, Luther, very helpful."

Luther cocked his head and asked, "Ain't you an uppity sumbitch? Got plenty of motive here. Sex, money, love, power, I could go on."

"You kidding me? This guy's like ninety years old. He might have money, but-"

"Eighty four. Three years younger than me. And he had it all, sport, trust me."

Luther started to bob his head and beat box, then started rapping.

"Read my book, bitchez, word for word, bitchez,

Eighty seven years, I be stacking my riches, bustin' my rhymes, full of anger and rage, 'cuz age is just a number on the top of every page. Better read my book, bitchez, every chapter every verse, I'll be the last mutha fucka, riding round in a hearse."

All Yvgeny could do was stare. The old man wiped his mouth, then cleared his throat.

"Words to live by, right there."

Yvgeny finally composed himself and asked, "You're a poet?"

Luther smiled, revealing a set of stained, brown teeth. His original set, not after market, like most of the corpses that end up on his table.

"Nope. That was the one and only Junior G, straight outta' Macon. Don't you know nothing?"

"An eighty seven year old rapper?"

"Well, I took a little poetic license on that verse."

"So you listen to gangster rap?"

"Everyone's got their vices, sport. I got your attention now?"

Yvgeny crossed his arms and said, "I'm listening."

"Earnest was in banking. Lost his wife back in the nineties. He got along OK for a while, but after his stroke, his kids dumped him off here. 'Bout two years ago, I reckon."

"Boy, he was a real player around here. Sealed the deal like nobody's business. Bought Viagra in bulk, if you catch my drift."

Yvgeny winced, but tried to remain stoic.

"So sex, there's your first motive," Luther said with a smile, a satisfied look on his face, then he continued.

"Money, too. They stuck him in here, then took control of the checkbook. Dropped him off in an old beat up Ford Ranger."

"They were out here a couple weeks ago, Ernie saw that putz of a son park outside in a fancy new Mercedes. You think that ass wipe earned it?"

"Next day, he talked to his accountant. Cut him off." After a pregnant pause, the old chief said, "There's your money."

Yvgeny remained quiet. The old man pushed off the gurney and leaned against the wall, then said, more softly, "love and power, those are more difficult under these circumstances. You can buy a little of both, but it ain't the real thing."

"What do you mean?"

"Well, none of us really work anymore, and we ain't royalty, so power's kind of a relative concept at this stage. And love? Well, we tend to take it day by day. We ain't much for planning futures, especially with each other."

"That's a fair point. So in this case, sex or money."

"You bet your sweet bippy! Maybe both!"

Luther turned and opened Earnest's door and walked inside. Yvgeny followed him, pushing his gurney. Luther walked toward the nightstand while Yvgeny looked on. Luther took each medicine bottle and brought them up, one at a time, to inspect. His vision was terrible, and he had to hold each bottle just a few inches from his face to read the label. He grinned upon reading the first one, then shook the bottle, the pills inside rattling like a percussion instrument.

"What I tell you? The little blue pills! That horn dog!"

Yvgeny moved closer.

Luther bent over slightly to look at Earnest's face, then lifted the sheets to look underneath. He grunted occasionally as he worked. Then he lifted the eyelids and studied his eyes.

"Cancer. He didn't have much longer. Poor bastard."

As Luther continued inspecting the body, Yvgeny wandered toward the dresser and opened the first drawer. Inside were a collection of socks, and a dinner plate, likely filched from the kitchen downstairs. On the plate there was a wedding ring, a wad of cash, and a few credit cards. Yvgeny glanced over his shoulder at Luther, still hunched over the body, then pocketed the cash. He left the ring and the cards- not worth the risk.

"Well, hard to say, you'd need an autopsy to make sure," the old man said to himself.

Movement outside got Yvgeny's attention, and he turned to look out the window. A cherry red older conversion van was backing into the driveway of Sunrise Manor. Yvgeny sighed. The driver gunned the accelerator, the glass packs rumbling, before turning off the engine. Jimmy Flowers, in the flesh.

"Oh goody, the coroner's here. Who called him?"

Luther looked at Yvgeny, then out the window.

"That ain't the sheriff!"

"Sorry, the *deputy* coroner is here."

"That dandy?"

Luther pinched his lips together in the universal expression of distaste, then took one more look around the room.

"Well, so much for proving a murder."

Yvgeny put his hands on his hips and turned to Luther and said, "Look, Luther, this ain't no murder, and even if it was, he was on his way out the door anyway. He needs to go in the ground by the end of the week or it's going to be closed casket, if you know what I'm saying."

"Listen here, sport, it's a murder until the coroner says otherwise. And until he says otherwise, Earnest goes to Macon, you catch my drift?"

"Have you met Jimmy? I'll be surprised if he figures out how to get up the stairs."

A few minutes later, the door to Earnest's room opened up, and Jimmy Flowers walked inside. Flowers wore a pair of jeans and a Hawaiian shirt, unbuttoned halfway, exposing a carpet of shiny black hair. He sported a thick mustache, and an affable smile. Flowers was a diehard Tom Selleck fan and a Magnum, PI, aficionado. He specifically chose the color of his van to match Magnum's Ferrari.

"Well, well, well, the undertaker himself."

"Good Lord, Flowers, who called *you*?"

Flowers straightened up and in a self-righteous snort said, "I am the deputy coroner and it is my solemn responsibility to declare whether this death requires referral to the medical examiner!"

Luther looked the doctor up and down, rolled his eyes, and walked toward the door. Ignoring Flowers, the old man turned back to Yvgeny and said, "motive, sport. It's all about motive," then with a wink, he was gone.

"What was that about?" Flowers asked.

"Don't worry about it. Look, just do your hocus pocus and go, I gotta get this guy in the fridge before the flies come."

"Gimme a break, Yvgeny, you can save your theatrics for someone else. I know your shuck and jive."

Yvgeny watched as the doctor glanced around the room, disinterestedly picked up one of the bottles on the nightstand, then looked at the body.

"Anyone touch him?"

"Yes, we cuddled for a while, then I brushed his teeth and made sure he was presentable for you."

Flowers glared at Yvgeny, but didn't respond. Yvgeny looked outside to check on Brianna.

"Seriously, what was that old fart talking about, 'motive?' Something I need to know about?"

"No, he was just saying you never have a murder without motive."

"Right. So, I hear Jezelda was here carrying on about some murder. She wasn't talking about this guy, was she?"

Yvgeny opened his mouth to begin unraveling a new story, then closed it. Flowers might already have spoken to Beatrice. Or Brianna.

"She was claiming some spirits visited her and told her he was murdered."

Yvgeny tried to sound as flippant as possible, but it fell flat. Flowers made a sound in his throat, then turned back to the body.

"You know what, I bet the sheriff would let me do this one-"

"No way, Flowers, this one's mine. I was here first!"

Flowers smiled and said, "It don't work that way, Geny, and you know it. This looks like a natural, and he's hospice, but all things considered, I betcha the GBI would let me do a limited autopsy. That's $600 bucks for about three hours' work!"

"Well, a decent funeral will net me over $4,000, minimum, so step off, cowboy."

"You know how silly that sounds coming out of your

mouth, with that Russian accent of yours?"

"It's Polish, you idiot."

Although Yvgeny was born and raised in the United States, his parents were first generation Americans, having left communist Poland before he was born. Unfortunately, they never taught him their mother tongue, so he learned English from birth, but with his parents' accent. He absorbed their culture, including their distrust of police, but not the language itself, much to his frustration.

"Whatever," Flowers said as he opened his phone and started scrolling through his address book. Speaking to himself, he muttered, "suspicious natural, just tell 'em a psychic said it was murder, but ain't no evidence, that should do it." He placed the phone to his ear, then glanced over at Yvgeny and said, "if I get a green light, I will be done tonight, you can probably get him by eight." Then he straightened up and said, "hi, sheriff?"

Yvgeny let out a frustrated breath and went back to the drawers, opened up the second one. Shirts. He opened the third as he heard Flowers say, "yes, just a limited should be enough for us to close the book on it." Yvgeny grumbled to himself wordlessly and opened the next drawer. He wrinkled his nose in disgust as he found a bottle of lubricant laying on top of some folded pants. He'd seen enough.

"Nope, no need to notify the GBI yet." Then there was a pause, then he said, "of course, I will give them a call." Then he pressed the end button.

"Jackpot!" Flowers called out as he shut his flip phone and stuffed it back into his pocket. "I got the green light for a limited. Come on, let me borrow that cart of yours."

Yvgeny hesitated, and Flowers let out a chortle and said, "Are you kidding me? You already have it up here, just give me a hand with the body. Damn, Geny, you're a pain!"

Yvgeny moved in closer with a sigh and stepped on the wheel brakes of the cart, then grabbed Earnest's feet. Flowers called out, "one, two, three, heave!" and they both lifted him up and dropped him on the gurney. As Flowers strapped him down under a sheet, Yvgeny sniffed, squinted his eyes, then leaned in and sniffed again.

"Damn, Flowers, it's not even 4 pm and you're already in the sauce?"

"It's my after shave."

"Yeah, right, *eau de* gin and tonic."

"Whatever," Flowers responded, then he turned and grabbed the prescription bottles from the nightstand.

"When are you going to be finished with him?"

Flowers looked at his watch, then back at the body.

"Like I said, probably by eight. I'm just going to run blood work, maybe a tissue sample, a quick external examination. Probably won't dig into him or anything."

"Then can't you just do it here?"

"You kidding me? In the middle of a nursing home?"

"Assisted living center."

"Whatever."

"What you're trying to say is you shouldn't perform autopsies when you're drunk."

"Stick it, undertaker."

Yvgeny followed behind Flowers as he struggled to push the cart toward the door. Once he finally got it into the hall, he stopped and turned back to Yvgeny.

"Um, maybe you can give the sheriff's office a call. Boss wants me to let the detectives know I'm taking Earnest here over to the shop."

"Any reason why you can't do that?"

"Because I kind of got my hands full!" Flowers cried out, filled with righteous indignation. Then Flowers patted Earnest on his chest and added, more calmly, "besides, the more I can focus on looking under the hood, the quicker I can finish and the quicker you can do whatever it is you do."

Yvgeny considered, then grudgingly nodded his head. "I suppose I can notify them."

"That's great, Geny, you're a real pal."

CHAPTER THREE

╬

After Flowers secured Earnest in the back of his custom ambulance and swerved onto the street, horns blaring behind him from the erratic move, Yvgeny rejoined Brianna and Beatrice on the lawn. It was February in middle Georgia, and it was brisk but sunny, low humidity with a moderate breeze. Yvgeny straightened his morning coat as he crossed the lawn.

"What happened?" Brianna asked.

Yvgeny looked at Beatrice and said, "Well, someone called the coroner's office."

Beatrice said, "Of course, we have to call. He was hospice, but the doctor wasn't around, and then Jezelda, well, people will start to talk, you know how it is in Comstock!"

Yvgeny didn't respond, turned instead to Brianna and said, "Flowers, that fool, he convinced the sheriff to let him take the body back to his shop of horrors. We will get whatever pieces are left after Dr. Ginsu finishes chopping him up."

"Is that normal?"

Beatrice interjected, saying, "Yes, when there is a

death of a hospice patient and the death is attended by a doctor, there's no need for an inquest or anything. But if the death is unattended, or suspicious in any way, then the medical examiner has to take a look. Usually they just let the county coroner decide whether the ME has to get involved. We are kind of unique here."

Beatrice glanced over at Yvgeny and asked, "You know Gilbert County is one of the few in the state that has a deputy coroner that is also on the GBI contract? Flowers actually has the authority to conduct an autopsy on behalf of the county. Pretty crazy, huh?"

"More than you know," Yvgeny added.

"And," Yvgeny said, turning back to Brianna, "he roped me into notifying our good friends at the Gilbert County Sheriff's Department, Office of Investigations."

"You mean those two-"

"Yes, those two."

Yvgeny turned back to Beatrice.

"Well, as soon as Flowers finishes playing with the body, I will take care of the rest. If you will kindly provide me the next of kin's information, I will-"

"I already have it," Brianna said, waving a slip of paper in the air.

"Splendid. Now I suppose we will have to go visit my friends down the street."

Yvgeny and Brianna piled into Cerberus and headed down the street to the Gilbert County Sheriff's Department's Headquarters in Comstock. The Office of Investigations was an office of two detectives, Harry Newsome and Bubba Johnson. They divided the county up in two, each one responsible for one end. In bigger cases, like murders or the other "seven deadlies," they banded together.

Yvgeny and the two detectives shared a mutual

dislike and mistrust for each other based on their previous interactions. On their way inside the precinct, Yvgeny turned to Brianna and muttered, "Here goes nothing," then painted a look of nonchalance on his face as he stepped inside.

A woman dressed head to toe in navy polyester greeted them from behind the front desk. He asked to speak with a detective, hoping against hope that perhaps one of them had been replaced. Unfortunately for him, he heard her side of the phone conversation as she called back to their work space.

"Yeah, Harry, some guy here says he needs to speak to you. I ain't even gonna try pronouncing his name."

She listened a moment, then glanced back at Yvgeny, inspected him up and down, and then nodded to herself.

"Yeah, that's about right."

A moment later she replaced the phone on the cradle, then looked at Yvgeny and said, "He'll be right out."

"Fantastic."

A moment later, Harry Newsome appeared. He looked like a Wild West sheriff's deputy straight out of central casting, with a bushy mustache, deep set eyes and longish graying hair. He wore cowboy boots, jeans, and a flannel shirt.

"Well, well, well, it's Count Dracula and his lovely assistant."

There was no humor in his voice.

"Lovely to see you again too, inspector."

Yvgeny preferred inspector to detective, just as he preferred undertaker to mortician, verbal anachronisms that might have originated with his parents' archaic English they picked up from old books and movies after fleeing communist Poland.

"To what do I owe this high honor? You come to tell me you've solved another murder?"

"Ah, inspector, jealousy is unbecoming on you."

Months previous, Yvgeny had found a body dumped in one of his open graves. He found a watch on the body that was far too nice to hand over to the deputies, who would no doubt have taken it for themselves or pawned it. Yvgeny dutifully notified the sheriff's department of the body, but he quickly realized they weren't nearly sharp enough to solve it on their own. Yvgeny had to take matters into his own hands to ensure justice was served.

He had grown quite fond of retelling his story to those willing to listen, regaling them with his epic tale of how he single handedly solved a heinous crime, how he drafted a unique and unstoppable group of confidantes to assist him in his zealous pursuit of the killers, all the while combating the two gumshoes and their haphazard and negligent manner of investigation.

"Jealous? Jealous of you and your team of retards interfering in an investigation?" Newsome quickly turned to Brianna and said, "Present company excluded, of course." Then he turned back to Yvgeny and continued, "And why would I be jealous of someone who obstructed that investigation from day one? Oh, that's rich. Bubba's gonna love this!"

Yvgeny took a deep breath, then shook his head.

"Anyway, inspector, I am here on a mission from deputy coroner Flowers, an important mission, dispatched from the sheriff himself."

"Oh, this oughta be good." Newsome announced,

then glanced backward at the woman behind the counter and called out, "Maxine, pay attention, you're gonna want to hear this!"

Yvgeny straightened his jacket again, placed his hands on his hips. He had rehearsed his lines in the hearse on the way over.

"Deputy Coroner Flowers wishes for me to inform you there has been a death at Sunrise Manor Assisted Living Center. The man was on hospice and the death was attended by a doctor. However, Madame Jezelda the Psychic-"

"Madame Jezelda? Oh, Maxine, please tell me we got the recorders going in here. I gotta play this for Bubba. OK, sorry Geny, go on."

Yvgeny cleared his throat.

"Madame Jezelda has been informed by reliable spirits from the other side that the victim has been murdered, so in an abundance of caution, Deputy Coroner Flowers has taken the body for a brief examination."

There was silence as Newsome stared at Yvgeny, expectantly. After a few seconds his smile faded and he said, "That's it? That's the best you got?"

"What were you expecting?"

"I don't know, maybe another dump job or something. Not some old fart in an old folk's home."

"Well, I consider you officially informed."

"Duly noted. Since when does an undertaker perform death notifications? Isn't that Flowers's job?"

"Yes, but he had his hands full with the body. God knows you don't want him multi-tasking."

"At least you got that one right."

Newsome looked at his watch, then clapped his hands together and said, "Well, look at the time. Great catching up with you, Geny. Make sure and not come back now, ya' hear?" Newsome turned on a heel and walked back behind the counter.

"A pleasure as always," Yvgeny responded softly. Then he turned to Brianna and said, "Let's go."

Newsome returned to his old battered metal desk, which was pressed up against Bubba's so that they faced each other. Space was at a premium in the office, leaving little room for privacy. Bubba was leaning back in his chair, his feet on his desk, and glanced up at Newsome when he walked by.

"That who you thought it was?"

"In the flesh."

Bubba nodded, then spit tobacco juice into a Gatorade bottle.

"What'd he want?"

"To inform us Flowers was examining some dead guy from Sunset Manor who was on hospice."

Bubba narrowed his eyes.

"Why would we care about that?"

Newsome smirked and said, "because Jezelda said it was murder."

"The freak with the bandana?"

"Yup."

"Whatcha gonna do about it?"

Newsome shrugged his shoulders and said, "If it was anyone but Geny, I'd say nothing. But if he's involved, something smells. Come on, Bubba, let's go for a ride."

Also by Jonathan B. Zeitlin

Death and Repair

Available in paperback and e-book

Michael Hart would do anything to bring her back.

Fate took her away from him, then, years later, fate pushes him to the town of Malway, a town with a secret. Michael, a retired policeman, believes he has stumbled across a crime, but soon discovers it is something far more incredible, something that could make his one wish come true. But it might come with a terrible price.

Death and Repair explores the power of love and the permanence of death. It is a re-imagination of the classic Djinn tales, part mystery, part science-fiction, part love story.

Praise for Death and Repair

"Zeitlin creates cinema with words." *Genevieve Kazdin, Rare and used book dealer.*

"Jonathan Zeitlin has crafted a tour de force supernatural mystery about love, loss, and an obsessive search for answers in a peculiar New England village where time may exist as more than a single dimension." *Bill Shepard, creator of www.filmblanc.info, and author of The Somewhere in Time Story.*

"Zeitlin extends the love-death-afterlife tradition in fiction, weaving science, theology, and the supernatural into a story of travel between overlapping dimensions, or parallel universes, in which a love that is lost can be regained, or lost more tragically than ever." *Richard Striner, Professor of History and author of Love in the Afterlife: Underground Religion at the Movies*

Made in the USA
Middletown, DE
14 December 2019